THE
SATURDAY
NIGHT
SAUVIGNON
SISTERHOOD

BY THE SAME AUTHOR

Why Mummy Drinks
Why Mummy Swears
Why Mummy Doesn't Give a ****
Why Mummy's Sloshed

Gill Sims

THE SATURDAY NIGHT NIGHT SAUVIGNON SISTERHOOD

HarperCollins*Publishers*

HarperCollins*Publishers*
1 London Bridge Street
London SE1 9GF

www.harpercollins.co.uk

HarperCollins*Publishers*
1st Floor, Watermarque Building, Ringsend Road
Dublin 4, Ireland

First published by HarperCollins*Publishers* 2022

3 5 7 9 10 8 6 4 2

Gill Sims © 2022

Gill Sims asserts the moral right to be
identifi ed as the author of this work

A catalogue record of this book is
available from the British Library

ISBN 978-0-00-854252-8

Printed and bound in the UK using 100%
renewable electricity at CPI Group (UK) Ltd

MIX
Paper from
responsible sources
FSC™ C007454

This book is produced from independently certified FSC™ paper
to ensure responsible forest management.

For more information visit: www.harpercollins.co.uk/green

To Lynn, Mairi and Tanya.
The original sisterhood.

1

Claire's phone buzzed as she was having what felt like the fifteenth argument of the week with Lucas about how she didn't care if tomato sauce DID count as one of his five-a-day, he was NOT substituting his lovingly cooked vegetables on his plate for a vat of ketchup, and actually, no, NO!, because she SAID so, and it was not up for discussion. Meanwhile Tabitha wittered on at her about ponies, about how a pony was all she had ever EVER wanted and of course she'd totally look after a pony if she had one, and please, Mummy, please, could she have a pony?

Claire glanced at her phone as she attempted to smile devotedly at her darling children. She took a deep breath and did not shout, 'Of course you can't have a fucking pony. Do you know how much they cost, and you said exactly the same about "looking after them" about the sodding guinea pigs, the existence of which you now ignore, you lazy little beast,' and instead explained in a calm, rational and loving way what a great expense and commitment a pony is, however much one might want one – and love one – and actually there is a big difference between playing with your My Little Ponies and looking after a real, live, pooping, snorting, hungry horse. Her phone screen showed a text from Andrew.

Sorry darling, meeting ran over, have to take the client for dinner now, I'll probably be late, see you when I get in. Love you xxxxx

Claire sighed. She knew, of course, that Andrew worked very hard. She knew it was not his fault he often had to work late, or that part of his job involved wining and dining his clients in nice restaurants while she sat at home wrangling broccoli down his darling children before supervising homework and bath time and bedtime alone. Sometimes, however, it was difficult not to feel resentful that she was always the one left picking up the slack of their home life. He huffed and puffed about how stressful it all was, but he was the one eating Châteaubriand and Bearnaise sauce rather than a packet of Monster Munch in front of *EastEnders*. Andrew frequently protested that he'd much *rather* be at home arguing with Tabitha and Lucas about the very real possibilities of them contracting scurvy, but Claire sometimes felt that was easy enough to say when you didn't actually have to do it.

She reminded herself, though, of how exhausted Andrew frequently looked when he finally got home and that he had almost been in tears when he discovered he'd be away on an unavoidable trip for Lucas's birthday last year. She was lucky he worked enough hours to enable her to pick the kids up from school one day a week and be there for them at dinnertime, etc, instead of having to work equally long hours herself. Claire gave herself a shake, because her cherubs were once more wittering on at her like budgies who'd had their Trill laced with speed.

'Mum, you're not meant to be on your phone at mealtimes,' clamoured Lucas.

'Yeah, Mum, no screens at the table. Remember, that's YOUR rule,' Tabitha chimed in. 'If you're on your phone, we should *totally* be allowed to watch our iPads. You're such a hypocrite!'

'First,' said Claire, 'I'm not actually eating, am I? I'm just keeping you two company while you eat. And second, I'm not "on my phone". I was just reading a text from Daddy, that's all.'

'What does Dad say?' asked Lucas.

'Just that he's going to be late again.'

'AGAIN?' wailed Tabitha. 'But he's *always* late! I wanted to show him the spreadsheet I made about why I should get a pony and how it *won't* be too expensive like you say, Mum, and how I'd *definitely* have time to look after it. I bet Dad would understand. Can I stay up and show it to him?'

'No.'

'If she's staying up, I'm staying up too,' said Lucas, 'or else it's not fair! And if she's getting a pony, I want a new PlayStation. And *Grand Theft Auto*.'

'No one is staying up. No one is getting a pony. No one is getting a new PlayStation. And definitely NO ONE is getting *GTA*, for the millionth time. You're too young and it's not suitable!'

'Toby has it!'

'I don't *care* what Toby has. Eat your dinner.'

'Emma's got a pony at her granny's; can I get a pony to keep at Granny's instead, then?'

'Granny lives in London. In a flat. Where exactly are you going to keep a pony at Granny's?'

'Can I get *Call of Duty* then?'

'JUST STOP TALKING AND EAT YOUR DINNER, PLEASE!'

'It's not fair, you keep telling us we aren't allowed to have our iPads at dinner because we're supposed to make conversation, and now you tell us to be quiet when we're just trying to make conversation!'

'Oh, for fuck's sake,' muttered Claire under her breath, as she opened the fridge to see what she could find for a solitary, no-effort dinner, since there didn't seem much point in going to the trouble of cooking the salmon fillets she had bought for her and Andrew if she was on her own (the children regarded any form of fish not encased in breadcrumbs as toxic, and were resistant enough to the delicious homemade fishfingers she had made for them, insisting they much preferred Captain Birdseye's version). The children continued to fight behind her. White wine was starting to look like quite an appealing dinner actually. Maybe just a small glass.

'Are you having wine, Mum? You know you're not supposed to have wine every night. We did about alcohol units at school. That's quite a big glass of wine – how many units do you think are in it?'

'Bet the bastards didn't tell you that wine is remarkably good at cancelling out whining though, did they?' muttered Claire.

'This is all cold. I don't like it cold, I don't want it now.'

'It's COLD because you've been pushing it round your plate for FORTY minutes while you babble on about ponies!' exploded Claire. 'If you'd eaten it in the first place when I put it on the table when it was HOT, it wouldn't have had time to get cold! JUST EAT IT!'

'You shouldn't shout at us, Mum.'

'It's against our rights. So's making us eat vegetables. Our bodies are our own and you can't make us do things we don't want to. We could report you.'

'Who to? Who are you going to report me to for crimes against broccoli?'

'The NSPCC,' said Lucas smugly. 'We had a lady come in at school and tell us never to let anyone make us do anything that makes us feel uncomfortable. These fishfingers make me feel uncomfortable. Why can't we just have the frozen ones? And vegetables make me feel *sick*, that's worse than uncomfortable.'

'Or we could report her to UNICEF,' chimed in Tabitha helpfully. 'Remember the assembly we had last week about the UN Rights of the Child? About how we're entitled to respect, and to have our opinions listened to? How do we report Mummy to UNICEF, do you think, because I definitely don't feel like I'm having my opinions respected right now!'

'Oh for FU-FIDDLESTICKS SAKE!' exploded Claire. 'Vegetables and homemade fishfingers do not contravene the UN Rights of the Child, nor is it a matter for the NSPCC. STOP being ridiculous, and EAT YOUR DINNER!'

'We could start a petition,' mused Tabitha. 'I expect Granny would sign it. And Grumble and Gramps. And we could ask the neighbours.'

'How do you even know what a petition is?' demanded Claire.

'I saw it on *EastEnders*,' said Tabitha.

'You're not allowed to watch *EastEnders*,' said Claire.

'Grumble and Gramps let me watch it when I'm at their house.'

'Oh, do they?' said Claire, reflecting that perhaps she needed to have a word with her parents about what was considered suitable viewing for their grandchildren. 'Just eat your dinner. You're not reporting me to the NSPCC, or UNICEF, or starting a petition round the neighbours about the iniquities of green vegetables, nor are you calling Childline.'

'What's Childline?' asked Lucas.

'It was a phone line that children could call if they were being mistreated at home and had no one to turn to for help,' said Claire rashly, as Lucas's eyes lit up. 'I don't think it still exists,' she hastily added. 'You had to call it from a landline.' She was well aware of both Lucas and Tabitha's bafflement at the *purpose* of a landline; the only thing that confused them more was when she tried to tell them about phone boxes and why they existed. Tabitha had howled with laughter one time when she was going through a box of Claire's old things, looking for dressing-up clothes, and had found an old address book. 'But why did you have to write their phone numbers down, Mummy? Why didn't you just put them into your phone?' A world without tablets and smartphones was utterly alien to her children.

Lucas heaved a martyred sigh and stared at his plate. 'I could probably finish my dinner if I could watch my iPad,' he offered.

Claire glanced at the clock. The prospect of dinner with her children continuing in this vein for another forty minutes was not a cheerful one.

'Fine. Watch your iPads. No, I'll not take the parental controls off. No, you cannot buy anything. Just watch Netflix or something, OK?'

Three hours, several arguments, a semi-flooded bathroom after the children's showers and a final threat of all internet disconnected for the foreseeable future if either child set foot outside their bedroom again later, Claire finally collapsed on the sofa. Andrew would not be home for at least another hour, possibly two. Claire considered what to do next. She had work to finish, but frankly, she was now so brain dead she could barely follow the plot of *The Crown*.

And, of course, there was still the laundry. There was always laundry. Sometimes Claire thought that laundry should be included in your marriage vows. 'Do you, Claire, take this man to be your lawful wedded husband, in sickness and health, for richer, for poorer, for full laundry baskets, and mountains of ironing because he thought his T-shirt "smelled a bit funny" when he took it out the drawer so he just chucked it in the fucking wash because apparently there is a magic fairy who comes and does the washing and folds it and puts it away again, and also does the ironing, so it is absolutely fine for him to take another shirt out the cupboard because he's "too hot" in the one he just put on, and no, obviously he's "worn it" now, so it can't be just put back in the cupboard even though he only "wore it" for about three minutes, and obviously any time he's asked to help with the laundry, despite being so Very Busy and Important as he never ceases to fucking remind you, he'll immediately become extremely incompetent and summons you to ask inane and STUPID questions to waste your time until it would have been quicker just to do it yourself, to have and to hold from this day forth, until death do you part, or you smother him with a pile of dirty towels?'

Claire was wearily sorting the darks from the whites, and swearing under her breath at discovering the entire pile of clean laundry she had put in Lucas's room the day before dumped back in the wash because he couldn't be bothered to put it away, when the doorbell rang. Claire continued to swear to herself as she stomped to the door to give short shrift to the Jehovah's Witnesses or chuggers or whoever had the temerity to ring her doorbell at 9 p.m. She flung open the door, tirade at the ready, and instead beamed with joy, because there stood Emily, brandishing a bottle.

'Ems! What are you doing here?'

'AUNTY EMILY!!!!' bellowed Lucas and Tabitha, charging down the stairs. 'Can we stay up now Aunty Emily is here?'

'No!' snapped Claire.

'PLEASE, Aunty Emily,' begged Tabitha.

'Yeah, it's not fair! Aunty Emily is, like, my godmother. I should totally be allowed to stay up,' argued Lucas.

'Not tonight, kids!' said Emily cheerfully. 'It's late, and I've come for a chat with your mum. How about I quickly tuck you both back in, and next time I come we'll have a *Frustration* marathon? How does that sound?'

The children, who would have argued with Claire for at least another twenty minutes, agreed immediately to Emily's offer and headed back up the stairs. Five minutes later, Emily was back down in the kitchen.

'So?' said Claire.

'I had another shitty date, and I left early again. It seems to be becoming a pattern,' said Emily. 'Where's the corkscrew, Claire? It's not in the drawer.'

'Oh God, I don't know. Andrew's probably moved it,' said Claire, as Emily rummaged round before triumphantly producing the corkscrew and swiftly opening the bottle – a rather nicer bottle than she was accustomed to, Claire noted with pleasure.

'So, what happened?' asked Claire, getting down two glasses.

'All men are pigs!' said Emily cheerfully. 'Only two glasses? I take it Lady Di is out again, then?'

'Client dinner.' Claire found that now Emily was here though, she didn't mind in the slightest that Andrew was out; in fact she was rather glad, as Andrew tended to be irritated by Emily and Claire's friendship, and had never lived down the fact that he had once drunkenly ranted that there 'were three people in this marriage', leading to Emily henceforth referring to him as Lady Di. Which didn't really help matters.

'Ah. The Busy and Important Client Dinners.' Emily nodded wisely. 'Still, right now, I'd take Lady Di and his client dinners over another evening listening to an Edgar boring on at me before lunging.'

'*Another* Edgar?' asked Claire in dismay.

'Yes. Oh God, how little did we know, Claire, when Edgar Trewarren asked me to dance at the Christmas ball when we were fifteen and just *pawed* at me with his disgusting sweaty palms, how many of his ilk there were out there? I'm starting to think that the only men left single now are Edgars. In fact, I'm just waiting for Edgar Trewarren himself to swipe right on me and send a dick pic.'

'No, he's married,' said Claire consolingly. 'Very plain woman, wears a lot of Boden.'

'How do you know that?'

'Andrew has a lot of client dinners. I get bored. I stalk people on Facebook.'

'You must have been very bored to have stalked Edgar Trewarren!'

'I was. I'd run out of anyone else to stalk, and I wanted to see how much more unattractive he'd got with age. The answer was – quite a lot.'

'Ugh.' Emily shuddered. 'I was going to say, "Show me," but I don't think I want to see. Those sweaty palms haunt me still. He left sweat marks on my favourite burgundy taffeta dress. I just thank the lord your mum had safety-pinned me in too stoutly for him to leave sweat marks on anything else! Have you stalked anyone else interesting lately?'

'Head-Girl-Hattie has her Facebook privacy settings locked down, but she updates her Twitter bio with the latest Very Important Company she's Very Important at. And I dip in and out of stalking Miranda Johnson, but you know that. I've a morbid fascination with how utterly unbearably smug she is, with her *Children of the Corn* offspring and her full-time job at "full-time mummy". They're thinking of getting a pony, you know. Most people are boring and have their privacy settings locked down, though, which is just rude. I assume Miranda doesn't because she actively wants everyone to see how smugly perfect her life is, just like at school when she'd make huge scenes in the loos about how *fat* she was because she thought she had seen a bit of cellulite, and everyone would have to gather round and assure her she wasn't. Bloody bitch knew she was perfect, she just wanted to make everyone else feel inferior. Not that *I'm* still bitter or anything,' Claire sighed.

'Oh no, nor me!' laughed Emily. 'I've *totally* forgiven her for snogging Peter Walker at the St Lawrence's dance. *Totally*. I don't sometimes sit alone and palely loitering, wondering if maybe we hadn't been drinking vodka out of Coke cans in the bogs, Miranda wouldn't have got in first, and then Peter and I would have been childhood sweethearts and I'd have married him, and now I'd live on a farm with six children and a flock of goats.'

'Goats?'

'Goats, yes. *Heidi* was a very formative part of my childhood!'

'Why are you talking about goats?' demanded Tabitha, who had snuck downstairs unheard. Claire hoped she hadn't been standing there too long before they'd noticed.

'BED!' said Emily authoritatively before Claire had a chance to say anything. 'Or you won't be getting to play *Frustration* with Lucas and me! And that goes for if I see you down here again tonight.'

To Claire's astonishment, Tabitha just gave a martyred sigh and trudged back off to bed with a sorrowful 'OK. Night, Aunty Emily. Night, Mummy.'

'How do you do that?' said Claire. 'She'd have argued with me about drinks of water and monsters under the bed and really important things she had to tell me for at least half an hour!'

'It's just the novelty. I'm not her mother, so it's not nearly as much fun to wind me up. Now, we've covered my shitty love life, and the fact Miranda is still a grade A bitch, so what's new with you? I feel like it's been ages since I've seen you!'

Two hours later, after much setting the world to rights, a good moan from Claire about Andrew's various ineptitudes, Emily bewailing the likelihood of her dying alone in a basement surrounded by the seventeen cats she had adopted to see her through her lonely old age ('You've got a lovely flat, you won't be living in a basement,' Claire consoled her) and a renewal of their pact that should Andrew die first, and Emily still be single, they'd set up home together in some sort of mini *Golden Girls* re-enactment, Claire felt a bit better about everything by the time they heard Andrew's key in the lock. Sometimes you just needed a grumble and to get things off your chest. Andrew was an arsehole, but he was her arsehole, and she was glad he was home at last.

'That'll be my cue to go, before Lady Di gets his knickers in a twist,' giggled Emily. Claire hastily ran her hand through her hair to try to tidy it up, and checked she didn't have vampire fangs round her mouth from the red wine, and they went out into the hall to meet him.

'Hello darling!' she said brightly.

Andrew was flipping through the post. 'Hi,' he grunted, ripping open envelopes and throwing them aside.

'Hi, Andrew!' beamed Emily.

'Emily.' He looked up in astonishment. 'What are *you* doing here? Claire didn't say anything about you coming over?'

'Surprise! I just popped by on my way home from another awful date.'

'What were you doing on a date?' said Andrew, looking duly surprised.

'Andrew!' said Claire. 'Don't be so rude!'

'OK, OK, sorry, Emily! Christ, this is *all* junk!' Andrew sighed, gathering up all his post and heading to the kitchen to hurl the lot in the bin.

Claire said a hasty goodbye to Emily, apologising for Andrew's rudeness, and followed him to the kitchen to retrieve the bundle of envelopes from the rubbish and put them in the paper-recycling bin.

'Darling, please try to remember that paper goes in the recycling, not the general bin.'

'Yes, yes, sorry! We must save the planet, or the children will nag me about the polar bears. Thank God for you, Claire. I can never get the hang of this bloody recycling and what goes in what bin.'

'Do you want anything to eat?'

'No, I told you, I was out with a client, had a disgustingly over-indulgent dinner. You know how it is – they like to take full advantage of my expense account, but don't want to look greedy if they order the caviar and steak and I have a salad, so I have to have something far too rich as well. I'll probably have bloody indigestion all night now.'

'You poor thing,' said Claire sarcastically. 'It must be so dreadfully hard for you!'

'It is, actually. It's not a jolly, Claire, it's *work*, and I'm knackered now.'

'I'm sure you are, you've had a long day.' Claire did actually feel much more sympathetic than usual towards Andrew after her moan to Emily about him. 'What did you have? Foie gras and *filet mignon*?'

'Smoked salmon and rack of lamb, actually. It was very good, I have to say. But yes, it *was* a long day and I'm *exhausted* now, you've no idea.'

Claire's sympathy ebbed slightly at the contrast between her evening meal and Andrew's, and being told she couldn't possibly understand what tiredness was.

'Gosh. I can see it *must* be exhausting sitting there, eating that. Do you know what I had? The cold leftover fishfingers and broccoli your children threatened to report me to UNICEF over for making them eat. You're not the only person who works hard, you know. *I've* been at work all day too, and then I come home and have to deal with the children and homework and domestic stuff and everything. And then *you* come home telling me how exhausting wining and dining is, and you don't even bother to ask about my day.'

Andrew sighed. 'This isn't a game of competitive tiredness, you know! I'm sorry I wasn't here to help tonight, but you seem to have had plenty of fun knocking back the vino with your pal there. And actually, mine hasn't been the shits and giggles you seem to think it was. Give me a fucking break, Claire.'

Claire opened her mouth to retort, but before she could, Andrew sighed again and said, 'I'm sorry. I shouldn't snap at you. Just been a bit of a day, that's all, but that's no excuse to take it out on you. I'm sorry I wasn't here, and I'm sorry for being a moany twat. Come here and give me a hug.'

'Is everything all right?'

'Yeah, everything's fine. Just clients, you know. They're dickheads. And fucking Uber drivers. I'd so much rather have been here with you and the kids instead of having to put up with some arsehole over an overpriced, too-rich dinner, you know that! Look, I'm going to jump in the shower, then we'll have a glass of wine together before we go to bed, OK?'

'All right,' said Claire, feeling bad for snapping at him, as Andrew chucked his usual detritus of keys, change and wallet over the kitchen table and went upstairs.

Claire picked up the coins and added them to her change jar, and put Andrew's wallet and keys on the hall table where he'd be able to find them in the morning instead of them getting hidden among breakfast dishes or being covered in milk or cereal or general matter in the kitchen, and poured another glass of wine for herself and one for Andrew.

Poor Andrew, she thought. He *had* looked done in. And she *must* try to remember that nice as these client dinners sounded, it wasn't like he could just kick back and get pissed and have fun. He had to concentrate and be in work mode the whole time. No wonder they gave him indigestion. And her having a go at him when he came home didn't help either. They snapped and sniped at each other altogether too much these days. Once upon a time,

Claire would have rubbed his shoulders sympathetically when he came home, and commiserated about his day, and they'd have laughed over their various woes together, before going to bed. Claire decided to take his wine upstairs to him so he could have a drink while he got dried and dressed after his shower.

In the bedroom, Andrew had abandoned his phone and a pile of receipts on the window ledge. Despite her good intentions and resolutions, Claire suppressed a moment of irritation. Of course, Andrew was tired, but did he really need to scatter his stuff around like this? He had always been messy, and he continued to ignore Claire's best efforts to explain that if he put things away properly instead of casually dumping them round the house, then he wouldn't lose his belongings with quite such regularity or forget essential items on the way out the door. Then their days could begin with some semblance of calm instead of Andrew roaring round the house bellowing and shouting because he had lost his wallet/keys/ phone/USB stick/other indispensable piece of equipment he couldn't possibly live without, accusing all and sundry of moving/ hiding/stealing said essentials until Claire found them in whatever random location he had abandoned them the night before.

Claire moved his phone from where it was half hidden behind the curtain, picked up the receipts that he'd doubtless need for his expenses and put them on the bedside table. As she put the phone down, it buzzed with a text. From Fucking Farquhar Ferguson, Andrew's appalling red-trousered best friend from school.

Looking forward to Sunday, old chap! Will I bring Bogg –

That was all that was visible on the lock screen.

Claire seethed to herself. Clearly Andrew had gone ahead and made plans with Fucking Farquhar without mentioning them to her, or checking that they suited, or consulting the complex colour-coded calendar in the kitchen that kept track of everyone's social commitments. How many times had she told him that if it wasn't on the calendar, it didn't count? Weekends were a complicated round of barbecues and Sunday lunches and dinner parties with nice couples just like them, who had nice children the same ages as theirs (though Claire tried not to wince when some of their friends referred to these dinners as 'suppers'), and the only way it could work and she could keep track of their social life and all the birthday parties and playdates for the kids was if it was all religiously added to the calendar. And now, a rare free weekend, and Andrew had arranged something without telling her! What if they had had something on? And it would appear that the Fucking Farquhar Fergusons were invited here, since Claire assumed the rest of the sentence referred to *Boggle*, Farquhar's favourite game, so she was in for an afternoon of slaving over a hot stove before being treated to Farquhar thinking there was nothing more hilarious than Rude Word *Boggle*, 'rude words' covering pretty much anything racist, homophobic and sexist, as well as the more standard rude words like 'willy'.

When Andrew came out the shower, Claire demanded, 'Did you ask the Fergusons round on Sunday?'

'What? Yes, I told you.'

'You *didn't* tell me. If you had told me, it would be on the calendar and it most assuredly is not on the calendar, is it? IS IT?'

'Oh, that fucking calendar. Can't we ever just do something spontaneous without referring to the FUCKING CALENDAR?'

'No! Because then the WHOLE SYSTEM BREAKS DOWN!'

'Well, it seems fine for you to make arrangements that aren't on the CALENDAR, like having Emily round tonight. So why can't I ask the Fergusons?'

'Emily just dropped in unexpectedly. I hardly made plans. And anyway, the Fergusons are –'. Claire bit her tongue in the nick of time before she said, 'the most loathsome arseholes I've ever had the misfortune to meet and I can't for the life of me think what you see in that revolting toad of a man.'

'The Fergusons are what?' demanded Andrew.

'Nothing,' said Claire. 'Nothing. You just need to *tell* me about these things, OK?'

'I'm sure I *did* tell you!' Andrew insisted. 'Look, I know you don't like them. But I put up with bloody Emily, so surely you can put up with some of my friends in return, can't you?'

Claire suddenly didn't have the energy to continue the argument. 'Yes,' she said wearily. 'Fine. Have the Fergusons over. You're quite right. I'm going to bed.'

Andrew caught Claire's hand. 'Don't go to bed,' he said. 'Not yet – I thought we were going to have a glass of wine together? Just one? I've not seen you all day, and all we've done is fight over broccoli and the Fucking Fergusons. Come on.'

'OK,' said Claire. 'That would be nice, actually.'

Downstairs, Andrew smiled at Claire.

'We should do this more often,' he said. 'Just have a drink together, instead of one of us always being busy on laptops or phones or dealing with the kids. Just sit, just you and me.'

'Like we will when we're old and grey and have bought a vineyard in Tuscany to retire to?' Claire smiled back.

'Exactly like that. You in your shady hat, me in a linen shirt, sitting on the terrace looking over the hills towards Florence.'

'You can do your own ironing if you're going to take up wearing linen shirts! Is Florence in Tuscany?'

'I think so.'

'A vineyard with views of Florence would be expensive, I bet.'

'We can dream, can't we?' insisted Andrew. 'If we're planning our perfect retirement together, we can have it exactly as we like it.'

'We could have a little *pied-à-terre* in Rome for weekends. Like Keats's apartment I saw on the Spanish Steps and wanted to go to for the weekend, and you said it would be too "peopley".'

'It *would* be very peopley,' Andrew objected.

'This is our perfect world, though,' Claire reminded him, 'in which both children have left home and settled down early, instead of living with us forever, or giving us false hope by moving out briefly and then moving back in complete with three children and several cats!'

'I'm allergic to cats.'

'You cannot refuse a home to your grandchildren's beloved pets.'

'OK, I think I prefer the fantasy version of old age. You can have your Keats's apartment on the Spanish Steps over grandchildren and cats living with us!'

'Thank you,' Claire smirked.

'We might as well dream while we can. In reality, we'll probably find we're lucky to afford a one-bed flat in Walton-on-the-Naze in our retirement,' Andrew sighed.

'Well,' Claire comforted him, 'we can't speak Italian anyway, and you're right, the novelty of weekends living on the Spanish Steps would probably get old quite quickly. And there would be no room for the grandchildren or their cats in a one-bed flat, would there?'

'True. Shall we have another one, or shall we go to bed?'

'We should probably go to bed. It's a Monday night and we have work tomorrow.'

'Bloody work,' groaned Andrew. 'Ah well. Roll on Walton-on-the-Naze and getting right off our tits on the cooking sherry every night.'

'To Walton-on-the-Naze and the cooking sherry,' said Claire
with a giggle, downing the last dregs of her wine.

Once they were finally in bed, Andrew snuggled up to Claire affec-
tionately and kissed her neck. 'Darling,' he murmured fondly. Claire
stiffened, much as part of Andrew was. One hand was now cupping
her left breast. She sighed. Her phone had binged her this morning
with the fortnightly reminder she had set to try to not let it go too
long without rebuffing Andrew's advances (since she could hardly
write 'Shag husband' on the colour-coded kitchen calendar). It
wasn't that she didn't *want* to have sex, it was just that she was so
bloody tired (especially after several glasses of ill-advised wine on a
school night). And Andrew was so bloody *predictable*. He never
cuddled up to her in bed just for the sake of a cuddle anymore; he
only moved in when he fancied a shag. And even then, it was always
the same. The snuggle. The neck kiss. The 'Darling' and then the
boob grope, followed by the hopeful nudge in the back. *Why* did
men think jabbing you in the small of the back with their erection
was erotic, Claire thought crossly.

Maybe if Andrew actually put a bit of effort in, tried to make her
feel a bit sexier, then she'd be more up for it. But then again, she
didn't exactly make a lot of effort herself. She kept promising herself
she'd cast aside her stout M&S gussets and wear sexy black-lace
thongs or something, but the thought of sitting at a desk all day in
something like that was always too thrushy to contemplate. Instead
she considered perhaps wearing some kind of skimpy silky number
to bed instead of her Boden jammies, but again, comfort and
warmth won the day every time. And then, he *had* tried to make an
effort earlier, asking her to have a drink with him, talking about
their plans, however wild, for the future together. Andrew nudged
her again and twanged the deliciously elasticated waist of said

Boden jammies. She sighed again. At least if she did it tonight, she could forget about it again for another two weeks. She suppressed yet another sigh and rolled over.

'Just a quickie, yeah?' she whispered.

'Yeah, yeah.' Andrew panted, pulling off her pyjama bottoms.

Claire lay there passively as Andrew beavered away. She wondered what had happened to the couple who had been so unable to keep their hands off each other that they'd had sex at every possible opportunity, in public loos, at Christmas parties, on a beach (only once, the sand got *everywhere*, and they both agreed that however unbearably horny they were, in future they'd at least wait till they got back to the car). Andrew had even once pulled off the motorway without warning and booked them into a service station Travelodge when they were driving to a wedding in Scotland because he declared himself unable to spend six whole hours in a car with her sitting beside him and *not* make love to her. They had arrived late for the wedding, and she had never quite got her hair right again the whole day, but they agreed, giggling in the back row of the ceremony, that it had been totally worth it. And then they had done it again in the loos during the groom's (very long and rambling) speech.

But now, sex was just another chore, another thing on the list to be ticked off. Collect dry cleaning, fill in school-trip forms, fuck husband, renew car insurance, ring parents and mother-in-law, make dentist appointments. Actually, Claire thought, that reminded her, she *did* need to make dentist appointments for everyone. Oh good. He was finished. Finally. Andrew proffered a romantic handful of tissues to her, patted her shoulder and murmured, 'Night, darling,' then immediately rolled over and started snoring, while she lay there, now wide awake, contorting herself to avoid the wet patch. 'Roll on Walton-on-the-Naze,' she thought to herself.

Emily said at least Andrew still *wanted* sex with Claire, and he wasn't on awful dating sites pretending to be single and trying to hook up with strangers. And Claire knew she should be grateful for that, and she was really. But however hard she tried, she couldn't quite ever convey to Emily the sense of ennui she now felt in her marriage. Claire loved Andrew, she really did. She couldn't even begin to imagine life without him. She had made him go to the doctor about a dodgy mole on his back last year, and she had been so worried until he got the all-clear that it was nothing at all. And *of course* Andrew loved her. But she couldn't help but wonder, was this all there was? Was this it? From now, until they died? Maybe things would change when they retired. Maybe when they were pensioners in Walton-on-the-Naze, or possibly a very bijou and especially tumbledown vineyard in a particularly cheap part of Tuscany, they'd finally have time to properly enjoy sex again and would turn into the sort of insatiably randy OAPs one reads about in the *Sun* sometimes?

But that wouldn't be for at least another twenty years. If ever. Even for another twenty years, was this really as good as it would get? And how could Claire change it? Where could she find the *energy* to change it, and improve things, when she couldn't even muster the energy to show enthusiasm for a – in the grand scheme of things – very quick quickie? Andrew snored on, blithely unaware of how much she wanted to just scream right now. Did he feel like this too? Did he look at her and think, 'Is this *it*? Where's the girl I married? Who *is* this woman wittering on at me about dentist appointments and buying yoghurt? Is this how I'll die? With a dentist-obsessed yoghurt freak? WHERE IS MY YOUTH?'

Claire punched the pillow and reflected bitterly that Andrew was so wrapped up in his own world these days that none of this had probably even occurred to him. 'Roll on Walton-on-the-Naze indeed,' she thought grimly.

2

On Friday morning, Andrew came downstairs carrying an overnight bag.

'What are you doing?' asked Claire.

Andrew looked shifty. 'I've got that team-building thing,' he muttered. 'I told you … yeah? In North Wales.'

'NO!' said Claire. 'Not this again. You did not tell me, because it would be ON THE FUCKING CALENDAR. And look!' Claire brandished the calendar at him quite violently. 'IT IS NOT ON THE FUCKING CALENDAR!'

'Mummy, you said "fuck",' observed Tabitha sweetly.

'Yes, Claire, please do at least *try* not to swear in front of the children,' said Andrew primly, attempting to regain the moral high ground that he had just bungy-jumped off with his announcement of an unscheduled trip away that he had most assuredly *not* mentioned to Claire.

'Anyway,' said Andrew. 'I'll be home tomorrow. It's only one night, you'll manage. Look, I must go. I'm picking up John and I'm late – I couldn't find my wallet.'

'Wait!' said Claire, preparing to launch once again into her tried-and-tested speech where she chuntered like a rabid squirrel, as she pointed out to Andrew the complex timetables, favours called in, hours spent filling the freezer and making sure everyone's laundry was up to date that she'd had to do in order to go on a two-day work trip a few months ago, and how unfair it was that Andrew was simply able to chuck some pants in a bag and waltz out the door. But before she had a chance to start, Andrew turned around, came over and kissed her.

'I'm sorry I forgot to tell you,' he said. 'Why don't I make it up to you? I'll take you away for the weekend. Properly, somewhere nice. We could even go to that place on the Spanish Steps you wanted to go to. What do you say?'

'Um,' said Claire, taken aback. 'Yes, that would be wonderful.'

'OK. Well, we can look into it when I get back, yeah? Anyway, I really *must* go now.' With that, he kissed Claire again and dashed out the door.

Claire was chivvying the children about their shoes and coats and did-they-have-their-PE-kits-well-why-not-how-many-times-had-she-told-them-to-make-sure-they-had-them, when to her irritation she saw Andrew's phone lying behind the local free paper on the hall table.

'FFS,' she thought. This was far from the first time Andrew had forgotten his phone, because he wouldn't *listen* when Claire told him time and time again to leave all his stuff in one designated place, and then he'd have it all together and ready to go, although recently he had been much better about not forgetting or losing things. She glanced at her watch. He'd probably just be picking up his colleague John now, so she could text John and tell him Andrew needed to come and get his phone before he was halfway to North Wales and realised he didn't have it, and they could avoid a repeat of the time he had got all the way to Bristol for an Important Meeting before he noticed he didn't have it with him. Claire, who Andrew complained was overly attached to her phone, couldn't imagine going so long without trying to look at her phone and realising it wasn't there, but Andrew had this weird thing about only checking his phone every hour, and 'not being a slave to it'.

Claire opened Andrew's phone to find John's number and message him. She was texting John, when to her surprise a message notification flashed up from Emily. Why was *Emily* texting Andrew? Was she OK? Had something happened to her and she was trying to reach Claire, and couldn't get hold of her and was hoping Andrew could pass on a message? Claire anxiously opened Emily's message to see what the problem was. Emily had sent a photo for some reason, two photos actually, that were downloading very slowly and filling the screen. Another text from Emily popped up below them, while the photos carried on downloading.

So excited. Can't wait to see you later. Do you want a sneak preview of what's waiting for you? I'm getting wet just thinking about spending the whole night with you and what I'm going to do to you …

Claire was confused for a second. Surely this was a mistake? Emily must have meant to send these to someone else, perhaps a Tinder date called Andrew? She'd be *mortified* when she realised though, as would Andrew. Though it was odd she hadn't mentioned anyone to Claire. Maybe Claire should just delete the messages. Another message pinged in.

And I'm getting even wetter thinking about all the things I'm going to let you do to me …

Send me a pic if these are making you hard xx

Another photo was downloading, very slowly. Oh God, this was awful. Poor Emily, how could she fuck up like this? She'd *never* live this down. Claire definitely had to delete all of this, before Andrew saw it. How would either of them be able to look each other in the face again? And Claire didn't want to see the photos that were *still* downloading either. It was bad enough reading Emily's dirty texts – they just made her seem a bit … desperate.

The children were clamouring something about money for a bake sale that they'd forgotten to mention to her, and she murmured, 'Just a second, poppets, I just need to do something' as she hastily scrolled up, to select Emily's messages to delete. No one need ever know. Well, she'd probably tell Emily next time they had a few drinks, and they'd piss themselves at the thought of Andrew's face if he had been driving to North Wales, listening to John the Motorway Bore droning on about the best route to take and why the sat nav was wrong when *these* popped up on the screen in the car! Poor Andrew. It was just as well he'd forgotten his phone.

But as Claire deleted the texts, she saw more messages from Emily that had been pushed up the screen by the photos, and replies from Andrew, and oh God, oh God – Claire felt sick – what did they say? All in the same vein, apart from one confirming the hotel they were meeting at tonight, and this was a mistake, this was a horrible mistake, that was all, and then Andrew's key was in the lock and he was walking through the door saying, 'Hello, you all still here, won't you be late, I forgot my phone, what are you doing, darling?' as he saw Claire clutching the phone and for reasons she wasn't sure of, she hit the lock button as she handed it to him and muttered, 'I was just about to text John to say you'd forgotten it,' and Andrew simply said, 'Thanks, sweetheart, must dash,' and was gone before Claire could say anything else.

Claire got the children to school on autopilot and made it into the office and logged on to her computer, though for the life of her, if you had asked her, she couldn't have told you what her username or password was. Or anything else really. All she had was ticker tape running through her head repeating, 'This is a mistake, it's all a misunderstanding, this is a mistake.'

Several times she picked up her phone, to call Emily, or Andrew, and have them reassure her. Tell her it was all a mistake, because surely it was. What else could it be? But each time as her finger hovered over the button, she stopped, because the other voice in her head was clamouring to be heard over the voice chanting 'Mistake, misunderstanding, mistake', and it was shouting, 'What if it's not, what if it's not, what if it's not?' If Claire didn't say anything, if she didn't let them know she knew, then it was a mistake, it wasn't real. It wasn't real until she heard Emily or Andrew say it was real. She didn't have to make it real. Maybe she didn't want to make it real. Because of course, it was all just a *mistake*.

Claire somehow got through the day until it was time to pick the children up from school. On Fridays she finished early, so she picked them up from the playground, straight after school, instead of from after-school club. Although Claire usually enjoyed the early finish and the children's faces as they hurtled out of school (well, Lucas was too cool to hurtle to her now. He tended to saunter over and chuck his bag at her and demand to go and play football with his friends until Tabitha appeared), she had never really got to grips with the whole 'chatting to the other mums' business. When Lucas first started school, she had gone for coffee sometimes with the other mums, and most of them had seemed nice. In good weather, some of them would go to the park after school and chat while the kids played on the swings and rolled in the mud. It had been fun getting to know people again after the toddler stages, when your attempts at friendships mainly consisted of half-snatched conversations over cold cups of tea and your offspring's rejected, soggy, half-eaten biscuits that went along the lines of, 'So, then I went to the – LUCAS! LUCAS! WE DO NOT HIT! Sorry, what was I saying? Oh yes, I went to – TABITHA, NO, TABITHA! TABITHA, IN THE POTTY, NOT IN THE CORNER! Oh Christ I'm so sorry – LUCAS, oh no! So sorry, so sorry, I'll replace it of course, oh shit, it was your grandmother's, oh no, I'm so sorry, yes of course, sentimental value, I understand, I really can't apologise enough, God, look at the time, we must get going – TABITHA, PUT YOUR PANTS ON. LUCAS, GIVE THAT BACK NOW! NO, DON'T LICK THAT! Sorry again, byeeee!'

Claire sometimes felt the toddler years with her children had mainly consisted of just repeating 'I'm so sorry, I'm so sorry' to people she didn't really know as she attempted to deal with the carnage her children seemed determined to leave in their wake wherever they went, and she'd had high hopes that once the children were (marginally) more civilised, she could actually make some friends instead of just issuing grovelling apologies.

But then, after Lucas had been at school for a couple of years, Tabitha started, and Claire went back to work. She was a senior risk analyst with a large bank, who made all the right noises about supporting parents and flexi-time, but in reality they were fairly inflexible. One early office finish a week to work from home was the best Claire had been able to negotiate, so she didn't get much of a chance to meet people in the playground anymore. And even though she was able to finish in time to pick them up on Fridays, there wasn't time for trips to the park because she was haring off to one or the other of the classes that she and Andrew had agreed would help them become proper well-rounded citizens, classes he was sadly never available to take them to (though Claire had dug her heels in when Andrew had suggested adding golf lessons to the rota and snapped that if he wanted them to learn bloody golf, *he* could organise it. She was playing no part in a game that she agreed with Mark Twain was a good walk spoiled, and there was such a thing as being *too* middle class and well rounded, you know). Every time Claire arrived at the school gates, the other mums already seemed to be in their own little groups, and though they were kind when she tried to join in the conversation, she couldn't shake the feeling that she was intruding and had missed the opportunity to actually make friends with any of them, rather than them simply being acquaintances that she shared lifts and arranged playdates with via WhatsApp.

Most of all, though, Claire couldn't help but feel that they were all so much better at being mothers than she was. They all seemed to have it so together – the wholesome snacks ready for their children, the apparent genuine interest in the inane stories their children told them when they came out of school. Claire, on the other hand, had a tendency to zone out of Tabitha's lengthy renditions of what Ella said to Olivia and why Miss Bateman was a poo-poo head and she hated her, interjecting the occasional 'Wow!' or 'Mmm!' at what seemed like suitable intervals. At least, Claire had always consoled herself, she had Emily. Emily had never made playdough or chia-seed porridge-bar bites in her life. In fact, compared with Emily, Claire often felt a tiny bit smug, like she really was a fully functioning adult, while Emily lurched from crisis to crisis.

Lucy Connor came over to talk to Claire when she walked into the playground, to arrange a lift-share to a party Tabitha and her daughter Ella were both invited to the following weekend.

'And are you doing much this weekend?' asked Lucy politely.

Somehow Claire kept the bright smile she had mustered when Lucy came over and fought the urge to be sick.

'Oh, not much on tonight. My husband's away for work, but we've got some friends coming for lunch on Sunday.'

'Lovely!' beamed Lucy. 'That'll be nice for you.'

'Yes,' said Claire, smile still plastered, while to herself she repeated, 'Mistake mistake mistake' to quash the urge to shriek, 'I think my husband is fucking my best friend and I don't know what to do, please help me, I can't cope, please tell me it's all a mistake mistake mistake.'

'Oh, here's Ben and Ella,' said Lucy. 'We must go. We've got swimming straight after school! Nice to see you, Claire!'

As Lucy hustled her children out the gate, Lolly Hughes appeared and made a beeline for Claire. Lolly Hughes was the most organically yoga'd up of all the little clique of organic yoga stay-at-home mummies that populated the playground. Not all the stay-a-home mums were like Lolly and her friends, of course – most of them were lovely – but Lolly's gang made it very clear they Disapproved of Working Mothers and believed if you didn't spend all your time between Sun Salutations whipping up batches of organic kimchi for your precious moppets to consume, then your darlings were indeed well within their rights to complain to UNICEF. And Tabitha had been at Lolly's for a playdate with her perfect twins, Ophelia and Gertrude, after school yesterday, but Lolly had been at a yoga class when Claire had collected them and she had only seen the au pair, so no doubt Lolly was making up for her missed opportunity to cast up something Tabitha had said or done last night. Lolly lived to make other parents feel inferior and was the last person Claire wanted to talk to right now.

'Claire,' Lolly cooed. 'SO nice to see you. I *did* want to have a little chat with you about Tabitha.'

'Oh?' said Claire, still smiling brightly.

'Yes,' continued Lolly, faux concern dripping from every perfectly cleansed, toned, moisturised and exfoliated pore. 'She didn't eat her supper last night, not a bite, and I wondered, have you considered the possibility that she might have an eating disorder?'

Claire blinked. In fairness, of all the things that she thought Lolly might be going to suggest about her failings as a mother, that hadn't been one of them. For a brief moment, the whirling in her head stopped as she attempted to process what Lolly was saying.

'I'm sure she's fine,' she replied, trying to edge away from Lolly.

'Claire, it's really important we're aware of the signs of disordered eating and tackle them immediately,' said Lolly firmly.

Claire resisted the urge to tell Lolly to FUCK RIGHT OFF, and instead asked, 'Well, what did you have for dinner?' (Tabitha, when asked the same question the previous night, as she inhaled three pork pies and a packet of Hula Hoops on her return from Lolly's, while wailing that she was STARVING, had replied only 'YUCK' to the same question: 'I don't *know* what it was, Mummy, apart from it was YUCK!')

'Oh, as you know, I like to keep it simple for visiting children, so we just had some natto and brown rice topped with avocado and kimchi.'

'Of course,' said Claire. 'Er, what exactly is natto again?'

'Oh, don't you know? It's fermented soy beans. SUPER-healthy and so delicious! It's why Japanese people live so long. Anything fermented is so marvellous for the gut. And the skin. And well, everything, really.'

Claire, reflecting that Tabitha wouldn't even eat baked beans, was unsurprised that she had rejected Lolly's offerings.

'Tabitha can be a little picky,' Claire admitted.

'I know, and I totally understand, of course, but I couldn't get her to eat *anything*. Even when I offered to make her some yummy scrambled organic tofu on my special cauliflower bread – of course, it's not *actually* bread because you know, toxins. We just call it that for a little bit of fun! That's Ophelia and Gertrude's favourite treat meal. They always choose on it on birthdays.'

Claire was lost for words. Lolly did not seem to notice and ploughed on regardless.

'And then, the children are always allowed a sweetie after dinner when they have visitors. And she wouldn't even have that.'

Claire tried to concentrate. 'Oh dear. No, that doesn't sound like Tabitha. What sweets did they have?'

'Well, obviously not SWEET sweets,' laughed Lolly. 'God, who would give their children *them*? I feel quite ill when I look at the ingredients on Haribos and Fruit Pastilles. No, they had a spoonful of chewable bee pollen. TREMENDOUSLY good for them, but Tabitha refused. So you see, I was worried. Is everything all right? You know, you do look very tired?'

Claire, thinking of the bare shelves in her fridge last night following Tabitha's return, thanked Lolly for her concern, and assured her Tabitha was *fine* and she, Claire, was also fine, but she'd keep an eye on Tabitha.

'Are you sure? Well, all right. And what about you, Claire? Have you thought about doing a total detox?'

'I need to go,' insisted Claire.

'It's just that you do look very drawn,' Lolly insisted. 'Have you thought about getting a jade egg, you know, for *down there*?'

Lolly's eyes flicked discreetly to Claire's crotch and back to her face. 'Just to keep everything in tip-top condition? It doesn't only do wonders for your sex life, though Harry says he can really notice the difference since I started using mine. It also really refreshes your whole body and system.'

'Err,' said Claire desperately, then saw another of the yummy-mummy crowd loitering nearby. 'I think Jacinta's looking for you.'

'Oh, gosh, so she is! She's got some new herbs for me, you know, for the vaginal steaming! I'll tell you about that another time. Anyway, before I go, I just wanted to check I can count on you to help at the coffee morning next week, yes? Good. We always need backroom people to come and lend a hand, so I'll put you down for washing up from 10 until 2, shall I?'

'What?' said Claire. 'Lolly, I don't know if I can –'

'Excellent,' said Lolly. 'That's that sorted. Jacinta! I'm over here,' and Lolly sashayed off to join Jacinta, who liked to think of herself as being 'alternative' because her £150 yoga leggings were branded as 'ethical' and she had once tried a joint ('but I didn't much like it. Maybe it was because they didn't use organic Rizlas?')

Lucas and Tabitha then appeared, to Claire's relief, and they all hurried out the gate, before Lolly and Jacinta could return and try to foist vaginal steaming herbs on her. Perhaps, she thought sadly, a scalded fanny would at least take her mind off things.

3

Post-playground, Claire marched the children home to ram snacks down them, since her subpar parenting skills obviously meant she hadn't brought any organic quinoa and date bars to the playground for her poor, starving offspring, and instead made them wait five minutes until they got home, like the absolute monster she was.

Tabitha voiced her displeasure about this inferior snack situation and again threatened to call Childline, adding helpfully, 'Because I asked my teacher about Childline after you were talking about it the other night, and she said it does still exist, so we *can* call it, actually. Miss Bateman asked if everything was all right at home and said if there's stuff I ever need to talk to her about, I can tell her anything in confidence. "In confidence" means I won't get into trouble and she won't tell on me, because I asked what it meant. I said, was it the same if you called Childline and she said it was. So there, Mummy!'

'What?' said Claire faintly. 'You've been asking your teacher about Childline? Oh God, she'll think we beat you or something.'

'You *can* be very unkind to me, Mummy,' said Tabitha tragically. 'Like now, starving me of snacks when I'm so very hungry. SO VERY hungry.'

'I'm going to have to go and see her and explain. What on earth must she be thinking? What were *you* thinking, Tabitha, asking your teacher about calling Childline? Lucas, please tell me you haven't done anything like that. I'm going to have social services at the door at this rate.'

'What? What are you talking about? What's social services? Can we order pizza for dinner?' demanded Lucas.

'Oh fine!' said Claire. Andrew was very against ordering pizza, declaring it to be naff, and felt takeaways should only be ordered from adorable Vietnamese places that no one else had heard of yet. But fuck Andrew, thought Claire.

By 9 o'clock Claire was done, in every sense of the word. She had attempted to distract herself and replace the soundtracks in her head with the mantra 'Keep busy, don't think about it, keep busy, don't think about it.' But now the children were upstairs, replete with greasy cheese and carbs and revelling in the glory of Friday night's unlimited screen time, and Claire had manically cleaned the house and done laundry for the last hour and a half.

She finally found herself sitting on the sofa, willing Andrew to ring, to hear his voice, have him complain about his day, what an arsehole John was and how he was never giving him a lift again, because his failsafe shortcut had added an extra hour to their journey, and how much he missed her and wished he was there. Andrew *always* managed to ring when he was away, no matter the time difference, no matter the length of his day. He always managed at least a brief check-in to let Claire know he was OK, to make sure Claire and the kids were all right, and to generally touch base with everyone. Sometimes if he was abroad, the call would be late and he'd miss the kids being up to say hello, but he was only in North Wales, apparently, so why hadn't he called? Not that Tabitha and Lucas had noticed, Claire thought, Netflix being so much more interesting than talking to their father, but still, why hadn't he phoned her? Again, she longed to call him, but a mixture of pride and fear stopped her. She got up and went to the kitchen to pour herself a large gin and tonic, then decided to clean out the cupboards as part of Operation Keep Busy. She took her phone with her, though, just in case she missed that all-important call, the only thing that could possibly stop this awful churning fear.

Claire woke up the next morning back on the sofa, with a dry mouth and a pounding head. Why was she here? Why did she feel so awful? She prised one eye open. The thought of actually moving her head was too painful to contemplate – even the daylight seemed to be causing some sort of vampiric shrivelling reaction in her dehydrated eyeballs. She attempted to focus. The empty gin bottle was on the coffee table in front of her, along with the tonic bottle. Gin. Sofa. Why was she here? Did she drink all that gin? Why would she do that? Then, suddenly, with a pain far worse than the sensation of an iron nail being pounded into her temple that was currently taking place in her head, Claire remembered why she had tanned the best part of half a bottle of gin. In fact, she now recalled exactly why she had brought both the gin and the tonic in here sometime after midnight after she'd finished deep cleaning the kitchen; getting up for another drink had become more effort than she could muster, and ice and lime seemed less important than the oblivion she was seeking – or failing that, at least some sort of numbness – as she tried over and over again to talk herself out of the thought of Andrew and Emily together.

Claire's stomach lurched. She shuffled into the downstairs loo with remarkable speed, given her hangover, and brought up the remains of the gin. If only Andrew had rung her last night, she could still convince herself the messages were all a mistake. But the call had never come. And as the evening wore on, as she ran out of things to do to distract herself, her conviction that it was just a silly misunderstanding had weakened and she'd been forced to face up to reality. Emily and Andrew. Together. Her husband and her best friend.

'Urrrghhhhh,' she groaned, resting her head on the cool, forgiving tiles of the floor, as she realised she really needed to clean behind the toilet. She tried to sit up. Why had she picked gin? Everyone knows about The Gin Fears, she scolded herself. Of *course* you're going to have The Fear if you drink too much gin! It's cause and effect, isn't it? Gin makes you overemotional and paranoid. She ran her head under the tap and gulped some water.

'That's better,' she told herself. It wasn't. She still felt awful. She looked in the mirror. She didn't look much better than she felt. Maybe she could go back to bed for a couple of hours and try to sleep it off. She looked at herself again. Her eyes were red and swollen where she'd been crying for hours. Hours long before there had been time for The Gin Fear to kick in. The Fear came after the gin, not before. The gin had not caused the hideous thoughts going round in her head. The thoughts had caused the gin. She wiped away some more tears, and then realised there was a commotion in the hall outside the door.

She wrenched open the bathroom door to find Lucas and Tabitha standing in the hall, looking at her reproachfully.

'Where were you, Mum?' complained Lucas.

'We're starving!' grumbled Tabitha. 'What's for breakfast? Can you make pancakes?'

Claire's stomach heaved again.

'No!'

'What about French toast, then?' demanded Lucas.

'Yes! With bacon and maple syrup!'

Claire fled back into the loo and spent a few more minutes in quiet contemplation. She rinsed her mouth out again, and finally exited when her darling offspring's clamours for food became so loud she feared the neighbours might call the NSPCC before the children had a chance to.

She stared at them both standing there helpless, squawking to be fed like a pair of baby magpies.

'What are you making for breakfast, Mum?' Tabitha said again.

'Cereal. You can get yourselves cereal.'

'What? But it's Saturday. You're supposed to make us a treat breakfast on a Saturday. We *always* have a treat breakfast on a Saturday.'

'You can have Coco Pops,' offered Claire, and when they opened their mouths to squawk their magpie objections, she added, 'And you can eat them in your bedrooms.'

This mollified them, as eating in bedrooms was Strictly Forbidden. It meant they could indulge not only in their iPads, but also computers and games consoles all at the same time. They were as easily distracted by shiny things as magpies, Claire reflected wearily.

'And you can go and get your own breakfasts,' she said. 'I'm going back to bed.'

'What? But what about swimming? And dancing?'

'And rugby!'

'Fuck them!' said Claire. 'Fuck them all. If your father's home in time he can take you.'

'Mummy, you said "Fuck"!' Tabitha exclaimed in the scandalised tones of a Victorian maiden aunt catching a glimpse of a piano leg. 'We're not allowed to say that and neither are you. Bad language is a sign of a poor vocabulary, remember? That's what Granny told Lucas when he said "Shit" at her house.'

'Fuck Granny too,' muttered Claire to herself, visions of her overbearing mother-in-law being more than her hangover could bear.

'Mummy! You can't say "Fuck Granny".'

'Watch me,' said Claire. 'And Lucas, why *did* you have to swear in front of her?'

'Dunno. Can't remember,' Lucas said thoughtfully. 'Oh yeah. It was all the dog shit in the park.'

'Lucas,' groaned Claire. 'Don't ever swear in front of her again.'

'I told you that, Lucas,' said Tabitha smugly. 'I did, I told him, Mummy.'

'Oh Tabitha, just –' Claire bit back the urge to tell Tabitha to shut up. Instead, she settled for 'Stop telling tales all the time, please. No one likes a tell-tale.'

'Ha!' smirked Lucas at his sister.

'I didn't even do anything! It was Lucas that said "Shit". It's not fair!'

'Tabitha, please. Not now. Lucas has been told not to do it again, and that's an end to it. All right? Now go and get some breakfast, both of you.'

Lucas, who had frankly expected far more of a bollocking when Tabitha dropped him in it for swearing in front of the Tyrant Queen – a little bombshell she'd been saving for some time – was taken aback both by his mother's lack of reaction and his sister's poor choice of timing. Usually she managed to slip these titbits of information to her parents at a moment calculated to cause him maximum trouble. He was a practical child, however, and one to make the most of situations if possible, and so, sensing weakness and deciding to take advantage, he asked, 'Can I have sausage rolls for breakfast?'

'Well, can I have Hobnobs then?' said Tabitha, recovering sufficiently from her fit of the vapours to make sure Lucas did not get something more than she got.

'Fine,' said Claire, as she heaved herself up the stairs.

By 12 p.m. Claire was feeling a little more human. A couple of hours' sleep, two ibuprofen, a Berocca, several pints of water and a shower, and a semblance of life was creeping back into her. A very expensive eye mask and face mask had reduced the worst of the puffiness and blotchiness and, really, thought Claire, you'd hardly know there was anything wrong. She stared once again into the mirror as she put on her make-up, ready to face Andrew.

The one conclusion she remembered coming to last night was that she *did* have to face Andrew. Despite the temptation to bury her head in the sand, pretend she had seen nothing, carry on as if everything was fine, Claire knew she couldn't. She could put on her game face for Lucy Connor and Lolly Hughes and for her work colleagues. But she couldn't, she just couldn't laugh and chat and sit across from Andrew at the table every night (when he wasn't out at 'client dinners', and how many of them were really 'clients' and how many were rendezvous with Emily, she wondered now), and act like everything was normal. Much less could she continue her friendship with Emily, knowing that she – Claire – had been stabbed in the back and betrayed. So, despite the fear of what the conversation would bring, of worries about money, where she'd live if Andrew went off with Emily and they had to sell the house, about what would happen to the children, Claire knew she had to face the worst, because things couldn't actually *be* much worse than they were for her right now.

*   *   *

Andrew finally waltzed in through the door at 12.30 p.m., bearing a large bouquet of flowers.

'Hello, darling!' he shouted merrily from the hall.

Claire walked into the hall and just looked at him.

'What are they for?' she asked.

'For you!'

'Why? You never buy me flowers.'

'Well, you know, to say thank you for holding the fort. I'm sorry I didn't put last night on the calendar, but you know, I'm not perfect. So sorry, darling! And I thought I'd take you all out for a lovely lunch now, and then we can look at that weekend in Rome.'

They were proper florist's flowers, Claire noticed, not a cheap garage bunch. She didn't think Andrew had bought her flowers like that since Tabitha was born.

'Where were you thinking for lunch?'

'Oh, maybe the Cat and Mouse,' said Andrew blithely, naming the new gastropub Claire had been wanting to go to ever since it opened and that Andrew had refused to countenance after looking at the website and declaring it to be extortionately priced hipster wank.

'The Cat and Mouse? Really? Why now?'

'I just thought you might like it.'

'Do you know what I'd really like? I'd like to know where you *really* were last night? And who you were with.'

Andrew barely missed a beat, but just for a second, in that pause, Claire saw the fear and guilt in his eyes.

'What?' he said. 'What are you on about? I had a work thing. In Norfolk.'

'You said North Wales.'

'You must've misheard me. You're being ridiculous. You know perfectly well where I was last night, I told you. Work do. Very dull.

John tried to make me go via the A14. Madness! Ha ha ha.' Andrew laughed just a little bit too heartily.

'You didn't have a "work thing". You weren't even with John. You were with Emily.'

'Emily? What a ridiculous thing to say. What would I be doing with Emily?'

'I saw your phone,' said Claire. 'I saw the messages from Emily. I thought they were a mistake at first, that she'd sent them to you by accident, she meant them for someone else. I even deleted some of them so you didn't see them, but there were more. And you were with her last night.'

'You're mad,' said Andrew, recovering from the initial shock and clearly deciding attack was the best form of defence. 'Quite mad. So, what, Emily texted me by accident and you deleted it, even though what were you doing snooping through my messages in the first place? And so because Emily sent me some stupid text, meant for someone else by your own admission, you've come up with this wild conspiracy? Talk about grasping at straws! Me and *Emily*? Why would you even *think* such a thing?'

Unfortunately, Tabitha chose that moment to bounce into the room.

'Hi Dad! Mum drank a whole bottle of gin last night *and* she said "fuck" this morning *and* she didn't take us to swimming because she went back to bed, AND she didn't even get cross at Lucas when I told her how he'd said "shit" in front of Granny!'

'What? Granny was here? Why didn't you go to swimming? And a whole bottle of gin?' said Andrew, in slight confusion at Tabitha's barrage of information.

'No, Granny wasn't here, Lucas said "shit" last time we went to see her, and I told Mummy, and all she said was he wasn't to do it again, and I think he should have got in more trouble, don't you,

Daddy? I bet I'd have got in *loads* of trouble if *I'd* done that. It's not fair, is it?'

'Right, well, I'm sure your mother knew what she was doing. But what's this about a whole bottle of gin?'

'She did, I saw it on the coffee table this morning. Pints and pints of it. I googled Childline, they've a section on helping someone with a drinking problem. Do you think Mummy has a drinking problem? I could call Childline about it,' offered Tabitha helpfully.

'Tabitha, go to your room please. I'm talking to your father,' said Claire.

'But …'

'Just do it!' said Claire, in a voice that not even Tabitha dared argue with.

'I really don't think that was very responsible parenting, getting shitfaced on a whole bottle of gin while you were alone with the children, Claire. Tabitha is clearly very worried about you. If she's talking about calling Childline, she must've been terrified!'

'She's obsessed with Childline at the moment. I told you she was going on the other day about calling Childline because I made her eat broccoli. And she was going to report me to UNICEF for the same reason, as apparently it violated her rights as a child. She doesn't exactly seem traumatised to me. And it wasn't a whole bottle of gin.'

'Well, it must have been a fair amount for you to come up with some mad paranoid accusations about me. For what? To make yourself feel better about your inadequacies as a parent? Punish me because I forgot to write something on your fucking calendar? A bottle of gin? Jesus! No wonder you came up with this crazy idea based on *nothing*!'

'For the last time, it *wasn't* a whole bottle of gin,' said Claire indignantly. 'She exaggerates. You know she does. And you didn't call me last night. You *always* ring when you're away, but you didn't last night. So I *know* something's going on, I *know* you're lying. So where were you? And who were you with, if it wasn't Emily?'

'You really shouldn't drink gin, Claire, it's clearly not good for you. For the last time, I had a work do. That I forgot to tell you about. And I said I was sorry and I've tried to make it up to you, and what do I get as thanks? You off your head on gin, accusing me of what? Shagging *Emily*? Because she still can't work her fucking phone properly? Because for the first time in God knows how many years, I lost track of time, it was a long day, and then I was having a few drinks with the guys, and before I knew it, it was late, I thought you'd be asleep, I didn't want to wake you, because you're always on about how tired you are. I'm sorry if that worried you, but I was *trying* to think of you.'

'I … I …,' said Claire uncertainly.

'Look, darling, I'm sorry I forgot to tell you about last night, that was stupid of me. And I do love you, you know that. There's no one else for me, there never could be. Can't we just put all this behind us, and have a nice day together? Forget I was a thoughtless twat, and forget you could even think such things about me? We've both messed up, so let's just say no more about it, and enjoy our afternoon instead.'

Claire tried to think about what he had said. She wanted so much to believe him. That this was all a big misunderstanding. For everything to go back to where it was just over twenty-four hours ago.

'OK,' Claire said. 'OK. I'm … I'm sorry. I don't know what I was thinking.'

'It doesn't matter, darling,' said Andrew gently. 'Let's not mention it again. We'll probably laugh about it one day, you know!'

Claire looked down at the expensive flowers in their swathes of cellophane and ribbon, lying on the table beside Andrew's phone and keys where he had dumped them as usual when he came in.

Something still wasn't quite right. though. She couldn't just let this go. Not without more than Andrew's word for it.

'I … I just … I guess I overreacted. I'm sorry. I was upset. But, please, just to put my mind at rest, can I look at your phone?'

'I thought we weren't going to talk about this anymore?'

'I know, I just … it looked bad from my point of view. It *seemed* very plausible. Please … if I could just look at your phone and know you were at a work thing and there isn't anyone else. So I was sure. I'm sorry. Please?'

'Really? Haven't you listened to anything I've just said? Why are you trying to spoil our day?'

'I just need to be sure. If there's nothing to hide, it won't be a problem?'

'It's not a case of there being something hide,' said Andrew, looking hurt. 'It's about you accusing me of being a liar and refusing to trust me.'

'I do trust you. I just need to be sure. Please.'

'If you can't take my word for it, then you don't trust me, do you? And I can't just let you scroll through my phone. There are highly confidential client emails on there!'

'I don't WANT to look at your client emails! It's just the messages I saw from Emily … they looked bad. I need to know that it wasn't what it looked like, that I misunderstood the other messages, the earlier ones that I didn't delete.'

'NO! No, I won't show you. You need to BELIEVE me. This is a matter of trust, Claire. I shouldn't need to *prove* myself to you every time you get some bizarre idea in your head. What next? You'll see me talking to a traffic warden and I'll have to show you my Ring-Go receipts so you know I wasn't driven crazy with lust by her neon tabard? If we haven't got trust in our marriage, what do we have? You *need* to trust me, OK?'

Claire snatched Andrew's phone off the table and opened it.

'Claire, give me my phone,' said Andrew furiously.

'No,' said Claire, bolting into the downstairs loo and locking the door.

'CLAIRE!' shouted Andrew, hammering on the door, 'Claire, this is ridiculous. Claire, please, just come out. Claire?'

Claire opened Emily's messages and scrolled rapidly through them. She didn't have to look far to have her fears confirmed. The messages between them were frequent and explicit, including photos of Emily from angles Claire had never expected to see her best friend.

'Oh my God,' gasped Claire in horror.

'Claire?' said Andrew again. 'Claire, please, talk to me? Just– come out and we can talk about this? I can explain, it's not what it looks like. Claire, please, you're scaring me, open the door!'

While Andrew hammered on the door and begged Claire to come out, Claire carried on scrolling until she couldn't bear it anymore and then she was sick. She picked up Andrew's phone to look again, but she couldn't. She didn't need to see anything else. She didn't want to see anything else. What was she going to do? She couldn't stay in the loo forever more. Could she? There was water. And facilities. How long was it you could survive without food as long as you had water? Tempting though the idea was, Claire knew she couldn't stay there. The noise of Andrew banging on the door and his increasingly panicked entreaties would eventually come to the attention of the children, and she didn't want him to scare them.

Claire unbolted the door, and looked at Andrew. He had gone very white.

'How could you?' Claire whispered.

'I'm so sorry,' said Andrew. 'Claire, please. I'm so, so sorry.'

4

Claire remembered very little of the drive to her parents' house. She probably shouldn't have been driving at all, but she had to get out of the house, away from Andrew's rambling, desperate attempts to explain that he hadn't meant to hurt her. As Andrew pleaded, Claire picked up her car keys and walked out the house.

Andrew caught her at the front door.

'Where are you going? What are you doing?'

He sounded panicked at the sight of Claire leaving, but she didn't care how he was feeling. After the initial shock and pain when she opened Emily's messages and realised that actually, knowing for sure hurt even more than her suspicions, she had felt oddly numb and detached.

'I'm going out,' said Claire, astonished by how calm her voice sounded.

'Where? Where are you going?'

'I don't think that's any of your business, do you? You can give the kids some lunch and then take Tabitha to dancing and Lucas to rugby.'

'What? Where? When? What do I do? What are they having for lunch?' quavered Andrew in confusion.

'That's your problem,' said Claire as she got in her car. Accelerating down the driveway, she caused Colonel Mousicles, her neighbour's fat and overindulged ginger tomcat, to leap out of the way in indignation, just as he was about to annihilate a pigeon. Colonel Mousicles was not at all pleased at such lack of consideration from the humans, and he hissed menacingly at Andrew, who was standing on the driveway looking in the direction of Claire's fast-disappearing car.

It was only when she arrived at her parents' house that Claire realised she had absolutely no idea how she was going to explain what had happened. She didn't think she could say the words 'Andrew and Emily have been having an affair' out loud. As it turned out, when her mother Tessa opened the door, took one look at her and said, 'My God, darling, what on earth has happened to you?' Claire couldn't say anything at all. She just burst into the hideous, racking sobs that she only then realised had been waiting behind a dam ever since she opened the messages. Eddie, her parents' Irish setter, was so appalled by the noise that he began to bay in sympathy.

Tessa dragged Claire inside, sat her down at the kitchen table, and put a box of tissues and a large brandy in front of her. Even through her tears, Claire's hangover rebelled at the smell of the alcohol and she pushed it away. Claire's father Jonathan came in to see what the noise was and Tessa waved him to leave as she rubbed Claire's back and murmured, 'Come on, darling, deep breaths. You can tell me, whatever it is. Just try to breathe, yes?'

Eddie, now he realised Claire was making that noise because she was upset, sat down beside her and put his head on her knee. A remarkably stupid dog but a very loving one, he hated to see anyone in distress.

Finally, Claire was coherent enough to choke out the words, 'Andrew. Andrew and Emily.'

'Andrew and Emily?' repeated Tessa, looking confused. 'What

about Andrew and Emily? OH!' Tessa sat back and gasped in horror as the penny dropped. 'Oh no, surely not, darling. Are you sure? There must be some mistake?'

Claire nodded soggily. 'Quite sure,' she snuffled. 'There were messages. I saw. There's no mistake.'

Jonathan reappeared. 'What on earth is happening?' he demanded. 'Claire, are you all right?'

'Emily and Andrew have been having it off, the dirty fuckers,' announced Tessa.

'Oh, for fuck's sake! What a pair of utter BASTARDS!' roared Jonathan, making Eddie jump.

'Mum! Dad!' protested Claire, shocked out of her despondency by her parents' furious reaction.

'What? Don't you start defending them. Bollocks to *that*, you don't owe them anything,' huffed Tessa.

'No, it's just … your *language*,' said Claire weakly. 'I've never heard you swear before. Ever. And now you're swearing like a trooper. Both of you are. When did this start?'

'We've always sworn, darling,' said Tessa fondly. 'Just, you know, *pas devant les enfants*. But frankly, this situation seems to call for it.'

'You young people think you invented bad language,' said Jonathan. 'Your mother in particular curses like a Marseilles docker.'

'Are the dockers of Marseilles particularly foul-mouthed?' wondered Claire.

'I've no idea. Just ignore your father,' said Tessa briskly. 'The point is, what are we going to do about all this? I really thought better of Emily – after all these years, after everything you've been to each other and everything you've been through together. I just don't understand *how* she could do this to you. I'll never forgive her for this. Never. If I could lay my hands on her, I'd –'

'Tessa, I'm not sure this is helping,' interrupted Jonathan. 'Emily, and what you'd like to see happen to her, are not our concern. It's Claire we need to be focusing on, not Emily.'

'The trollop!' put in Tessa helpfully.

'How long have you known?' asked Jonathan gently.

'Since about two hours ago, for sure,' said Claire, and then the whole story came spilling out, with more tears, and more furious indignation and chuntering from Tessa, until Claire finally got it all off her chest and was sitting dry-eyed at last, twiddling Eddie's silky ears between her fingers and feeling drained and weary. More than anything in the world, she'd now just like to crawl into her old bedroom, lie down on the Laura Ashley eiderdown and sleep for about a week. But Jonathan was having none of that.

'Right,' he said firmly. 'First things first. Drink that brandy your mother has given you, it will make you feel better. Not least because I see that she has decided this occasion is beyond her cooking brandy and has poured you a hefty measure of my good Rémy Martin. Thank you for that, Tessa.'

Tessa shrugged. 'It was clearly an emergency.'

'Well, there's no point in it going to waste, is there? That's it. Good girl. Don't gulp it, *sip* it!'

Claire obediently sipped the brandy and felt it did provide a comforting warmth, but it made her even more inclined to go to sleep.

'Now, to practicalities,' said Jonathan. 'Where are the children now, and where is Andrew?'

'At home,' said Claire. 'I simply had to get out of there. Andrew just kept saying how sorry he was, like if he said it enough it could change things and –'

'OK, so Andrew and your children are all still in *your* marital home? Yes?'

'Yes. I told you, I couldn't stand it. I had to get out. I wasn't really thinking where to go, but if I could just stay here for a few days? Though I haven't even brought any clothes or anything, so I'll need to buy some.'

'No,' said Jonathan firmly, and quite unexpectedly. 'No, you can't stay here.'

'What?' said Claire in disbelief.

'Jonathan, for God's sake, *of course* she can stay here, for as long as she likes! What are you on about?'

'No,' said Jonathan again. 'Claire needs to go home. This needs to be sorted out. Whatever happens, Claire needs to be there. And if things are over with Andrew, if she lets Andrew stay in the house now she'll have a much harder time getting him out later and keeping what's rightfully hers. Especially if he's got the children too. And what's to stop him moving Emily in? Is that what you want? Emily, living in *your* house?'

At the thought of Emily living in Claire's house, Tessa now passed beyond the point of rational speech and instead made furious noises reminiscent of a rabid squirrel, the only words that could be made out being the occasional 'A GOOD SLAP!' or 'THE NERVE!'

Claire shook her head. 'No, of course not. But he wouldn't. Would he?'

'I don't know, darling. How serious is it between them?'

'I … I've no idea. He just kept saying he hadn't meant to hurt me.'

'Well, you need to know how serious it is, and what they're intending. And for that, you need to be at home, I'm sorry.'

'I should have *known* he was a wrong'un from the off,' said Tessa sadly. 'The man didn't like gravy. You can't trust a person who doesn't like gravy. They should put that on a fridge magnet.'

'Anyway,' said Claire, 'I can't go back there. I can't. I can't *do* this on my own, that's why I came here!'

'Don't be silly,' said Jonathan. 'You're not doing anything on your own. We're coming with you.'

'How could you think we'd let you do this on your own?' said Tessa. 'Come on, darling, chin up. We're not going to let those bastards win. You're better than that. Finish your brandy, and wash your face and have a wee – it's a long drive home – and then Daddy will drive you back in your car and I'll follow in ours with Eddie. He gets car sick in strange cars, but we can't leave him because he'll eat the furniture if we do.'

Claire tottered into the loo to wash her face and have the maternally mandated wee that must be undertaken before a journey, and started crying again, looking at the photos that plastered the walls. They were fairly dreadful in the most part, which was why they had been relegated to the downstairs loo, but they showed Claire and her older brother Mark at various stages of their childhood, with buckets and spades on windy beaches, tea towels on heads for nativity plays, Mark looking glowering and spotty in his rugby kit among fourteen other glowering, spotty boys (at least twelve of whom Claire had been hopelessly in love with at one time or another in her adolescence), Claire with a truly appalling perm, off on her first school trip abroad, where she had snogged a French boy called Michel when they had *allezed à la discotheque*.

Michel had written to her every week for a month after she came home, letters that she had very little idea what they said, because he wrote in French and Google Translate hadn't been invented yet and she could hardly have shown them to Miss Bosomworth, the French teacher, and asked for help with translation. Poor Miss Bosomworth, reflected Claire, how they had tortured her. But then again, what on earth induced someone to go into teaching with a name like Bosomworth? Claire had thought life was so complicated then, but really it had been so simple. When did it get so complicated? And when did all the promise and hope life had held in those photos vanish and get replaced with a never-ending carousel of laundry and bastarding oven chips?

The drive home with her father was an even more surreal journey than getting to her parents' house had been. Jonathan stopped for petrol and bought a tin of travel sweets which he pressed solicitously on Claire, and he didn't even object to the car radio being on Radio 2. It was the concession to Radio 2 and the munificence with the travel sweets that really brought it home to Claire that this was real, that this was serious, and that Jonathan was very worried about her. As a child, Radio 4 was the only station allowed in the car and the tin of travel sweets was a coveted thing, safely locked in the glove compartment, with only ONE allowed, despite Claire and her brother Mark drowning out Radio 4 with their constant pleas for *just* one more. Only on journeys of more than five hours was a second travel sweet ever permitted. To be presented with a whole tin and urged to have as many as you wanted was unheard of.

When they got home, Andrew burst into the hall as Claire walked through the front door, flanked by Jonathan, Tessa and Eddie.

'Claire!' he gasped. 'Thank God you're back. I've been so worried! I'm so sorry, so sorry about everything. Please, we need to talk!'

'About what?' said Claire wearily. 'Really, what can you *possibly* say?'

'Claire, you need to let me explain!' pleaded Andrew. 'It's not how it looks. Emily … she wouldn't leave me alone. She pursued me! I … it was a moment of weakness. Madness! I don't know what I was thinking, it's *you* I love …'

'So what you're saying is that it's all Emily's fault?' asked Claire.

'Yes!' said Andrew in a relieved voice. 'Yes, that's exactly it! It was all Emily. *She* came on to *me*.'

'Right, I see,' said Claire. 'I think I understand now. It was a moment of weakness, you say? Weakness in what, exactly? Did Emily take all her clothes off and you were standing there, NOBLY resisting, saying, "No, Emily, I can't do this, I love Claire, this is wrong," and suddenly there was a moment of weakness where what happened? That old rugby injury started playing up again and your gammy knee gave out, and you fell over and your dick *landed* in Emily? You didn't *mean* to fuck her, it just all happened accidentally because of your *weak knee*. Before you knew it, there you were, balls deep? Is that how it went?'

'Claire!' hissed Andrew in horror. 'Mind your language. Your parents are standing here.'

'It's hardly the first time I've heard the word "dick", you know,' said Tessa stoutly. 'Or "fuck".'

'Nor the first time I've heard some self-justifying little weasel trying to squirm out of taking his share of the responsibility for screwing around and trying to blame the other woman,' put in Jonathan. 'And I can assure you, I'm *not* going to stand by and let you ruin one more minute of my daughter's life! Pack your bags and get out.'

'Claire!' objected Andrew. 'This is between you and me. We need to *talk*, by ourselves. Please, darling, be reasonable, you need to let me explain, and I *can* explain. I told you, this is all Emily's fault.'

'I don't want to talk to you,' snapped Claire. 'What can you possibly say?'

'Sweetheart, please, I know you're upset, and I know I have a lot, a *lot* of making up to do, but we've so much to lose. All over one little mistake, that's all it was, a *mistake*. You can't finish things over this! We have a whole life together. Please, please, just let me talk to you. The children –'

'Where are the children, by the way?' asked Claire.

'I told them to go upstairs and put their headphones on, and gave them a family bag of crisps each. Since I've done the dancing and rugby runs, I thought it would be good for us to have some time to talk,' said Andrew virtuously.

'But there's nothing to talk about,' repeated Claire, with less certainty than before.

'Claire, *please*, darling, you just need to give me a chance here. You're not even listening to what I'm trying to tell you.'

At this point, Tessa gave up the unequal struggle of keeping Eddie under control and let go of his lead. Eddie, with a remarkably feline intuition for anyone who disliked him (he'd had a good growl at Colonel Mousicles on the way in, before deciding discretion was the better part of valour after Colonel Mousicles stood his ground, spat at Eddie and had a swipe at his nose), took a flying leap at Andrew, catching him off balance and knocking him over, before proceeding to enthusiastically lick his face.

'Oh dear, I am sorry,' said Tessa in an entirely unapologetic voice. 'And he was licking his balls all the way here too!'

Andrew spluttered from the floor, but any attempt he might have made at retaining dignity and composure under the circumstances had been ruined by being pinned down by seventy pounds of very overexcited Irish setter. VERY overexcited Irish setter, in fact, as Eddie promptly got his lipstick out and started dry humping Andrew, still prone on the floor.

'Bad dog, Eddie,' said Jonathan unconvincingly. 'Stop that!'

'You're right, I haven't given you a chance to actually explain,' said Claire over Andrew's protestations. 'So go on then, explain. Is that how it happened with Emily? Are you like Eddie? You fell over, and before you knew it you were screwing her?'

'I told you,' shrieked Andrew, as Eddie embarked on one of his oddest habits, which was to start howling when he was becoming uncontrollably aroused.

'Right, Eddie, that's enough,' said Jonathan eventually, hauling him off Andrew before actual penetration occurred. 'You might catch something nasty off this one, old fella! Come on!'

An indignant Eddie removed, Andrew sat up.

'Now, tell me honestly,' said Claire. 'How long has this been going on?'

'Just last night.'

'Never before?'

'No, no, I swear it.'

'Nothing at all between you?'

'No, no, well … Look. Can't we talk about this in private? Not, you know, in front of your mum and dad?'

'You don't have to do anything you don't want to do,' Tessa reminded Claire.

'I don't know what I want to do,' Claire said miserably, choking back more sobs. Oh, if only Andrew *could* explain. Maybe he could. Maybe, if she gave him a chance, there would turn out to be a perfectly reasonable explanation and everything could go back to how it was, and since her mum and dad were here they could babysit, and she and Andrew could go out for a romantic dinner together, since it was now too late for lunch, and plan the trip to Rome, and everything would be all right, and they'd laugh, they'd actually laugh at this, and reassure each other of how much they loved each other and it would all be like it once was again. In fact, that was all Claire wanted. Never mind Rome, or romantic dinners, she'd settle for it just being like it was before, laundry piling up, no one apparently able to put dishes in the dishwasher apart from her, and Andrew losing his keys and forgetting to write things on the calendar and asking the Fucking Fergusons over without discussing it with her. Everything would just be ordinary again. Just ordinary. That would be enough.

'Grumble! Gramps! What are *you* doing here? And Eddie!' shrieked Tabitha from the top of the stairs in delight. 'LUCAS! Grumble and Gramps are here!'

'Um, we've just popped by to say hello!' said Jonathan quickly.

'But you don't live anywhere near here,' said Tabitha in astonishment. 'Did you know Mummy drank a whole bottle of gin? Grumble, have you brought me a present?'

'No, darling, but if you're very good I might give you £5,' offered Tessa. 'Actually, do you know what you and Lucas could do? Go and make me and Gramps a cup of tea. Do you think you can do that?'

'Oh yes,' said Tabitha importantly. 'And then will I get my £5?'

'And me,' said Lucas.

'You're only getting £5 if you help,' Tabitha objected.

'Well, I'm older than you, so I'm more responsible, so I'll actually be doing more of it, so actually I deserve the £5 more than you,' argued Lucas.

'Go!' said Tessa sternly. 'Make tea. Or I shall donate your £5 to Children in Need.'

The children safely in the kitchen, Tessa turned to Claire. 'Darling, do you want to talk to him?'

'I don't know,' said Claire miserably. 'There is so much to sort out.'

'Please,' said Andrew. 'Please at least let me try to explain.'

Claire nodded at Tessa. 'I think I should talk to him,' she whispered.

'Right,' said Tessa briskly. 'Why don't we take the kids back with us for the night then? Give you two some space? What do you think, Claire?'

'Yes … yes, that would be good, actually. Thanks, Mum.'

When her parents had finally hustled the now very overexcited children out of the door, Claire collapsed on the stairs, head in her hands. Andrew sat down beside her and attempted to put his arm around her. Claire pulled away.

'Look, let's go into the sitting room,' he suggested.

Claire trailed after him into the sitting room, dimly registering through her misery how tidy it looked, and also that, somewhat tactlessly, he had put the Guilt Flowers in a vase and plonked them on the mantelpiece in pride of place. Claire slumped on the sofa. Andrew sat opposite her, then got up and went into the kitchen and came back with a bottle of wine and two glasses, the last two remaining from the set they had been given as a wedding present, she noted. She didn't know if that was a sign she should or shouldn't throw them at him. Andrew handed her a glass and sat back down again. He was clearly waiting for her to open the conversation.

'Go on then,' she said. 'The truth, this time. How long?'

'Last night. That's all. I swear.'

'Only – I saw your phone, remember?' said Claire. 'I saw how many messages there were going back and forth. I saw some of the photos she sent you. And I saw the photos you sent her. So I know you're lying.'

'I'm not. I'm not. Last night was the first time I slept with her. I … the rest … that was just stupid virtual stuff. It … it was only for a few weeks. I know, I know. It was wrong, it was so wrong of me. I was just flattered, I suppose, that she wanted me so much. I shouldn't have. I'm sorry. I'm so sorry.'

'Really?'

'Really. That other stuff on the phone, it wasn't real. It was, oh God, I dunno, just like watching porn or something, I guess.'

'Why didn't you delete her messages? Why did you leave them there on your phone? Your phone you're always fucking losing? If you'd only done that, maybe you'd have got away with this. Did you get a kick out of going back over them?'

'I don't know. I suppose … I didn't think you'd ever go through my phone. And yeah, I was being a lot more careful with it. But I was so stressed about going to meet her … of all the times to forget it! I'm sorry, Claire, I'm so sorry.'

'You keep saying you're sorry, like being sorry can fix it. Like Lucas when he was a toddler and he thought sorry was a catch-all get-out-of-jail-free card to do whatever the hell he liked, as long as he said 'sorry' when he was caught. In fact, this is *exactly* like that! How did it start? How did this happen?'

'Oh God, Claire, please, do we have to do this?'

'Do what? Talk about you fucking my best friend? Do you expect me to just brush it under the carpet and move on? *Forget* about it?'

'No, of course not. I just mean, do you need every forensic detail?'

'Yes. Yes, I do. I need to understand *how* this happened. *How* you and my BEST FRIEND ended up in bed together. And, ideally, WHY. So, again, how did it start? I assume she didn't message asking how to repressurise her boiler and you responded with a dick pic?'

'No. I just … how is this helpful for you to know?'

'I think I get to decide what is helpful, not you.'

'OK, OK. I guess it was maybe about three months ago. I'd had another client dinner. We'd had another huge row about it that morning – you said I hadn't told you, and you'd had plans and now you'd have to cancel them, and there had been a lot of shouting and you basically telling me what a shit father and husband I was.'

'How many times? This is WHY we have the fucking calendar!'

'OK, yes, this is why we have the calendar.'

'Anyway, you were telling me what happened?'

'Well, I had a few drinks with dinner, and then after the clients had gone back to their hotel, I thought, "Fuck it." I didn't want to go home. I didn't want to have you having a go at me again. I just felt like everything I did was wrong, you pushed me away all the time, I just wanted to forget that, forget work, forget everything for an hour. So I went to this bar in town. It was a nice bar, you know, posh whisky, cocktails, cigar terrace. I thought I deserved a treat. I'd got a big contract out of those clients, but you wouldn't have cared. You'd just have started on me again. So, I walked in, and Emily was sitting at the bar. She'd had another crap date that she'd bailed from early, and also had decided she needed cheering up instead of going home. I didn't know she was going to be there, I swear it. It was sheer coincidence. We had a couple of drinks together. I told her about my contract, and she ordered us champagne. Then we had a whisky, and I think it was me who suggested we went out to the cigar terrace and had a cigar. Because we deserved it. And then we had another whisky, and we talked. And Emily really listened to me, in a way that you hadn't listened to me for a very long time. And when the bar was closing and it was time to go, I don't know who kissed who, but we kissed. And I felt so guilty. So awful. What was I doing?

'I went home to you and you were asleep, and you looked so beautiful lying there, and I told myself I'd been pissed, I'd just been pissed and it would never happen again. Emily messaged me the next morning to say the same thing. A pissed mistake. Must never happen again. But then a few days later, you turned me down for sex again. And I couldn't help but remember how *fantastic* it had felt, sitting there with Emily, having her *listen* to me like that, and I texted her. Just a joke I'd seen, that I thought would make her laugh, and it did. And she messaged me back.

'And it started quite innocently. Jokey messages. And then it sort of started being less jokey, more serious. I met her for a drink a couple of times, but we just talked. Nothing happened. We both agreed nothing could happen, because we couldn't hurt you. And then one Friday night, I was a bit pissed, you were dicking about on your phone and ignoring me, and I messaged Emily and she was a bit pissed too. I asked her what she was doing and she said she was in the bath. So …'

Andrew paused and swallowed hard. 'I asked her to send a photo. And she did. So I sent one back, and well, you know.'

Claire drained her wine glass and refilled it. 'So how did you go from grubby little texts to shagging your tart?'

'Claire, don't.'

'Don't what? Make it seem as sordid and pathetic as it is? Should I respect your love affair and speak of it only in polite and pleasant terms, instead of calling it what it is, which is the pathetic mid-life crisis of a dirty old man and a desperate old slag? Or is that not how you saw yourselves? Were you star-crossed lovers? Were you *making love*, not *shagging*?'

Somehow Claire thought that the viler the names she could call Emily, the better she might make herself feel.

'No. No, of course not. I … we kept trying to stop. But something would always start it again. And we felt so wretched about you. It wasn't fair to you.'

Claire spluttered a mouthful of Montepulciano over the La Redoute rug that had been so in last year and said, 'It wasn't *fair* to me? FAIR? Is that what you call it? Shagging my best friend was a bit UNFAIR of you? Unfair is when you eat all the Kettle Chips and don't leave any for me! Unfair is cheating at *Scrabble*, not FUCKING EMILY.'

'All right. That was a bad choice of words. Not unfair. We knew it was wrong, but we couldn't seem to stop it. So we … we thought if we just slept together, we might get it out of our systems. And we could forget about it and move on. Go back to being friends.'

'Get it out of your systems?'

'Yes. You were never meant to find out. Hurting you was the last thing on our minds. In fact, we were trying to protect you!'

Claire attempted to laugh a hollow, bitter laugh. Andrew looked at her in concern. 'Are you choking?' he asked.

'No. So what if it hadn't got it out of your systems? What if I hadn't found out? Would you have carried on fucking her?'

'Please stop saying that. It sounds so awful.'

'THAT'S BECAUSE IT IS AWFUL!' Claire screamed. 'IT IS FUCKING AWFUL THAT YOU FUCKED MY BEST FRIEND! And no doubt if you hadn't been caught, you still would be!'

'No! No, absolutely not! We both agreed. It was a one-off, one-time thing only.'

'But I thought you agreed exactly that about the first kiss. So I very much doubt it would have ended there, would it?'

Andrew looked miserable. 'I don't know. I want to think it would have.'

'And what about Monday night? Talking about us growing old together? About our vineyard in Tuscany or retiring to Walton-on-the-Naze. Our future. Our future I was looking forward to. And all the time you were planning to go off and screw Emily?'

'I … I don't know. It was a shock seeing Emily here, I wasn't expecting it. And it reminded me that however much I fancied Emily, I love *you*, Claire. I've only ever loved *you*.'

'But you still went off and fucked her.'

'I know. I know. I … we were getting on so well that night. I thought, I can't do this. Seeing you together. I realised it was you, not Emily. But then … later, in bed. We'd had a nice time, talking and drinking wine, I thought finally, you might be interested in sex with me. But you still weren't. "Just a quickie" to placate me, keep me quiet for another few weeks. And I thought, don't I deserve one night with someone who actually wants me? Just one night? But … I see now that was so wrong. I should never have done that.'

'Oh, now you see it was wrong. Now you've had your dirty week-end, you see it was wrong. And all that "let's go to Rome" before you went away yesterday? What was that? Guilt?'

'Yes,' said Andrew simply. 'Yes, it was. I suppose I thought it would balance it out. If I could just have this one thing I wanted, then I could make it up to you, without you even knowing it had happened at all.'

'But I do know it happened. I can't ever *not* know, now. How could you *do* this to me? How could either of you do this to me? Were you laughing at me behind my back the whole time?'

'Of course not. God, Claire, we'd never have … hurting you was the last thing we wanted. I just … I was so sick of waiting for it to be our time. We joked about Tuscany and retirement, and that seemed so far away. So long until we got to be *us* again, instead of parents, instead of chauffeurs, instead of our job titles, instead of this man whose idea of an exciting Saturday is doing DIY badly. I just wanted to feel like *me* again.'

'Don't you think I felt all those things too?' said Claire incredu-lously. 'Christ almighty, it's been so long since I've felt like *me* I don't even know if I know who that is anymore. But it's OK for you to screw my best friend because you wanted to feel like *you* again, and once you'd got what *you* wanted, you thought you could make

it up to me with a weekend in Rome, because somehow you enduring a few tourists was the same thing as me enduring you fucking
my best friend, and so that would *make it up to me*!' Claire was
crying again now.

'No, no, of course it's not the same. But I still want to make it up
to you. All I want to do is make things right with you. I never ever
want to see Emily again in my life.'

'Well,' said Claire grimly, 'at least we've got one thing in common.
So what do we do now?'

'We can get through this. We've so much to lose, Claire, we can
sort this out. We can go back to how we were.'

'How we were was pretty shit,' sobbed Claire. 'And it's a shame
you didn't think about how much there was to lose when you were
FUCKING EMILY and disregarding my bloody calendar!'

'I know, I know, things haven't been great. I mean, we could go
back to how it was when things were good. I love you, and I want to
make this right, and we can, we *can* fix this, and the children as
well, Claire, we need to fix this for them.'

'How can we fix this?' asked Claire sadly. 'I just don't see how we
can possibly come back from this.'

'Let me try. Please, I'm begging you. At least let me try to fix this.
For you, and for the kids. For the children's sake, you can't end this
without at least giving me a chance to try to fix this.'

Claire shook her head. All she wanted to do was sleep. For about
a hundred years. She got up. 'You're sleeping in the spare room,' she
said. 'Until I say otherwise.'

'Does that mean you're not kicking me out?' Andrew said hopefully.

'It doesn't mean anything,' said Claire. 'Except that you're right
about one thing. I do need to think of the children as well as what I
want. So you can stay, for now, until I work out what is best for the

children and me, and see if there is any way at all we can keep this family together for their sake after what you've done.'

'Thank you, darling,' babbled Andrew in relief. 'Oh God, thank you so much. You won't regret this, I promise you!'

'I very much doubt that,' said Claire. 'I'm going to bed.'

'I love you!' Andrew called after her as she trudged up the stairs.

'Oh, go fuck yourself,' snarled Claire.

5

Claire was astonished by how well she slept that night. As she crawled into bed, she didn't think there was any chance of sleep, but as soon as her head hit the pillow, her mind and body, exhausted by the stress and emotion of the day, shut down completely and she fell into a deep and dreamless sleep. The next morning she woke up and stretched, and for a brief moment reflected on how well she felt, before everything came crashing down again as she remembered the events of yesterday.

Downstairs, a hollow-eyed Andrew was sitting at the kitchen table and ostentatiously drinking black coffee to signify his exhaustion. He looked, Claire was pleased to note, like utter shit.

'Farquhar's texted to ask what time they should come over today,' he announced.

'Farquhar?' said Claire in confusion. 'What? Come over?'

'Farquhar and Felicity are meant to be coming for Sunday lunch today. Remember?'

'Farquhar and Felicity?' repeated Claire. 'Coming for *lunch*? Are you serious?'

'Well, it's all arranged,' said Andrew, 'so I assumed we'd be going ahead. We can't just cancel at short notice. It will look very odd – what will they think?'

'I don't care what they think,' said Claire, thinking that the last person in the world she could cope with putting on a united front for was Farquhar Fucking Ferguson and his vapid wife Felicity, who giggled when Farquhar smacked her on the arse and simpered when he made chauvinistic comments about women Knowing Their Place. It was a friendship Claire had never been able to fathom, other than the fact that Andrew and Farquhar had been at prep school together.

'If we can just get through today, darling, it will avoid any awkward explanations, and once this has all blown over –'

'Blown over?' said Claire. 'BLOWN OVER? You think I'm going to pretend this has never happened and we're all going to play HAPPY FUCKING FAMILIES with your pompous prick of a school friend Farquhar Ferguson, which is a stupid bloody name by the way, who calls their child Farquhar Ferguson, and his racist wife Felicity, sitting there pretending everything is fine like I've done far too many times while Farquhar complains about benefit scroungers and Felicity goes on about immigrants? I've put up with their shit for years, and I'm certainly not doing it today while you carve the roast beef like nothing has happened! Do you know something, I *hate* Farquhar and Felicity.'

'What are you talking about? You adore Farquhar and Felicity.'

'No, I don't. I loathe them. They're awful people and I've never been able to stand them. I put up with them for your sake and because you put up with Emily, but since you've rather moved the goalposts when it comes to how we put up with each other's friends, and since I've no intention of shagging Farquhar because the only thing probably more repulsive than Farquhar *wearing* his red trousers is probably Farquhar not wearing *any* trousers, though it would serve you right if I did go out and screw someone else, sauce for the goose is sauce for the gander and all that, but anyway,

I'm not going to screw anyone else today, so at the very least, I think I cannot be forced to endure FUCKING FARQUHAR AND FELICITY, OK!'

'I thought you liked them. You never said you didn't like them. Do you really mean it that you're thinking of sleeping with someone else to hurt me?'

'I don't know! I don't know what I want to do.'

'Who would you sleep with?'

'I DON'T KNOW! Ideally, yes, it would be your best friend so you can see how that feels, but much as I hate you right now, I don't hate myself enough to shag Farquhar, so maybe I'll just give Tom Hardy a call and see if he's free.'

'You're hurt, I understand,' said Andrew in an irritatingly soothing voice. 'You're saying things you don't mean.'

'I do mean that I'd totally shag the fucking *arse* off of Tom Hardy, given the chance, actually,' said Claire. 'And I also mean that I hate your friends, and do you know what, it feels bloody marvellous to say so after biting my tongue and being polite all these years.'

'All right, all right. It was a bad idea to suggest they still come round. What will we tell them, though?'

'I dunno. How about that they can go fuck themselves? No? Well then, you can tell them whatever you like. I never want to see the fucking Fergusons again.'

'Of course, of course,' Andrew said, looking flustered. 'I'll tell them something's come up and I didn't realise you didn't like them, you're right, they're awful people, don't know why we see them, we won't any more, I'm so sorry, you should have said something before, I totally see what you mean, I'll sort it, don't worry.'

Five minutes later Andrew announced he had told the Fergusons that Claire had a migraine. Claire snorted, and Andrew then announced he was popping out for five minutes and walked out the door. Claire was immediately clutched by a cold dread and horror that he had gone to see Emily, or to ring her out of earshot. By the time he returned fifteen minutes later, smugly clutching a bunch of petrol-station red roses, Claire had worked herself into a semi-hysterical state.

'Where were you?' she howled when he walked through the door brandishing his booty.

'I went to buy you flowers,' Andrew said in confusion, thrusting the sad plastic-wrapped roses at Claire.

'More flowers? Why? Why would you do that? Was it just an excuse to go and ring her? You bought flowers because you're feeling guilty about ringing her, but it was only a phone call, not actual sex, so shitty petrol-station flowers will do for the guilt. I only get the nice ones if you do the deed, is that how it goes?'

'No! No! I thought it would be romantic.'

'A dozen half-dead flowers? It was just an excuse, an excuse to go and ring her,' Claire sobbed, before collapsing on the sofa.

'It wasn't. It really wasn't. I'm trying to do the right thing, but I don't know what that is.'

'Let me see your phone then.'

'Fine.'

Andrew reluctantly handed over his phone, and Claire scrolled frantically through it. What had he been doing? There were no messages to Emily, nor any calls logged.

'I've blocked Emily's number,' said Andrew quietly.

'Why? Were you afraid you might not be able to control yourself and stop calling her if you didn't?'

'No. Of course not. I just … I don't know. I wanted to wipe the slate clean. I didn't want any reminders of it all in my phone, any part of her in our lives. So I've deleted everything.'

'So I wouldn't have a chance to read your messages properly?'

'What good would that do? You'd be hurting yourself all over again.'

'NO!' screamed Claire. 'YOU'D BE HURTING ME! YOU! YOU DID THIS! YOU AND THAT BITCH! And how do I know you've deleted everything because of that? How do I know you've not just started covering your tracks now you've been caught? Now I've fucking REMINDED you that the sensible thing to do when having an affair is to delete the calls and messages after you've made them? Oh my fucking God, do I even have to tell you how to have an affair?'

Andrew slumped wearily into an armchair.

'Check my phone records,' he suggested. 'I'll give you the login details and you can go through every fucking call I make, every text I send.'

'You could be whatsapping. You could have a burner phone. A secret email.'

'I could,' Andrew agreed sadly. 'There are a thousand ways I could contact her without you knowing. But why would I do that? If I wanted Emily, why would I be here?'

'I don't know,' wept Claire. 'I don't know anything anymore.' She continued to cry and cry, suddenly seemingly unable to stop, until she began to laugh hysterically. 'Now do you see why I didn't think it was a good idea to have to the fucking Fergusons over?' she hiccupped. 'All these tears, Farquhar's beef would have been over-seasoned. And we couldn't have that, could we? WHY DID YOU REALLY GO OUT?'

'I told you, I went to get you flowers. I thought it would be romantic. You know, making an effort. I mean, what do you want me to do? Do you want me to stand naked in the street with a rose up my bum and serenade you?'

'No, I most definitely don't want you to do that, and even that's not an original idea. You've stolen it from *Cold Feet*.'

'Which I remembered you loved, which makes it romantic!' said Andrew. 'Do you know what I want, Claire? I want this marriage to work. I don't want to go back to how we were before, two people snapping and snarling and too busy for each other. We've lost sight of *us*, these last few years with the kids. Emily, this thing with Emily, it reminded me who *I* am, it made me feel alive and special and wanted, but afterwards, that night with her, I realised that it wasn't Emily I wanted to be making me feel like that, it was you. It's always been you. I miss *you*. There's more to life than the calendar, and I want us to find that again, I want us to find *us* again, to be more than parents, more than a husband, more than a wife, I want us to be Andrew and Claire again. Don't you want that too?'

'I just want this never to have happened,' wept Claire, and she didn't know if she meant Andrew's affair, or the loss of themselves, buried under ParentPay emails and invitations to trampolining parties and chimney bastarding sums and trying to teach Lucas the importance of commas and persuading him why a *Minecraft* manual was not a suitable choice for a book review.

'Oh Claire, so do I. More than anything. More than I could ever tell you. If I could put this right, I would.'

Andrew moved over and put his arms round Claire. She was so lonely and heartbroken and in need of comfort that she leaned into his chest as she sobbed on and on, while he stroked her hair and murmured soothingly to her.

6

For the next few weeks Claire and Andrew struggled on. He tried very hard to make it up to her. He arranged a babysitter and took her out to dinner, but she ended up crying into the panna cotta because he had inadvertently picked the restaurant that she and Emily had been planning to have lunch in soon, and they had to leave abruptly.

Claire made heroic efforts to get over his affair as well, but try as she might, every time Andrew was out of her sight she was gripped with terror that he was contacting Emily, and nothing he said could convince her otherwise. When Claire was with him, she could just about calm down and believe him when he assured her that he was doing nothing he shouldn't be doing, but every time he nipped out to the shops, or was ten minutes late home from work, or, worst of all, had a client dinner, the gnawing fear was back, whispering in her ear. How did she really know where he was? He had lied to her before – if he hadn't forgotten his phone, if he'd been a better liar, if he'd had the sense to cover his tracks, she'd never have known about Emily and him, they'd still be carrying on their relationship, and Claire would be none the wiser.

So who was to say they *weren't* still seeing each other? She only had Andrew's word for it, after all. She checked his phone relentlessly, sometimes several times a day, sometimes in front of him, sometimes secretly when he was in the shower, going through emails and messages and websites, searching for anything, the slightest clue that he'd been with Emily.

Andrew, in fairness, bore all this without a word, but he eventually snapped one day when Claire was sobbing again because he'd been delayed by roadworks.

'For Christ's sake, Claire, can't you even TRY to trust me?'

'How can I trust you?' screamed Claire. 'You screwed my best friend and now you just expect me to move on and be over it. Just forget it and TRUST you on YOUR say-so? How can I ever believe a word you say again?'

'You can try to meet me halfway! I'm TRYING to save this marriage and I feel like all you do is knock me down. I can't save it on my own!'

'You wrecked it well enough on your own,' Claire said nastily.

'That's not fair. That's SO unfair. I know what I did was awful, I know, but if things had been better with us, it would never have happened. Maybe if you'd ever noticed I existed, instead of always being "tired" or "busy" it would never have come to this. Christ, you had a bloody alarm set on your phone to REMIND you to throw me a pity shag every couple of weeks – that's how little interest you had in me! It's not *just* my fault things got into this state!'

Stung by Andrew's accusations, Claire had hurled fury and bile at him, refuting any possibility that she might bear some of the blame. Yes, their marriage had not been perfect, yes, she too had been bored and felt neglected and in need of some excitement and spice in her life sometimes, but *she* had managed to keep her knickers on, so why couldn't Andrew have done the same? And if he was so fed up, found their marriage and sex life so stagnant, why hadn't he done something about it? It was all very well to complain that she'd had no interest in sex, but maybe that was because Andrew's quick tit squeeze and cock nudge was so very predictable and it didn't exactly scream 'burning with lust and desire for you, O glorious goddess of my heart', did it? When was the last time he'd tried to initiate sex with anything a bit more innovative? Christ, Claire would have settled for him trying to squeeze her right boob first instead of her left one!

Despite all this, Claire thought she could have coped with Andrew's betrayal, with the fury and hurt and misery she seemed to cycle through on an hourly basis, if only she'd had Emily to talk to about it, Emily's shoulder to cry on, Emily to make her laugh and feed her Creme Eggs and remind her there was nothing so bad with boys that Emily and Claire couldn't get through it together. Claire felt like she had no one to talk to at all about it, apart from her mother, and Tessa was so outraged that she just made Claire feel even worse. She had contemplated talking to one of the other women in the dinner party and barbecue circle of friends that had filled their weekends so effectively until now, but she couldn't bear the thought of them going back to their husbands and relating Claire's confidences and laughing at her together.

Andrew had suggested that perhaps a counsellor would be beneficial, and they had duly trooped off to see one, a dreadful man with a droopy moustache and leather patches on the elbows of an even droopier cardigan, which looked distinctly whiffy. He wittered on a lot about non-judgemental safe spaces, and no blame being apportioned, and Andrew had talked earnestly about his feelings and Claire had vaguely thought she should have been paying more attention to what Andrew was saying, but she was too fascinated by the bowl of rocks the counsellor had placed on his fireplace hearth. Just rocks. Not pretty, shiny, ornamental stones, but just ordinary shitty rocks like Claire sometimes turned out of Lucas's pockets when she was sorting the laundry, Lucas claiming he had picked them up because they looked 'useful'.

Claire couldn't help but wonder if the counsellor also collected rocks that looked 'useful' (useful for precisely what, Lucas had never been able to clarify) and had no one to chuck them out when they were discovered in his pockets (though he looked distinctly like he still lived with his mum – shouldn't it be a rule or something that you couldn't be a marriage counsellor unless you were actually in a long-term relationship? Claire couldn't imagine anyone burning with lust for Peter the Counsellor with his 'tache and elbow patches and *rocks*). Maybe, Claire mused, he had seen a Top Tip in his mum's *Take a Break* about creating a 'fun feature' that 'all your friends will love' and 'didn't cost a penny' by putting rocks in a bowl and he'd decided to give it a whirl. Claire got the giggles at the thought of Peter sitting solemnly, poring over *Take a Break* and piling his Useful Rocks into a bowl. He probably also tore the lingerie pages out his mum's M&S catalogue to interfere with himself over.

Claire snorted to herself and thought, 'Oh God, I can't *wait* to tell Emily about this.' Then her laughter turned to tears and she stumbled out of the room to lock herself in the loo and sob, while Andrew banged on the door in exasperation and reminded her that this was costing £90 an hour. But all Claire could do was sob harder, because she didn't want to talk to fucking Peter and his rocks in a safe, non-judgemental space. She wanted to be sitting on her old bedroom floor in Tessa and Jonathan's house with her back against the bed and Counting Crows playing (to demonstrate that she was feeling meaningfully unhappy), with her mouth open as Emily lobbed Maltesers into it while assuring her that she wasn't going to die of misery over this – she'd survived Take That breaking up, and she would survive this.

What could a counsellor possibly say that could help Claire fill the gaping hole in her life that Emily had left? Once or twice, Claire had weakened, and thought about unblocking Emily's number and calling her, just for the sheer relief of having someone to talk to. But every time she did, she remembered those photos of Emily on Andrew's phone, and her resolve hardened again.

With Emily had also gone a certain amount of Claire's sense of self, and of self-worth. Claire was ashamed to discover that deep down, though Emily had always been the one all the men stared at when they walked into a room together, she had nonetheless felt slightly superior to Emily, on account of her own far more success-ful love life. Yes, a Italian conte *had* once whisked Emily off to Venice on their second date for a weekend of passion in a splendid palazzo, but on the second night he'd appeared in the bathroom – while Emily was in the bath – with an escort in tow, whom he wanted to join them for a threesome. Claire had been horrified when Emily rang her from the airport in floods of tears about this, but even as she consoled Emily, she'd been thinking 'Poor Emily' and 'How lucky *I* am to have Andrew.' Emily's relationships all tended to be equally disastrous, if not quite as sordid as the conte, leading even Farquhar Ferguson to remark on it, declaring, 'Pretty girl, that Emily, cracking tits! Can't understand why she can't keep a man,' and Claire had felt smug once again, if irritated with Farquhar's casual sexism. And anyway, she thought, maybe my tits *aren't* as cracking as Emily's (though Farquhar had at least possessed the bare minimum of tact required to prevent him from comment-ing on Claire's breasts right to her face, so she was blissfully unaware of his thoughts on the subject), but at least she, Claire, could keep a man. But now? Well, could she? Was this her comeuppance for that smug complacency?

* * *

Work became a sanctuary, a respite from the whirling thoughts in her head. At work she could switch off the pictures going round in her mind, and focus only on her computer screen and the figures scrolling past on it. Even previous irritations such as the fact that the email about arranging a leaving present for Nigel Dawson was now up to three thousand messages and counting came as a welcome distraction. Maybe Nigel *would* like a voucher for *World of Golf* more than he'd like one for *Golf World*, after all? It was a valid point, well made by Tom from IT. Or maybe Debbie from HR was right, and you couldn't go wrong with John Lewis vouchers? Claire set the cat among the pigeons and suggested a *Hello Fresh!* subscription. They were up to 3,500 messages by the time she logged off at the end of the day.

On a Friday evening about a month after Claire's discovery about Andrew and Emily, Tabitha and Lucas were at Lucy Connor's house after school. Lucas had always been good friends with Lucy's son Ben, and Tabitha had recently announced that Lucy's daughter Ella was her best friend. Claire did not hold out much hope of this lasting, as Tabitha changed Best Friends weekly, but Ella seemed to be sticking so far. Claire was just relieved that the era of being Best Friends with Lolly Hughes's practically perfect twins, Gertrude and Ophelia, was over, as Claire was not sure how much longer she could have borne their sad little faces on playdates, avidly watching every mouthful of ketchup-slathered chicken nuggets Tabitha and Lucas consumed, while they dejectedly contemplated the bento boxes full of organic, sugar-free, gluten-free, joy-free, vegan delights Lolly sent everywhere with them, lest they become corrupted by such horrors as taste and texture in their food.

At least, Claire reflected wearily as she parked outside Lucy's house, picking up the children slightly delayed her inevitable return home to an empty house and wondering what Andrew was really doing, as opposed to what he said he was doing. He had told her earlier in the week that he had clients to take to dinner tonight, and Claire had suffered another meltdown, accusing him of romancing Emily, until Andrew showed her the reservation email for five people from his secretary. Nonetheless, there had still been a horrible atmosphere when he left this morning, and Claire knew she'd spend another miserable evening crying after the children had gone to bed. She had tried ringing her mother for reassurance, but even Tessa's internal Angry Squirrel seemed to be losing patience with Claire, and instead of the furious chunterings, Tessa said instead, 'Darling, have you thought maybe you need to start trying to move on?'

'Move on?' Claire had spluttered in outrage.

'Well, it's just, there comes a point when this constant rage and hurt, darling, it starts to seem a bit like you're *wallowing* in it.'

'*Wallowing*? I'm upset about my husband and my best friend's affair, and my own mother says I'm *wallowing* in it? Really?'

'Well, maybe "wallowing" wasn't the best word to choose. But Claire, it does seem like you're not making any effort at all to get past this. And I know this must be dreadfully hard, darling – I can't imagine it – but you can't keep dwelling on things like this. You need to buck up and get on with your life.'

'BUCK UP?'

'Oh, you know what I mean. Just, you're hurting yourself as much as Andrew with this constant anger and suspicion. If you're trying to punish him, it won't work, it'll only drive him away.'

'Back to Emily, you mean?'

'NO. Claire, darling, you're not listening.'

'I have to go, Mother,' said Claire curtly. 'I'm picking up the kids.'

Claire got out of the car and trudged up the path to Lucy's house, feeling like she had just lost her last ally. 'Wallowing!' 'Buck up!'

Lucy flung the door open before Claire had even rung the doorbell.

'Claire!' she beamed. 'Come in!'

Claire entered nervously. The door being opened that promptly at the end of a playdate usually boded badly, so she immediately wondered what the children had done. Had Tabitha convinced Ella to call Childline? Had Lucas traumatised Ben by introducing him to the Urban Dictionary, despite Claire's strictures that he was NOT allowed to look at it?

'Everything OK?' Claire asked tentatively.

'Oh yes, fabulous! I've hardly seen or heard them. They've pretty much entertained themselves, it's been great. Threw pizza and garlic bread at them for dinner, they inhaled it, then vanished again. Tabitha and Ella are covered in glitter, though, I must warn you. They've been playing "makeovers" and are definitely of the "more is more" approach when it comes to make-up, but other than that, all good! Can I tempt you to stay for a glass of wine?'

Claire was exceedingly tempted. A glass of wine, a bit of normality, it sounded bliss.

'I can't,' she said sadly. 'I've got the car.'

'Oh, ditch it!' said Lucy. 'It's not raining. It'll only take you ten minutes to walk home with the kids, probably not even that. You can come and get it tomorrow. Go on, it's Friday night, after all.'

Claire thought about it. Lucy was right on all counts. In fact, she was already brandishing the bottle and a glass at Claire. And what did she have to go home for anyway? Her husband was off gallivanting and thought she was a hysterical bitch, and her own *mother* thought she was 'wallowing'.

'OK,' she said. 'You've convinced me.'

'You didn't take much convincing. I like that in a person! Sit down. There's pizza left if you're hungry. I hid it from the ravening beasts.'

Lucy handed Claire a brimming glass, waved at her cluttered kitchen table and shoved a plate towards Claire, but Claire shook her head.

Claire liked Lucy, but she had never got to know her very well. She knew she was divorced, but she didn't know any more than that, as until about six months ago Lucy had been part of Lolly Hughes's little coven of yummy mummies, though she had never struck Claire as having much in common with the clean, green yoga machines like Lolly and Jacinta, and their third 'chum' Figgy. Then all of sudden, one day, she had been cast out, and Lolly refused to even stand on the same side of the playground as her. Claire was dying to know what had happened but felt she couldn't just ask outright.

They chatted back and forth over the first glass of wine about the children, about work, about the endless pleas from their children as to why they needed a smartphone and their insistence that 'everyone else has one'. Claire found herself starting to relax and laugh, and yes, have a good time. 'Wallowing' indeed! She still knew how to have fun. She could still be a good laugh. She didn't need to 'buck up'; she was *perfectly* bucked, thank you very much. She just needed Andrew to not be a twat.

Lucy refilled their glasses, and Tabitha and Ella charged into the kitchen and demanded that Tabitha be allowed to sleep over.

Lucy shrugged. 'I don't mind, if you don't? She can borrow pyjamas and clean clothes for tomorrow and I've got spare toothbrushes.'

'Pleeeeease, Mummy,' beseeched Tabitha.

'All right,' said Claire.

'Thank you, Mummy, you're the best!' and Tabitha and Ella departed in a cloud of glitter and sickly faux-fruit body spray.

'That's very kind, Lucy,' said Claire.

'Might as well keep all the glitter in one location,' Lucy said. 'Oh hello, Ben, Lucas. Yes, Tabitha and Ella *are* having a sleepover. Well, I don't mind if Lucas sleeps over – the more the merrier, as long as you don't mind, Claire?'

'Not at all,' said Claire, who was feeling really quite merry herself, as after the first hideous weekend she had barely touched a drop of alcohol, unsure whether she'd be able to keep control of herself if she did.

'What's your husband up to tonight?' Lucy asked as the boys thundered away back upstairs. 'Do you want another glass of wine, or now you're childfree for the night, do you want to rush home for a lovely romantic evening with him? Oh shit, Claire, what's wrong, what did I say?'

Suddenly all the warmth and merriment Claire felt, sitting in Lucy's cosy, cluttered kitchen, chatting away like a normal person, had drained away at the mention of Andrew and what he might be doing right now, let alone the idea of her wanting to rush home for a romantic night with him. Lucy's words were like a pin stabbed into the fragile balloon of Claire's fleeting happiness and she could physically feel herself deflating as her eyes filled with tears. She needed to go, she needed to stand up and find her bag and get out of here now, but she couldn't see through the tears spilling down her cheeks. Although the warmth of the wine had abruptly left her, the slight befuddlement it brought had not, and everything seemed like a terrible, huge effort, except she couldn't just sit here at Lucy's table, crying her eyes out, much though she wanted to.

Lucy got up and shut the door, then sat back down next to Claire, putting a box of tissues in one hand and a refilled wine glass in the other.

'Do you want to talk about it?' Lucy asked quietly.

Claire shook her head violently.

'It's too awful,' she sniffed. 'I can't.'

'Is Andrew ill?'

Claire shook her head snottily and realised she had better blow her nose before she actually dripped snot over Lucy's table.

'Has he left you?'

Claire shook her head again and mumbled, 'I wish he had, really.'

'It is something to do with him, then?'

Claire nodded miserably.

'Look,' said Lucy, 'you don't have to tell me anything if you don't want to, but sometimes it helps to talk to someone about things. And I swear nothing you tell me will leave this room. If it makes it easier to tell me, well, my husband left me two years ago. For our au pair. Which was nice. I came downstairs for a glass of water one night after I'd gone to bed early, and found him screwing her on the sofa. It was pretty grim. I hadn't forked out the extra to have the sofa stain-guarded for a start. And then he announced that he was in love with her, and it was over, and he upped and left. Fifteen years of marriage, two children, a mortgage. All over in the time it took to leave one jizz stain on my dream sofa.'

Lucy laughed, but it was a bitter sort of laugh. 'Anyway. Whatever he's done, whatever's happened, I might understand. Or at least you might feel better if you got it off your chest.'

Claire sniffed and blew her nose again, then took a big gulp of wine. The wine, and Lucy's kindness, and the weeks of bottling everything up were all too much for her. The temptation to put it all out there was irresistible. The need for some sort of confessional –

to just see what someone else thought, if it was as bad as *she* thought it was – was overwhelming. Claire wiped her eyes and sniffed again.

'He had an affair with my best friend,' she announced.

'Your best friend! gasped Lucy. 'Oh, that's low! That's shitty. That's worse than ruining my sofa. Well, it's his sofa now, I didn't want it. *She* can sit in the spunk stains. Sorry! So how did you find out? And what's happening now?'

Over several more glasses of wine, Claire told Lucy the whole sordid story, and at the end she felt a sense of calmness that she hadn't felt in weeks. It really did seem like a weight had been lifted.

'And what now?' asked Lucy.

'Now? We're trying to "save our marriage", as they call it. But I'm just so angry with him. I can't trust him, I don't think I can ever forgive him, and not only has he ruined our marriage, he's cost me my best friend.'

'So what's happening with Emily?'

'Gone. Blocked her. Told her I never want to see or hear from her again.'

'Can I ask you something? Why are you punishing Emily more than Andrew? She's been cut out of your life, but you've stayed with him.'

'He persuaded me we should try to get through this, for the children's sake. But sometimes, sometimes I hate him. And sometimes I wonder whether I only agreed to him staying because I was so afraid of being alone. Especially without Emily as well. Maybe I was scared I couldn't lose them both at once, no matter what he's done. And also, it almost felt worse, Emily doing that to me, than Andrew. At least things were already shitty between me and him. But Emily and me, we were great. And she STILL did this!'

'There are worse things than being on your own,' said Lucy gently. 'Being stuck in a miserable marriage for one. It's been really hard since Matthew left me, but I've managed. The thing is, only *you* know what is right for you and your marriage, only *you* know that. What I will say is that at least you have the option of choice. You can decide what you want – if you want to stay with him or not. Not everyone gets that. So you need to use that choice wisely, and think about what you really want from life. And if Andrew, and getting through this, are what you want, marriages have survived much worse. It *is* possible. Not easy, but possible. None of the choices you have are straightforward, though, that's why no one else can tell you what you should be doing. But sometimes talking about it helps you see more clearly. Have you been to see anyone?'

'Like a counsellor? Yes. It's awful, I hate it. He has these rocks and oh! I can't concentrate when I'm there. My mind wanders, not least because he's always wearing the same cardigan and I don't think he ever washes it, and possibly not himself either. There's a distinctly goaty whiff in his room, but ultimately he's not the person I want to talk to, neither him nor his cardigan, which I'm genuinely concerned is starting to take on a sentient life of its own. I don't *want* to tell a stranger all my darkest thoughts and have them analyse me. Though I suppose that's what I've done with you, isn't it? Oh God, I *am* sorry. You kindly invite me in for a glass of wine, you offer to keep both my kids overnight, and I repay you by getting pissed and crying all over you and dumping all my tales of woe on you.'

'You haven't dumped anything on me. It's nice to hear someone actually being honest about their relationship, instead of pretending it's all perfect happy families and there are no cracks in their smug, smiley marriage at all. Too many of those swishy-haired bitches in that playground do that.'

'Like Lolly and Jacinta?'

'What have you heard?' asked Lucy guardedly.

'Nothing. Only they're the swishiest of swishy-haired bitches. Sorry, I know you were friends with them.'

'"Were" being the operative word. And yeah, I suppose I was referring to them.'

'What happened? Sorry, I'm being very nosey, you don't have to tell me.'

Lucy sighed. 'I was only really friends with them because Matthew works with Harry, Lolly's husband. After Matthew left me, the social invites dried up, but they'd continue to graciously bestow their patronage on me in the playground. Until the night Harry stopped by with a bottle of wine and told me how he'd always fancied me, and he could tell I was "up for it", which I most certainly was not. I sent him packing with a flea in his ear and told Lolly what he'd done. But Lolly insisted Harry was totally innocent. If anyone had come on to anyone, it was clearly me trying it on with *him*. She was very nasty. Basically called me a slut and a complete fantasist. As if anyone would fantasise about that sweaty oaf. So now we no longer speak.'

'Crikey.'

'Yeah. The downside of the world of the single woman – every man thinks you're gagging for it, and most married women think you're after their balding, paunchy sex machines. As Loretta Lynn once said about divorcees, if you're a woman, you're rated X! Not that Lolly and Jacinta and Figgy were a great loss anyway, but it still stung. And now every time I'm in the playground, I'm wondering what they've said and if everyone's whispering about me.'

'Well, I've not heard anything,' Claire comforted her. 'I shouldn't think it's the sort of thing St Lolly would want people knowing anyway.'

'Nor do I, really. Promise you won't tell anyone?' said Lucy anxiously.

'I promise. I don't know who I'd tell anyway, not that I would!'

'Well. Shall we have another glass of wine, then? It's been a bit of a night, hasn't it? Sure I can't tempt you with a delicious slice of cold, only slightly rubbery pizza?'

Claire suddenly found that actually, she was hungry. The cleansed lightness from telling someone outside the circle of her family and Stinky Peter what had happened had given her back the appetite she had lost on the morning Andrew forgot his phone. Lucy poured more wine, they ate cold pizza and sang along to Loretta Lynn.

Finally, on the doorstep, Lucy hugged Claire and said rather drunkenly, 'Think about another counsellor, yeah? Stinky Pete isn't the only one in the world. Maybe go yourself, instead of with Andrew? And even if you don't, think about what you want, what you need, what would make you happy. OK? And if you want some time tomorrow to talk to him about stuff, anything, there's no rush to pick the kids up. Text me when you're home. Byeeeee!'

Claire walked home slowly, turning over what Lucy had said. Andrew came in the door about five minutes after Claire, looking wary and braced for another row. He blinked in surprise when Claire simply said the children were at a sleepover and she was going to bed, and headed up the stairs.

Claire didn't sleep much that night, there was too much to think about. Mostly she thought about what Lucy had said about having a choice. Claire had spent the last month focusing almost entirely on how many choices had been taken away from her by Emily and Andrew, but Lucy was right, and so, annoyingly, was Tessa (apart from the 'wallowing' bit). As long as Claire kept dwelling on all the things she didn't have, and feeling sorry for herself, she could never move on and start putting her life back together. She had been betrayed by her best friend and her husband, yes, and that was a terrible thing, but dwelling on it wouldn't help, because she couldn't change the past. She could only change what happened in the future. About 4 a.m., having made several spreadsheets of pros and cons to weigh everything up, Claire finally fell asleep. She was too tired to think now, and was even more confused than ever.

7

Claire woke to the sound of Andrew clattering about downstairs making coffee, and thought about going downstairs to see him. She looked at the spreadsheets she had made last night, and considered a day of at best awkward silences and forced politeness, and at worst rows and recriminations. She thought of the next twenty years, and she finally knew what she wanted. She got up, had a shower, got dressed and made up her face with extra care. This was not a conversation to have in your pyjamas with bed hair. She went down and found Andrew drinking his coffee in the kitchen.

'Coffee?' he offered tentatively. 'I made a big pot?'

'Thanks,' she said. 'That would be nice.'

'There's croissants too?'

'No, no thanks. Andrew, can we talk?'

'We're talking now,' he said brightly.

'Please, you know what I mean.'

'Well, that depends. Are we going to actually talk, or are you just going to scream at me and throw more accusations around? I can't face another row, Claire. I'm exhausted.'

'So am I,' said Claire quietly. 'That's what I want to talk about. And yes, I do mean talk. I can't take any more rows either.'

Andrew sat down at the table, looked at Claire and sighed wearily. 'All right. Go on then.'

'I'm sorry, Andrew. I can't do this anymore. The rows, the anger, the suspicion. I just can't. I want us to separate.'

'But why? I thought we were making really good progress with Peter … if you just give it time …'

'I hate Peter. And even if I saw another counsellor, one that might help me – us – find ways to deal with the anger and to stop thinking about what happened all the time, how long is that going to take? Things are getting worse, not better. Yes, maybe, if we gave it enough time, we'd move past this all-encompassing THING that poisons every aspect of our lives, but how long will that take? We're not getting any younger. I don't want to spend years hating you, feeling so much anger, only to find that after that finally subsides, all that's left is indifference. I want to move on, Andrew. I've been thinking about this all night, and I can't do that when I'm with you. This isn't a knee-jerk thing, but I honestly don't know where else there is for us to go with this.'

'Like Elvis said, we can't go on together, with suspicious minds?'

'Pretty much. Andrew, this is destroying us. Us, as people. Look at us. We're both drained, shattered, living on our nerves. We're tearing ourselves to pieces, and it's not making either of us happy.'

'So your mind is made up?' asked Andrew despondently.

'Yes. I'm sorry.'

Andrew sighed. 'No, I'm sorry. I'm the one who fucked all this up. You've nothing to be sorry for. I just … I don't want this to be the end. I wish I'd sat you down like this and had a real conversation with you, instead of blaming you for all the failings in our marriage.'

'Well, I could have done that too. But there's no point dwelling on what we *could* have done now, is there?'

'Do you think you can ever forgive me?'

'Maybe one day, I don't know. All I know is I can't live with you at the moment. Until that time comes, if it comes, I don't want to spend every morning wanting to smash your face into your bowl of cornflakes and hold your head in it till you drown in the semi-skimmed.'

'Not sure you can actually drown in a bowl of cornflakes.'

'You can drown in two inches of water!'

'I know, you never ceased to remind me of this when I took Tabitha and Lucas to the park when they were little.'

'Well, you take a lot of milk on your cornflakes. And you always managed to let the kids fall in a puddle or a pond.'

'I didn't *let* them. Anyway, what happens now?'

'I suppose we see how it goes. And then at some point we have to think about what to do with the children, and the house and money and pensions and everything.'

Andrew looked round the kitchen sadly.

'God, what a mess. What a stupid fucking mess.'

'Please don't,' said Claire. 'Don't start. I know it's going to be a mess, but it's a mess *now*. And at least once we get through this messy part, we might start to be able to be happy again.'

'I know. I wasn't starting. I just wish things were different. I assume you want to stay here with the kids? Do you want me to go now?'

'No,' said Claire, surprised by Andrew's capitulation. 'No, stay until you find somewhere to live. And thank you.'

'What do I do about somewhere to live?'

'I don't know. Rent somewhere, I suppose.'

'But for how long?'

'I don't *know*!'

'And when should we tell the kids?' Andrew asked.

'I don't know that either. Why do you think I have all the answers? I suppose when you've found a flat and can move in.'

'Right. Yes, that makes sense. Is that what people do, then? And what do we tell them?'

'I don't *know*, Andrew. I don't know how any of this works. I'm going to be finding my way just as much as you are.'

'Of course. Well, I suppose I'd better get another cup of coffee, then it's a day on Rightmove for me. What are your plans?'

'Pick the kids up, take them to swimming and everything else, I suppose.'

'Do you want me to help with that? If you give me this morning to have a look for flats, I could do the afternoon shift?'

'Yeah, that'd be good, actually. Thanks.'

'Claire,' said Andrew as she walked out the kitchen, 'is there really no chance for us? No hope? None at all?'

Claire stopped and looked at him. Half her life was there, sitting at the kitchen table with a cold cup of coffee, the sun catching his hair, and if she looked really hard she could still see the boy with the bluest eyes she had ever seen, there beneath the tired man looking back at her. A hundred thousand memories stood between that boy and that man. After all her certainty, *could* she really throw it all away? End it just like that? As Claire wavered, the sunbeam Andrew was sitting in faded, and so did the vision of the boy he had once been, and there was just a middle-aged man sitting at the table, with a strained smile.

'I don't know,' said Claire sadly. 'I really don't. I wish there was. All I know is that right now, living with you, no, there's no hope. I know it's a cliché, but I know I can't live with you, and I don't know if I can live without you. But I guess we'll find out.'

As Claire walked back to Lucy's to collect the kids, she reflected on how strange it was that after all the years she and Andrew had been together, after the last weeks of screaming emotion and rage and feeling like she just wanted to smash every breakable object in the house (she *had* flung a rather hideous vase that Andrew's mother had given them at the wall, and it had been extremely satisfying, albeit very briefly), it was all over in one short, calm and rational conversation.

Obviously, there was a lot more to be done, and eventually there would be lawyers and letters and papers to deal with and quite probably further arguments and acrimony, but the months of getting to know each other, moving in together, the excitement of his proposal in Sorrento, planning a wedding, Claire's pregnancies, everything that had gone into their relationship, all this now had a line drawn under it. Whatever happened, nothing would be the same again. All the little things that over the years had built up their life together, all the bits and pieces and hideous souvenirs with 'Love From Majorca' on them that the children had insisted on buying on holiday, all the half sets of Ikea glasses and worn-out sheets that weren't worn out enough to throw out but were too worn out to use but still might come in useful for something, one day – all those jigsaw pieces of their life together that had taken so much effort for so long to build, all that was gone. Whatever their new lives might be, that one was no more.

Claire felt a sense of peace that had been missing for a long time, and she also felt a new sense of pride that however sad it was that this life was now over, it was finishing on *her* terms, and at *her* say-so. She had let herself drift along at the mercy of other people's whims for too long, and now it was time to take charge of her own life again. Quite how she was going to do that, she wasn't sure, but she was determined that she was. Right after her day had been dictated by Tabitha and Lucas's whims, obviously.

* * *

Lucy was kind, if a little hungover, when Claire arrived at her house.

'You look like you've barely slept,' she said as she opened the door to Claire.

'I haven't. You gave me a lot to think about. And I decided to ask Andrew for a separation.'

'Shit! Wow, that was fast! When I said you had choices, I didn't mean you had to make them immediately!'

'I know. But the more I thought about things, the more I knew what I needed to do, and I woke up this morning and knew for sure, so there didn't seem any point hanging around. So I may yet wake up *tomorrow* morning and think what the fuck have I done, but well, at least I've done *something*. I've been drifting for far too long.'

'Well, congratulations for being proactive. And you know, I'm here if you need to talk or anything,' Lucy offered.

'Thanks,' said Claire, slightly awkwardly. She was so grateful to Lucy for her advice, but after all her tears the night before, she was worried Lucy was only being nice to her and offering help because she thought Claire was having a nervous breakdown. The last thing she needed was people's pity.

'Um, I'd better get the kids. Swimming, you know!'

'I know,' said Lucy. 'It never stops, does it? I mean it, though. I'm here if you need me.'

8

For the next couple of weeks Andrew and Claire were exceedingly polite to each other. There were a lot of 'No, after you's at the bathroom door (Claire regretted her civility the day after she had made an unexpectedly spicy curry) and 'Are you using that? May I's?', etc. Then, thirteen days after the Big Conversation, Andrew told Claire he had managed to get a lease sorted on a small flat, and that he could move in anytime from the following day. Claire suddenly felt like she was standing on the edge of a precipice that was rapidly crumbling under her feet. This was really happening. Andrew was leaving. Their marriage was over. Was this what she really wanted? *Really?*

'Right,' said Claire. 'I suppose we'd better tell the children. Do you need any stuff for the flat?'

'It's fully furnished,' Andrew said. 'So there's no need to start counting out the cutlery *just* yet. What do we tell the children, though?'

'Well, we can hardly tell them the truth,' snapped Claire. 'I mean, it's going to be hard enough for them, without knowing what you did!'

'I was hardly proposing we mentioned that,' sighed Andrew. 'But, you know, what do we say?'

'Why do you always assume I know what to do, and what to say? Why do I always have to have all the answers? I don't KNOW! I've never had to tell my children that their father and I are separating, have I? There's probably a Mumsnet board about it, if you want to go and look. They must have plenty of experience, given their posters always advocate LTB and insist that him leaving the loo seat up is a clear sign of emotional abuse.'

'What? What does LTB mean? Why are we talking about Mumsnet?'

'It stands for "Leave The Bastard". It's their solution for everything.'

'Is that why we're separating? Because of Mumsnet?'

'Of course not. Mumsnet say LTB about everything. If I'd listened to what they say on Mumsnet, I'd have left you years ago for squeezing the toothpaste out of the middle of the tube. According to them, that's emotional abuse *and* gaslighting. I just really resent that you seem to think that because I'm a woman, I must have all the answers about everything to do with the children, that … that I get some, I dunno, some secret signal from my uterus that automatically tells me what to do, so you don't have to think about it because you can just LEAVE IT TO ME!'

Claire knew she was lashing out at Andrew because of the sudden fear of what actually being on her own was going to be like, but after a fortnight of tiptoeing round each other like new housemates, she didn't seem able to help herself.

'I don't leave it all to you!' Andrew protested.

'You do! You assume I just know what to do. It's been the same ever since Lucas was born. "Why's he crying?" "What does he need?" "Should he be eating that?" You've never taken any initiative with the children. You've always just sat back and let me do all the boring stuff, while you got to be the Fun Dad! And now it will probably be even worse, They'll go to you at weekends and you'll get to do all the good stuff like going to the park and getting pizza and I'll get all the shitty stuff like nagging them about homework and taking them to the dentist, and so they'll love you best and not realise that I'm the one keeping them fucking ALIVE!'

'I'm sorry. I'm sorry that apparently I've been a shitty father as well as a shitty husband. OK? Are you happy now? Jesus Christ, I'm so fucking TIRED of being sorry, though. Meet me halfway, Claire. I've done everything you asked, I've found a flat, I'm moving out, you're getting to stay in the house, WHY are you suddenly dragging up old transgressions to throw in my face?'

'I don't know,' Claire muttered sulkily. 'I don't know anything anymore. But everyone still expects me to. And I don't know how we're going to tell the children, or get them through this, and it's annoying that you expect me to.'

'OK. Yes, why should you know any better than me. But fighting me won't make it easier for them, will it? That's supposed to the point of this separation, to stop us fighting and tearing each other to bits. This is still what you want, isn't it? You can still change your mind, you know?'

'I DON'T know.' Claire burst into tears. 'Yes, I want this. But I don't want it to have had to happen. I wish we could just turn back the clock.'

'Oh Claire.' Andrew stepped closer to her and tried to pull her into a hug. 'So do I. More than anything.'

'Don't!' Claire jerked away. 'Please don't. It makes it harder.'

Claire shut herself in her bedroom and cried for a while, before she was calm enough to go back downstairs and discuss with Andrew the best way to tell Tabitha and Lucas that Andrew was moving out. In the end, they went with the old chestnut of 'Mummy and Daddy don't love each other anymore, but we're still friends and most importantly, we still both love you very much.'

Tabitha burst into tears and clung limpet-like to Andrew. 'Don't go, Daddy,' she begged. 'Please, Daddy, don't leave us.'

Andrew looked helplessly at Claire. What good would it do Tabitha to let him deal with this alone, she thought?

'Daddy's not leaving you,' Claire said gently. 'He's not leaving anyone. He'll be living really nearby and you'll see him every weekend and any other time you want. If you think about it, you don't see Daddy much during the week anyway, because he has to be at work so much. So it won't be that different.'

'It will,' howled Tabitha. 'I'll KNOW he's not here. WHY are you going, Daddy? Why don't you love Mummy?'

'I … I do love Mummy,' said Andrew awkwardly. 'Just … I love her like a friend. And that's how Mummy loves me now. And well, friends don't usually live together, do they?'

'They could,' insisted Tabitha. 'I'd LOVE to live with Ella. Why can't you stay, and you and Mummy can live together as friends?'

'Because that's not what happens when you're a grown-up,' Claire tried. 'It's just not that simple, Tabitha. I'm sorry, darling.'

Lucas barely reacted to the news at all, simply shrugging, and saying, 'Can I get an Xbox at Dad's then?' before shuffling off to his bedroom while Tabitha continued to cry for another hour, before calming down and apparently forgetting all about Andrew's imminent departure.

When Claire went upstairs to check on Lucas, though, she found him sitting hunched and miserable in a corner of his room.

'Are you OK?' she asked tentatively.

Lucas nodded bravely, and tried to say something, but it ended in a gulping sob, before he choked out, 'Dad won't want us anymore.'

'Of course he will!' said Claire in horror. 'Why would you think that?'

'Ben's dad doesn't want him. He never sees his dad. He's got a new baby now, and he doesn't care about Ben and Ella.'

'Who told you this?' said Claire, shocked that Lucy would have said such things to Lucas.

'Ben. He said his dad usually cancels when he's supposed to see them, and his mum tries to pretend it's because "something came up", but Ben said he knows it's because his dad doesn't really care about them or want to see them. And when they do see him, it's all about the new baby. They never do anything Ben and Ella want to do – they can't go to the cinema or anything, because what about the baby? Is Dad going to have a new baby with some-one?'

Claire felt guilty about assuming Lucy must have been badmouthing her ex to the kids, when it seemed he did a perfectly good job of blackening his character to his children all by himself.

'No, sweetheart, he's not,' she said firmly.

'He might. You don't know what will happen in the future. Ben didn't know his dad would have another baby with someone else, so he *might*. And then he won't want us.'

'He will. I can promise you that whatever happens, you and Tabitha will always be the most important thing in the world EVER to your dad, OK?'

Claire went back downstairs and sent Andrew up to reassure Lucas. He came down half an hour later.

'Well, I've never met Ben's dad,' he said. 'But the man sounds like a colossal prick.'

'Well, that's one thing we can agree on,' Claire nodded.

'Look, I hope you don't mind, but Lucas was so convinced that I was abandoning them, like Ben's dad, that I said he could come with me tomorrow to the flat and spend the night. Start as we mean to go on? Tabitha too, if she wants.'

'Oh,' said Claire in surprise. 'Tomorrow? I just … you won't be ready for them. You're only getting the keys tomorrow.'

'I know. But it's a Saturday, so why don't they come and stay? I've warned Lucas we'll basically be camping, and he's fine with that. He's already suggested we had better order pizza then.'

'I didn't think they'd be staying so soon, that's all. But if that's what they want, then I suppose I need to let them do whatever works for them.'

'I'm sorry, Claire. I hadn't planned it like this, but Lucas was so upset. I just blurted it out, and he cheered right up. You don't mind, do you?'

'Of course not!' said Claire brightly. 'Not if it's what they want. They're the most important ones, after all!'

Now Andrew was actually going, the Separation, which Claire had pinned all her hopes on as being the answer to everything, suddenly seemed very real, and more than a little bleak. Claire suddenly wondered if it was too late, if she could tell Andrew she had changed her mind, ask him to stay, say she'd had second thoughts. She did not want them to end up like Scarlett O'Hara and Rhett Butler, a marriage ruined by both of them being too proud to tell the other how they really felt. But Claire suspected that her sudden eleventh-hour desire for Andrew to stay had more to do with a fear of the unknown, of standing on the edge of a chasm, than an actual sudden change in her feelings for him.

9

In the event, Tabitha declined to go to Andrew's flat and 'camp', as the lure of Milly Taylor's birthday sleepover and unlimited glitter and cake pops were far more enticing than even the notion of all the pizza she could eat.

After Claire had dropped Tabitha off, she went home to an empty house. Of course, she'd been in the house plenty of times on her own, but somehow it had never felt quite so empty. Despite everything, seeing Andrew walk out the door, and knowing he was not coming back later, had felt like a knife in her heart. She wondered what the hell she had been thinking? Had she actually just waved him off straight into the arms of Emily? But then again, if he went straight back to Emily, which was probably the worst-case scenario Claire could think of, at least she'd *know* she'd done the right thing, and she could get on with her life.

Without thinking, and not for the first time, Claire reached for her phone to call Emily, then realised that she couldn't pour out her problems to her. She considered ringing Tessa, but Tessa hadn't been as supportive as Claire had hoped regarding her decision to separate from Andrew, saying that was not what she had meant *at all* by telling Claire to pull herself together and stop wallowing, and was Claire *sure* she was doing the right thing? Claire certainly wasn't sure she could stand another of Tessa's brisk Pep Talks.

She thought about texting Lucy Connor to see if she was free to do something. She had hoped to see her at the drop-off for Milly's party, but she'd already left Ella there and gone, obviously hoping to make the most of her time before the very real chance that at least one parent would get a phone call within the hour to come and pick their daughter up due to over enthusiastic consumption of cake pops, resulting in glittery rainbow-hued vomit (unicorn puke, Claire had once described it as to Lolly Hughes, who'd recoiled in horror).

It would look too needy to text Lucy, Claire decided. She didn't want to Lucy to think she didn't have any other friends, and of course Claire had *plenty* of friends. Until recently, Claire and Andrew had never stopped socialising – either their house was full of people or they were out at an endless round of barbecues, dinner parties and boozy 'suppers' in their friends' tastefully renovated kitchens, admiring the built-in Miele appliances and the £1,200 boiling-water taps, because apparently kettles were *so* over, darling! The pair of them had been part of a busy network of couples at the same stage in life, and although she hadn't actually heard back from anyone in response to the polite email she and Andrew had drafted explaining that they were separating, Claire was quite sure that Jen or Julia, or Louise or Sarah would soon be round for an afternoon chat, and maybe even free to pop round for a glass of wine in the evening.

Claire texted Jen, but got no response. When Louise and Sarah failed to respond to her messages, she bit the bullet and actually called Julia.

'Claire,' said Julia, sounding less than thrilled. 'Hi.'

'Hi Julia,' said Claire. 'Is this a good time?'

'Um, well actually, we're at Tim and Jen's. All the gang's here, Jen's doing Ottolenghi, and it's not really a good time. Did you want something?'

'Oh. Oh right.'

Claire could hear everyone chattering in the background, and the clink of glasses and cutlery. They could have bloody asked her, couldn't they?

'OK,' Claire gulped. 'I was … I was just ringing to see if you fancied catching up sometime. We could maybe do a girls' night?'

'Errr, yeah … um …'

'Maybe next weekend?'

'Oh, I'm sorry, we can't do next weekend. It's Simon's birthday and everyone's coming over.'

There was an awkward pause, as Claire waited with shameful hope to see if Julia would issue a pity invitation to her, since she was clearly not included.

'I *would* ask you, Claire, but it's a bit difficult. We've asked Andrew, you see, and now you guys are, well, you know …'

'Right, right, of course! Not at all, it was short notice anyway. What about the weekend after?'

'I think Joel and Louise are having everyone round to try out their new pizza oven.'

'Oh.'

'Claire, look, I need to go, Jen says the smoked aubergine won't wait. Great to chat, must catch up soon. Bye!'

And Julia was gone. Claire poured a glass of wine and buried her face in it in mortification. Was this it, then? Was this what it was like to be a Single Woman? Julia couldn't get off the phone fast enough and she could just imagine them all now, sitting round Jen's bastarding original Ercol dining table, which frankly Claire thought looked like something her mother had sent to the charity shop in the eighties, discussing Claire's desperation in not getting the message when they had not answered her email or her texts, and being so embarrassing as to *call* Julia. She could almost see them shaking their heads sorrowfully over the vegan, gluten-free panna cotta. And Andrew being invited to Simon's birthday made it very clear whose side they'd decided to take. Single men were an asset. Single women, as Lucy had tried to warn her, were deemed a liability.

Claire really hadn't expected this. All right, she hadn't been waiting for the Fucking Fergusons to call her; they were very much Andrew's friends and no great loss, but the others? Tim and Jen? They had been on holiday with them half a dozen times. Simon and Julia? They saw them at least once a month. Joel and Louise, Sarah and Nigel? Had she been cast out by all of them? It certainly seemed so.

Claire suddenly realised that all the people they had surrounded themselves with for years had really been Andrew's friends and their wives. Claire, secure in the cocoon of Emily's friendship, had never really felt the need to make any other friends to introduce to the group. They were all nice people, and Claire had liked them and got on well with them, had, in fact, thought of them as 'their' friends, and indeed they had been. That is, until the chips were down and they had to choose, at which point they reverted to being Andrew's friends.

Claire poured another glass of wine and tried to put on a brave face, to remind herself that if they were so shallow and didn't even care about how she was coping, then they hadn't ever been real friends in the first place and they were no loss at all, and she didn't even *want* to be friends with them because they were HORRIBLE POO-POO HEADS (she was finding more and more these days that there was great satisfaction to be had in very childish insults). But it stung nonetheless, and added even more to the intense loneliness she feared in her new life without Emily or Andrew.

After she finished her second glass of wine, Claire decided that she was not going to wallow in self-pity, she was going to take control. She pulled down the stack of photo albums from the shelf, stomped into the garden with them and dumped them on the patio.

Every year, since they were twelve, Claire and Emily had each selected their favourite photos from the past year and put them in an album, which they gave each other for Christmas. The first ones were rather small, tattered, plastic-covered Woolworth's photo albums, followed by slightly classier ones, and then in the last few years, smartly bound photo books they had made online. It was a Christmas tradition, looking through the photos, picking them out, wondering which photos Emily would have chosen. Ironically, Claire had once thought that after the children, those albums would be the next thing she'd try to save in a fire, but she now doused them in barbecue lighter fluid and set them alight.

'I AM MOVING ON!' she bellowed up at the sky, contemplating the pyre of her friendship.

Next door's upstairs window flew open.

'Keep the noise down, you're frightening Colonel Mousicles,' howled her neighbour. 'And why are you having a bonfire at this time of night? I'm sure it violates the by-laws.'

Colonel Mousicles, sitting on the fence giving his arse a thorough wash, merely gave Claire a hard and very unfrightened stare.

After another two glasses of wine, Claire deleted everyone's numbers from her phone.

'Ha! Poo-poo heads! Fuck you!' she sniggered to herself. Mainly, of course, it was to stop her convincing herself that she had misunderstood Julia's awkwardness and the ghosted texts and emails, and trying to get in touch next time she was at a low ebb, and having to go through the whole miserable pantomime again, and hearing pity as well as embarrassment in their voices.

As soon as she had cleared all the numbers, Claire immediately panicked that she had overreacted, that she had read too much into it, that she *had* misunderstood. Still, she comforted herself, if that was the case, they could easily get in touch with her if they wanted.

As she emptied the remains of the bottle into her glass, Colonel Mousicles appeared at the patio doors, miaowing imperiously. Claire opened the door.

'What?' she said.

Colonel Mousicles stalked in and made himself at home on the sofa.

'Oh, it's like that, is it?' said Claire. 'Well, you can stay till we hear your mistress calling in you for the night, and no longer. I'm not risking her wrath.'

Colonel Mousicles gave Claire a look that made it clear that *he* would decide when he went back out, not Claire, and they settled down companionably to watch *The Crown*. As Olivia Colman as the Queen was wearing an unflattering headscarf and being emotionally repressed at Prince Charles, Claire realised how very comforting the solid, purring, warm presence of Colonel Mousicles was, and thought maybe she should get a pet. They had never been able to – apart from the guinea pigs in the garage that the children had long since abandoned to Claire's care – because Andrew was allergic, but now, surely, there was nothing to stop her.

10

The Saturday morning after Andrew had left, Claire looked out of the window when she was hoovering the sitting room while the children were supposed to be getting ready for their father to pick them up – but were probably actually faffing around and still in their pyjamas – and she saw Emily's mother Lydia pulling up outside and parking.

Had Emily sent her mother to plead her case? Claire quailed a little. Lydia was very hard to say no to. Lydia had always been the most glamorous woman Claire had ever seen when they were growing up. A hotshot corporate lawyer, Lydia's power suits and designer heels had always made Tessa look slightly faded and frumpy beside her, however dressed up Tessa was herself. No one could quite compete with Lydia's sharp bob and dramatic red lipstick. Claire was rather in awe of Lydia, who was extremely brisk and no-nonsense. She was now divorced from Emily's father, who had run off with his secretary (clichés and moral turpitude both obviously running strong in Emily's family), probably because he also found Lydia rather intimidating.

Age had made Lydia no less glamorous or terrifying, and Claire wondered if she had the nerve to tell Lydia to go if she had come to tell her why she had to forgive Emily and be friends with her again.

There was something about Lydia that made Claire feel eternally an awkward twelve-year-old.

'Claire, darling,' said Lydia as soon as Claire opened the door. 'Emily told me what she did. I'm so dreadfully sorry. I can't imagine what she was thinking. I'm appalled by her! May I come in?'

'Of course,' said Claire politely, standing aside to let Lydia through the front door.

Claire took Lydia into the kitchen, it being the tidiest place in the house at the moment as she had already cleared away the chaos of breakfast time. After Claire had made coffee, Lydia attempted to give Claire the most awkward hug of her life. Lydia was not a hugger. In thirty years, Claire did not think she had ever been hugged by Lydia. Even on Claire's wedding day, Lydia had wafted up to her in a covetable vintage Chanel dress and vaguely waved her cheek in Claire's direction in lieu of an actual embrace. Claire thought she'd probably actually prefer the imminent 'Why Emily Is Very Sorry Speech' to being hugged by Lydia again.

'Anyway,' Lydia went on, releasing Claire to both their palpable reliefs, 'I came to see if there was anything I could do. Your mother told me that you had kicked the bastard out, and so I assume you'll be needing a lawyer, and so I took the liberty of making some calls to a few friends and colleagues, and I've a shortlist of the best family law lawyers out there for you.'

Lydia handed Claire a folder containing a sheaf of neatly typed papers. Claire was stunned but not really surprised. Lydia was a doer, not a talker. She liked to fix things. She had evidently assessed the situation in her usual unsentimental way, realised that Emily and Claire's friendship was beyond salvaging, and decided to concentrate on what could be fixed instead. If Lydia's daughter had ruined Claire's life, Lydia's solution was to understand that apologies would achieve nothing and instead focus on getting Claire the best divorce possible.

'My secretary put this together for you. Victoria Dean is the best, she's the first one in there. The others are just back-ups in case you don't gel with her,' said Lydia. 'I hope you don't mind, I've already made sure she can take you on, and well, I might have overstepped the mark, but I negotiated her rate for you. Got a very good deal too!' she added in a burst of pride. 'Anyway, she's an absolute shark. Andrew will be lucky to have a pair of underpants to call his own by the time Vicky's finished with him.'

'I … Lydia … I don't know what to say. Do I need a lawyer?' asked Claire uncertainly.

'Yes!' said Lydia, aghast. 'Of *course* you need a lawyer if you're getting divorced. And a good one!'

'Oh. I hadn't really thought about all this yet. Do I need to? It just all seems so … final, and *aggressive*, lawyers and all that.'

'Claire, are you quite sure this is what you want?'

'What do you mean?'

'Divorce.'

'Please stop saying "divorce". We're *separated*. We haven't even talked about divorce.'

'Well, it's the natural next step. You separate, and then you either get back together or you get divorced. Do you want to get back together?'

'No …?'

'Well then, you'll need to get divorced.'

'Will I really?'

'This is why I asked if you were *sure*, Claire darling. You need to be very sure about these things. You can't just go around getting divorced on a whim,' Lydia said sternly.

'It's not a whim. And yes, I'm sure. I just don't know what the rush is.'

'The rush is to get a good lawyer to protect yourself, your children and your assets.'

'I haven't got any assets.'

'Well, the house and all that. Everything is an asset.'

'But I don't want it to be like that,' said Claire. 'You know, wrangling over everything down to who gets the Debbie Harry CD, and fighting over the fact we've nine forks left from the set of twelve, so who gets four and who gets five? We're trying to be civilised about this – he's still the children's father, after all. And he's said I can keep the house, and we're working out proper access for the kids and all that. In fact, he'll soon be here to pick them up.'

'Of course,' said Lydia. 'I quite understand. You do get divorces like that. Sometimes. And let's hope he feels the same and this can be concluded like grown-ups. But from what I've seen, more often than not it all starts out with great promises of generosity and civility, and then when the buggers see how much it's going to cost them, things turn ugly. So, if he decides to be difficult, you need a good lawyer who will go for the jugular before he knows what's happened, and it's best to be prepared and have one lined up. That's all. You need to protect yourself. And also, you need to accept help when people offer it, darling. Being a single mother is not easy. I've been there. I've no doubt about your capability to do it, but why make things harder for yourself? There's nothing wrong with needing or taking help. So let me help with this, and go to the lawyer I've found you. Just to be on the safe side.'

'OK. Thank you. It's just … lawyers. Looking round at everything and wondering how we're going to divide it up. How do you divide a LIFE? It's just making it all very real.'

'It is real,' said Lydia sternly. 'And this is your life more than his, so make sure you get the good bits. And the Debbie Harry CD. Cheating bastards don't deserve Debbie!'

After Lydia left, Claire sat on in her kitchen in the cloud of Lydia's Chanel No. 5 and wondered if she could actually do this. She had known, of course, that at some point it would all have to become official and lawyers would be involved, and there would be paperwork to be signed and twenty years of shared experiences would be divided in two, but sitting there with Lydia's neatly typed sheet detailing the best woman to do this for her made it seem very cold and clinical.

What would happen to things like the little painting she had fallen in love with in an antiques shop window when they had first moved in together and were utterly broke? Claire had stopped to gaze at it every morning on her way to work, until the day she was heartbroken when it wasn't there anymore. Andrew had beamed that night as he handed her a small, square package, and she'd thought she'd explode with joy when she found her painting inside. He had sold his grandfather's gold cufflinks to pay for it, and Claire had been horrified when she found out, but he had insisted that they were hideous and he had never really liked either them or his grandfather, and that Claire's joy was worth far more to him than a pair of ugly old cufflinks. She suspected he was lying, but her heart lifted every time she looked at the painting. Though now she thought about it, it hung at the top of the stairs and she hardly ever looked at it any longer. Maybe she should have looked at it more, she reflected, and she suddenly felt crushed under the weight of all the 'maybes' that had led her here. She finished her coffee and went to get the children ready for Andrew to pick them up, but she stopped at the top of the stairs and looked at her painting again for the first time in a long while.

11

Claire wasn't sure if she was supposed to tell Andrew about the lawyer when he picked the children up. She had been surprised enough that he wanted to have them, given that it was Simon's birthday party that night, though obviously she couldn't tell him that, as it would reveal that she knew she hadn't been invited. There had been a small part of her had hoped that if Andrew had declined, then maybe she'd be invited instead. Was being B list better than being NFI, she wondered? Probably not, actually, but it would at least give her the satisfaction of haughtily declining. In lieu of Emily and the PooHead friends, Claire had decided she needed to find something more constructive to do on a Saturday night than getting pissed by herself and burning things, so she had answered a post on the local Facebook group advertising that someone was starting up a new book club. A book club, reflected Claire, sounded just the ticket. Literary discussions, and new friends, and maybe just a tiny glass of wine, and no setting things on fire. She'd be a highbrow and cultured person before you knew it.

Claire wasn't quite sure what to wear to the book club. She didn't want to look done up to the nines, but neither did she want to look 'My husband cheated on me so my life is over and now I've given up ever making an effort apart from putting on clean pants' drab. She also quite fancied projecting an air of literary intellectuality. To that end she tried on a beret and black polo neck, but had immediately taken them off as she looked like a tit. She tried FaceTiming her mother, but Tessa wasn't much help either, suggesting 'You can't go wrong with a little black dress and pearls, you know. And you're single now, you need to keep standards up. Don't let people get the wrong idea about you.'

'Mum, on both those counts, I need to remind you it's not 1950,' Claire pointed out.

'I know, darling. I just think people looked much nicer then. Hats and gloves! Properly dressed.'

'Mum, you barely even remember the 1950s. You weren't born until 1955. Have you been watching *The Crown* as well?'

'Maybe. But I remember my grandmother never went anywhere without a pair of gloves and a hat,' she said stubbornly.

'I'm not sure that's totally the right look for a book club, though,' insisted Claire.

'But you always look lovely, whatever you're wearing,' said Tessa in surprise. 'Why are you getting yourself in such a tizz about it tonight?'

'I just want to look right,' said Claire miserably. 'Like I fit in. It's scary enough going to something like this on my own, not knowing a soul. I just want to look like I'm someone they could be friends with, like I could be part of a group. Like an antelope,' she added vaguely.

'Like an antelope? Why do you want to look like an antelope?'

'I don't want to *look* like an antelope. I want to blend in, like an antelope. Like, if you've got a herd of antelope and then a … a … I don't know, a *zebra* tried to join the antelope gang, they'd immediately see it wasn't an antelope and they'd be all, "No, you can't sit with us." You know? Even if it was a really nice zebra, and had loads in common with the antelopes, like being eaten by lions and eating grass and stuff. But they wouldn't get to know the zebra first and find all that out about the lions and grass, they'd just see it was different and not want it to be there. But *maybe* if the zebra had put on a pair of antlers and an antelope skin, well maybe not, because where would it get them? It would have to be off a dead antelope and that probably wouldn't endear it to the other antelopes, but if it somehow came up with an antelope disguise that wasn't a dead antelope, then by the time the other antelope realised that it was a zebra, they'd all have bonded over lions and grass and they'd be friends with it.'

'Why doesn't the zebra just live with the other zebras?' said Tessa in confusion. 'Why does it want to be an antelope? Was all its zebra family eaten by the lions? It should just tell the antelopes that, and they'd understand. They could unite and rise up against the lions. Form an army with the wildebeest!'

'It was just a metaphor, Mum. I hadn't really thought through the zebra's full back story, let alone the politics of the grazing animals of the African savannah. I just meant that I want to fit in tonight. I don't want to be the zebra. I need friends, Mum. I hadn't properly realised until all this that I don't have any friends anymore. All I had was Emily, and Andrew and his friends. And now I don't have them either and I'm on my own. I know, I've got you and Dad, and the children. But I need actual other people as well. People that aren't my children or my parents. People maybe I can talk to about things that I can't discuss with my parents or my children.'

'Like sex?' said Tessa.

'Well, I suppose so,' said Claire in horror. 'Not that there's exactly anything *to* discuss right now!'

'I think you're quite right,' said Tessa. 'Of course you need friends. I just don't understand why you're so worried about not fitting in.'

'I'm just scared … and I just feel if I can look right, then at least they'll give me a chance and get to know me before shunning me, and then maybe they'll like me enough to overlook any terrible shortcomings and flaws in me.'

'You obviously don't have any terrible shortcomings or flaws, darling. Don't be silly!'

'But you're my mother. You have to say that.'

'Well, maybe some of them are zebras too and are hoping you'll be a fellow zebra to bond with against the antelopes, though I honestly think you're working yourself into a state about nothing. I do understand it's daunting, but it's also an opportunity. Now, get dressed. No, maybe the black top, sweetie, that one's a bit "I'm sadfacing in the *Daily Mail* because I gave my life savings to a twenty-three-year-old Turkish waiter because he said I had nice eyes," I think.'

Claire deliberately arrived bang on 7.02 p.m., not wanting to be the first one there, and not wanting to be immediately deemed the late scatty one if she wasn't on time. The book club was run by someone called Stella, who had bravely offered to have it in her house. Claire wasn't sure she'd have invited a group of strangers into her home; she'd be worried about them stealing things, or murdering her, or pooing in her toilet, so she rather admired the mysterious Stella for her courage. At the end of Stella's path, Claire encountered a tall, anxious-looking woman, like Claire clutching a bottle of mid-price wine and the book-club book.

'Is this the book club?' she asked.

'I think so,' said Claire. 'I've not been before.'

'Oh good! Me neither. I think it's the first one, isn't it? I was worried everyone would know each other really well.'

'I don't know a soul! I'm Claire, by the way.'

'I'm Kate. Lovely to meet you. Shall I ring the bell? At least if we've got the wrong house we can make tits of ourselves together!'

A moment later, a woman – undoubtedly Stella – opened the door and looked sternly at Kate and Claire's bottles of wine as they thrust them at her and introduced themselves.

'Thank you,' she said limply. 'I've made herbal tea. I thought it was better we didn't drink, you know, so our minds were clear to focus on the book. But everyone seems to be bringing wine, I don't know why. It's very worrying you know, the extent of alcohol dependency in modern society. Do you *want* wine?'

Claire and Kate immediately assured Stella that absolutely not, herbal tea was just fine, lest Stella assume them to be dependent on alcohol.

'You'd better come through,' said Stella, who despite being the person who'd started the book club and offered to host it, didn't actually seem very keen on the idea now it was happening. 'One person is here already, and we're waiting for another two. I thought six was enough. Gives a chance for everyone to really contribute *properly* to the discussion. Right, here's two more, this is … what was your name again?'

'Lucy,' said Lucy Connor, who was sitting forlornly on Stella's rather hairy-looking sofa, cradling an enormous mug that was giving off a strong smell of pond.

'Lucy!' said Claire. 'What are you doing here?'

'Broadening my horizons,' said Lucy valiantly, going to take a sip of steaming pond and thinking better of it. 'What about you?'

'Well, the same, I suppose. This is Kate, we met outside.'

'Hello,' said Kate shyly. 'I'm sorry, I don't know anyone.'

'I didn't think I would either,' said Lucy.

'I'll get the door,' sighed Stella as the doorbell rang again. A woman in complicated glasses and a man with corduroy trousers and an unhygienic-looking beard were ushered in.

'This is Morag and Neville. I'll get everyone more tea,' announced Stella. 'Lucy, do you need a top-up?'

'No!' yelped Lucy quickly. 'Thank you. It's, errr, very unusual.'

'It's organic dandelion and nettle. I make it myself from the plants in the garden,' Stella said smugly.

Once everyone was settled with their vats of pond – Claire sipping hers tentatively, convinced that for all Stella's burbling about the botanical origins of her tea, she was pretty sure she could taste a definite hint of cat piss under the general sludginess – Stella announced that she thought it would be fun if they all played a little game to start things off in which they went round the circle and told everyone a bit about themselves. Claire's heart sank. Luckily Stella volunteered to go first, so at least everyone could get an idea of just what level of sharing was expected.

'Right, I'm Stella, as you all know. I've just moved into the area from London, where I ran a very successful book club, which I hope to replicate here. I had a waiting list to join in London, but we had to move for my husband's job – he's in charge of opening a new regional office for Chalmers & Scott. Have you heard of them?'

Stella looked disappointed at the blank faces and ploughed on regardless, leaving them none the wiser about her husband's occupation.

'I have two children, Melissa and Edwin. They've both left university now, but when they were young I stayed at home to support them, as unfortunately they were both so gifted and talented that mainstream education wasn't enough for them and they required a lot of extra stretching! Anyway, they're both doing awfully well now – Edwin is in Thailand, in underwater recreation work, and Melissa is in hospitality in Australia. So now I've got a bit more time on my hands I've started my own business, making ethical, eco, upcycled jewellery. These earrings are from my new collection.'

Stella tossed her head to show off some alarming creations.

'Gosh,' said Morag. 'They're so unusual, Stella. What are they made of?'

'Orange peel,' said Stella proudly.

Claire had just braved a sip of the pond tea and promptly choked. She did not dare meet Lucy's eye.

'OK, who's next? Morag?' Stella said warmly, Morag's admiration of her earrings clearly having bumped her up in Stella's estimation.

'Hi guys! I'm Morag! I'm a ceramic artist, specialising in pre- and post-birth vulva sculptures. I find it an amazingly empowering way for women to chart the changes in their vulvas from giving birth. I have five children, and I got the idea from making my own vulval casts before and after each birth. I've had them framed as keepsakes for my children, but a lot of women like to gift them to their husbands as well. And I homeschool too, because my children are also so gifted and talented, but I manage to fit in my art around that. My husband is very supportive.'

'Sorry,' said Lucy. 'I need to ask. Vulval casts? Do you mean …?'

'Yes,' said Morag brightly. 'So I take a cast of your vulva in early pregnancy, and then in late pregnancy, and then after the birth. It's up to the mama when they have it done afterwards. I prefer to do it immediately post birth, like I did with my own, but obviously I had home births, and midwives can be so closed-minded. So it's usually about a week afterwards. They're really beautiful things. I can show you some examples if you're interested.'

Even Stella and her orange-peel earrings looked nonplussed.

'No,' squeaked Lucy. 'Thank you!'

'What if you have a C-section?' asked Claire curiously.

'My mamas don't have C-sections,' said Morag contemptuously. 'There's no need for C-sections. Birth has become over-medicalised.'

'Well, that may be true, but some women do still need a section,' Claire argued.

'Nonsense,' huffed Morag. 'They just need to *listen* to their bodies. It's like these women who claim they can't breastfeed –'

'No, sections save women's lives sometimes,' Claire insisted.

'Claire!' snapped Stella. 'This is a fascinating debate and I'm *sure* it's helping us all to get to know each other much better, but maybe we could move on? Why don't *you* tell us about yourself?'

'Um, I'm Claire. I have two children, still at school. I work for a big bank. Risk management, which *sounds* exciting, like there should be tigers or high-wire-walking across gorges, but is actually very boring. That's it, I think!'

'And are you married, Claire?' Stella asked sweetly.

'Um. Separated, actually.'

Neville licked his lips.

Stella moved on to Lucy, who kept hers short and sweet as well. 'Lucy. Two children at school with Claire's, which is how I know her. I'm an accountant, which is also very dull. And I'm divorced. Who's next?'

Neville shot his hand up and a waft of BO was released into the room, fighting with the aroma of pond-weed tea.

'I'll go next!' he beamed. 'I'm Neville. Aren't I lucky, the only chap here with all these ladies! I'm a music teacher at St John's High School. My interests are cycling and jazz, and I'm also single and ready to mingle, as my wife left me last year for a geography teacher.'

With that he aimed lascivious winks at Lucy and Claire, and they were forced to bury their faces in their mugs to pretend they hadn't noticed.

'Hi. I'm Kate. Er, no kids. I'm a freelance marketing consultant. Also not very exciting.'

'And are *you* divorced too?' Neville asked eagerly.

'Um, no. I'm … I'm widowed, actually.'

'Oh dear! I'm so sorry!' everyone twittered at poor Kate, who just looked mortified.

'And how long ago did you lose your husband?' demanded Morag, head on one side in the universal 'caring' pose that allows you to ask impertinent questions under the guise of 'concern'.

'My wife.'

'What?'

'I didn't have a husband. I had a wife. Her name was Susan, and she died six months ago. Cancer. Shall we talk about the book?' Kate said desperately.

'Oh yes! The book!' said Stella. 'Of course! *Yellow Lorries*. What did everyone think? I thought it was *marvellous*. Profoundly stunning. Such intensity in the writing. The urgent power of it really came across incredibly.'

'Mmmmm,' said everyone. Claire, who had thought it rather a boring book about a man driving a lorry across South America and having a lot of sex with women who just appeared at truck stops and were apparently immediately overcome with desire for his big truck, nodded along, trying to look wise.

'I thought it was stunningly profound,' said Morag. 'Powerfully urgent. And so moving. That passage where the service station has run out of doughnuts, I wept. Wept!'

'I do that when Greggs runs out,' muttered Lucy.

'Sorry, Lucy, didn't catch that,' trilled Stella. 'What did you think about the book?'

'Um, well, yeah, profound. And, er, moving,' floundered Lucy. 'The pampas grass was a very good metaphor!' she finished triumphantly.

'Of course, the *whole thing* is a metaphor for the penis,' said Stella solemnly.

Claire caught Kate's horrified eye and they both suppressed a snigger, as Morag argued heatedly that the *lorry* was obviously a penis metaphor, but the truck stops were clearly metaphorical *vaginas*.

Neville seemed to be getting quite hot under the collar about the metaphorical discussion, and had been forced to place one of Stella's hairy cushions on his lap.

Claire had zoned out as Morag and Stella continued to debate, when Lucy suddenly exclaimed, 'Oh dear! Look at the time! I'd better go. Babysitter. This has been great, thanks, Stella. Claire, do you need to get back for your babysitter?'

'No, Andrew is –. Actually, yes, yes I do,' said Claire, as she realised what Lucy was hinting at.

'Me too,' said Kate, scrambling to her feet. 'Cat sitter,' she offered feebly.

'Gosh, are all you lovely ladies leaving?' said Neville. 'Well, don't want to overstay my welcome. I'd better be going too.'

'Oh, is everyone off?' said Stella in surprise. 'Morag, do you want to stay and see the rest of my jewellery collection? Anyone else want to see it?'

With many regretful apologies, Claire, Lucy and Kate headed for the door, while the noxious Neville, still trailing behind them, picked up his cycle helmet from the hall.

Out on the pavement, helmet safely strapped on, Neville beamed at them. 'Well, that was fun, wasn't it! What say we repair to the local hostelry for a pintage of ale, fair wenches? Eh? Who's up for it?'

'Oh no,' said Claire sadly. 'Babysitter.'

'Me too.'

'Cat sitter,' Kate reminded him.

'Not even a swift half?' pleaded Neville.

'So sorry. Another time. Which way are you going, Neville? That way? Oh, what a shame. We're all this way, aren't we?' And Lucy swept them off in the opposite direction to that indicated by Neville, who was still standing on the pavement looking rather deflated all round.

Lucy hurried everyone along the pavement as Kate made vague protests about living in the other direction, until they were safely round the corner and Neville was out of sight and earshot.

'Well,' said Lucy. 'What about the pub? It's still only just after half eight?'

'I thought you both had to get back for babysitters?' said Kate.

'Only in as much as you have to get back for a cat sitter,' grinned Lucy. 'I just needed to escape, and no one can ever argue with babysitter problems. So, pub?'

'Yes, please,' said Claire, who wasn't relishing the thought of going home to her empty house already.

'Why not?' said Kate. 'Let the cat sitter wait!'

'Do you really have to get a cat sitter to go out for the evening? What sort of cat do you have?' asked Claire in astonishment.

'Of course I don't. But I'd already told everyone I had no dog or child, so I wasn't left with many excuses to make a sharp exit, was I? Oh, what about this pub? It looks nice.'

Five minutes later, Claire, Kate and Lucy were sitting down with a bottle of Sauvignon Blanc, having wisely agreed that really, it was *far* more economical to get a bottle than buy it by the glass.

'Well, that was interesting!' said Claire valiantly.

'Yes. Very interesting,' Kate agreed doubtfully.

'Do you think you'll go back?' asked Lucy.

Claire sighed. 'I feel like I *should*. But what if it's all Stella and Morag still insisting everything is a metaphor for penises and vaginas? And Neville could benefit from a can of Lynx, and a bottle of Head & Shoulders, not to mention the fact he called us *fair wenches*! Was I the only one who didn't get that the book was actually all about rude bits?'

'No,' said Kate. 'I thought it was a bit dull and far-fetched, and if it hadn't been written by an Important Author everyone would have said it was rubbish.'

'Oh, thank God!' Lucy cried. 'I thought it was just me. I'd hoped it would be all literary salon-esque and we'd all be terribly impassioned, and it would be a chance to meet people outside of the playground cliques, because I realised recently that these days my selection of friends is largely dictated by who my children are friends with, and it would be so nice to talk to people about things other than bitching about who got the solo in the dance recital and is it too soon to start finding tutors if we want them to get into a decent secondary school.'

'Instead you got me. Sorry,' said Claire. 'Should I be finding tutors? Where do you even *find* tutors? Sorry, sorry, this isn't what we're supposed to be talking about! I just thought it would all be a lot more *fun*. I didn't think there would be quite so much showing off of how *clever* everyone was.'

'But of course they're very clever, with their gifted and talented children.' Lucy shook her head.

'Are your children gifted and talented?' Kate enquired politely.

Lucy shook her head again. 'Nope. Astonishingly average.'

'Lucas got stuck in a hedge on the way home from school yesterday. I think he might actually be considerably below average.'

'Stuck in a *hedge*?' said Kate. 'How do you get *stuck* in a hedge?'

'I don't know,' said Claire. 'He claims he thought he saw a piece of Lego he'd dropped on the way to school, so he hurled himself into the hedge to get it, and then apparently he couldn't find his way out. I extracted him and hustled him up the street only just in time before the hedge owner came home and demanded to know either why there was a boy stuck in his hedge, or, once I got him out, why there was a large boy-shaped hole in his hedge.'

'Oh,' said Kate. 'I see.'

'I doubt you do, unless you have a ten-year-old boy,' Claire sighed. 'But you said you didn't have children?'

'No. We … we talked about it. But we never got round to doing anything about it. And then Susan became ill, and now she's gone and well …'

Kate gave one of those very shiny-eyed tight smiles that are only just holding back the tears.

'Shit. I'm so sorry,' Claire said in horror. 'I didn't mean to pry. Oh God, you must think me such a rude cow.'

'No, no, it's fine.' Kate swallowed hard. 'Just … it still takes me by surprise that she's gone. And all the decisions we were supposed to make together, I'll have to make on my own.'

'I'm sorry,' said Claire again.

'That must be so hard,' said Lucy.

'No, I'm sorry. I try to talk about other things and be normal, but whatever I do I just seem to end up talking about Susan. I thought if I tried to press on with life, meeting new people, making an effort to do all the things Susan and I always meant to do but never got round to doing, it would take my mind off it. But here I am – I met you less than two hours ago and already all I can talk about is Susan. Enough.' Kate wiped her eyes furiously. 'Look, let's talk about something else. How awful was that "Tell us about yourself" bit? I hate things like that.'

'I know,' agreed Claire. 'I can never think of a single interesting thing about myself when people make me do that. "Tell me about yourself," blah blah. We had to do one of these at work recently, and all I could manage was "I like toast."'

'Well, toast is good, isn't it?' agreed Lucy. 'I mean, I'd probably definitely put someone on the potential Kindred Spirit list if that was what they shared about themselves. Certainly they'd be way above someone who announced they were a free-spirited go-getter who loved extreme sports and kale. People like that never appreciate toast for the important food group that it is. There is something wrong with people who don't like toast. With Marmite or without?'

'With?' said Claire, unsure of the correct response.

'OBVIOUSLY with!' said Lucy in delight. 'I knew you were a Kindred Spirit. And I'll tell you one good thing about husbands leaving. You can eat Marmite toast for dinner whenever you want. You can eat Marmite toast for dinner *in bed* if you want! We have to look for the positives where we can.'

'I take it with all this talk of Kindred Spirits, you're an *Anne of Green Gables* fan?' asked Kate.

'Of course. Who isn't? Well, my miserable daughter. I thought it would be so magical, reading the stories I loved to my little girl. We'd bond. It would be amazing. But all Ella wants to do is make TikTok videos. I tried her with *Heidi*, and she asked was the grandfather a paedo, is that why he had to live alone up the mountain and avoid children? What is this world coming to? And what do they teach them at school?'

'Tabitha's the same,' sighed Claire. 'TikTok is life and I'm ruining hers by not letting her have her own account to post videos of her gyrating in hotpants to terrifying music about bitches and pussies. Though I think she's still under the impression some of those are confusing songs about cats. And to think, when *I* was young, my mum wouldn't even let me read the *Sweet Valley High* books. She said they were inappropriate. Oh God, *sorry* Kate. Here we are being stereotypical mummies, unable to talk about anything apart from our children. You must be bored rigid.'

'Not nearly as bored as if they were gifted and talented,' smiled Kate, relaxing a bit now the conversation had moved on to less emotional topics.

'I loved *Sweet Valley High*,' enthused Lucy. 'Though it was quite a jolt from the innocent courtship of Anne Shirley and Gilbert Blythe. Did you read the new *Sweet Valley* a few years ago where they were grown up?'

'Yes,' shuddered Claire. 'There were sex scenes. I wasn't antici-pating sex scenes. I mean, Jackie Collins, Jilly Cooper, Penny Vincenzi, you expect a bit of sauce.'

'It's the closest I get to sex,' sniffed Lucy. 'A good dirty book. Judith Krantz was always good for a bit of raunch too. If I don't get a shag soon, though, I'm going to have to resort to reading *Fifty Shades*, and then I'll feel dirty, but not in a good way.'

'Is it really hard to meet another man at our age?' asked Claire anxiously. 'Are we destined for a future of celibacy and cats? Is being Neville's *fair wench* as good as it gets?'

'Judging by some of the men I've encountered online, Neville could possibly be regarded as quite the catch!' said Lucy darkly.

'Even with the BO?' said Kate, wide eyed. 'I mean, it was quite pungent. At least, I think it was Neville, and not Stella's tea.'

'No, I'm pretty sure it was Neville,' agreed Claire. 'The waft from him was more polecat, the reek from the tea was more tomcat.'

'Oh fuck, did you smell that too?' exclaimed Kate. 'I hoped it was just me thinking Stella's tea wasn't as 100 per cent botanical as she claimed.'

'Definitely a whiff of tomcat.'

'Oh dear,' said Lucy sadly. 'We've finished this bottle. Shall I get another one? Just to make sure Neville is safely behind closed doors before we brave the streets to go home. Though we could probably smell him from three blocks away!'

'Oh no!' said Claire. 'I should be getting back. Look at the time, it's –'

'Half past nine,' said Kate, looking confused. 'Will you turn into a pumpkin?'

'No,' said Claire indignantly.

'Well then,' said Lucy. 'Do you have anything to get back for?'

Claire thought about her empty house. There was a tin of tuna in the cupboard she could try to entice Colonel Mousicles in with, though he'd made it clear that he much preferred salmon.

'No,' admitted Claire.

'Another bottle it is then!' Kate said in glee.

'Why not,' said Claire. 'I can't actually remember the last time I didn't have anything at all to get back home for. I might as well make the most of it. Perhaps this is a night of new beginnings! I'm out out, I've read an Important Book – all right it was shit – but I can't remember the last time I did that, and I think it would be wrong not to have fun.'

'That's the spirit!' cackled Lucy. 'Maybe we'll even have *shots*.'

'Oh, steady on,' said Claire, in mock alarm.

12

Claire woke up at five the next morning with a dry mouth and a thumping head. She was grateful to find she'd had the foresight to bring two pints of water to bed with her, and promptly downed them both. She woke up again at nine, when Andrew texted to ask if he could keep the children for the day and bring them home after dinner. Claire looked at her screen. God, she had loads of missed messages from Lucy. Claire opened them in some trepidation. The first one was sent at 12.39 a.m. that morning.

[Lucy] Home now efsgrkjthy34i You home now SSD?

Was it a code, wondered Claire. What did it mean? Then there were three messages sent at 2.46 a.m. The first simply read:

Arse sdfg bum

and the others were a string of random letters and numbers.

The next lot of messages were from 8 a.m. onwards:

Claire, are you OK? Did you get home OK?

Claire? Claire, message me when you get this and let me know you got home all right?

CLAIRE! Claire, I'm very hungover and very worried about you, please let me know you're alive!

Please don't be dead Claire, my hangover can't deal with this. Also, I'd be very sad as well, but I'd probably have to go and be sick while giving a statement to the police, and then they'd judge me, so CLAIRE, DON'T BE DEAD!

Claire suddenly remembered guiltily that Lucy had given her a very drunken hug when they parted ways and had insisted they all message each other so they knew they were home safely, and indeed, Lucy had checked in and Claire had utterly failed to.

[Claire] I'm so sorry! I completely forgot to message when I got back.

[Lucy] Yay! You're alive! I can go back to feeling sorry for myself again. Will you bring me a bacon sandwich since you're not dead? I was wondering if I could've asked the policeman to make me one when I was giving my statement about you, after I'd finished being sick but since you're OK, that won't be necessary. Obviously I'd rather you weren't dead than that I had a policeman to make me a bacon sandwich. Eurgh, I wish Greggs delivered.

[Claire] I feel awful too. Have you heard from Kate, is she OK? When did we leave?

[Lucy] Yeah, I got a message from Kate just after 12.30 saying home. I dunno when we left. I don't remember an awful lot at the end, do you?

[Claire] I do remember we came up with an incredibly astute and profound observation on the nature of the patriarchy and a groundbreaking theory on how we could best dismantle it and change the entire social structure of the world for the better. It was completely earth-shattering.

[Lucy] Wow. What was it?

[Claire] I don't remember. I know you wrote it into Notes on your phone, so we could refer to it again.

[Lucy] Hang on, I'll check.

[Lucy] All it says in the note I made last night is asldkjfhwpiuhrgo-0348u93q8hg rnkjenasnvfkla'sdkngsf'lk'nlk'n'l fuck.

Reading all the nonsense texts from Lucy, Claire suddenly felt that the sensation of someone stabbing her through the temple while she was also suffering a bout of seasickness was actually worth it. She couldn't remember the last time she had ended up with a hangover from having *fun*. She hadn't had many hangovers at all in the last few years, as the Jen/Tim/Julia crew were always rather miserly about topping up your glass, and though visits from the Fucking Fergusons generally had involved a degree of self-medicating leading to general fragility the next day, one could hardly claim *fun* in the getting of the hangover. And obviously there had been no fun involved in obtaining the skull-splitting hangover the night that Andrew had spent away with Emily. But last night had been a reminder for Claire that there was life still out there, if she could find the courage to go out and get it, and she was very glad that Kate and Lucy had not let her leave early, and in fact that Lucy had got her way, and shots had indeed been involved.

*   *   *

The rest of the day was really rather pleasant. Since Claire still felt a bit fragile, she spent the afternoon lying on the sofa watching old films and eating an out-of-date box of Celebrations she'd found at the back of the cupboard, obviously having hidden them from the children at some point and forgotten about them, and messaging Lucy and Kate as they compared notes on the various states of their hangovers (Lucy had stopped by Greggs on the way to pick up her children from a rare visit to her ex-husband, and a cheese and onion pasty had helped, though she still had The Fear and was having flashbacks).

It had been, in short, a lovely Sunday afternoon of the sort Claire had never enjoyed with Andrew, as Sundays, far from being a day of rest, always seemed to be spent either with hordes of the Fucking Fergusons, and the likes of Tim and Jen, etc., over for a 'family' Sunday lunch, or staging a barbecue, which meant feeding and entertaining what felt like dozens of picky children as well as various adults all on alkaline diets, or low GI, or trailing off to someone else's house for the same, while Claire tried to stop Lucas and Tabitha making rude comments about the food and their hosts' Wi-Fi connection.

Sunday evenings were usually spent washing PE kit, trying to tidy up the house, shouting at the children about getting homework done, and ironing work shirts for Andrew for the coming week. His one attempt at ironing had been so stressful that it had eventually resulted in the fire brigade appearing, so it was actually easier for Claire to do it herself. Meanwhile, she had long ago decided her own workwear could easily be things that didn't need ironing, and Marks & Spencer's non-iron school uniform was surely one of the greatest inventions in the world ever.

Until Andrew left, Claire reflected, it had been a very long time since she'd had a day off. Andrew would have scoffed and said that she was being ridiculous, that she had weekends off, just like he did, but the reality was very different. Somehow the weekends, when they were supposed to have their 'downtime', ended up being just as busy, if not busier, than weekdays. Not only were Sundays the roast or barbecue days with the Friends of Doom, but Saturdays were usually even busier.

Claire would spend Saturdays ferrying the children around to all the activities they had somehow agreed were necessary for them to partake in, and attempting to snatch a moment to start on all the jobs around the house that needed catching up on from the rest of the week. Andrew, meanwhile, cut the grass, faffed around doing unnecessary DIY badly or vanished with his laptop because he had 'some work to do' on account of his great Busy and Importantness, before she gave the children an early dinner, saw them to bed, and then either had to make herself look respectable and cook a three-course meal for whichever adults they had invited round, or frantically apply make-up and try to find a clean top to wear to a dinner party with their friends. All the while, Andrew would be jingling his keys and demanding why wasn't she ready yet, *he* was ready, but she still had to shout last-minute instructions to Tamsin the teenage babysitter and hope she wouldn't have sex on the sofa with an unsuitable boy while they were out.

So a day off was a definite positive, Claire reminded herself. She was free to do whatever she wanted today. She could lie in the bath for three hours and tan a bottle of champagne. She could switch off *Dead Poets Society* (not least because although technically fancying Ethan Hawke was not *actually* wrong since he was older than Claire, she still felt like a bit of a randy old lady fancying Ethan Hawke when he was only nineteen and playing a schoolboy) and go to the cinema to watch something French and intense, where people gave a lot of meaningful looks and sighed about obscure metaphors and she didn't need to wear bastarding plastic 3-D glasses that had cost a fortune even though she had a whole DRAWER of the damn things at home that she always forgot to bring to the cinema. Yes, Claire thought firmly. She had longed for years for more time for herself. Now she had it, so she should make the most of it. What about taking up Spanish lessons? She and Emily had always talked about learning the language, then abandoning Andrew with the children to go on an epic road trip in South America.

Claire bit her lip and swallowed hard to keep the tears at bay as she realised another dream had vanished along with Emily. OK, *not* Spanish lessons. What about … archery? She had been quite good at archery the time she'd gone on an otherwise disastrous Outward Bound trip at school with Emily.

'Oh FUCKING FUCKING HELL,' yelled Claire suddenly, sitting up and hurling the remote in the general direction of the TV. Did everything have to come back to Emily? Her phone buzzed again with another message from Lucy, and Claire couldn't hold the tears back, because however nice Lucy and Kate were, they weren't *Emily*. And all Claire really wanted to do with all this new time on her hands, was to call Emily and do all those things she now had the freedom to do with her. And at the same time, she knew if she so much as laid eyes on Emily, she'd at the very least punch her repeatedly in the face while frothing at the mouth with rage.

How was Claire ever going to get to know anyone again as well as she had known Emily? How was anyone ever going to know her again like Emily had? Even Andrew hadn't known her as well as Emily. And now, at the moment when Claire needed her most, Emily wasn't there for her. Claire had never imagined a life in which she wouldn't be there. They had been so much more than best friends. When Emily's ratbag fiancé announced the day before their wedding that he was calling it all off because he'd met someone else, it had been Claire who'd sat with Emily while she sobbed, Claire who called the register office, reception venue and one hundred and one other people, and Claire who at very short notice took two weeks off work, kissed Andrew goodbye (pre-children) and went to Antigua with Emily for a fortnight on her honeymoon, where they got rat-arsed on cocktails and agreed all men were bastards, except Andrew. When they came home, Emily moved in with them for three months until she got herself back together. This hadn't entirely thrilled Andrew, but as Claire had explained, Emily was her best friend and they came as a package, so if you wanted Claire, you got Emily too. Well, he'd certainly ended up taking *that* literally, thought Claire with a sob.

Claire wanted nothing more than to curl up on the floor in a foetal position and cry until she had no tears left, but even that brought back memories of Emily. Claire had been terribly depressed both times after the children were born, and Andrew had been at a loss as to how to reach her, how to help her. It had been Emily who had stepped up, Emily who had sat holding Claire as she sobbed hopelessly for hours, persuaded her to take a shower, convinced her that she was not a terrible mother or an awful person, that she was just unwell and needed help, and finally took Claire to the doctor to get that help.

After the children as well, Emily was her reminder that there was more to herself than being a wife and mother. That there was more to life than wiping noses and bums and shouting about scurvy and filling in forms for school trips and finding lost shoes and emptying festering lunchboxes abandoned under beds for the summer holidays. Only when she was alone with Emily could Claire feel like *Claire*. Only Emily wasn't constantly clamouring for a part of Claire's soul, for her to come and look at something, to want to know where the garage key was, or whether she had renewed the house insurance, or who did she think would win in a fight, Gertrude or Ophelia Hughes? With Emily, Claire had felt she knew who she really was. And now, without Emily, and without Andrew, and without her children every weekend, Claire didn't know who any of the many Claires she was to various people were. And how was she supposed to find out?

The future may hold all sorts of possibilities, Claire thought sadly. New friends. A new life. Maybe even one day, a new man? But did she really want them? Or did she just want her old life back? And could she trust anyone again after what Emily and Andrew had done? Yes, she decided. Just because Emily and Andrew were awful people, didn't mean everyone was awful. Most people were good, she reminded herself. Like most dogs were wonderful. And since she couldn't have her old life back, she'd better make the best job she could of the new life ahead of her.

Claire was wiping her eyes, and sternly chanting 'Think of the positives' to herself when the doorbell rang.

Andrew was on the doorstep, with two muddy, wet and frozen children. Tabitha was particularly bedraggled and appeared to be covered in pond weed.

'Oh my God,' said Claire, aghast. 'Tabitha, upstairs and straight in the shower. Lucas, shoes and clothes off, go and put on your dressing gown and in the shower after Tabitha, please. What *happened*?' she asked Andrew. 'I thought you were keeping them till after dinner?'

'She fell in the pond!' said Andrew crossly. 'I told her not to fall in, but she did, and they've no more clean clothes.'

'Well, yes,' said Claire. 'They like falling in the pond, that's why you shouldn't let them go near it.'

'You might have told me! As for the rest, they just appeared to *roll* in the mud. You should see the state of my car.'

'It's probably similar to the state of my car. And they're *your* children, Andrew. I shouldn't need to issue a set of instructions every time you take them out, though I've told you for years about them falling in ponds and puddles. But they still always do it on your watch.'

'Please don't start, Claire,' Andrew sighed. 'It's been a long and very trying afternoon.'

'Taking *your* children to the park.'

'Claire, please, I am *trying*. Anyway, I need to talk to you. Can I come in?'

'Come on then,' Claire sighed. Then blood-curdling screams rang out from upstairs.

'Shit, I'd better go and see what's happening.'

Upstairs, Tabitha was having a complete meltdown because Lucas had 'breathed at her' when she came out of the bathroom.

'The lady who gave us the talk about living and growing at school said we must not let anyone do anything that makes us feel uncomfortable, AND I FEEL UNCOMFORTABLE WHEN HE BREATHES AT ME!'

'He … can't not breathe, Tabitha.'

'HE CAN! HE BREATHES AT ME AND I DON'T LIKE IT!'

'How does he breathe at you?'

'I DON'T BREATHE AT HER! I DON'T EVEN WANT TO LOOK AT HER STUPID FACE!'

'YOUR FACE IS STUPID, NOT MINE! AND YOUR BREATHING IS STUPID. STUPID STUPID STUPID, AND YOU SMELL LIKE POO AND THAT'S WHY CARYS JOHNSON WON'T BE YOUR GIRLFRIEND.'

'MUUUUUUUM! I HATE HER. Can she just go and live with Dad?'

'Lucas loves Carys, Lucas loves Carys.'

'I DON'T! WHY CAN'T YOU JUST DIE IN A HOLE?'

'LUCAS! *Don't* say things like that to your sister.'

'Why not? Why do you always take her side?'

'That's a death threat. Mum, he gave me a death threat. I can call the police about that. Then you'll go to prison and then Carys Johnson will NEVER do snogging with you, HA!'

Claire finally, by dint of the usual threat of changing the Wi-Fi password if the children DID NOT STOP FIGHTING NOW, managed to end the battle and trudged back downstairs – reflecting that maybe despite everything that had happened, some things never changed – to see what Andrew wanted. He was sitting in an armchair doing his best Brooding Look. Claire remembered that once she had found Andrew's Brooding Look to be irresistibly Heathcliff-esque. She wondered when that had changed.

'Right,' Claire said briskly. 'What did you want to talk to me about?'

Andrew slowly raised his eyes, clearly playing out Brooding for all it was worth, and said, 'This is hard, on my own. I miss you. The kids miss you. Doing things by myself with them, it's not how I thought it would be. They talk … a lot. About really random stuff. And they fight, all the time.'

'I know,' said Claire. 'I deal with it all week. They're kids, that's what they do.'

Andrew sighed deeply, and looked for a moment like he was going to Brood harder, but instead he attempted a soulful face and caught her hand.

'Oh Claire!' said Andrew passionately. 'It doesn't have to be like this, you know. I made a mistake. A terrible mistake, and I'm so sorry, but we can get through this. I only ever loved you, and I still love you. I'm willing to try again,' he finished nobly, sounding rather as if he was making a great concession to Claire.

Claire was suddenly glad Andrew's Brooding Look actually made him look rather silly, because after the afternoon she'd just had, it would have been so very easy to agree with him and claw back at least a little of her old life.

Instead she just said, 'Andrew, it's too late for ifs and ands. I just … I need to get the kids' dinner and get them to bed. I think you should go. I'm sorry you're finding it hard. So am I, but it will get easier. At least, I hope it will.'

After Andrew had left, Claire was faced with the option of another crying jag on the sitting-room floor or doing something constructive, so she pulled herself together and chivvied Tabitha into her pyjamas, Tabitha having decided the best garb for a Sunday evening was her flounciest party frock. She also had to chivvy Lucas into *his* pyjamas, having discovered him sitting naked on his bedroom floor playing Minecraft, and then mopped up the flood in the bathroom caused by allowing the children to use the shower unsupervised.

After she'd done all this, and ladled out cheesy pasta to the ravening maws of her cherubs, Claire looked at her phone again. There was a text from Kate.

It was really nice to meet you both last night. I wondered if you'd like to go for a coffee or something sometime.

A new friend, thought Claire. New beginnings. I need to at least try to move on.

13

Over the next few weeks things settled down into a sort of routine. Sometimes Claire couldn't quite believe how much her life had changed in such a short time. She did her best to soldier on, but there were still a lot of bad days, of course. Days where despite everything she missed Emily so much it hurt, and the betrayal felt like a stab wound in her soul, and days where she wondered if she'd done the right thing after all, when Lucas or Tabitha cried and said they just wanted Mummy and Daddy to live together again, and why couldn't that happen, why wouldn't Mummy let Daddy come back, why was Mummy so mean, and it took all of Claire's strength not to cave in and ring Andrew and say, 'Come home.'

It took even more not to ring Emily, but Claire knew there was no way for them to go back to how it used to be. Whatever Andrew's betrayal had done to her was nothing to Emily's. Andrew was a husband, he knew Claire better than anyone except Emily, he had been part of her heart and the children would always tie them together, whether they liked it or not. But Emily – Emily was Claire's best friend, part of her soul. Sometimes they joked that they were two halves of one soul, and so Emily she could not forgive. Hearts, after all, could be transplanted, replaced with another in extremis. You could not do that if you lost half of your soul. Instead,

Claire focused as hard as possible on the new life she was trying to build.

Thus Claire did take one huge, positive step, one that went a long way towards not only salving her bruised and battered heart, but doing what she had thought impossible, and easing the ragged pain that Emily had left in her soul. For years she'd been trying to persuade Andrew that a dog was in fact a necessity in a family, but he always had some reason why they couldn't get one. But after Colonel Mousicles' initial visit, and realising the huge comfort to be found in the company of an animal, Claire had registered with some dog rescues.

After much research and reflection, she had decided a rescue Staffie was the way forward – there were so many of them dumped and abandoned. Claire had once broached the subject of a rescue Staffie with Andrew, but he'd been horrified and insisted they were 'dangerous dogs', which was utter nonsense. They were big-hearted softies! Staffies used to be known as the nursemaid dogs, she had told him, because they were so good with children, and Nana in *Peter Pan* was allegedly a Staffie. How could Nana be considered vicious?

Vaguely, Claire wondered if a Staffie could look after the children after school and save her money on childcare. Probably not. It was all very well for the Darlings to leave their children to be brought up by a dog, but Claire suspected that this sort of thing would be frowned upon by the mothers at the school gates. Mrs Darling was probably quite judged for it by the other Edwardian mummies in any case, not to mention the whole 'children flying away out of the nursery window' thing. What would Mumsnet have made of such a carry-on? Claire was thrilled though when a lovely lady rang up one day and said they'd found a dog they thought would match with Claire.

'I'm afraid at the moment it would be a foster situation,' she explained. 'Sadie has too many issues for us to look at permanently rehoming her with anyone until we see how she settles in. But it occurred to me that your circumstances would suit Sadie very well.'

'What do you mean?' asked Claire. 'What issues? And why would my circumstances suit her so well?'

'Ah, I was coming to that,' said the nice lady. 'Sadie, well, she has issues with men. She's OK if she's out of the house, but someone, a man, has obviously abused her very badly, and she's utterly frightened of men in the house. Her last placement has had to return her because she was so terrified of the husband – who is a lovely man, I must add. He didn't do anything to her, he's absolutely devasted by this, but she just couldn't cope living with him there. It's a terrible shame. But I believe I'm right in thinking that you live alone, with your children?'

'Yes,' said Claire. 'But I can't guarantee there will never be any men in the house. What happens when my son gets older, or I need a plumber or something? Or if my dad comes to stay? Or even – and I admit this is a long shot, and quite unlikely, but I'd like to think it's not something I'm ruling out altogether – what if I meet someone and I want him to move in?'

'I know,' said the lady soothingly. 'It's a tricky one. I don't think your son will be a problem. Sadie's last placement had a boy about the same age, and she was fine with him. And as your son gets older, Sadie will see that happening and will know it's still him. And we're very hopeful that with time and love and work, Sadie's phobias will ease. But right now, she can't cope in our kennels. We have three young men working here, and we try to make sure they don't clean her kennel or walk her, but she's still terrified when they're here and she can hear their voices when she's in her kennel, which of course is supposed to be her "safe space". As far as plumbers and all that go, like I said, with time, hopefully she'll be able to cope better, but for the time being she'd need to be in another room, or ideally even out on a walk. Your father? Again, introducing him gradually would be an idea, and the same would go for if you met a new partner. The trouble is, you can't really introduce a man gradually if it's HIS home too, which is why we thought that a home that doesn't currently have a man living there full time would be more suitable for Sadie while we work with you to try to help her.

'We wouldn't throw you in at the deep end to do this yourself. But apart from the man thing, she's perfect for your circumstances. She's a Staffie, which you said would be your preference if possible, and she's the gentlest soul – actually I should have said, her issues with men don't involve any aggression from her, she's just *terrified*. Which can sometimes lead to her having an accident, I'm afraid. But she's an older girl too, we think probably about ten, and apart from the accidents when she's frightened, she's very clean and quiet and is fine to be left for a few hours, which I think you said was going to be a necessity. But her age is a reason we're keen to at least get her into a foster home instead of our kennels.

'We do our best here, but we're very aware we don't, we *can't*, however hard we try, provide a home environment, which is what most of them really need. And we know for the older ones, they don't always have that long to go, and living their final years in a kennel … well, it's not ideal. But Sadie is such a sweet girl. All she really wants is a sofa and some love and a belly rub and an ear scritch. Would you be willing to consider her, Claire?'

'Um, can I meet her first? Would that be OK?'

'Of course. When can you come?'

Claire had feigned Women's Troubles and taken the afternoon off sick, Linda at the next desk having heard the whole conversation and offered to cover for her. As Claire left the office, she heard

Linda dramatically saying, 'Poor thing! She said the clots were like *liver!*' to Steven the office manager, who was entirely unable to cope with anything gynaecological and thus was willing to sign off any absences as long as he didn't have to hear the words 'ovaries', 'hormones', 'uterus', 'cervix', 'menstruation' or 'menopause'.

At the rescue centre, Claire sat anxiously in the meeting room while Nicola, the lovely rescue lady, went to get Sadie. Sadie came into the room, nervously hiding behind Nicola's legs, unsure what was happening to her now or where she was going. She peered round Nicola's knees and ducked back again.

It took everything in Claire to stay calmly on her chair and hold out her fist for Sadie to sniff, when every single muscle in her body was straining to fling herself on the floor, throw her arms around Sadie and say, 'You're my girl now.' This was because as soon as she saw her – fear brimming out Sadie's big brown eyes in a broad white face with a black patch over one eye, and one black sock, her whole body shaking with terror, but her tail still bravely trying to wag, to show she was a good girl, she was good girl, please, please, she was a very good girl, she'd do anything, just please don't hurt her – Claire knew, she just knew, that Sadie was Her Dog and she was Sadie's Person. They had found each other, and nothing and no one was going to keep them apart.

Sadie sniffed Claire's fist tentatively, and looked up at her, and wagged a little harder. Claire choked back tears and scratched Sadie's ears. Sadie sighed in bliss, and although she knew it was the wrong thing to do, that she needed to give Sadie space, Claire couldn't help herself. She slipped off her chair and wrapped her arms around Sadie. Sadie leaned into her, and rested her head against Claire's shoulder.

'Well?' said Nicola. 'What do you think of her?'

'Yes,' sobbed Claire. 'Oh yes, please. You are my girl, aren't you, darling? You are my girl now.'

Sadie obligingly licked the tears off Claire's face, and made a small noise that clearly indicated she agreed, and Claire was now *her* girl too. Two sad souls who had been battered by the world had found each other, and would be able to start healing each other.

Sadie came home with Claire for good a week later. Although she was still officially only fostered with a view to potential adoption, Claire, Sadie and Nicola all knew that Sadie was not going anywhere ever again.

Lucas and Tabitha were utterly enchanted with Sadie. They squabbled over who was going to feed her, sit next to her, hold her lead on walks, fill up her water bowl and coax her to play with the entire toy stock of Pets at Home that Claire had enthusiastically bought on the way back from her first meeting with Sadie, and that Sadie, heartbreakingly, had no idea what to do with. This fascination lasted exactly two days, and then they both reverted to type and declared themselves busy and unable to do anything with her because Reasons.

Despite the children's utter lack of interest in Sadie, they were not above using her for their own purposes, such as being unable to do the task Claire had asked them to undertake because Sadie was sitting on them and shouldn't be disturbed. They were also shameless in their use of Sadie to distract Claire when she was berating them for their latest foul and unhygienic misdemeanour, such as Tabitha's staunch insistence that she absolutely had not removed her latest attempts to become a TikTok make-up sensation by simply bypassing such old-fashioned notions as soap and water and rubbing her face over Claire's white Egyptian cotton towels, leaving liberal smears of glitter, violently hued eyeshadow and what looked suspiciously like Claire's treasured Chanel foundation.

They had only to say, 'Look, Mummy, look what Sadie's doing, isn't she sweet?' or 'Mummy, I don't think Sadie likes you shouting, she's getting upset,' and Claire's ire over the ruined towels or the identity of the Phantom Shitter who constantly left large offerings unflushed in her toilet bowl were instantly forgotten at the sight of that sweet little face staring up her.

Sadie added another layer of work to Claire's life, obviously, not to mention an additional strain on her bank balance, which was already feeling a little tense, but the comfort of that solid presence beside her in bed made the nights feel far less long and lonely, as did that black and white head resting on her knee in the evenings. Sadie's love and gentle hopefulness did a lot to soothe Claire's shattered heart, and she had someone to talk to again, a shoulder to cry on again, someone whom she knew loved her utterly unconditionally and this time, would never, ever let her down.

Sadie in return was so blissfully happy to be with Claire – sleeping in a soft bed at night, and curling up in her cosy crate to await the lovely dog walker Claire had found, who also adored Sadie so much that she kept her out with her most of the day, instead of for the hour Claire paid for – that within a few weeks she was a very different dog indeed to the terrified, anxious bundle of bones Claire had brought home.

The only person not delighted with this whole new arrangement was Colonel Mousicles. Claire had tried to explain to him that she had very much enjoyed his visits, but he couldn't stay with her all the time, his owner would miss him, and thus Claire had got a dog instead. Colonel Mousicles had said very rude things to Sadie from the top of the wall, and made his rage at Claire very clear too, hardly being able to bring himself to eat the conciliatory salmon fillet she'd offered him to try to make up for her terrible behaviour.

There was another advantage to Sadie's arrival as well. Andrew, faced with the constant round of activities on his weekends with his children, and like Claire, a dwindling amount of disposable income, had readily agreed to Claire's suggestion that perhaps they should listen to the kids and let them drop all the things they'd insisted they were 'desperate' to do and after three classes had declared to be boring, but that Andrew and Claire had urged them to carry on with to make them into well-rounded people. This freed up both a bit more cash, and a lot more time for Claire on the weekends the children weren't with Andrew, and she started to spend Saturday mornings going for long dog walks with Lucy, who was proudly possessed of a sex-obsessed and malodorous Border terrier named Bingo.

Claire and Lucy's children would accompany them if they were at home, usually moaning about being cold and bored and being unimpressed at the lectures about how it was character building, and Kate, who had kept in touch after the ill-fated book club and booze-up, often joined them too. The long walks in the fresh air and the chats they had as they marched along, children wailing about socks coming off in their wellies, did them all a world of good.

Somehow, it was much easier to talk about things when you were walking, rather than sitting on a sofa or at a table, even if you did occasionally have to break off what you were saying to stop Bingo humping Sadie, or to stop Sadie wheedling a croissant from a toddler in a pram. Kate shared her fears about becoming a single mother if she went ahead and had the baby she and Susan had always planned, but also her feeling that if she didn't, she was some-how letting Susan down. Claire confessed her guilt that she missed

Emily so much more than Andrew, and that if someone could wave a magic wand and erase what had happened, but on condition she could only have Emily *or* Andrew back, not both, that she'd unhesitatingly choose having Emily in her life over Andrew.

Lucy kept everyone entertained with her tales of attempted revenge against her cheating husband, explaining why it was a terrible idea to ever try to stuff potatoes up the exhaust pipe of someone who had wronged you.

'It's meant to wreck the car. But it's really hard to find a potato that's exactly the right size, and so you end up sitting in a car park, crying over a bag of King Edwards because they're all either too big or too small, and passers-by think you're mad, which at that moment you possibly are a bit, and then someone calls security and you have to pretend potatoes just make you *really* emotional, and that's why you're sitting there crying with your spuds. Anyway, there are far better methods of revenge, like signing his email address up to loads of really dodgy websites.'

For all Lucy's laughing and joking and insistence that she was totally over her ex and was now fine, Claire noticed that she always had a funny story rather than really opening up, in the way that both Claire and Kate didn't seem able to stop themselves from doing. In many respects she envied Lucy her ability to carry on pretending everything was all right, even though Claire knew from her own experience that Lucy must have been horribly hurt by her husband's behaviour. Claire still had too many moments of crying into Sadie's scruff at night, or starting what she thought would be a light-hearted conversation with Kate and Lucy about something and finding herself instead talking about Emily and Andrew and pouring her heart out again.

'Do I overshare?' she asked one day.

'No, of course not,' said Kate.

'Definitely not,' insisted Lucy.

'Only sometimes, I feel like all I do is moan about my life and I know I'm still luckier than about 99 per cent of the world, and I don't mean to, but it just seems to all come out.'

'I feel like all I do is moan too,' said Kate.

'You don't moan,' said Claire. 'You've had an awful time. Talking about it isn't moaning.'

'Well, the same goes for you,' Kate pointed out. 'I never think you're moaning.'

'Neither do I,' put in Lucy. 'I feel like all *I* do is whinge on too, going on and on about that useless twat.'

'But Lucy, you never whinge at all,' said Kate in astonishment. 'You're always so upbeat.'

'Yes, I wish I could be more like you,' said Claire. 'Even when shit happens, you pick yourself up and get on with it, and turn it into a funny story.'

'Really,' said Lucy doubtfully. 'I feel pretty moany.'

'Well, you're not. I suppose we all cope in different ways.'

'This is true,' sighed Lucy. 'That is why I stopped going to that counsellor after Twatface buggered off. She said it wasn't constructive to always use humour to deflect my feelings, and I asked if she'd rather I used interpretive dance and her mouth went all cat's bummy, so I didn't go back.'

'Why did you suggest I went to a counsellor, then?' demanded Claire.

'Well, I assumed it was just me. Other people seem to swear by them. Or if it wasn't me, then maybe it was her. Either way, I just said "a" counsellor. I wasn't going to recommend Mrs Cat's Bum. Oh bugger, talking of bums, Bingo is trying to shag that Doberman. BINGO! BINGO, THAT'S NOT NICE!' and Lucy raced off after him.

'Do you think she's OK?' Claire asked Kate.

Kate shrugged. 'I doubt it. But I suppose she'll cope in her own way and in her own time. She does talk about it all, though, just in a different way to us. I just hope if she ever needs us, she'll tell us.'

14

Claire was at work when she received a mildly hysterical WhatsApp from Lucy.

[Lucy] What the actual buggering bollocks of fresh shitting hell is this?

[Claire] ???????

[Claire] Are you OK? What's happened? Do you need me?

[Lucy] Have you read your emails?

[Claire] No, I'm at work, I'll check them at lunch.

[Lucy] CHECK THEM NOOOOOOW!!!! WE'RE DOOOOOOOMED!

[Claire] Calm down Lucy. It can't be anything that bad if it's in an email? The kids are OK?

[Lucy] Oh yes, the kids are OK. It's us that won't be.

Claire was now too intrigued to wait until lunchtime and opened up her emails on her phone. There was an email from Lolly Hughes, who was of course the class rep, and one from the school. Claire opened the school email first.

Dear Parents,

We are delighted to inform you that after careful consideration, and appropriate risk assessments, that the proposed parent and children camping trip for Year 4 will be going ahead. We would like to thank the Parent Council reps for suggesting this trip, and for their hard work in the planning of it. Thanks to the Parent Council reps' negotiations with the campsite, we are pleased to inform you they have secured a discounted rate. The cost of the trip is £175 per adult and £150 per child. This covers your camping accommodation and dinner on Friday, all meals on Saturday and breakfast on Sunday. Additional siblings not in Year 4 are welcome to join the trip, though additional spaces are allocated on a strictly first come/first served basis. The trip will take place from Friday 2 June to Sunday 4 June at the Forest Fields Campsite. Further information on the facilities available at the Forest Fields Campsite can be found here: www.forestfieldscamping.co.uk. Extra activities on the trip will incur additional charges.

This is a really unique chance for Year 4 to bond with each other, and work on their resilience and interpersonal skills while supported by their parents and guardians and we strongly encourage all families to participate. Please sign up via the ParentPay link here: www.parentpay.co.uk

Meadowgate Primary School bears no liability for any accidental injuries or losses during this trip.

Yours sincerely,

Eleanor Cartwright,

Headmistress

With some trepidation, Claire then opened Lolly's email:

Hi Guys,

Isn't it amazing news about the camping trip? I have put SO much work into this, and I really think it is going to be a very special weekend. This has been a project super close to my heart, and I know you are all going to get so much out of it. We did a presentation to Year 4 this morning about it, and they are all SO SO keen to go and can't wait. They are going to benefit so much from this, as are we as parents. It's a great opportunity for us all to learn and grow together, while really getting to enjoy the beautiful countryside. And we managed to get it for SUCH a reasonable price, so there is no reason that the whole family can't come, as we have made sure it is totally affordable! Harry and I are so looking forward to it. As a special bonus, some of you may know that I am opening my own yoga studio very soon, and so I am THRILLED to announce that on Saturday morning I will be offering a unique opportunity for a taste of parent and child yoga in the forest. Normally in my new studio I would be charging £25 per person for this class, but I am doing it at a discounted rate of only £20 per person as a goodwill gesture for us all to be able to get to know each other better. I know you'll all want to sign up, but places WILL be limited, so get in touch ASAP!

   Love and peace, friends
   Lolly

Claire's immediate reaction was to text Emily to help her come up with excuses as to why she couldn't possibly go on such a trip. Emily was the queen of plausible excuses. If things had been different, they could have concocted a plan to send Andrew on the trip with both children and had a lovely weekend to themselves, thought Claire sadly. As it was, she was not convinced she'd be able to persuade him that he wanted to spend the weekend sleeping in a field listening to Tabitha wittering on about Smiggle and TikTok, but maybe this was one of these new opportunities she kept telling herself would be so good for her, and she should suck it up and get on with it. Surely it would, at the very least, be character building.

[Claire] OMG. A class camping trip! It sounds fun!

[Lucy] Are you fucking serious?

[Claire] Do you not want to go?

[Lucy] No, I do not want to go.

[Claire] Do you think it will really be that bad? It might be fun!

[Lucy] Fun! I'd rather spend the entire weekend rimming Jacob Rees-Mogg!

[Claire] I take it that's a no, then?

[Lucy] That's a no. I'm sexually frustrated, not perverted.

[Claire] What IS rimming anyway?

[Lucy] I'm also at work. Look it up in the Urban Dictionary.

[Claire] LUCY! That's disgusting. I mean, each to their own. But imagine doing
THAT to HIM!

[Lucy] Well, yes, that's rather the point. That's HOW MUCH I do NOT want to go on
a class camping trip organised by Lolly Twatting Hughes!

[Claire] Oh come on. How bad can it be?

[Lucy] What was the last thing you went to organised by Lolly?

[Claire] That PTA coffee morning a few months ago. She railroaded me into it.

[Lucy] And how was it?

[Claire] She made me spend four hours washing tea cups and then shouted at me for not counting them into the boxes correctly because she has a SYSTEM and also I got in trouble for putting the almond milk in the same fridge as the cow's milk because she might have been contaminated with filthy dairy, and then I put my back out putting chairs away because she was yelling at everyone to work faster because she had someone coming to balance her chakras at 3pm. She had a whistle. It was awful.

[Lucy] And now she's going to do all that, but with added mud and mosquitoes.

[Claire] It's not going to be fun, is it?

[Lucy] No, Pollyanna, it is not.

[Claire] How are we going to get out of it?

Later, as Lucy sat at Claire's kitchen table, despairingly pretending to bang her head on it repeatedly, occasionally looking up to take another slug of wine, they concluded that there was no getting out of it. They were indeed doomed. Ella and Tabitha were hugely excited and had talked of nothing else from the minute they got out of school, and Lolly Hughes, the smug bitch, had been preening and smirking in the playground, and accepting the congratulations of the many parents who also shared Claire's initial optimism that this was a GOOD IDEA and were thanking Lolly for her enterprise in organising it.

'What is *wrong* with them?' hissed Lucy to Claire.

'Dunno,' Claire whispered back. 'Stockholm Syndrome?'

Lolly, clearly deciding that it was worth crossing to Lucy's side of the playground to ensure that no one escaped without acknowledging her great generosity in taking the time to ruin their lives, and determined to force every parent to commit to coming in front of their cherubs so they could not wriggle out of it without causing immense emotional trauma and requirements for future therapy, bounded over to Lucy and Claire.

'Claire! And Lucy!' she said disdainfully. 'So nice to see you *single* gals are pals now. Much *safer* for everyone that way, no one can get any silly *ideas*. And can we expect you on the camping trip? I've gone to so much trouble arranging it that we do really feel everyone should make the effort to come so we can all pitch in.'

'Oh yes, Mummy, I really, really want to go. There is zorbing and everything,' said Tabitha.

'What is zorbing?' asked Claire doubtfully.

'Dunno,' said Tabitha. 'But I really want to do it.'

'And me, Mummy, please, Mummy, please say we can go,' Ella begged Lucy.

'We'll see,' muttered Claire.

'Maybe,' snorted Lucy.

'Are Lucas and Ben coming too?' demanded Ella.

'Fuck, no,' said Ben, an expression of horror crossing his face.

'BEN!' said Lucy, equally horrified.

'It's hardly surprising, poor child,' cooed Lolly in tones now dripping with saccharine spite. 'I do *try* to understand how difficult it is, with your … circumstances. I think the camping trip will be especially important for children like *yours*' – she nodded at Tabitha and Ella, who were chanting some song they had learnt off TikTok, and Ben and Lucas, who were covered in mud as per usual and wearing particularly truculent expressions, reminiscent of William

Brown upon being made to join The Band of Hope, and lowered her voice to a dramatic whisper – 'who come from *broken homes* to see what *normal* family life is like, don't you? It will give them hope to see what proper families are like. Despite people's attempts to spoil those families, some of us are stronger than that.'

Claire and Lucy both stared at Lolly, gobsmacked at her utter insensitivity, but she had already turned on her heel and stalked off.

Before Claire knew what she was saying, she yelled 'FUCK YOU VERY MUCH' at Lolly's retreating back.

'What was that?'

'Nothing,' said Claire meekly, her sudden burst of courage deserting her.

Lolly narrowed her eyes and glared at Claire, before walking on.

'Bravo,' said Lucy loudly. Lolly's back stiffened, but she carried on walking.

Lucy had chuntered all the way back to Claire's house about Lolly's rudeness and had made several comments along the lines of 'that bitch needs a good slap!' Claire had been too stunned that she had finally said anything like that to any of the Playground Coven, let alone Lolly, that she had drunk quite a large glass of wine rather quickly when she got home. It had been very childish and very rude, and exactly the sort of thing she'd once have done with Emily when they were young. And it had also felt rather good, that she had done it by herself, without Emily egging her on. That brief flash of excitement had been quickly dimmed by the prospect of Lolly's revenge at Forest Fields.

So now here they were, slumped in despair at the kitchen table, desperately trying to think of a way to get out of the class camping trip, while Ella and Tabitha chattered on like demented monkeys about how excited they were, and Ben and Lucas made dire threats about running away in the night if they were forced to join the Year 4 trip with a 'bunch of stupid babies', which had predictably made Tabitha and Ella screech with rage that they WERE NOT stupid babies, and only Claire's swift intervention had prevented Tabitha blacking Lucas's eye with a Nintendo Switch.

'Thank God,' she said to Lucy. 'Can you imagine Lolly's face if he came to school looking like a battered child after her comments today?'

'And Ben's swearing! Why? Why in front of Lolly, of all people? Oh God, Claire, I can't go. Lolly hates me. She'll have a shallow grave dug in the woods and will lure me out there to be bludgeoned to death with a vegan sausage roll! No, not a sausage roll, far too gluteney. I dunno, she'll smother me in my sleep with organic tofu or something. I just CAN'T go, Claire.'

Unfortunately, Ella had come in at that very moment and overheard Lucy declaring she could not go.

'But if you don't go, I can't go, Mummy,' she wailed.

'I know, darling, but do you really want to go? Actually? We could do something lovely ourselves that weekend for a treat? Go camping somewhere else? Tabitha and Claire could come too! Wouldn't that be fun?'

'But *everyone* else is going on the family camping trip. Even Amy, and she's only just started at school,' said Ella, big eyes brimming with tears. 'Please, Mummy. Please can we go? Or don't we have enough money to go, like Daddy said was why he couldn't take Ben and me on holiday with them when he took Celeste and her new baby to Tenerife? It's OK if we don't have enough money, Mummy, but I'd really like to go if we could. I could give you the money Grandma gave me for my birthday for it?'

Lucy sighed. 'It's OK, Ella darling. I don't need your birthday money. If it means that much to you, of course we'll go.'

'But why did you say you couldn't go, Mummy?'

'Oh, I was just being silly. A silly joke with Claire. Of course I can go.'

'Are you sure?'

'Yes. I'm quite sure, darling. Don't worry about it.'

'Well,' groaned Lucy, as Ella skipped out the kitchen, 'it looks like I'm going to Forest Fields. The things you do for your children. You can't abandon me now, Claire! Though it is galling to have to spend £350 to sleep in a fucking field for two nights.'

'£325. You're supposed to be an accountant, Lucy!'

'See? Despair at the very thought of it has clouded my ability even to do basic arithmetic. I can't believe that woman thinks £325 to sleep on the ground in the fucking mud is considered good value.'

'MUMMY,' bellowed Tabitha. 'Ella says she's definitely going on the camping trip. Are we DEFINITELY going too, Mummy? Please, please, please, Mummy. I want this more than anything in the world, Mummy, PLEEEEEASE? I think I'll die if I can't go!'

'You said yesterday that you wanted a TikTok account more than anything in the world and you thought you'd die if I didn't let you have one,' pointed out Claire.

'That was *yesterday*,' replied Tabitha scornfully. 'Yesterday I didn't know about the camping trip, did I? Please can we go, Mummy? I'll be so good and I'll keep my room really tidy and I won't tell Lucas to die in a hole EVER AGAIN, and I'll even be nice to him, and I'll walk Sadie every day and brush her and feed her and bring my laundry down when you tell me and everything.'

'All right, all right,' laughed Claire. 'We'll go! Happy now?'

'Yes, I'm so happy, thank you. Lucas isn't coming, is he?'

'I thought you were going to be nice to him?'

'I AM, but I just don't think he'd enjoy it, so this IS me being nice to him. There might be a lot of holes in a campsite for him to die in. That's all.'

'And me,' muttered Lucy.

'No, I don't think Lucas will come,' Claire assured Tabitha.

'Good. I mean, I'm just thinking of him.'

'You shouldn't actually tell your brother to die in a hole ever,' Claire pointed out, 'not just when you're trying to be extra good. Remember when he said that to you and you tried to phone the police to report a death threat?'

'No,' said Tabitha. 'I definitely didn't do that. Anyway, Mummy, have you signed us up yet? You need to sign me up, they might run out of places. Ophelia and Gertrude's mummy said places were *strictly limited*, Mummy, so can you sign me up NOW?'

'LATER!' said Claire. 'GO and play with Ella and let me talk to Lucy.'

'Can I have some crisps?'

'Fine.'

'Can I have the nice crisps not the rubbish ones?'

'What do you mean?'

'These ones,' said Tabitha, brandishing the Good Crisps, aka the Sea Salt and Balsamic Vinegar Kettle Chips, at Claire.

'No. Here.'

Claire thrust two bags of own-brand Hula Hoops at Tabitha.

'WHY can't I have these nice ones?' Tabitha whined. 'It's not fair. You never let me have anything nice. Are you and Lucy going to eat them? That's discriminating against children.'

'Tabitha, not even five minutes have passed since you were swearing dramatically that you'd be good forever if I took you on the camping trip, and already you're whinging at me about crisps.'

'Well, that's because you've not *actually* signed me up yet, isn't it? I can't start being good until I'm definitely going, because otherwise it would be a waste.'

'You could just try being good for the sake of it?' Claire suggested wearily.

'Why?' said Tabitha. 'What would be the point of that?'

'Just go and take Ella those crisps. And here, take some for the boys too.'

'Why do I have to do everything? Why can't Lucas come and get them? You're so unfair! I'm not a servant!'

'JUST GO, Tabitha! Now. Before I change my mind about camping.'

Tabitha opened her mouth to continue arguing, thought better of it and went.

'The things we do for our children indeed,' Claire said. 'Shall we have more wine?'

'Lots more,' Lucy said despondently. 'Though I don't think there's enough wine in the world to make this better!'

Within a week it became apparent that the rest of the class parents were also having some misgivings. The class WhatsApp was on fire. Claire wasn't really a big fan of WhatsApp groups; she had long since muted the class groups for Lucas and Tabitha, which mainly consisted of a small number of mums humble-bragging about what a terrible job their precious moppets had made of the latest homework project while proudly displaying intricate scale models of the Coliseum that quite clearly their little darlings had never been anywhere near, as well as random requests that were nothing to do with the school and could have been answered with a brief Google: 'Hi, does anyone know how to make rhubarb crumble/if there are any local window cleaners/what time the post office opens?'

The neighbourhood WhatsApp wasn't much better, consisting largely of questions about which bins were going out this week and furious accusations from Colonel Mousicles' owner next door, insisting that other people were CLEARLY feeding her cat and to desist IMMEDIATELY (Claire was relieved Colonel Mousicles' last supper with her had been her guilt salmon fillet for Sadie's arrival, and so her conscience was clear on this score, as she hadn't fed him in months – though he was looking rather stout) before she involved the police, and complaints about dog poo.

Now though, the Viking longship competition was forgotten, as were the arguments for and against competitive sports at Sports Day ('Poppy is *extremely* sensitive and is distressed by the concept of failure, therefore competitive sports shouldn't be allowed as Poppy will be very upset if she doesn't come first'; 'Noah is training at county level tiddlywinks. It's completely unfair if there's no competitive element for children like him,' etc., etc.), as rumours swirled about the camping trip. Some parents were furious to find, not having read the original letter properly, that the extortionate fee didn't cover any activities and that these would be charged as 'extra'. In an attempt to mollify them, Lolly offered to further reduce the cost of her forest yoga class to only £18 per person. The mob remained unmollified.

Then, a message arrived from Caroline Northfield.

[Caroline N] I've just been looking on the Forest Fields website and there's a glamping area, with luxury bell tents and separate toilet facilities and electricity. Is there an option to upgrade to this?

[Natalie F] That sounds good, I'd also be interested in upgrading.

[Lizzy P] And me. That sounds a bit more like it.

[Lolly H] Actually, we've booked the whole of Forest Fields, as for safeguarding reasons we decided it was better if we had the exclusive use of the entire site.

[Caroline N] So does that include the glamping area?

[Lolly H] Yes, of course.

[Sally B] So who gets to have the glamping tents and nice toilets?

[Susan F] Yes, good question. How do we get one of them?

[Lolly H] Well, ladies (and gents, must be inclusive 😊, I know there's some chaps on this WhatsApp), we decided that the fairest thing was just to draw lots for it.

[Sally B] And then whoever gets picked pays the extra? But what if they don't want to pay the extra? What if they can't afford it, or just don't want the fancy tents? Do you draw again? Is there a list to work your way down?

[Lolly H] Oh no, there won't be any extra to pay for the glamping tents.

[Caroline N] Did you manage to get them to throw them in for the same price? Even so, bit unfair if we're all paying the same and some people have luxury tents with hair straighteners and phone chargers and some people are roughing it?

[Lolly H] Well, no, I didn't exactly get them for the same price. It's because they're more like permanent structures, whereas the rest of the tents we'll be hiring from Forest Fields and putting up ourselves. We did talk about people bringing their own, but it was too complicated and they could have been potential fire risks. We have been very vigilant about fire risks, and Forest Fields can rent tents and equipment for everyone, you see, all you need to bring is sleeping bags, though you can rent them for extra too. We did do an extensive risk assessment and we decided the best thing to do was to hire Forest Fields tents because they're big enough to sleep a number of people, possibly two families in some cases, so we thought that would be much cosier and friendlier you see, and more in line with the sort of team building and bonding we're hoping to focus on this weekend. So actually it should all be really great fun and I hope you're all looking forward to it as much as I am!!!!!!!!!xxxxxxxxx

[Caroline N] What do you mean 'not exactly' for the same price?

[Lolly H] Well, I explained above, it's because they're permanent structures really, and so it's something to do with insurance and fire risk, and I can't really spend any more time explaining because I need to take Ophelia and Gertrude to their bonsai class now.

[Caroline N] So are the people in the ordinary tents, which no one mentioned we had to put up ourselves by the way, paying to subsidise the extra cost of the people in the glamping tents? I don't think that is very fair.

Claire messaged Lucy separately.

[Claire] Are you watching the class WhatsApp?

[Lucy] Hell yeah!

[Claire] Do you think we should join in?

[Lucy] Fuck no, they're doing fine on their own. Let them get on with it.

In the time it took for Claire to have that brief exchange with Lucy, eighteen new notifications had pinged up from the class group, and when she checked the message thread, they were all along the lines of how very unfair this was that most of the group should be subsidising a minority, as well as a host of demands to be put in the glamping tents.

Lolly was conspicuous in her silence, but her sidekick Jacinta was valiantly attempting to fight a rearguard action, trotting out the same lines about insurance, fire risk and safeguarding, none of which made any sense, and explaining that it would simply have been TOO COMPLICATED to have had a two-tier system, and finally announcing that it was not in fact 'unfair' to have one price across the board. This was *actually* the fairest way, as she and Lolly had been *so, so* worried that if they had not done it like that, if they had altered the pricing system so that some people could book and pay more for the glamping tents, then how would the children in the 'other' tents feel? Lolly and Jacinta had been very worried about the children in the 'other' tents feeling *stigmatised* if their parents couldn't afford the nice tents, and so the best thing had been to charge everyone the same and then allocate the posh tents accordingly, so no one felt bad about how expensive they were. Lolly and Jacinta had ONLY BEEN THINKING OF THE CHILDREN, so there was no need to be so rude.

Tempers continued to fray and feelings run high as the weeks counted down towards the Famous Trip. Claire had at least persuaded Andrew to have Lucas and Ben for the weekend, as Lucy's ex could not look after his son because Reasons. Andrew had been reluctant at first, but had finally agreed when Claire had pointed out that two ten-year-old boys would be perfectly happy plugged into an electronic device of some kind or another all weekend, and virtually no interaction from him would be required for either boy, apart from providing regular supplies of crisps, fizzy drinks and pizza. He'd still been somewhat anxious, though.

'What do I with someone else's child? What if I break it?'

'Well, for starters, try not calling him "it". Always helps. And second, try very hard not to break him. The rules are quite clear. You must not break the visiting child. It doesn't matter how many limbs your own cherub may break or lose, as long as you do not break the visiting child.'

'Really? Why?'

'Well, because it's a lot less embarrassing taking your own kid to A&E than having to explain to another parent why *their* kid is in A&E. Honestly, Andrew, how have you never dealt with someone else's child before?'

'I don't know. You always did it. You were so good at it, and I didn't know what to do and I was scared they might think I was a paedo.'

'Why would they think you were a paedo?'

'I don't know. You just hear stories, don't you? Comments being misconstrued. And like I said, you always seemed to know what you were doing better than me, and I thought I'd probably get in the way, so I just left you to it.'

It was true, Claire reflected. Visiting children, whether on play-dates or the offspring of the Jen/Tim/Julias, or even worse, the vile fruit of the Fucking Fergusons' loins, like everything to do with the children, had always been Claire's department, while Andrew disappeared for 'work' or busied himself playing Mein Host, dispensing beers and bonhomie while Claire shovelled out oven chips that she lied were homemade with olive oil and attempted to ration the tomato ketchup.

'Just don't break Ben, or make any comments that might sound paedoey, OK?' she sighed. 'Look, I really do appreciate you doing this and helping out, though. I know you didn't have to take Ben as well, but it's very kind of you, and the boys are really looking forward to it. Thank you.'

'I feel I've got the lesser of two evils,' Andrew admitted. 'Since Tabitha has her heart set on going, someone has to take her, and since she decided you were it, oh dear, what a shame, how sad I am not to be the chosen one. Looking after Lucas and whatshisname for the weekend is definitely better than being drilled by the PTAstapo.'

'The PTAstapo is quite funny, I'll give you that. Though mainly because it's true.'

'Yep. Have fun.'

'It's going to be hell, isn't it?'

'No, no, you'll enjoy it. Remember how much you enjoyed that time I took you camping in Cornwall?'

'We drove for six hours to get there and I was so miserable that I cried all the first night and we had to book into a hotel because I was convinced I had beetles in my hair.'

'Yes. Character building,' Andrew chortled.

'Bastard,' said Claire, but with a lot less rancour than when she'd recently been calling him that.

Luckily Claire found it a lot easier all round to sort out accommodation for Sadie, who was spending the weekend with the lovely dog walker. When she had asked Lolly about bringing Sadie, Lolly had made it clear that so intent was Claire on blinding all the children there by bringing a DOG that would POO, that she might as well bring a red-hot poker and just put the children's eyes out there and then.

15

By the time the camping trip took place, Claire was already very much over it. Lucas had announced on Friday morning that he hated Ben, he never wished to speak to Ben again and that Ben was a 'shithead'. Claire's frantic remonstrances over both Lucas's language and his very inconvenient timing had fallen on deaf ears, as Lucas insisted that it was no good, Ben's transgressions in Minecraft could not be forgiven and if he never set eyes on Ben Connor again it would be too soon, and so why couldn't he come on the camping trip instead of going to Dad's with stupid Ben? The camping trip sounded *fun* and it wasn't *fair* that he was being excluded from it.

Deciding that forewarned was forearmed, Claire didn't tell Andrew about the Great Minecraft Row until they were both in the playground picking up the children, Claire to go straight to Forest Fields with Tabitha, and Andrew heading for home with the boys to place a mega Domino's order.

'What?' said Andrew desperately. 'They're fighting? But I thought they were friends. I thought that was why I agreed to do this. Now you tell me they're sworn enemies. So what am I supposed to *do* about that?'

'I don't know!' said Claire. 'I'm sorry. Just … referee or something. Take them on some kind of male-bonding exercise. You're always going on team-building days at work. Use what you've learnt on them to help the boys reconcile their differences.'

'We mainly just play paintball and then get pissed,' said Andrew. 'Anyway I'm not sure the corporate-wank-speak team-building pep talks and exercises included anything on ten-year-old boys falling out over Minecraft. Here they are. Which one is Ben?'

Claire stared. Ben was the one wandering along with Lucas, chatting nineteen to the dozen and acting like they were the best pals in the world. They were both covered in mud and looked slightly bruised and battered.

'What happened?' said Lucy, running into the playground late. 'I thought you two had fallen out?'

'We had a fight at lunchtime behind the wildlife garden where the teachers can't see us, and now we're friends again!' explained Lucas cheerfully.

'FFS,' thought Claire crossly. She'd felt it would be very character building for Andrew to have to try to resolve his son's issues for once, instead of leaving it to her.

'Oh well,' said Lucy. 'Sorry, you must be Andrew. I'm Lucy. I don't think we've met. Anyway, thank you *so much* for taking him this weekend.'

'No problem,' said Andrew, Mr Charming now he had an audience. 'My pleasure.'

'DAAAAD,' moaned Lucas. 'Can we go? I'm like *starving* and you said we could get pizza. *And* garlic bread. Mum doesn't let me get both, she makes me eat *vegetables* with pizza.'

Both boys made retching noises at the very thought of vegetables.

'Come on then, boys,' said Andrew, in jovial Hunter-Gatherer mode. 'Bye Tabitha, darling, have a lovely trip with Mummy! Say goodbye to your mums, boys.'

Claire and Lucy's attempts to say a fond farewell to their first-born and only sons were met with horror and revulsion, especially the requests for a hug, and the boys slouched off, the epitome of ten-year-old cool, with a casual 'Laters, Mum' and not so much as a backward glance.

'Wow,' said Lucy. 'He's hot!'

'Is he?' said Claire doubtfully.

'Oh yes. Don't you see it?'

'Not really. He's just … Andrew.'

'Trust me, he's hot. But don't worry, I'm not that desperate I'll do an Emily and shag him. It's lucky Lolly's not here right now, though. For all her "Harry is my hunky sex god" talk, she's always ALL over any hot dads in the playground. But alas, she awaits us, having bravely gone ahead to pathfind the way to our weekend of fucking expensive fun. Come on. Forest Fields it is! Best we can hope for to save us now is a small and very localised meteor strike just before we arrive. Obviously, it would be a dreadful shame if it hit Lolly as well as the campsite.'

Claire stared after Andrew as he walked out of the playground ahead of them. Andrew? Hot? OK, he hadn't gone bald or got fat, but Claire realised she hadn't looked at Andrew as a man rather than just Andrew for a very long time. He had just always been there, like a plant stand in the corner that occasionally was irritatingly horny. Well, maybe a plant stand was a bad analogy. He did still have a nice arse, though, she noticed. When had she stopped noticing that? When had they stopped noticing each other? Claire was annoyed to find she felt really quite jealous of Lucy's statement that Andrew was hot. Just because she didn't want him, didn't mean anyone else was allowed to have him, after all. Especially not Lucy.

* * *

Lolly was indeed ready and waiting at Forest Fields, doing her best Jo Whiley at Glastonbury meets *Footballers' Wives* impression, showing off very tanned (and annoyingly toned) legs in denim hotpants and glittery pink Hunter wellies, a pink cowboy hat and her expensively highlighted hair in cascades of artful 'beachy waves', which looked suspiciously like she'd spent the morning having it done at the hairdressers. She was also clutching a clipboard and a whistle, and looking extremely officious, and was accompanied by a dejected-looking man in a polo shirt emblazoned with the Forest Fields logo.

'Welcome, welcome,' she trilled merrily to the mutinous parents who were trudging in from the carpark, most of whom had already spent the day at work, not having beachy waves curled into their hair and berating the Forest Fields employee until he'd lost the will to live.

'I've the list of accommodation here,' Lolly continued, waving her clipboard, 'and have tried to consider all the sharing requests wherever possible.'

'What we want to know,' said Caroline Northfield and Sally Baxter, 'is who gets the glamping tents?'

'Well, you'll NEVER guess what happened when we drew the lots,' laughed Lolly merrily. 'It came out as Jacinta and Hugo, and Harry and me getting the first two glamping tents, and how we laughed when it was Figgy and Huxley's names next out the hat! We couldn't believe it, could we Figgy?'

Lolly nodded to the third member of her coven, Figgy, who was wafting around in a white cheesecloth dress and leaning against trees, attempting to recreate a White Company advert.

'I know,' giggled Figgy. 'What were the chances?'

Caroline frowned. 'So you and your two friends got the glamping tents?'

'I know,' beamed Lolly. 'What were the chances, eh?'

Caroline narrowed her eyes. 'What about the other glamping tents?'

'What other glamping tents?'

'It said on the website there were six glamping tents. That's three accounted for. What about the other three? Who's in them?'

'Our children, of course,' said Lolly sweetly. 'I mean, the glamping tents only have a double bed. The children couldn't sleep in that with us, and we can't have them miles away on their own in another part of the campsite, can we?'

'The website said the glamping tents sleep six,' insisted Caroline.

'Yes,' put in Sally. 'One double bed, a sofa bed, and two air beds. So why *can't* your children sleep in the same tent as you?'

'Sally, I really don't think that our private sleeping arrangements are any of your business,' said Lolly. 'Though I must remind you that since I've gone to all the trouble of arranging this trip for the benefit of you and your children, I *don't* think it's a lot to ask for Harry and me to have some privacy over the weekend to enjoy a little downtime and relaxation to ourselves after everything I've done for you all, do you?'

'I do when we're paying for it,' said Sally indignantly.

Lolly sighed, her voice full of pity. 'Sally, I didn't want to make you feel bad, but the fact is that Gertrude and Ophelia actually have a serious medical condition that means they have to sleep in a proper bed. They couldn't possibly sleep on a sofa bed or an air bed. They could become very unwell.'

'They slept on an air bed at mine last week at Maisie's birthday sleepover,' objected Fiona Dixon.

'That was different,' snapped Lolly. 'We were within easy reach of emergency medical services. Now we're in the countryside and I simply *cannot* take the risk!'

'What's wrong with them? You've never mentioned this before.'

'I don't have to tell you that.'

'What would you have done if your name hadn't been drawn, then?'

'I'm sure someone would have been kind enough to swap when I explained the situation,' simpered Lolly. 'But luckily I didn't need to.'

Sally was not giving up that easily. 'What about Jacinta and Figgy's children? Why can't *they* share the tents with their children?'

'Because Innes has allergies, so she can't sleep on an air bed either, and Figgy has just managed to finally cure Olly's separation anxiety, so to have him sleeping in the same tent could cause a *serious regression*. NOT that that's ANY of your BUSINESS!' snapped Lolly, the sugary-sweet welcome smile definitely a thing of the past. 'I'm NOT discussing this any further, so can everyone *please* gather round, and I'll allocate your pitch numbers and who you're sharing with, and Mark –'

'Matt,' put in the Forest Fields man.

'What?'

'My name's Matt. Not Mark.'

'Right. Mark here –'

'Matt.'

'That's what I SAID. He'll give you your tents and instructions on how to put them up.'

Claire and Lucy reached the front of the queue and received the joyous news that they were at least sharing a tent, though the slightly less joyous news was that they were also sharing with someone called Mary Thompson and her daughter Amy.

'Who?' said Claire. 'I don't even know who she is.'

'She's new,' said Lolly shortly. 'Look, can you just go and get your tent off whatever-his-name-is? I've got a lot of people to get through. Caroline, what's wrong now?'

An hour later, as Lucy and Claire wrestled with tent poles and enormous flapping sheets of nylon, and Lucy muttered as she tried to insert a pole into a hidden tent flap – 'For fuck's sake, maybe I should have been nicer to my first boyfriends as they fumbled around down there. This must be what sex is like for men!' – Lolly sashayed over to them, the Welcome Beam back in place now that she had someone to swank in front of.

'Hello, ladies, I've brought you Mary and Amy.'

Lolly waved a gracious hand at a small, nervous and very young-looking woman behind her, clutching the hand of a child who presumably was her daughter, Amy.

'Now, I put you all together because I thought it would be nice for all you single gals to be in the same tent,' smiled Lolly.

'I'm not single,' objected Mary.

'Now, where are your girls? In the play park? Why don't you pop off and join them, Amy? I really think this weekend will be so good for children like yours,' ploughed on Lolly, completely ignoring Mary's comment. 'Really let them see what a proper hands-on father figure is like. Harry has very kindly offered to lead some dad-based activities, which will be fun for everyone. *Such* a shame your boys couldn't come,' she carried on, turning to Claire and Lucy. 'I really think *they* could have especially benefitted. But never mind. And of course, it will be so good for little Amy, experiencing a positive male role model too!'

'What are you talking about?' said Mary in confusion.

'And what are "dad-based" activities?' asked Claire. Lucy said something muffled and fortunately indecipherable from inside the folds of nylon in which she had become trapped and was trying to fight her way out.

'Oh, you know, orienteering and things,' said Lolly vaguely. 'SO kind of him.'

'Why can't women do orienteering?' demanded Claire. 'Why is that suddenly a Dad Activity? I can do orienteering.'

There was a sound from Lucy that sounded like 'For fuck's sake'.

'Oh, girls! You know what I mean, stop being silly. Now, have you signed up for my Forest Yoga on Sunday morning yet? Places are going fast.'

'I'm fine,' said Claire.

'Me too,' sniffed Mary. 'And I'm *not* single.'

Lolly tipped her head to one side in a particularly affected and annoying way, and looked at Mary patronisingly. 'How sweet you've found a chap to take you on as a single mum. And you've got other little ones too, haven't you?'

'No one has taken me on,' protested Mary.

Lolly was already walking away again, though, and paying no attention. As Claire and Mary saw her wiggle off, golden brown buttocks peeping out from the bottom of her very short shorts, a large horsefly landed on one bum cheek. The subsequent yelp from Lolly and accusing look back at Mary and Claire suggested it had wasted no time sinking its nasty jaws into the peach it had so fortuitously found. Claire and Mary looked at each other and burst into laughter.

Lucy finally crawled out from under the tent, looking red-faced and furious.

'I'M FINE,' she shouted. 'Don't worry about me! Just leave me to die under there, it's FINE!'

'Well, at least you missed Lolly,' Claire comforted her. 'And this is Mary.'

'Hello, Mary. I could hear bloody Lolly wittering on about something even through my death folds of doom. She has the *most* annoying laugh, like a very smug hyena!'

'Whereas we're antelopes, but nice ones who admit zebras to our midst,' said Claire dreamily.

'What?'

'Nothing. Do you actually know how to put up a tent, Lucy, or were you just hiding from Lolly under there?'

'I *can* put up a tent!' insisted Lucy.

'I can *try*,' said Mary doubtfully. 'How hard can it be?'

An hour later, it turned out it was *quite* hard. They were all now as red-faced as Lucy and on the verge of tears, as Lucy read again: 'Insert Pole A into Seam B, while lifting Flap C overhead.'

Any amusement at the thought of Flap C had long since dissipated under the utter unrelenting bastardry of the fucking tent. Claire flung her tent pole away and collapsed on the ground, head in hands.

'I can't do it!' she snapped. 'I hate tents and I hate camping. I wish Andrew was here to do it, and I hate myself for not being able to do it and wishing he was here, and I hate doing everything on my own, and I hate that we're the fucking sad singletons' tent despised by Lolly, and I HATE ALL OF THIS!' And she burst into tears.

Lucy and Mary looked at Claire in concern. Lucy rummaged in her bag and produced a gin in a tin, opened it and hastily handed it to Claire. Claire sniffed at the can hesitantly, then took a swig. Lucy rummaged further and produced another two cans for Mary and herself.

'Sucks to be us,' said Lucy, sitting down and putting an arm around Claire. 'Drink your gin. We can do this, OK. We don't *need* men. None of us do. They're nice to have, and don't hate yourself for wanting help, but we *can* do this, can't we, Mary?'

'Absolutely,' said Mary awkwardly. She was hovering off to one side, clearly, Claire thought, wondering what the hell she had let herself in for.

'Everything all right, girls?' boomed a hearty voice, as Lolly's loathsome husband Harry swaggered up. 'You little ladies needing some help?'

'NO!' snapped Claire, Lucy and Mary in unison. 'We're just fine!'

'Having a little break, are we?' sniggered Harry. 'Didn't you get Lolly's email about no booze?'

'Yes,' said Lucy. 'And as we're grown adults we chose to ignore it, since the campsite is actually licensed. Now piss off, Harry. We don't need help, and certainly not from the likes of you.'

'Just trying to be friendly,' grumbled Harry, as he sloped off with a last pervy look at Mary's legs.

'Come on,' said Lucy. 'How hard can it be if a fucking sleazy cretin like Harry thinks he can put up a tent. Let's *do* this! We just need to put Pole A into Seam B while holding Flap C aloft. We've pushed human heads out of our hoo-has. We can definitely put Pole A into whatever and keeps our flaps in the air!'

Another hour later and they were triumphant.

'WOOOO!' shouted Claire exultantly. 'WE DID IT! You were right, Lucy. Fuck men! Yay us! Jesus, what's that noise?'

'I think,' said Mary, consulting the lengthy list of times and activities Lolly had handed them, 'that that is the signal that we're to go and have dinner. We'd better try to find the girls, I suppose, and try to make them wash their hands.'

The various children had all abandoned the relative civilisation of Forest Field's tasteful wooden playground area in favour of going feral in the woods while their parents wrestled with the tents, as Claire, Lucy and Mary had not been the only ones slightly stumped by the instructions. And thus the children were unsupervised while their parents wrestled with the acres of nylon and colour-coded poles and flaps that made no sense whatsoever.

Lolly's Ophelia and Gertrude ('We just really love Shakespeare'), and Jacinta's Innes and Hamish ('Hugo's great-great-grandmother was Scottish, actually') and Figgy's Olly ('It's not short for Oliver, it's short for Oleander') and Mallory ('No, it's not a girl's name, it's unisex) hadn't vanished, their parents not having had to put up tents on account of nabbing the posh glamping tents. Instead they'd been playing a wholesome game of rounders in the field behind the campsite with their caring parents, until an angry farmer had chased them out of his field, pointing out they 'have a whole fucking campsite to play in. Now get to fuck. That's a pedigree cow your little shit nearly knocked out with a ball.'

The various other children were eventually tracked down. Ella and Tabitha were in a ditch, building a dam. Amy was up a tree with Caroline Northfield's son and attempting to push him out of it for saying girls were rubbish at tree climbing. Sally Baxter's daughter, being an enterprising sort, had saved her allowance of sweets for several weeks before the trip and had been selling them on to the other children at an extortionate mark-up, the campsite shop being closed for the evening. Natalie French's son, meanwhile, had clearly watched too much Bear Grylls and was building a den to live in for the weekend, and was only found when he returned to base to request a bottle to wee in so he could have something to drink, as he had 'tried catching it in his hand and it didn't really work'.

The Glamping Gang were sitting reproachfully in front of cooling plates of something unidentifiable in the communal dining room when the posse of bedraggled children and stressed adults finally made their way in.

'We waited for you,' sniffed Lolly. 'Though I can't think why you don't all keep track of your children better; *we* didn't have any problem.'

The Glamping Children looked rather gloomy about this. Oleander in particular was casting envious glances at Toby French as he related tales of his hour living rough in the woods, and how he'd planned on catching rabbits to eat and dress in the skins.

Dinner was surprising tasty, given the condition of the Glampers' plates. Unfortunately, Forest Fields had rejected Lolly's request for a gluten-free, all-vegan menu from the canteen for the weekend as being beyond the budget she was willing to pay, and so there were vats of pasta instead, and Lolly had been forced to provide her own food for her 'brood' because obviously Ophelia and Gertrude's delicate systems could not be poisoned with cheesy pasta. As they pushed their Edamame Bean Surprise around their plates, they too looked jealously at the other children.

'Now!' Lolly clapped her hands for attention. 'First things first! A few housekeeping points. Have you all had a chance to look at the rota? I've pinned it up on the board by the door. It will be so much fun if we all just really muck in and help. Second, I think a lot of you have forgotten to sign up for my Forest Yoga session on Sunday morning. Third, I think I made it quite clear in the email I sent on my camp rules that there was to be NO processed sugar brought to the camp.'

The canteen staff, in the process of serving up jelly and ice cream for pudding, looked surprised by this.

'Yet I've overheard several children talking about the sweets they've been eating! It's regrettable that we can't be fully vegan, but I think we should all take the opportunity this weekend to be really *mindful* of what we put into our bodies, which was why I made it very clear there was to be NO sugar and NO alcohol. But when I popped into Sarah Harley's tent before dinner, what did I find? Sarah and Judith, drinking gin and tonics!'

There was a general murmuring of 'Good for you' from most of the other parents, and Judith shouted, 'I asked Matt when we arrived if alcohol was allowed and he said of course it was. So I still don't see what the problem is. He even said they sell it in the shop if we run out.'

'Forest Fields may not have a no-alcohol policy, but this is supposed to be a *family* weekend, which is why I imposed the no-alcohol rule. Please be so good as to stick to it,' Lolly replied tartly. 'NOW,' she beamed, turning the megawatt grin back on, 'it's not all boring old rules, of course. I've a treat for you all. After dinner we're going to have a BONFIRE and a good old-fashioned campfire singsong. Won't that be fun?'

The mutterings issuing from the rest of the parents suggested that they'd call it something other than fun. The words 'Utter bollocks' definitely came from the general direction of Caroline Northfield, but Lolly was not to be dissuaded. THEY WOULD HAVE FUN, GODDAMMIT!

'Will there be marshmallows, Mummy?' said Tabitha in excitement.

'Yes, and S'mores!' said Amy, who luckily had turned out to already be good friends with Tabitha and Ella, and not a sworn enemy.

'Oh yeah, S'mores!' said Ella.

'What *are* S'mores?' asked Lucy.

'Dunno,' said Ella. 'They had them on *The Thundermans* one time.'

'I doubt it,' said Claire regretfully. 'Not with Lolly's no-sugar rule.'

'Nooooo,' wailed Tabitha. 'I just want to toast marshmallows on a campfire like they do on TV! It's not FAIR!'

'Well, luckily I brought some,' said Claire smugly.

'Me too,' said Lucy.

'Me three,' said Mary.

'Yay,' said Tabitha. 'Now I won't have to call Childline!'

'You can't call Childline anyway. First, not being able to toast marshmallows is not a form of child abuse, and second, there's no phone signal here anyway.'

'No signal?' said Tabitha, aghast. 'But Mummy, how will we watch Netflix?'

'You won't. You're here to have wholesome outdoor japes and frolics.'

'No YouTube?'

'No YouTube.'

'Not even BBC iPlayer?'

'Not even iPlayer.'

'But what will we DO?'

'Same as you've done all afternoon. Play outside. JAPES AND FROLICS, like I said.'

'Yes, Mummy, but for the WHOLE WEEKEND?'

Tabitha was nearly weeping, and Ella and Amy were also demanding to be shown their mothers' phones to have this hideous situation confirmed to them.

Amy shook her head sorrowfully. 'Not even 3G,' she intoned gloomily. 'We're doomed. They'll probably make us play *board-games* like in the Olden Days.'

16

The campfire proved controversial. First there was Lolly's impassioned plea to the other parents to please *not* furnish their darlings with marshmallows, Haribos and other foul sugar-laden horrors, which fell on deaf ears. Caroline Northfield was ripping open the Fangtastics even as Lolly wailed, 'It's really not fair to Gertrude and Ophelia, though' and 'Will no one think of the children?'

Then there was the matter of the singsong. Lolly rejected 'Kumbaya' as 'too representative of Abrahamic religion' and 'Ging Gang Goolie' as 'problematic' on account of its mentions of 'gangs and well, you know, slang words for *genitals*. It's absolutely not appropriate.' The Girl Guiding classic 'Black Socks' was deemed 'possibly racist'.

'But it's about *socks*,' protested Claire. 'How can a song about socks be racist?'

'We can't take any chances,' insisted Lolly. 'These are impressionable young minds here.'

'Five Little Speckled Frogs?' someone suggested.

'Mmm, the use of "frogs" is also a little unfortunate. It could be seen as a song about wanting to be rid of French people.'

'Alice the Camel?'

'Fat-shaming. It's suggesting Alice is trying to lose humps in order to change her own body image to make herself into a more acceptable version of herself for society.'

'What the fuck?'

'Lucy! Language!'

'We're Going on a Bear Hunt?'

'Glorifies hunting, and thus our colonialist imperialist past.'

'She'll be Coming Round the Mountain?'

It took Lolly a moment to think of an objection to this, before declaring that 'I feel it might have pronouning issues. What if some people here prefer to use gender-neutral pronouns? We must be inclusive.'

'Well, what CAN we sing then?'

'Ah.' Lolly flashed that smile again. The glare of the campfire off her brilliant white teeth was starting to give Claire a headache. 'I anticipated the problems with the traditional campfire canon, so, ahem, I've actually written a politically correct singsong song for the twenty-first century.'

'Oh fuck.'

'Sally! I must ask you all to moderate your language in front of the children.'

After one round of Lolly's unspeakably dreary song about a brave little boat sailing down a big river, everyone abandoned the 'singalong' and fell to gossiping instead, once all the children abandoned their parents to sit together on the opposite side of the campfire, since, even at the age of eight or nine, to be seen willingly associating with your parents was Social Death.

Poor Mary had suffered the bad luck to end up sitting between Lolly and Claire, and Lucy had vanished on a mission for a wee, and now Lolly was clearly determined to show generosity even to the less fortunate around the fire, and therefore engaged Mary in conversation.

'So, Mary,' she cooed. 'We've all been wondering – you look so very young. Just how old are you?'

Mary tensed. 'Twenty-six,' she admitted.

'TWENTY-SIX,' shrieked Lolly loudly. 'Oh my GOD. But that means you must have been –'

'Eighteen,' snapped Mary. 'I was eighteen when I had Amy, OK? And I don't regret it, before you ask.'

'Of course not,' said Lolly in her best Sympathetic Voice. 'Why would you regret it? I expect it was to get a house, wasn't it?'

'What?'

'You know, that's why all these young girls get pregnant, isn't it? So they get fast-tracked for a council house. Everyone knows that.'

'Lolly,' said Claire warningly. 'I don't think that's really appropriate.'

'Well, why then? Jacinta, did you know Mary was only *eighteen* when she had Amy? Imagine!'

'Eighteen!' said Jacinta in horror. 'Goodness, that means you didn't even have a gap year! Oh! Unless … did it happen *on* your gap year?'

'No,' said Mary furiously. 'It didn't *happen* on my gap year, and it wasn't to get a house.'

'Oh, you DID have a gap year then,' said Jacinta in relief.

'Actually, no, I didn't. Not everyone has a gap year.'

'Don't they?' wondered Jacinta. 'I couldn't imagine not having a gap year.'

'*I* didn't have a gap year, Jacinta,' said Claire.

'Oh. Poor you. I loved my gap year. I built a school in India and then I went backpacking round Thailand. Oh my God, it was just *amazing* and such a total cultural experience, and I got this tattoo. Look!'

Mary relaxed slightly, now the subject seemed to be about Jacinta's gap year, which in fairness was probably the most interesting thing to have ever happened in Jacinta's life, and not about Mary the Teenage Slut. But Lolly was not letting it go that easily.

'I can't imagine having a baby at eighteen. I mean, why would anyone do that? How would you travel? What about university? Your career? You've missed out on an awful lot, Mary, don't you think? I simply couldn't have even considered having children before I was thirty-five. I needed to put myself first and do all the things *I* wanted to do, so I could be a fully present mother for my children. Don't you agree, Harry?'

'What?' said Harry, who had been looking at Mary's boobs from across the campfire.

'I'm saying, darling, we agreed not to even think about children until we were thirty-five because we wanted to be able to enjoy life and be US first, so that when we had children we could give them all the benefit of our time and the wisdom we had learned over the years.'

'Oh yah, yah, definitely,' said Harry. 'Why?'

'Because Mary had a baby when she was eighteen. I'm just saying I couldn't even have thought about that. I didn't even get married till I was thirty, and I made you propose four times, remember, so I knew you were really sure, and we were *ready*.'

'Well, not everyone's life works out the same,' said Mary furiously. 'We didn't all have our perfect life plans turn out the way we thought they would, and things *happen* and you deal with them. And I've not missed out. I still went to university. I've a sodding first-class chemistry degree, actually. I'll have a career one day. I'm just doing things in a different order to you.'

'How did you go to university with a baby?' said Jacinta in astonishment.

'With difficulty,' ground out Mary.

'I think that's amazing,' said Claire. 'That's a real achievement, much more than getting stoned on a beach in Thailand and then getting a 2:2 in media studies while Mummy and Daddy bankroll you. And chemistry too, Mary. That's incredible. Chemistry is *hard* at the best of times, let alone with a baby.'

'Thank you. It *was* hard, but it was all worth it.'

'But Amy's dad, what happened to him? Is he still in touch?' persisted Lolly.

'I met this amazingly gorgeous chap on my gap year when I was eighteen and I never heard from him again. Hung like a … well … anyway,' sighed Jacinta, as Hugo turned purple.

'Oh, yah, me too,' said Figgy. 'But I looked him up on Facebook, and he's sooooo fat and unattractive now.'

Looking over at Huxley, who was not exactly an Adonis, Claire wondered how fat and ugly Figgy's gap-year crush must have got to be more unattractive than Huxley.

'It was so freeing, being on a gap year,' Jacinta wittered. 'This is a bit like it, like a beach party in Thailand. Only without –. Anyway, what were you saying, Lolly?'

'I was asking Mary if she still hears from Amy's dad? And your two younger children? Are their dads still around?'

'Amy's father is now my husband. And the father of my two younger children. Not that it is ANY OF YOUR BUSINESS, Lolly.'

'Really?' said Lolly in amazement. 'You're still together?'

'I didn't know people did that,' said Jacinta, jolted back from her gap-year reveries.

'But you're with the same boy as when you were eighteen,' Figgy helpfully pointed out, in case Mary hadn't noticed.

'Yes, is that so odd?'

'Well, it's a bit like me being married to Farquhar Ferguson, who was my boyfriend when I was eighteen,' Figgy said, clearly still under the impression that Mary needed her own relationship explained to her. Somehow, it didn't surprise Claire that Fucking Farquhar Ferguson had once fucked the frigging awful Figgy.

'Figgy, people do form lasting relationships with people they meet in their teens,' Claire pointed out. 'Lots of people do it.'

'I had no idea. I thought at the very least you'd be at university when you met them.'

'You can always meet someone at university when you're eighteen.'

'Is that what happened, Mary?'

'Was it a Fresher's Week fling?'

Mary looked close to tears, and Claire felt awful for not putting a stop to this hideous interrogation sooner.

'Lolly, look, I think Ophelia and Gertrude are eating marshmallows,' she hastily put in, and Lolly was off with a squawk to rescue her darlings from the hell of processed sugar and gelatine they were happily burning on the other side of the fire, followed by Jacinta and Figgy, equally keen to prevent their cherubs ingesting anything involving flavour or joy.

'Come on,' said Claire. 'I think we've done our bit. Let's get the kids and go back to the tent – it's way past their bedtime anyway. Ah, there you are, Lucy. We're going back to the tent, are you coming?'

Claire's announcement about bedtime gave all the other parents an excuse to escape as well, and everyone collected up their sugar-hyped children with relief and shuffled off to their respective tents, trying to suppress their rage as Lolly and Figgy and Jacinta wondered whether they'd turned on the fairy lights in their glamping tents before they went to the campfire, and did anyone actually know if the bed linen was organic cotton or not. Sally Baxter had to restrain Caroline Northfield from storming the glamping tents and smothering Lolly with a potentially non-organic whimsical print cushion.

Back at the tent, the girls objected strenuously to the proposed sleeping arrangements, whereby each set of mothers and daughters occupied one of the three 'sleeping pods' off the main body of the tent. They wanted to sleep together, not with their loving mothers. The girls therefore ended up being bedded down in the main 'living area' of the tent, which meant, Claire reflected, that she might at least get *some* sleep without Tabitha kicking her relentlessly all night.

'So,' said Claire over the shrieking-hyena soundtrack coming from the girls, which was apparently laughter, 'I don't think sleep is going to be happening any time soon, do you? Shall we go and sit outside while they calm down? It must be time to open more of the extra "supplies".'

'Extra supplies? Well, what are we waiting for?' said Lucy briskly.

All across Forest Fields drifted the happy sound of corks popping and cans opening, apart from in the glamping tents, where the sound of what seemed suspiciously like the mother of all rows was coming from Lolly's boudoir. As best as the eavesdroppers could establish, Harry was being berated for failing to prevent Gertrude and Ophelia stuffing themselves on marshmallows, and Lolly had taken exception to Ophelia's puking up pink and white sticky goo over her doting mama's purple vegan Veja trainers.

'That's better,' said Claire, taking a huge slug of Cabernet Sauvignon from her blue and white enamel mug, which she had bought especially for rustic outdoor wine drinking, so she still had some standards despite resorting to functional alcoholism to get through the weekend.

'Mmmm,' said Lucy, closing her eyes in bliss. 'Sweet, sweet booze, come to Mama. Drown out the horrors of the evening. Wash away the thought that Ella still has ditch slime in her hair, and fuck knows what that is going to smell like by the time I get her in a proper shower on Sunday night!'

Mary, however, was just staring into her mug gloomily.

'What's the matter?' asked Claire in alarm. 'Don't you like it? I know it's a bit cheap and cheerful, but it's really quite nice once the burning sensation passes.'

'It's not the wine,' said Mary. 'I just … before I drink anything, can I ask you something? Do *you* think I'm a feckless slut for having Amy when I was eighteen? Do you agree with Lolly and all her lot that it was a stupid decision and I've ruined my life?'

'NO!' said Claire in horror, as Lucy chimed in equally vehemently a beat behind her.

'I just feel like for years, for *years*, everyone has been looking at me and saying "Stupid Mary. What did she do that for?" The other people on my course, other mums at the baby group. I thought now I was a bit older, people would stop looking at me like I was still a teenage mum, you know, but Lolly automatically assumed I was a single mum and put me in with you two. Not that there's anything wrong with being a single mother, obviously. I just resent the assumption that I *must* be one because I'm young.

'So I've done things differently. So I didn't have a gap year, and I haven't been to Thailand. So what? I've worked hard, I've been to uni, and then James and I, we knew we wanted more kids, and to wait until I was ahead in my career would have meant such a big age gap between Amy and any more kids, so we just decided to have them and then I could think about work. But it's not been easy, and people go on at me like I'm such bad mother, just because I'm young. And I'm not, I'm really not!'

Mary was crying a bit now.

'Drink your wine, Mary,' said Claire. 'We don't look down on you, do we, Lucy?'

'Of course not. Lolly and all that, they can't comprehend anyone who lives their life in a different way to them. I know they think it's my fault my husband left me, for example. If I'd only not insisted on having a job, if I'd done more yoga, been more toned, even turned a blind eye to what he was up to. Being part of a couple, being seen as #CoupleGoalz, is more important to them than actually being happy.'

'No one cares what they think, not really,' added Claire.

Mary considered this for a while, head down, then turned to both Claire and Lucy. 'But what do *you* think, really? Maybe you don't look down on me, but secretly, are you thinking, "Why didn't she just get rid of it?" I see it in people's faces all the time. "Why didn't she just get rid of it?" But that "it" isn't an "it", it never was. "It" is Amy. My daughter!'

'I think you must have been incredibly brave and strong to go through with a pregnancy at that age,' Claire said. 'Not many people are that brave. I couldn't have done it. Christ, I remember having a scare when I was about the same age as when you had Amy, and the panic of peeing on that stick and the relief of there only being one line.'

'Oh Christ, yes, me too!' said Lucy. 'No way could I have gone through with it either. Those scares were the worst moments of my life back then! Funny, isn't it? Because you fast-forward a few years and you're *desperate* to see that second line!'

Mary sniffed again. 'I was pretty horrified too, the first time. But I knew, even before I saw the second line, that I couldn't not go through with it if I was pregnant, no matter what people thought.'

'Fuck what people think,' said Claire stoutly. 'Anyway, who's to tell anyone what is a right decision and a wrong decision? Look at me! I did everything by the book. Married a nice man, waited a nice, respectable amount of time before having children, banged out the proscribed nice, tidy number in a nice, matched pair, got the nice surburban house, in a nice town. Everything was perfect. Well, everything *looked* perfect. Until I found out he was fucking my best friend. My very best friend! So that wasn't so nice.

'And here I am in my forties, single, trying to navigate life on my own, without my husband or my best friend. Which is a bit shit. No one knows how life will turn out, regardless of the choices we make. I never thought I'd be single again. I certainly never thought Emily would screw me over like that. And every time I think I'm doing OK, I'm fine, I'm a strong independent woman, I'm coping OK, something knocks me back down and I end up crying in a fucking Forest Fields campsite because I can't put up a tent and I want a man to do it for me, and Lucy has to apply medicinal gin in tin.'

'Oh Claire!' said Lucy. 'Any man, or Andrew specifically?'

'I dunno,' said Claire morosely. 'You know what it's like, doing everything yourself. And then earlier, in the playground, when you said Andrew was hot, it just made me look at him properly, you know. Like I hadn't looked at him for a long time, and maybe he hadn't looked at me. And I thought, maybe if I'd taken the time to look at him and appreciate that actually, yeah, he's still an attractive man, instead of just another *chore* to be done, things would be different. I've spent so long blaming Emily and Andrew for this, but maybe I could have done things differently too. But then I started wondering why you'd never seen Andrew before to notice he *was* hot, and I realised that it was because he was always too Busy and Important to do school pick-ups or playdates or birthday parties, and then I just became fucking ANGRY with him again for never pulling his weight and then making me feel guilty for not having enough time for him when actually I was just BUSY picking up his slack, and now I just feel drunk and confused, and I wish being a grown-up wasn't so fucking HARD! And that my soon-to-be ex-husband didn't have such a nice fucking arse.'

'Hear, hear!' said Lucy and Mary.

'Sometimes I dream of just walking out the door and running away to a desert island,' said Mary.

'Don't we all,' groaned Lucy. 'Being a grown-up sucks. Still, in the meantime, at least we have lovely wine to drown out the endless whining! Top up?'

'Cheers!' said Claire. 'Oh God, we're so going to regret this after we have to sleep in a field on the ground, aren't we?'

17

The next day over breakfast ('Ophelia! Gertrude! Step away from the Coco Pops and come and have your lovely chia seed porridge RIGHT NOW'), it appeared as if most of the other parents had also rather overindulged the night before.

'We're out of booze, *and* out of sweets to bribe the children,' Claire pointed out gloomily.

'The campsite shop has sold out of both,' said Mary sadly. 'Apparently everyone else was more organised and went before breakfast.'

'Morning ladies!' said Lolly brightly, stopping by their table. 'Goodness, I don't know what's *wrong* with everyone this morning. All this fresh air, I'd think you should be bright-eyed and bushy tailed, and everyone seems very tired and cross this morning. Now, have you got your itineraries for today? And you all know what you're supposed to be doing on the rota?'

Everyone nodded sullenly. The rota had caused some controversy, with Caroline, Sally and Lucy all down on toilet-cleaning duty, Sarah and Judith on litter picking, and Lolly, Jacinta and Figgy's names not appearing anywhere on the rota at all – 'Because how can we, when we're co-ordinating it all, and I have my yoga class to prepare for as well?' Claire and Mary weren't sure if they'd done better or worse than loo cleaning and litter picking since they'd been dragooned into assisting Harry and Hugo with their 'orienteering' walks.

The children's itinerary had also gone down like a cup of cold sick. After much clamouring from the girls over the previous few weeks about the absolute essentialness of the extra activities, Tabitha and Ella were doing zorbing at 10 a.m. and archery at midday, and Amy had archery at 10 a.m. and the climbing wall at midday, all at vast added expense. Now, though, they were grumbling that they just wanted to play in the woods together and make dams in ditches, and their loving mothers were cruel and unfair for forcing them to participate in the activities they'd paid for.

'Marvellous,' cooed Lolly, ignoring the mutinous faces.

The orienteering started not too badly. Claire was assigned to Harry's group, and once she showed Harry the right way up to hold a map, they were able to set off. Their unfortunate charges, who had been pressganged by Lolly into coming along to admire Harry's Manly Skills, were unimpressed, though, and despite repeated pleas to 'stay together' insisted on scattering to the four winds at every opportunity. It was in fact more of an exercise in herding cats than navigation. Claire sighed with relief every time she did a head count.

By the time they got to the halfway point to stop for a drink and a snack, she was exhausted, as Harry's Demonstration of Fatherliness seemed to consist of being even more useless and determined to get lost than the children. He also took it quite badly when he attempted to show the children how to find their way by looking for moss growing on the north side of a tree and Claire was forced to point out that the moss was in fact growing on all sides of the tree. Harry brandished his Swiss Army knife quite menacingly at her for spoiling his own Bear Grylls fantasies.

Claire collapsed against a tree and wished very much that there was vodka in her water bottle. Harry sidled up and sat down next to her. Very next to her. Far too next to her for comfort, in fact. He pressed his sweaty leg against hers, and cleared his throat importantly.

'Well done, Claire,' he said warmly. 'You're doing really well at the orienteering. Nice to see a woman getting the hang of something like that.'

'What do you mean?'

'Maps and stuff. Easier, of course, with a chap to explain it. Must be hard for you, without a chap.'

'Not really.'

'Lonely, I mean. All by yourself of a night.'

'No, not really. I've got a dog.'

'Brave. So brave. Thing is, I er, I could pop round one night, if you fancied a bit of company. We could share a bottle of wine. Get to know each other.'

Harry winked, a hideous leering wink, and put his clammy paw on Claire's knee and squeezed it.

Claire stared at his hand in horror.

'What about Lolly?'

'Oh, don't worry, I'd just tell her I was working late.'

Harry slid his hand from Claire's knee up her thigh, just under the edge of Claire's shorts.

That damp palm against her upper leg gave Claire a sudden flashback to her old headmistress Miss Pearson's 'self-defence' classes at school. In truth, they had not been particularly helpful, as the primary advice for discouraging an over-ardent admirer was to remove his hand from your knee (Miss Pearson did not cover the possibility of him pawing another part of your anatomy) and return it to him with a loud and firm 'NO'. Claire had never had the opportunity to put this into practice in the last thirty years, unwanted advances having tended to more take the form of arsehole men in bars trying to snog her, and builders shouting 'Nice tits, love', but now that the moment had arisen, it seemed rude not to put Miss Pearson's training to use.

Claire picked up Harry's hand and thrust it back at him. 'NO,' she bellowed.

All the children immediately looked up from their juice boxes and crisps (Ophelia and Gertrude were doing a guided meditation in the glamping tents with Lolly) to see what was going on.

'Keep your voice down,' hissed Harry, as Claire loudly and firmly repeated 'NO' again ('Never be afraid to keep saying it till he gets the message, girls, even if you're in a cinema').

'Are you … are you *propositioning* me, Harry?' asked Claire in horror.

'No, no. Of course not. Ha ha ha. I was just being *friendly*.'

'It *sounded* like you were propositioning me.'

'That's feminism for you,' complained Harry. 'A chap can't say *anything* these days, can't even make a friendly remark and some feminazi takes it the wrong way. I was just trying to be pleasant to you, that's all, and you misunderstood.'

'Oh, I see. I *misunderstood*. My mistake. Goodness, won't we have a good chuckle about this later! Can't wait to tell Lolly how I *misunderstood*. She'll find it hilarious, won't she!'

'Errr. No need to tell Lolly, is there? Like I said, a simple misunderstanding, that's all. Might as well keep it between us, eh?'

Harry licked his lips nervously as he edged away from her.

Claire didn't bother to reply, and instead went to summon the children to find their way back to Forest Fields, leaving Harry trailing behind them. She had half hoped they might lose him to be eaten by bears or wolves, or at least maybe a particularly malevolent fox, but unfortunately you can't get up much speed while shepherding nine eight-year-olds along.

Once Claire's rage at Harry, fuelled by the years of the shouts of 'Nice tits, love' from sleazy men and pleas to 'Give us a smile, darling,' wore off, she felt a great weariness and sadness. At least when you were married you were spared the advances of dickheads like that. Was Lucy right, and this was the future? Married men assuming you must be 'up for it'? Constantly having to explain that you were not in fact 'gagging for it' and you were just fine on your own, because however lonely one might get at night (considerably less so since the arrival of darling Sadie, though), Claire did not think she'd ever be so lonely or desperate to consider making the Beast with Two Backs with the likes of Harry Hughes.

Maybe this was why the Julias and Jens and Sarahs stayed in their marriages, though. Maybe this was the price you paid for not being sexually harassed by your friends' husbands. Is this what Emily went through, Claire wondered. She'd never said. Surely she'd have said? Unless … maybe that was how it started with Andrew? No. She had seen the texts. And Andrew wasn't like that. But then again, Lolly didn't think Harry was like that. Maybe Emily hadn't been quite so guilty in all this as Claire had automatically assumed. Maybe she *had* just been lonely and Andrew had been lonely because Claire didn't notice he had a nice arse anymore, and so he told Emily his wife didn't understand him and she fell for it?

Claire gave herself a shake. Maybe it *was* more Andrew's fault than Emily's, but it didn't *matter*. Claire had still been Emily's BEST FRIEND! Andrew wasn't some random married man she'd picked up in a bar, he was her best friend's husband, and however lonely Emily might have been, however disillusioned with dating, however charming Andrew might have been, Emily had broken the code. You just don't do that to your friends.

Back at the tent, she filled in Lucy and Mary on the afternoon's events.

'I told you Harry's a total letch,' said Lucy, shaking her head. 'Hugo and Huxley merely aspire to Harry's levels of lechery. Huxley kept hanging around the bathroom block to stare at our arses when we were cleaning, but he's too scared of Figgy to do anything more.'

'I thought Hugo was a bit over-familiar with his insistence on helping me over streams and logs, but I kept telling myself his hand must have just slipped,' said Mary, shuddering.

'But Harry actually suggested telling Lolly he was working late and popping over with a bottle of wine,' Claire protested.

'Only one! Tight bastard. Not only propositioning, but treating you like a cheap date! That seems to be Harry's signature move, that's pretty much what he did to me too,' snorted Lucy.

'Would it have been better if he'd offered to bring a case?'

'Well, at least then you could have lured him over with your womanly wiles and then booted him out, and we could have drunk his case of wine!' Mary pointed out pragmatically.

'I'm not luring Harry Hughes for the sake of a case of wine. That's … no. Anyway, the point is, I should tell Lolly what he's like, what he tried, shouldn't I? Maybe if *enough* of us tell her, she'll finally see the light.'

'There's no point,' Lucy sighed. 'I tried to tell her, and look what happened. He tried to snog Caroline Northfield at the PTA Halloween Disco three years ago, Sally Baxter *saw* him lunge at her behind the fortune-telling booth, and Lolly also refused to believe either of them, accused them of being jealous of her perfect marriage and trying to stir up trouble. They told me when we were scrubbing the bogs. That's why they all hate each other so much. And because Lolly's a glamping tent thief.'

'How has Harry managed to make a pass at half the mums in the class and Lolly refuses to believe he's the problem? What happened to female solidarity?' demanded Claire.

'Some women don't believe in it,' said Lucy regretfully. 'Surely you, of all people, must realise this, after what Emily did? And Lolly is one of those people who genuinely thinks being part of a couple is the most important thing in life and she'll do anything to hang on to that. She'll refuse to believe you, and she'll just resent you for pointing out the flaws in her perfect marriage. Greatest trick the patriarchy ever played was brainwashing women into thinking other women are the enemy.'

'Fucking patriarchy,' snapped Claire. 'I hate the fucking patriarchy.'

'One day we shall disassemble it, one creepy motherfucker sleazy bastard at a time,' declared Lucy.

Later at the campfire, after a couple of glasses of wine, Caroline and Sally and Lucy having done a very half-hearted cleaning job in the bathrooms and instead spending the rest of the afternoon on an emergency booze and sugar run to the big Sainsbury's down the road while Claire and the others were orienteering, and everyone having made a silent pact to ignore Lolly's cries of disappointment at 'Alcohol! In front of the *children*', Mary shyly made a suggestion to Claire and Lucy.

'Would … would … either of you be interested in coming to see Louisa Russell with me? She's doing a night at the community centre in a few weeks, and I think it would be really interesting.'

'Who's Louisa Russell?' asked Claire.

'She's Ellen Green's sister-in-law,' explained Mary, then when Claire still looked blank, asked, 'Haven't you read Ellen's book?'

'Oh God, Claire, you must!' said Lucy. 'Especially after our chat this afternoon. She wrote this amazing book called *The Patriarchy*

Can Go Fuck Themselves: Why Women Ended Up Doing It All, Not Having It All. It was on all the bestseller lists, No. 1 in *The Sunday Times* and *The New York Times* at the same time. It's brilliant, all about how the patriarchy sold us the myth that we could have it all, work and families, and all the while it was just a ploy to make us DO it all – go out to work, have a career, and still have to shoulder almost all the domestic and emotional labour of a family, while the men just carried on like before, and why this needs to change.'

'I think I remember seeing it and thinking it looked interesting, but also thinking I could just imagine how Andrew would laugh if he saw me reading it,' admitted Claire.

'Oh, I'll lend you it,' exclaimed Lucy. 'It really is brilliant. It does make you see how we've been sold such a fucking lie for so many years. But I don't think I've heard of her sister-in-law, Mary?'

'Louisa Russell is a radical intersectional feminist poet and best-selling author,' Mary read out from her phone.

'Have you got signal?'

'No, I took a screenshot of it a few days ago when I saw it adver-tised so I wouldn't forget, but I didn't have anyone I thought would want to go with me. Anyway, it carries on:

Louisa's poetry explores many of the themes also covered in her sister-in-law Ellen Green's popular book, and in her own *Sunday Times* bestselling tome *WombBeats*. Louisa's work casts an unflinching look at what femineity, feminism and femininity mean for real women. Where Ellen Green's inexplicably celebrated book looked only at capitalist ways of how to live as a woman, both Louisa's written poetry and spoken-word performances drill down into the essence of what it means to actually exist as a woman. Louisa's work is a raw, powerful, unique and above all *essential* exploration of what it is that defines the female spirit. *The Sunday Times* bestseller *WombBeats* is the book all women around the globe needed, craved and thirsted for, a lifechanging and seminal book that shocked women and men everywhere into acknowledging the inner power of the Goddess in all our wombs. Now Louisa is bringing her *Sunday Times* bestselling book *WombBeats* to the stage in a brand new and exceptional one-woman show for the first time, which is something Ellen Green couldn't do with her book. *Louisa's Womb Still Beats* is a *Vagina Monologues* meets *Fleabag* for the twenty-first century and is a truly unmissable experience.

'I'm not sure,' said Lucy doubtfully.

'It might be fun?' said Mary. 'I couldn't get tickets for Ellen's book tour last year, it had sold out, and I thought this might be good instead.'

'She really doesn't like her sister-in-law's book, does she?' said Claire. 'Is she *actually* a *Sunday Times* bestseller as well?'

'I suppose she must be, if she says so,' said Mary. 'I don't think you can just say that if you're not, can you? Otherwise it's fraud.'

'I expect she probably is,' said Lucy. 'I think I remember seeing her on various podcasts and interviews last year, desperately piggy-backing and cashing in on being Ellen's sister-in-law. I suppose if she plugged it enough, the association with Ellen could have given her enough publicity that she might have scraped onto the list.'

'Did she sound all right? Like it would be a fun night out?'

'She seemed quite … intense,' said Lucy carefully.

'Well, even so,' pleaded Mary, 'I think it sounds interesting. We might learn something about getting rid of the patriarchy. We'll be cultured and literary. And we can go to the pub afterwards.'

'Oh, why not. It's something different to do!' said Claire. 'I've never been to see a … a radical –. What was she, Mary?'

'Intersectional feminist poet.'

'See? That's definitely different!'

'Oh, go on, as long as I can get a babysitter. Down with the bastarding patriarchy and all that!' said Lucy.

'What about Kate? Should we ask her? She might enjoy it too,' said Claire.

'Good idea. Do you mind if we ask our friend Kate, Mary?'

'No, the more the merrier. Oh wonderful! Shall I book the tickets, then?'

'Why not! Also, have you noticed Lolly's arse?' whispered Lucy.

'Well, it's hard to miss when she's prancing around in hotpants half the time,' complained Claire.

'She's not wearing them tonight though, is she? I noticed earlier that she had a huge red lump on one buttock, where that horsefly bit her. And she's sitting distinctly lopsidedly, look. I think the bite has got infected.'

'You mean she literally has a septic arse?' sniggered Claire.

'I reckon so!'

They erupted in laughter, as they gasped about karma and how it couldn't have happened to a nicer person. Caroline Northfield leaned over and demanded they shared the joke, and Claire, sitting next to her, whispered it in her ear. Caroline snorted with glee, and immediately passed it on to Sally beside her, and in no time at all news of Lolly's septic arse had spread round the campfire via one of the most bizarre games of Chinese Whispers ever. And every time Lolly, wincing slightly, attempted to shift position, hilarity broke out again.

* * *

The rest of the camp passed without any other great incident. There was a minor standoff when Figgy and Jacinta attempted to stop Caroline and Sally using the special glamping toilet block, but they dodged past them and locked themselves in the cubicles for a very long time. Everyone else coming out of the glamping loos for the rest of the night looked vaguely horrified, and Caroline and Sally seemed cheered up that they had effected some small revenge on the glamping gang.

Lolly was forced to call off her Forest Yoga class on Sunday morning, as the horsefly bite on her bum was now the size of a tennis ball, despite Jacinta's careful application of crystals to the afflicted area, and the cancellation was definitely because of this, Lolly insisted, and not due to lack of interest, as she knew how disappointed everyone would be. There was, however, a distinct absence of disappointment in the dining room, but Lolly's septic arse seemed punishment enough without anyone pointing this out.

Despite the demise of Forest Yoga, the death stares from Lolly, and the unfortunate incident with Harry, Claire was astonished to find that she was actually really enjoying the weekend and would be sorry when it was over. It had been so different to anything she'd ever done with Andrew, although when they first met and he'd tried to get Claire to go camping, he'd insisted it should be wild camping, declaring campsites 'naff' and 'full of people'. Claire's reasonings that they may be full of people but they were also possessed of lavatory facilities fell on deaf ears, which was why Claire had previously found camping so unpleasant; there was something just too primitive about digging yourself a little hole to poo in.

Claire now thought she might actually take the children on a camping holiday sometime. It would be a cheap and fun way to get away. Andrew would have been horrified at the notion – he had very clear ideas about holidays, and people. Andrew didn't like hotels, because there were strangers in them. Despite their busy social life, Andrew was very clear about the people he did and did not want to associate with. He *did* want to associate with anyone he'd chosen and deemed suitable. He did *not* want to associate with anyone else. Early in their marriage they'd gone to Portugal for a week, and a nice lady from Kirkby Lonsdale had attempted to make a passing remark to Andrew from the next sun lounger. He'd been so appalled at the idea of a stranger trying to strike up a conversation with him (all she'd actually said was, 'Oh, it's lovely to get some proper sunshine, isn't it?') that he refused to ever go to a hotel again, and insisted on villas henceforth.

The villas were usually shared with at least one other family, sometimes two, which meant that instead of a chilled-out, relaxing time, the fortnight would be spent refereeing fights between children about the myriad 'unfairnesses' that only children can take umbrage at – 'Well, why CAN'T I have four ice creams for dinner like George has?' – and negotiating the simmering resentments between the adults. These usually took the form of one couple feeling the other had bagsied a better room or weren't pulling their weight, or arose from differing approaches to parenting.

And yet, year after year, instead of saying 'Fuck this, we need time to ourselves,' Claire and Andrew and the others would book themselves delightful villas in Menorca or Corfu or Provence and traipse off, assuring each other afterwards that they'd had the *best* time and they couldn't wait to do it all again next year. And somehow, like childbirth, each year they forgot that Tim was quite racist when they were abroad and Jen had an uncanny knack of vanishing when it was time to make the children's dinner, or that when you spent a whole week with them it was quite noticeable that Simon and Julia were functioning alcoholics, and that Joel and Louise actively hated each other, and that Sarah and Nigel had such loud sex every night that *surely* they had to be faking it to make everyone else feel inadequate. Andrew and Claire used to feel rather smug when they came home, though, because compared to their friends, they really seemed to be quite good people and to have it all together. Ha, thought Claire. Oh, the irony.

This weekend, though, with everyone being united in their rage at the Glamping Gang and at Lolly's diktats, there had been a proper camaraderie between the rest of the campers, even when on toilet-cleaning duty, and as well as meeting Mary, Claire had finally got to know some of the other parents better, which was a bonus she'd not expected.

On the way home, with an exhausted and filthy Tabitha, as Claire pondered that for a weekend that was supposed to be about her and Tabitha bonding, she'd barely actually seen her daughter, Claire was astonished to hear her pipe up, 'Thank you, Mummy.'

'What for, darling?'

'Taking me on the camping weekend. I had the best time. And we've decided Amy is our best friend too. It was brilliant! I love you, Mummy, loads and loads. You are the best mum in the world!'

Tabitha hadn't said an unsolicited thank you for anything in a long while, usually preferring to complain about the gross unfairness of her life. Maybe there was more than one way to bond with your child, thought Claire, feeling quite heartwarmed by the whole thing, and even slightly grateful to Lolly for organising it all. She'd probably feel even more grateful when she'd had a bath and washed the field out of her hair, she reflected.

'And Mummy,' Tabitha said importantly, 'I've decided I'm going to keep on being good, like I said I would be if you took me to the camp.'

'Really, darling?' said Claire in surprise, as despite Tabitha's grandiose promises, there had been very little alteration to be seen in her behaviour.

'Yes,' said Tabitha firmly. 'Because that would be a nice thing to do for you, wouldn't it, Mummy? Because you always do nice things for me and Lucas, and you don't have anybody to do nice things for you, do you, now you don't have Daddy anymore. So I'm going to be nice to you by being very good, like I've been before the camp. Will that make you happy, Mummy?'

'Yes, darling, thank you. But you already make me happy, just by being you! You don't have to do anything else.'

'Don't I? Oh well, I'll see how I get on with being good then. Maybe I'll be good except for being nice to Lucas, because he's a bumhead. How about that?'

Although, to be honest, the best thing Tabitha and Lucas could have done for Claire was to stop fighting, she didn't really feel she could turn down Tabitha's generous offer, not that Claire had any hope she'd actually be able to detect any discernible difference anyway.

'Thank you, darling, that would be wonderful,' Claire said, as she wondered if perhaps a bit more emotional maturity from Tabitha was actually a positive consequence of her separation from Andrew, a sign that Tabitha was growing up a bit, or just one of those moments when your children suddenly reveal that there's a chance of them growing up to be decent human beings and you feel quite proud that you're #NailingIt and #WinningAtLife and #AcingParenting, before they immediately revert to being feral pig trolls, lest you get any ideas about the whole 'decent human being' thing happening properly anytime soon.

18

Over the next couple of weeks it became apparent that Mary was definitely a Kindred Spirit as well. It helped, of course, that Tabitha, Ella and Amy had all also decided they were Kindred Spirits, but when your circumstances meant you mostly ended up socialising with the parents of your children's pals, it was much easier when your children befriended people who you liked as well. Claire had struggled somewhat with Tabitha's brief friendship with Ophelia and Gertrude, as it was much more relaxing when Tabitha had friends you could just feed pizza to and whose mummies accepted enthusiastically when you suggested a glass of wine when they picked up their cherubs.

Finally, the much-anticipated night arrived for the trip to see Louisa Russell, Radical Intersectional Feminist Poet Extraordinaire. Not all the anticipation was entirely positive, but Mary was still young enough to be idealistic and had rallied Claire and Lucy with a pep talk about not being closed-minded and needing to Support the Arts, and Kate, who had enthusiastically accepted the invitation, had separately given them a similar talk.

Claire had at least objected that her mind would be more open if she had a swift gin first, and also it would be a good chance for Kate and Mary to meet in the pub before they went to hear Louisa do her Artistic Thing, and so, thus fortified, they arrived at the community centre and took their seats. Due to the gins being slightly less swift than originally planned (i.e. Mary saying brightly, 'God, I haven't been Out Out in ages. I'm sure we've time for another,' and everyone else enthusiastically agreeing that yes, there was definitely time for another), by the time they arrived the performance was about to start.

The hall was remarkably full, which Lucy unkindly pointed out might have been something to do with Louisa's posters all declaring her to be 'Ellen Green's Sister-In-Law'. They therefore had to spread themselves over three rows, perched on the end of each, Claire craning her neck around a tall lady in front in order to be able to see. Claire would soon be extremely grateful for the tall lady's impediment to her view.

Once the hall was plunged into darkness, a single spotlight shone on the stage and a husky voice intoned solemnly from offstage.

My Womb BEATS
[A dramatic pause]
My WOMB beats
[Another pause]
MY womb beats
[A longer pause]
YOUR womb beats

A really quite pointlessly long pause followed that caused someone to clear their throat loudly and wonder if they'd paid good money to sit in the dark in silence. They were shushed by someone else.

Finally, the voice spoke again.

'OUR WOMBS BEAT,' it roared, and someone, presumably Louisa Russell, erupted onto the stage. She was stark bollock naked.

Worse, some kind of dark, viscous fluid appeared to be seeping down her thighs. Surely … surely … it couldn't be?

The naked woman bounded into the middle of the stage and flung her arms wide, causing her tits to nearly have someone's eye out in the front row.

'Friends,' she cried. 'Nay, SISTERS. Welcome. I'm Louisa Russell. Tonight, our wombs shall beat together. Each and every one of you, your wombs shall feel the power of my womb, and together we shall feel the powerful pulse of our WOMB-ANHOOD moving through us all as one!'

'Well, I very much doubt that,' muttered a woman behind Claire, 'because I've had a bloody hysterectomy and what's more, I can't say I miss my uterus one bit. I was quite over it! Fucking fibroids.'

'ARE WE READY? ARE YOUR WOMBS READY?' bellowed Louisa.

'Is this some surreal episode of *Gladiators*?' hissed Lucy. 'What the fuck is going on? What *have* you brought us to, Mary?'

Louisa was now pacing up and down the stage. Something splattered onto the ground.

'Sisters,' she announced. 'I must share with you that this is my most powerful time. For yes, my womb is making its monthly cry of POWER, telling the world, "I AM HERE, HEAR ME SPEAK" and marking its message to us all in blood!'

'Oh Christ, she IS on the blob,' moaned Mary in horror. 'I thought I must be imagining things and surely that couldn't be what I thought it was. Please make it stop.'

Claire could only stare at the stage in speechless shock.

'At least we're not in the front row,' Claire finally offered.

'So, my sisters, I want to share this power with you. My womb has been channelled for many years to come to its full power. I want you to have some of that power. Therefore, I'm proud to tell you that my books will be for sale in the foyer afterwards and I'll be signing in the blood of my womb, so you can take home some of that essence, and through it learn to bring your own womb to power and take ownership of your WOMB-anhood!'

'Did I hear right?' whimpered Kate. 'She's going to sign books in *her own period blood*? How is that allowed? How is that hygienic? Surely it's against health and safety regulations?'

'And I don't know what the hall committee are going to say about the mess she's making,' added Lucy.

The lady next to Claire covered her eyes with her hands as Louisa began to declare her first poem. Then she thought better of it and put them over her ears.

'This poem is about BIRTH!' Louisa informed us. 'The miracle, the wonder of BIRTH! I call it – BIRTH!'

My yoni stretches
Wider wider
My womb clenches
Wrenches wrenches
My body writhes
My breasts drip
Back arching in ecstasy
It is like fucking fucking fucking

'How the fuck is giving birth like fucking?' Lucy gasped. 'It is nothing like it!'

Everyone else in the hall was now clearly too shocked to shush her, and in fact there was a murmur of agreement. But Louisa was still going. She'd paused in the centre of the stage, eyes closed and fists clenched at her sides as she continued with her poem.

The blood spills spills spills
Shit comes. I come. I shit and come
I come and shit
While blood and liquid gush

'Enough,' said the lady next to Claire, standing up. 'I can't do this. I'm going. This is awful.'

'Do you think we can go?' said Lucy from the row behind. 'I'm one hundred per cent on board with women being open and comfortable with their bodies and demystifying periods and child-birth, but this is just … grim. Some poor bugger's going to have to mop that stage, you know.'

Claire was torn. She didn't want to leave Mary and Kate alone together when they had only just met, especially after the Stern Talks from them both about Supporting the Arts, but no part of her wanted to stay either. Louisa was now on all fours, panting loudly, with her back to the audience, simulating giving birth, which actually meant they had a very clear view of her arsehole. Claire was no longer attempting to crane around the tall lady in front in order to see the stage. Maybe Kate and Mary *could* Support the Arts together, without Claire and Lucy?

Louisa gave a final triumphant bellow and sprang to her feet again.

And then my womb, my womb
Heaving, shaking, thrusting like my lover's penis
Sowing seed within me

'Oh, for fuck's sake,' said Mary. 'That doesn't even make sense. How can a womb thrust? It's a physiological impossibility. Come on, let's get out of here.'

'Thank God,' said Kate, scrambling to her feet.

Claire and Lucy were already at the door.

Louisa did not give up that easily, though.

'SISTERS!' she howled, as Claire put her hand on the door handle. 'WHERE ARE YOU GOING?'

They all froze, like naughty schoolgirls, caught by matron on the way to a midnight feast.

'People are looking,' moaned Mary. 'Oh God, there's going to be a scene.'

'SISTERS, you must stay and HEED MY MESSAGE,' Louisa insisted. 'You must NOT leave.'

'Just GO,' hissed Lucy. 'Come ON.'

'You find me too powerful,' screeched Louisa. 'I understand, sisters, I understand. You've been brainwashed by the patriarchy. You're afraid of your own wombs. Do not be afraid! I'm here to help. To de-programme you from the teachings of society. To allow you to be as wild and free as I am! Watch, I shall demonstrate how FREE you can be with my next poem, called 'Vulva Music'. Hear the song of my vulva! Can I get another microphone, actually. I need one for my vulva? So you can properly hear the music it makes,' she called offstage.

Mary gave Claire a shove from the back. 'GO!'

'Don't forget to buy my book on the way out,' Louisa yelled hopefully after them, still waiting for her vulva microphone, which the sound tech from the hall committee seemed strangely reluctant to hand over.

In the foyer they stared at each other in horror.

'Pub,' said Claire firmly.

'Yes, please,' the others gasped in relief.

*　*　*

'I guess it's my round,' said Mary, as they went through the door of the pub across the road. 'What are we all having?'

By the time Mary returned with a bottle and four glasses, there was a steady stream of people fleeing Louisa's poetry.

'Oh God,' wailed Kate. 'Maybe she got her vulva microphone in the end.'

'My daughter goes to drama classes in there,' Claire shuddered. 'I'm probably going to have to disinfect her afterwards if she's been on that stage.'

'The Stage of Dooooom,' intoned Kate. 'Maybe it'll be like Lady Macbeth. Louisa's blood will be so POWERFUL they'll never get it out.'

'It was more than a damned spot,' said Claire. 'There was buckets of it. I think she needs a good gynaecologist. Useful, though, to have a plentiful supply for the book signings. She wouldn't want to run out, after all.'

'I don't think there's much danger of that,' Lucy said, peering at the exodus now pouring forth from the community centre, most of them pale and horrified and making a beeline for the bar. 'How do you think she does it? Does she like, collect it first in some sort of inkwell, or does she just pop a quill right up there?'

'Oh God, no,' spluttered Claire.

Kate gave a horror-struck giggle. 'Christ, can you imagine? I wouldn't put it past her to just, you know!' She gestured at her lap and mimed writing.

'How many people do you think buy her book after that?' said Mary.

'There's probably some weirdos that follow her round everywhere and buy a monthly copy for their collection,' shuddered Kate. 'Oh God, we need another bottle already.'

'Thank God we left early. This place is packed now. Look, the only man that was there is at the bar with a large double whisky, and he's actually crying!'

Three hours later, the table was littered with bottles and glasses. Kate and Mary had firmly declared each other to be Kindred Spirits. There had been tears, there had been laughter, there had been tears of laughter, there had been complaints about ineffective pelvic floors.

'No one says, "Have children and you'll *literally* piss yourself laughing," do they?' yelled Lucy in fury. 'I mean, those fucking soft-focus Tena adverts don't say that. They're all hand-in-hand walks on the beach. Well, I've never pissed myself on the beach, although I've had to go behind a rock a few times. And there was a time when Ben was little and he needed a shit, and I whipped him behind a rock and he curled out a turd the SIZE OF HIS OWN FUCKING HEAD, I SHIT YOU NOT, if you'll pardon the pun. And it wasn't till after I'd wiped his arse and pulled up his swimming trunks that I realised that particular rock was over-looked by the eighteenth green of a very exclusive golf course, and two appalled golfers had witnessed the whole thing. Then I had to suffer the indignity of having to borrow a poo bag from a passing dog walker so I could pick up the offending article. So yes, I've been very humiliated on a beach, but not by pissing my pants, so the adverts should show a bunch of drunk women able to laugh and sneeze WITH FUCKING ABANDON WITHOUT PISSING OURSELVES! It's like BLUE PERIODS!' she finished darkly.

'Blue periods?' said Mary in confusion.

'You know! The adverts where you go roller skating in white jeans when you've got your period, *like you do*, and then, then Claire Rayner pops up with a test tube of blue liquid and pours it onto the sanitary towel, but it's all OK because it's got WINGS!' Claire explained.

'I think you've just combined every period advert from the eighties and nineties into one there,' said Kate. 'And I think Mary's maybe too young to remember them?'

'Well, they were all the bloody same! If, again, you'll pardon the pun,' insisted Lucy. 'There was one where she went skydiving. Bet she was glad of Claire Rayner's wings then!'

'I remember that one!' cried Kate, wiping tears of laughter from her eyes. 'I'm sure it was a Bodyform one – oooooh Booooodyfoooorm,' she warbled.

'Boooodyfooooormed for YOOOOOUUUUU,' Claire joined in, as the rest of the pub looked rather startled at the table of women crooning the jingle from an ancient sanitary towel advert.

'Oh, this is fun!' said Kate suddenly. 'It's been a long time since I've had *fun*. Nothing tells you how to learn to have fun again. All the articles on how to cope with bereavement tell you to take up meditation or "Join an evening class", and I don't think evening classes are even still a thing. And everything else on how to change your life just tells you how to start a six-figure internet business or how to meet men, and I don't *want* to meet men, obviously, and I don't want to meet women either. I mean, not like that. Obviously *you're* women, and I'm glad I've met you, but if I met someone romantically, they'd have to be special, really special, and I can't ever imagine meeting someone that special again.'

'I used to feel to like that,' sighed Lucy. 'Now I'd just settle for being banged like a barn door in a storm.'

'LUCY!' protested Mary.

'What?' said Lucy. 'It's true! What is wrong with admitting that sometimes women DO just want nothing more than a good fuck? It's finding one that's the trouble! Oh, not a man *willing* to do it –

they're ten a penny – I mean finding one who's any good at it, and knows which buttons to press and realises his cock is not some magic wand, and actually it takes some effort on his part for a woman to have a good time!'

'Lucy, please,' choked Mary again, gesturing wildly at Kate.

'Well, I know that's not what Kate wants, even from a woman. But I'd so like to have actual sex, you know? You don't realise, when your husband fucks off with someone else, that that last indifferent, hurry-up-will-you-because-I-want-to-go-to-sleep fumble might have been the last sex you ever have. And I just didn't realise how much I'd miss it. Jesus, most of the time when I was married, I couldn't be bloody doing with it. I just wanted him to leave me alone to go to sleep. But now, really, I'd give anything just for a shag. Well, not anything. But it would definitely beat getting hot and bothered while watching *Bridgerton*, you know? Sorry. More wine?'

'Of course you haven't had your last shag, Lucy!'

'I might have. I mean, I suppose I could do meaningless sex with one of the randoms off the internet. I've tried all those websites – Plenty of Fish, Matched.com, MySingleFriend, even Tinder – but there are times when you match with someone who seems nice and normal, and you think, well, maybe they're not a soulmate but they could do as a fuck buddy. Yet when you start messaging them, it turns out they want you to wee on them or something, and quite apart from how unhygienic the whole thing is, if someone talks about weeing on people in sex, it does just make me remember the allegations about Donald Trump. And you can't feel sexy thinking about him, can you? Not that I had any intention of weeing on anyone. There needs to be a website just called 'Normal Shags' or something, where you can just have some ordinary casual sex! Though invariably that would be full of sleazy married men too.'

'NormalShags.com!' said Claire. 'I like it. You should start it. Make your fortune. Oh no, we've finished the bottle, again. Sorry!'

'I'll get another one,' said Lucy. 'Maybe I'll pick up a man at the bar. What? Accountants have urges too, you know,' she said menacingly.

'Oh God,' said Kate weakly through more tears of laughter. 'Oh Lucy. "Accountants have urges too." I'd forgotten what it felt like to laugh this much.'

Another two bottles later, and Mary was slightly tearful. 'I jus' wanted to try something new and I'm sorry it was shit,' she sniffed. 'It's always the same, my life – school run, wipe arses, make dinner. Always the same. So I wanted something new, and it was rubbish, and I'm sorry.'

'NO!,' bellowed Claire. 'It wasn't rubbish. WAS BRILLIANT!'

Claire banged on her glass with a spoon she had mysteriously acquired from somewhere. She wasn't sure where it had come from, but since it was there she'd been using it as a microphone and singing nineties hits into it.

'This,' she slurred. 'This has been a brilliant night, an' we all thought it would be a bit shit at the start! But it wasn't, it was BEST NIGHT! And it's all 'cos of Louisa and her poems. Awful poems. But we, we were all there. An' all of us there tonight, we're … we're like wossit, Henry V. Agincourt!' Claire nodded wisely.

'Wha'?' said Kate in confusion 'Wha's Agincourt got to do with awful poems and seeing her arsehole?'

'Well,' said Claire. 'S'like this, you see. S'Agincourt, an' he says, "We's brothers now, all of us here."'

'"We few, we happy few, we band of brothers"? That what you mean, Claire?' asked Kate.

'Yesh,' said Claire firmly. '"Band of brothers". 'Cos they all had shit time together. 'Cos of the French. You know.' Claire nodded wisely again before going on. 'And us. We've all had a shit time. Not 'cos of the French, though. 'Cept that time Mary was telling us about when she got food poisoning in La Rochelle. Anyway, Louisa's poems were shit too. And also, she was *ewwww*. BUT, we all survived. We survived the poems. An' her shouting at us. *An'* all the other shit in our lives. That's what I'm saying. WE's a band of brothers.'

'Sisters!' pointed out Mary. 'Band of sisters. Like Smelly Louisa said.'

'YES,' said Kate. 'SHISTERS. Doing it for ourselves. 'Cept Lucy who wants a burly man to press her buttons, ha aha hahaha!'

'Can still do it for myself too,' said Lucy. 'I's been to Ann Summers.'

'Will you LISTEN?' shouted Claire impatiently. 'I saying something ver' profound an' you're not LISTENING. We're SISTERS! An' I love you!'

'A sisterhood. Yesh. S'what we are,' slurred Mary, attempting to pour another glass of wine from a bottle with the lid still on. 'S'broken, this bottle. S'not working.'

'A Sisterhood,' said Lucy, taking the bottle off Mary and opening it. 'Our oath sealed in Sauvignon, not blood.'

'Yes!' cried Claire. 'That's US. The Saturday Night Sauvignon Sisterhood!'

'The Saturday Night Sauvignon Sisterhood,' echoed the others. 'Yes!'

'A toast,' said Claire, standing up unsteadily. 'To us. The Saturday Night Sauvignon Sisterhood. We're divorcees and widows and marrieds an' all, an' here's to us! AN' to doing new things like Mary made us do this, 'cos then who knows what happens!'

They clanked glasses with wild abandon. Quite a lot of Sauvignon went over the next table, who fortunately were in a similar condition to the newfound Sisterhood after also attempting to blot out the memory of Louisa's poetry. Claire managed to catch Kate as she attempted to sit back down and nearly missed her stool.

'The Saturday Night Sauvignon Sisterhood,' repeated Claire.

'And new things!' cried Mary. 'Come on, what are we going to do? I picked Louisa, so that's my thing. Claire, what about you?'

'Noooo, this is like that awful "Tell us about yourself" circle thing at that awful book group!' wailed Claire.

'Oh, don't be silly. Just pick something! Something new and exciting and different,' said Mary sternly.

'Arrrghh! I dunno! OK, wild swimming!'

'Really? BASIC! Everyone on Instagram is wild swimming. You're more unusual these days if you HAVEN'T been wild swimming.'

'What? It looks fun. And it's s'pposed to be good for you. I might develop a passion for it and turn into a wholesome, clean-living person who drinks green tea an' goes hiking, and doesn't drink wine anymore,' Claire insisted, waving her wine glass around.

Everyone looked deeply unconvinced by this, but Kate said, 'OK. Wild swimming for Claire. If I get hypothermia, you can provide the brandy. Oooh, shall we have brandy now? Or shots? Lucy? What's yours?'

'Oooohhhhhh, yeah, I've got one!' shouted Lucy in excitement. 'I wanna try life drawing. I loved art at school but my parents wouldn't let me go to art school, said artists never made any money, and I'd starve in a garret, and I should get a proper career and art could be a hobby. But then, children, time, blah blah, so yeah. A life-drawing class. An' we should *definitely* have shots!'

'I can't draw,' said Claire anxiously.

'It doesn't *matter*,' said Kate. 'It's about the whatsit, the *experience*, what we learn from it. Not the finished product.'

'Will there be willies?' Mary asked.

'I don't think they'll have willies, no,' Lucy assured her.

'But what if there is a funny willy and we get the giggles?' Mary wanted to know.

'It's about ART,' Kate said disapprovingly. 'Not looking at willies and sniggering like schoolgirls.'

'But willies are FUNNY,' Claire insisted. 'How do you not snigger if there's a willy, especially like Mary said if it's a funny winkle? Or looks like a turnip?'

'Well, you two can sit at the back then,' said Kate crossly. 'And Lucy and I will sit at the front like whaddyacallits? Mature and responsible adults.'

'I mean, I's can't rule out tittering at a knob,' said Lucy thoughtfully. 'No, no, I know, this was my idea, Kate, I promise not to laugh at the willies. Or the boobies … heh heh. Boobies!'

'For fuck's sake. You's all ver' childish! If *I* can look at a knob without tittering at the sheer ridiculousness of it, I don't see why you all can't,' said Kate, 'Mary. What's yours?'

'Nope. I told you. Louisa was mine, I've done my bit.'

'Noooo. You're not getting out of it that easily. Come on.'

'Ummmm, oh I know, I'd love to try boxing. I bet punching people is really good fun. HiiiiYA! There you go! So what about you, Kate?'

'Urghm, this is also so basic, as well, but a climbing wall. I'm terrified of heights! So, yeah. Climbing wall. Feel like I've overcome something. We're not a ver' adventurous lot, are we?'

'Well, the thing is,' Claire pointed out, nodding wisely as she poured another glass for everyone. 'We don't have to stop at these new things. New things are new to all of us, so maybe it's good we're starting small and working up to other things. Once we've done these things, there's loads of other things to do. You're starting with a climbing wall, and we could end by conquering Everest or something.'

'To Everest!' roared Mary, and they all clanked glasses.

'To New Sisterhooding experiences!' added Claire, and they clanked again, sending more waves of Sauvignon Blanc over the pub.

'I's made a new WhatsApp group,' announced Lucy. 'I put us all on the group. So's OFFICIAL. There!'

Everyone's phones flashed with a garbled message from Lucy, announcing that the WhatsApp group was now henceforth the Saturday Night Sauvignon Sisterhood, and they were going to do NEW THINGS!

'To the SISTERHOOD!' they all roared again.

19

The day after the glorious night when the Saturday Night Sauvignon Sisterhood came into being, Andrew dropped the children home and rather diffidently suggested that he'd like to have them for a couple of weeks during the approaching summer holiday.

'Where did this come from?' Claire asked in astonishment, because Andrew had previously insisted he was too Busy and Important to have the children over the holidays, apart from their usual weekends.

Andrew looked awkward. 'Well, it was something Ben said.'

'Ben? Lucy's Ben? Lucas's friend?'

'Yeah. I knew his dad was a knob. But Ben was just so … casually accepting that his dad didn't have time for him. That he and Ella are the B team to his father's new family. I don't … I don't ever want Lucas or Tabitha to feel that. I've not been the best dad up until now, I realise that. The weekends with the kids – it's made me see how much you did with them. And I want to change that. If nothing else good comes out of all this, I want the kids to grow up knowing I always had time for them and was always there for them. So can I have them for the first two weeks?'

'I've already booked that time off. Have you booked it too? I mean, if you want them for those weeks, I can save my holidays and take time off later in the year, it won't be a problem. Everyone always wants time off in the summer holidays, so I'm sure I can swap with someone if you're already off.'

'Oh yes,' said Andrew proudly. 'I've arranged the time off. I mean, I can't say it was *easy* getting that time off, but I did it,' he went on, looking at Claire expectantly.

He continued to stare at her soulfully until she finally said, 'Are you feeling quite all right, Andrew? Have you got indigestion from a client dinner again or something?'

'No,' he said, looking hurt. 'I just thought, you know, you might say, "Well done" or something, you know, for managing to arrange all this.'

Claire sighed. 'Well done, Andrew. Yay you.'

Andrew did his indigestion face again. 'I *am* trying, you know, Claire.'

'Yes, I know, I just wish you'd tried like this a long time ago. That's all.'

'That's the worst of it, really,' said Claire to the rest of the Sisterhood a few days later, as they shivered on a chilly beach ready to embrace Claire's New Thing of wild swimming. 'He thinks he's demonstrating what a great guy he is, being this new caring, sharing, helpful Andrew, and all it does is make me angry that a.) it's no more than I've always had to do with no thanks, and b.) if he was capable of this all along, why has it taken till now for him to be this person? Why did it take the end of our marriage for this to happen? Why the fuck couldn't he have stepped up years ago? Maybe it's me, maybe *I'm* the problem. Maybe he's just a better person without me.'

'Of course he's not,' everyone reassured Claire quickly.

'It's probably just him having to spend all those weekends with his kids that has eventually made him see how much you did,' suggested Lucy. 'And maybe he's finally appreciating that.'

'How the fuck couldn't he see how much I did when he lived in the same bloody *house* as me, though?' raged Claire.

'Sometimes we don't see what's under our noses,' said Kate gently. 'I never realised how much Susan did until she was gone. All the boring stuff like life insurance and house insurance. Maybe you just made it look so effortless that he didn't understand how much time and energy you put into running the house and dealing with the kids.'

'Effortless?' snorted Claire. 'Hardly.'

'It's a fair point,' said Mary. 'James is the same. Half the time he seems to genuinely not even notice the things that need to be done, though how the fuck you can "not notice" four boxes of Duplo strewn across the hall I do not know, and the rest of the time he seems to have no idea how long things actually take to do. He thinks everything is just a "five-minute job" and can't understand why I complain I never have any spare time. Quite apart from the fact that even if everything that needed to be done was in fact a "five-minute job", there are still a fuck of a lot them to be done in a day.'

Claire sighed. 'I know, I know. I *know* he's not an inherently bad man. Just an annoying one. And I know he's trying, and I suspect he thinks if he tries hard enough, everything will go back to how it was. But how can it, because there's still the problem of Emily, isn't there? We should start a lovely matriarchal society,' said Claire dreamily. 'On an island. Like that one,' she added, pointing out into the lake. 'With no men, apart from for the drains.'

'Can I have one visit for a shag?' asked Lucy.

'Why not? He can fix the drains at the same time.'

'I don't want to shag the drains man, he'd smell all drainy. I want a clean one.'

'Fine. You can have a clean one. And we'd all just be nice and jolly and happy, and even people like Lolly would probably be happier because they wouldn't be worrying about sleazy bastards like Harry, and maybe I could make up with Emily if there were no men, and all the children would romp merrily and be raised communally by the village.'

'What about boy children? What will we do with them when they grow up? Will they be banished, to be kept somewhere for when the drains need fixing?'

'Depends if they grow up to be arseholes or not.'

'I wish we *could* bring up children in some sort of communal matriarchal society,' said Kate. 'I think that would be wonderful. Dozens of mothers, instead of one or two. Do you think children really need two parents?'

'It's certainly easier with two,' said Lucy. 'My ex is barely involved, and yes, it's hard.'

'I know I just had a moan about him, but I couldn't imagine doing it without James,' said Mary. 'But then I've never tried to.'

'Yeah, I suppose I'm lucky that he's wanting to spend more time with the kids, not less,' said Claire (who had not had the heart to tell Lucy that it was Ben's heartbreaking acceptance of his father's lack of interest that had sparked Andrew's desire to be more involved).

'Oh,' said Kate. 'So you don't recommend being a single parent?'

'Oh shit,' said Claire. 'Kate, are you pregnant? How? When?'

'No,' said Kate. 'I'd hardly be about to plunge into a large body of cold water for the very first time ever if I was, would I? But I told you that Susan and I had been talking about it before she … she died. Before we knew she was sick. About having a baby. I wasn't sure I was ready. I wanted more time with just us. And Susan felt she *was* ready, and we should go ahead before we got any older, because it was going to be harder for us to get pregnant than a straight couple and so we should start trying. But there was always a reason not to. That holiday we'd just booked. A promotion at work. And now ... Susan's gone. And she never got to have her baby. And I don't know what to do.'

'Oh Kate. It's totally possible to have a baby on your own,' Claire assured her.

'It's never easy having a baby, there's never a right time. I of all people should know that,' said Mary. 'But people would help. Friends and family.'

'Really?' said Kate doubtfully.

'Really,' everyone insisted.

'We would be your matriarchal society,' Claire insisted. 'What could possibly go wrong? Us, a baby, a drains man. All you need!'

'*Four Middle-aged Women, a Baby and a Drains Man* doesn't sound quite as snappy as *Three Men and a Baby*. But it would certainly be in keeping with the spirit of trying new things,' said Kate thoughtfully. 'Anyway, I feel like I'm just procrastinating now. That water does look quite chilly. Are we sure this is safe? What about cold water shock? Maybe someone should stay on shore just in case? I don't mind staying behind, really I don't.'

'It's summertime,' Lucy reminded her. 'You can't get cold feet now.'

'It's cold everything else as well as my feet I'm worried about,' said Claire. 'And no one's staying behind. One in, all in. Come on, then. LET'S DO THIS! On three? One ... two ... THREE.'

And they hurled themselves into the sullen grey choppy water. There was a lot of shrieking. A pair of dog walkers on the beach stopped to watch anxiously as the four women splashed and attempted to swim in the cold water.

'At least they can call the coastguard if we start drowning,' chittered Mary.

'We're in an inland lake,' Claire pointed out. 'I don't think there's a coastguard. Are we feeling exhilarated yet?'

'Well, it depends what you mean by exhilarated,' shivered Lucy. 'If you mean, "Have your nipples gone numb?" then yes, yes, I'm FUCKING exhilarated.'

'I'm a bit numb too,' admitted Mary.

'Maybe we should get out,' said Claire anxiously, 'before we get hypothermia.'

Everyone gladly agreed, and they swam back to the shore.

'Well?' demanded Lucy through chattering teeth. 'What did you think, Claire?'

'I should really say how amazing it was, how free and unfettered I feel,' said Claire sheepishly.

'But?' prompted Mary.

'But mostly I feel fucking freezing. But also, I feel really glad I've done it, partly so I *know* I don't like it, and partly because now I can smugly drop my "wild swimming experiences" into conversations with people like Lolly. Mainly, though, just because, well, I've been in a rut for so long. And this was not "fun" in a way I used to think of fun, but it was fun because it was new and different, and it was just out of that comfort zone, you know? And also because you were all here with me. That made it fun. It wouldn't have been fun on my own. But I've said "fun" too many times now and it no longer sounds like a real word.'

'It would also have been very dangerous to do on your own,' put in Kate sternly. 'You could have got a cramp and drowned, like they were always worrying about in *Malory Towers*.'

Lucy looked up from drying herself and giggled. 'I think there is one perk of wild swimming,' she announced. 'Quite literally. It was so fucking cold my tits have gone almost perky again!'

'Really?' said Claire in astonishment, as everyone peered down their swimming costumes and agreed that yes, it did seem to have had a most bracing effect on one's bosoms.

'Probably only temporary,' sighed Claire. 'But it definitely means we deserve cake, and lots of it, since we've been so very wholesome and outdoorsy!'

20

Claire had decided to give herself the enormous treat of keeping one of the weeks she'd booked off work in the summer holidays for herself, even though Andrew would still have the children all that week. She suspected she'd regret this indulgence when she was tearing her hair out trying to eke out her remaining holidays to be able to attend the myriad 'Open Afternoons' and school concerts and assemblies and everything else parents were summonsed to and guilt-tripped into attending.

Claire reflected that it was strange that during her childhood, when far fewer women worked than nowadays, there had been no requirement for her mother to traipse into school every couple of weeks to sit through excruciating presentations on *Why Bullying Is Bad* or *Why Recycling Is Good*, or to admire the various misshapen papier-mâché lumps hanging from the classroom ceiling that were allegedly the solar system.

But now that almost every parent at the school was holding down a part-time job at the very minimum (even Lolly had her Forest Yoga classes now, Figgy painted rocks and attempted to sell them, and Jacinta had her crystals and herbs business), suddenly they were expected to be there making appreciative noises about their precious moppet's touching performance as 'Bingo the Dog Who Hurt His Leg', which mainly consisted of falling dramatically to the ground and lying there unmoving for the next ten minutes.

Nonetheless, Claire decided she deserved a bit of time properly to herself. Her weekends when Andrew had the children always seemed to be spent rushing round trying to catch up on all the things she hadn't had time to do during the week, and so she had promised herself some proper Time Off.

As the Week Off loomed, though, Claire started to wonder what on earth she was going to do with herself for seven days all on her own. She also realised she was actually going to miss the children. Although there hadn't been much tangible evidence to show for Tabitha's declaration post-Forest Fields that she was going to be good from now on, her frequent proclamations that she was being very good for Mummy had spurred Lucas on to try to behave in a slightly less Dorito-smeared-Neanderthal way too. Lucas had even made her a cup of tea the other day, unasked for. It had basically been lukewarm milkwater that had briefly had a teabag waved near it, and was so disgusting Claire was forced to pour it down the sink when he wasn't looking, but the thought was there. And it is the thought that counts.

The children were to go to Andrew's on the Sunday, and on Saturday morning Claire woke up full of plans for the many Happy Memories she'd make with the children that day before they went off for the fortnight. Sadie had sneaked up the bed again in the night and was beaming at Claire from the pillow next to her.

'Sadie,' remonstrated Claire feebly, 'you're meant to sleep at the end of the bed, not with your head on the pillow.'

Sadie thumped her tail apologetically and promised not to do it again. They both knew she was fibbing, as Claire scratched her head and pulled her in for a snuggle.

'You silly old thing,' she crooned. 'Are you my girl? Are you?'

Sadie made a groaning noise to agree once again that she was indeed Claire's girl, and Claire was her girl.

'And you're never going anywhere, my love, are you? Never again,' Claire whispered in her ear.

This was Claire and Sadie's morning routine now. With hindsight, Claire wasn't sure that the sight of Andrew's head on the pillow next to her had ever filled her with such happiness and love every morning as Sadie's did. Claire reflected, not for the first time, that rescue dogs are well named, as they rescue every bit as much as they are rescued. Sadie gave Claire a nudge, to remind her that these cuddles were very nice, and very welcome, but Sadie was not as young as she once was and so could do with a wee. And also, it was breakfast time.

Claire trotted downstairs with Sadie, and stepped in a puddle. She looked suspiciously at Sadie, but Sadie denied everything and pointed out she'd been upstairs with Claire all night. Claire could hear Lucas thumping around in the kitchen. She knew it was him, not Tabitha, because it sounded like a herd of elephants had been let loose in there.

'Lucas!' yelled Claire. 'LUCAS!'

Lucas finally shuffled out, a cereal bowl brimming with Coco Pops and milk in his hand (Claire had given up on the faffy fancy weekend and holiday breakfasts now the children came from a broken home. Occasionally, she even took them to McDonald's for pancakes, because if you're letting your standards slip, you might as well do it properly).

'Wha'?' he mumbled through a mouthful of cereal.

'Lucas, was this water here when you came down?'

'No.'

'Well, why's it here now?'

Lucas crammed in another shovelful of Coco Pops and thought about it.

'Probably the downstairs loo?' he finally suggested. 'The toilet's blocked.'

'What? How is it blocked? Why didn't you come and tell me?'

'I'm *telling* you now!' said Lucas indignantly. 'And I *tried* to fix it.'

'How did you try to fix it?' enquired Claire in despair.

'Kept flushing it,' said Lucas smugly. 'To clear the blockage. See?'

And before Claire could stop him he nipped into the loo and flushed it again, sending further cascades of dubiously coloured water over the floor from the brimming bowl.

'Lucas! Stop flushing! All you're doing is making it worse,' wailed Claire, as she looked in horror at the waves gently lapping at the foot of the stairs, where Sadie stood on the bottom step looking down in horror and whining gently at the thought of getting her paws wet.

'Oh God. Right, Lucas, I won't be cross, but I need to know. Did *you* block the toilet?'

'What do you mean?'

'Was it you? With one of your large … er … deposits?'

'You mean with a big shit?'

'Lucas! Language!'

'Well, but I was watching this programme on YouTube and it said it wasn't swearing if it was what the word was for, like the Elizabethans used "fuck" and "shit" all the time to talk about those things and it wasn't swearing, so it's actually OK in context. And it said in Chaucer, he even says "Cu –"'

'RIGHT! OK, I don't need a history of profanity, I just need to know if you blocked it.'

'No, I just had a piss, and "piss" is in Shakespeare, so it's definitely OK, and so is "bastard", because remember when you took us to see *Richard III* to try to make us more cultured, and he said "bastard" all the time.'

'Yes, but he was talking about the alleged illegitimacy of his nephews, not just throwing round insults,' said Claire.

'And he said "bloody" all the time, and then he murdered everyone. It really wasn't a very suitable play for children.'

'No. You're right. But at this moment in time my maternal failings in taking you to see *Richard III* are not really at the top of my priority list! Can you please take Sadie out for a wee while I try to sort this?'

'Shakespeare's very rude, actually. There's all sorts of puns about sex,' Lucas helpfully informed her.

'Great. I'm very happy you're watching such informative programmes instead of rotting your mind with Minecraft. Sadie. Wee. NOW, please.'

'Come on, Sadie, let's take you for a piss,' said Lucas smugly, clearly determined to mine this rich seam of historical profanity for all it was worth.

Two hours later, Claire had failed to unblock the toilet and the day of #HappyMemories was a distant dream. She had wrestled her hand down the U-bend, she had waved a wrench hopefully at it, she had tried poking a coat hanger down – and nothing. All this had been done with constant interruptions to inform her that Sadie had peed on the kitchen floor because Lucas had not let her out, having got sidetracked by a bowl of Crunchy Nut Cornflakes after his Coco Pops; with complaints from Tabitha that Lucas had used all the milk so what could she eat because she was STARVING; and with outraged objections from Lucas about how unfair it was that Tabitha was eating the chocolate brioche that were only for special treats and why couldn't he have one, and how was he supposed to know that it was unreasonable to use four pints of milk for a single individual's breakfast?

She had broken up fights, she had tried sixteen times to make the children get dressed, she had stopped to feed Sadie because no one else seemed able to, she had come as close as she had ever been to telling Tabitha to actually just FUCK RIGHT OFF when Tabitha burst into the very small and enclosed space that was the downstairs loo to squawk like an electrocuted parrot (about the absolute total, incredibly important, earth-shattering necessity of Claire downloading this app for her now. Like RIGHT NOW, Mum. Well, why can't I just have your iTunes password, Mum? Oh my God, this is so unfair, and last night you let Lucas get a game and now you won't even let me have this, and you love Lucas more than me), all while Claire was groping about in the murky depths of the bog, the marigolds she had donned now full of toilet water that her hands were squelching in unpleasantly.

She had soothed Tabitha's screaming when Lucas told her to fuck off, and now realised with a sinking feeling that Lucas's current topic at school was in fact the Tudors. He was supposed to be doing a presentation on them that she'd somehow have to stop him filling with obscenities on the basis that the Elizabethans were prolific pissing, shitting fuckers. She had also fielded a call from her mother-in-law, complaining about how little she saw her grandchildren and when was Claire going to arrange for her to see them and no, she couldn't call Poor Andrew about it, because didn't Claire *know* how stressed and busy Poor Andrew was?

She had rung six plumbers, none of whom had answered their phones, despite all their adverts promising a twenty-four-hour call-out service, and she was sweaty, soggy and at the end of her tether. Doing everything on your own all the time was *hard*. All right, Andrew wasn't very good at DIY, but at least another adult in the house meant one of them could deal with the children and one of them could deal with the problem, even though Andrew's method of dealing with it would doubtless have involved breaking the toilet further while insisting he knew what he was doing, before finally calling in a plumber about a week later, muttering that he *had* known how to fix it, he just hadn't had the special tool the plumber had. But even so, at least she might not have been quite as frazzled and pulled in four directions at once by the two children, Sadie, her mother-in-law and the stupid, fucking, broken toilet.

Claire slumped on the stairs, head in her hands in despair, and Sadie gave her a sympathetic lick.

'I know, darling,' sniffed Claire, 'I've been ignoring you. But I need to get this fixed, because the damn thing is still dripping water onto the floor, even though it's not been flushed in hours, and the only way I've found to stop it is to turn off all the water in the house. Now that's all very well, but we can't use the garden as a toilet like you, and it will be frowned upon if I hose the children down with the outside tap instead of letting them wash indoors. It's true, we can be strong, independent women all we like, but the chips are down, we *do* need a drains man! Oh God, *why* won't any of these plumbers answer their phones?'

Sadie looked at Claire gravely. She didn't know why the plumbers wouldn't answer. But she hated seeing Claire upset. Claire got up and squelched back into the loo to stare at the recalcitrant toilet despondently.

'MUUUUUUUUM,' came another bellow from outside the door.

'WHAT NOW?' yelled Claire.

'I THINK I CAN FIX IT!' Lucas yelled back.

'How?' Claire demanded, wrenching the door open to find Lucas there brandishing a sink plunger and his iPad.

'I've been googling it,' announced Lucas. 'I can unblock it with this.'

'But that's a sink plunger?'

'Yes, but it'll work on a toilet too,' Lucas insisted. 'There's loads of YouTube videos about it. I've watched quite a few and I know what I'm doing.'

Claire sighed. She wasn't sure she really had many other options left, apart from ringing Andrew to ask for help, and she was damned if she was going to do that. And after all, she thought to herself, what was the worst that could happen? A small voice whispered that the worst that could happen was that Lucas could make the entire situation worse, completely break the toilet and flood the house even more, and then she'd be beyond the aid of just a plumber and would probably have to claim on her house insurance. Then the insurance man would ask what had happened and Claire would have to explain that she'd let her ten-year-old son try to fix the loo with the aid of a YouTube video, and the insurance man would laugh sardonically and turn down her claim on the spot. This would mean she'd probably just have to burn the house down or something because it would be in such a state of disrepair, but that was arson, so she'd undoubtedly end up in prison and the children might get taken into care. But *apart* from that, Claire reasoned, what was the worst that could happen?

'Go on then,' she said, with some trepidation.

Lucas approached the toilet with the air of an expert. He plunged vigorously several times, splashing a great quantity of toilet water over himself, the floor and the walls. Nothing happened. He plunged again a couple of times, and the loo gave out an almighty gurgle. Claire tensed, unsure if the gurgle was things going down or coming back up. But her lack of faith was misplaced. The toilet was draining and Lucas was looking extremely smug.

'Oh my God, you fixed it,' said Claire in wonder.

'It's easy when you know how,' said Lucas airily.

'But why did it keep overflowing even when it wasn't being flushed?' said Claire.

'Ah, that's probably because the cistern was dripping into the bowl. I'll have to adjust the float before you turn the water back on. If that doesn't work, I'll need you to take me to B&Q to get some new seals and washers.'

'OK,' said Claire. 'Whatever you need.'

Going to B&Q with Lucas was not quite the japes and frolics she'd planned, but it seemed like an excellent substitute for the apocalyptic scenario she'd been envisioning just moments ago.

As it turned out, adjusting the float fixed the dripping too, much to Lucas's disappointment. Sensing weakness in his mother, however, he persuaded her to take him to B&Q regardless. Now that he was a fully fledged YouTube qualified plumber he found her small selection of tools somewhat wanting, and insisted he needed his own equipment. Since this still worked out much cheaper than the cost of an emergency plumber on a Saturday, Claire happily agreed to his demands, much to Tabitha's indignation, until she was placated with a selection of paint charts and a promise from Claire that she'd *think* about repainting her bedroom.

21

The day before the children were due home was a trying one for Claire. Her grand plans for relaxation and pampering had gone awry on day one, when she realised it had been so long since she'd done nothing that she was no longer capable of it. She'd booked a massage, then found herself lying on the massage table growing tenser and tenser because she wasn't relaxed enough. She'd gone home and decided to gut the children's squalid pits of hell in their absence, so they'd have delightfully clean and tidy rooms waiting for them on their return.

Unfortunately, once she'd spent hours and hours picking up tiny bits of Lego and sorting L.O.L. doll accessories, she realised that the extreme tidiness of the bedrooms just showed up how shabby and grubby the walls were. So off to B&Q Claire had gone once more, having texted Andrew to instruct him to tell the children to go online and pick a paint colour, and she'd spent the rest of the week redecorating their bedrooms. She was very nearly finished when she realised she was just fractionally short of having enough paint to finish Tabitha's room. Claire cursed to herself and wished she'd not bothered moving the wardrobe to paint behind it, because she was really only lacking about a wardrobe's worth of paint. Back to B&Q it was.

Claire was standing, covered in paint and gazing longingly at the tastefully middle-class colours on offer on the Farrow & Ball shelves, instead of the lurid flamingo pink Tabitha had requested and Claire had capitulated to on the basis it was Tabitha who had to live with it, when she heard a familiar voice shriek, 'Claire! How are you? Gosh, I haven't seen you in ages. What are you doing here?'

Claire plastered on her best Bright and Cheerful Smile and turned round to beam at Jen bearing down on her, as if she'd been round for a barbecue the week before and Claire had not been cast into the chill world of Singledom alone.

'Just picking up some paint for Tabitha's room,' said Claire, Bright Smile still firmly in place.

'Oh, isn't that sweet,' said Jen. 'And lucky, lucky you, able to come out to the shops on your own! What a lovely treat.'

Jen gestured vaguely to her own offspring, who were attempting to twat the everlasting fuck out of each other with a pair of mops they'd stolen from the homeware aisle.

Claire wondered whether she should say something along the lines of, yes, wasn't she SO LUCKY that her husband had had an affair with her best friend, thus ending their marriage and leaving her attempting to rebuild her life on her own? With, might she add, no assistance from Jen et al., but what was all that compared with being able to go to B&Q by herself while her traumatised children attempted to adjust to their own new lives of being shuttled between Mummy and Daddy's houses on account of them coming from a Broken Home? Indeed, yes, she, Claire, was truly #SoBlessed. Instead, Claire settled for a non-committal 'Mmmmm …'

'It's been ages since we've seen you,' Jen said again. 'It's all such a shame, you and Andrew, isn't it? He was over last week. Tim's got the sweetest new girl who's joined his team, and she's a single gal too, so we invited her over for Andrew to meet. They seemed to get on like a house on fire!'

Claire's smile became slightly less Bright at both Jen's hideous phrase of 'single gal', and her merry revelation that she and Tim were match-making for Claire's husband. She clenched her fingers hard round the tin of paint she was holding, to prevent her from putting it down and punching Jen right in her smuggety smug face.

'Oh gosh,' Jen trilled. 'Sorry, was that tactless of me? I mean, you don't *mind*, though, do you? After all, *you're* finished with him, aren't you?'

Claire ground out furious assurances to Jen that of course she didn't mind, and absolutely she was finished with him, the Bright Smile continuing to dim considerably as she did so.

'And how *are* you?' said Jen with faux concern. 'You look … tired. Must be hard, being single again at your age. Oh! I've just had the most super idea! Once we get Andrew fixed up with someone lovely, we must do the same for you! I'll see if Tim knows any single chaps, bit more of an ask of course than finding some single gals, there's a lot of you about.' Jen pulled a rueful face and gave a little tinkling laugh. 'And then you can come to supper too, and we'll get you matched up with someone, and who knows! One day maybe Andrew and you and your new other halves can all come round together. Doesn't that sound *fun*?'

Claire, who could not help but think that sounded about as much *fun* as shitting in her hands and then clapping, made another non-committal noise.

'Do you need to find a single man for me to come to supper, though?' Claire asked, more out of curiosity than a desire to return to Jen's hand-painted kitchen to eat Seitan Surprise at her fugly expensive marble dining table while Jen and Tim pretended they hadn't just had a massive row before everyone arrived.

Jen looked at Claire blankly. 'Well, yes,' she said in confusion. 'Because otherwise it would be all couples … and you. That would be odd. All couples. And a single woman. It would mess up the *Boggle* teams afterwards.'

'Of course,' said Claire. 'The *Boggle* teams. Silly me, I wasn't thinking. Anyway' – she held up her paint tin again – 'better go. Need to get this finished before Tabitha's home tomorrow.'

'Oh yes,' said Jen, looking relieved. 'Bye then. If I hear of any nice single men, I'll give you a ring. Rafferty! Barnaby! Stop that!'

And Jen took off in pursuit of her little darlings, who had progressed to trying to knock over a Ronseal display by walloping paint sample pots at it with their mops.

Claire's emotions were mixed as she drove home. There was an element of relief, that she no longer had to convince herself that she really liked Jen, and also a lot of hurt that Jen hadn't so much as suggested they went and got a cup of coffee together sometime. It seemed that until Claire could be safely paired up with some 'lovely chap', she was still persona non grata, fit only to be a pawn in Jen's matchmaking game. Mostly, though, there was rage at the sheer *effrontery* of Jen, going around offering up Andrew as a prize in said game. Andrew was *Claire's*. And just because she might not want him, that didn't mean she wanted anyone else to have him, let alone a 'sweet girl' from fucking Tim's team.

If and when Andrew happened to meet someone on his own, that was one thing. But Jen, who was supposed to be Claire's friend, pimping him out to all and sundry was quite another thing. And why? Had Andrew asked her to do this? Had he announced he was ready to move on and please line up the ladies for him to take his pick, since as Jen had so kindly pointed out, single men were at a far higher premium than single women at this point in life, and, as Lucy had reminded Claire, Andrew was still quite hot?

Claire was still thinking about her old friends as she finished painting Tabitha's room. Seeing Jen had stirred up memories of their old busy social life, and she couldn't help but wonder if the frenetic pace of their lives was partly what had driven Claire and Andrew apart. Or was the constant whirl of people and events and socialising a vain attempt to cover up the fact that there wasn't much of a marriage left – that they were just two people who shared a house and a couple of kids?

As long as they were busy, busy, busy, doing the same as everyone else, going on the right holidays, sending their children to do the right hobbies, cooking the right show-off dinner-party food from the right Ottolenghi cookbook, they never had to look at their relationship and think about what was lacking. When was the last time they'd had a *proper* conversation about anything, for instance? Even that last good night talking about their retirement had hardly been an in-depth discussion. And what about that extended dry patch in their sex life, which had become more arid than Claire's mouth after drinking sambuca with Lucy? As long as they were busy, they could pretend everything was fine. And maybe, Claire thought, while trying to get splatters of pink paint off the light switch with a wet wipe, that was why Julia and Jen and all the others had been so quick to distance themselves from her.

The end of Andrew and Claire's marriage made them the boat rockers, the ones disturbing the comfortable status quo, and to get involved in the breakdown of Claire and Andrew's relationship would mean their friends might have to examine their own comfortable, white-washed, middle-class, miserable lives too.

Claire wondered if she was any better than them, though, deep down. She'd been happy enough to judge them post-holidays and feel smugly superior. She'd known her marriage was not in a good place, had known she wasn't happy, but she hadn't done anything about it until her hand was forced. Had it not been for the perfidy of Andrew and Emily, instead of being covered in pink paint, even now she'd probably be getting ready to go out for an evening of agreeing that yes, you really do get what you pay for, and no, it was never too early to start thinking about tutors, was it?

And if it had been someone else who'd upset the apple cart? If, say, Jen had stood up one day and hurled a Sophie Conran plate full of swede gnocchi with miso butter at the wall and screamed that if she had to spend one more night listening to Tim snoring she'd go mad, and that was IT, she was OFF, would Claire have reacted any differently than everyone had to her?

Would she also have been embarrassed and angry at Jen for making her look at the deficiencies in her own marriage, and instead of admitting that her outwardly perfect marriage was also crumbling and possibly having to face up to hard truths and hard work to fix it, would she have just frozen Jen out and pretended she had never existed and nothing had ever happened? Claire would like to think no, she wouldn't have been so shallow. But in her heart of hearts, she wasn't so sure.

'Fuck,' she thought, as she realised she'd been so deep in thought that she'd forgotten to stop rollering the wall when she reached the ceiling and had painted a long pink stripe over it, and would now have to go back to B&Q for stain block and more white paint.

All in all, by that evening Claire wasn't in the best mood, slumped on the sofa with Sadie and an enormous glass of red, when the door-bell rang unexpectedly. She huffed crossly into the hall, expecting a double-glazing salesman or Jehovah's Witnesses. Instead, Emily stood on the doorstep, soaked by the pouring rain and shivering.

'Please don't slam the door,' said Emily quickly. 'Just two minutes, that's all I need. Please, Claire, please.'

In fact, Claire's first feeling on seeing Emily was joy – far more joy than when Jen had appeared in B&Q – and she had to resist the urge to fling her arms around her and drag her in for a glass of wine and a good chat. But Emily's plea for her not to the slam the door was a brutal reminder of where things stood between them.

Sadie peered round Claire's legs and studied Emily suspiciously as she rooted through her bag. Sadie was unsure what to make of Emily. She gave a small bark, and Emily looked up.

'Oh Claire! You got a dog!' Emily cried. 'You wanted one for so long, and a Staffie too. She's just beautiful, aren't you, darling? What's her name?'

This was very unfair, thought Claire. Emily was not supposed to say Sadie was beautiful. It made it even more difficult to hate her, as how could anyone who recognised Sadie's intrinsic wonderfulness at first sight be a bad person?

'Sadie,' said Claire grudgingly.

'Sadie! Hello, sweetheart. Hello. You are lovely, aren't you? Aren't you just? Aren't you just the bestest girl?' crooned Emily, extending her hand for Sadie to sniff. Sadie thumped her tail approvingly, and shuffled out from behind Claire to say hello to Emily properly.

'Emily, what do you want? Sadie, stop being so disloyal,' snapped Claire to a blissfully beaming Sadie as Emily scratched her ears.

'Sorry, sorry, I just wanted to give you these, but I put them right at the bottom of the bag so they didn't get wet, because I wanted to make sure the kids weren't here first so it wasn't awkward for them. But I can't find them …'

'For Christ's sake, you'd better come in for a minute,' sighed Claire. 'Sadie's getting wet with all this carry-on.'

Claire stepped back for Emily to come into the hall, but Sadie had other ideas and belted into the sitting room where she had a nice snug blanket on the sofa, and barked imperiously for them to follow her. This was Sadie's new trick. She didn't like Claire being in another room, but she also liked her blanket, so she had taken to barking to get Claire to come and see her, which obviously Claire did, so Sadie barked more to summon her, and so it went on.

'Is she OK?' asked Emily anxiously.

Sadie barked again.

'She wants us to go through,' said Claire. 'We'd better go, or she'll get stressed.'

'Is she a rescue?' babbled Emily nervously. 'I'm honestly so happy for you that you've finally got a dog, and she's perfect.'

Sadly, Claire remembered that Emily genuinely did love dogs, and it had always been a great source of disappointment in their youth that Lydia had insisted that it wasn't fair to leave a dog alone in their flat while they were out all day, and that Emily had always travelled too much for work to get one when she left home. Really, thought Claire, Sadie was being *very* disloyal. She wasn't meant to remember any good points about Emily, and Sadie was not exactly helping.

In the sitting room, Sadie smugly surveyed them from the sofa, delighted she had so easily trained her human slaves to do her bidding, and Emily gazed round in surprise.

'Where's all your *stuff*?' she said. 'The pictures from that wall and the clock on the mantelpiece?'

'They were Andrew's grandmother's,' said Claire, 'so he took them for his new flat. That's what happens when people are getting divorced, didn't you realise? They don't just lose their marriage and their partner, they usually lose half their possessions as well, and in many cases their home, though thankfully it hasn't come to that. Yet.'

'Oh shit,' muttered Emily, as she looked around again. 'I never … I didn't mean to … and all your photo albums, Claire, where are they? Surely he didn't take *them*?'

'I burnt them,' said Claire bleakly.

'You *burnt* them?' wailed Emily in horror. 'But Claire, why? They had so many memories. And they were the only old photos you had, after the removal men lost all your other boxes of photos when you moved here.'

Claire shrugged. 'I didn't want to be reminded of most of the memories in the albums. Of *you*! How can this surprise you?'

'I know, of course, of course, you wouldn't want to be reminded of me, but there weren't just photos of me in there. There were photos of all the parties, of everyone from school, of the school dances, and the taffeta dresses, and the university balls, and so many things. The kids' christenings and birthday parties. And now they're all gone. I'm so sorry, Claire.'

Claire, who had actually rather regretted her impromptu bonfire as soon as it was too late to rescue anything, and wished she'd just cut Emily out of the photos instead, didn't really want reminding by Emily, of all people, that she'd been wrong.

'What do you want, Emily? Why are you here?'

Emily finally extracted a crumpled envelope from her bag and held it out to Claire.

'It's tickets for *The Lion King*,' she said. 'It's touring, and I promised Lucas and Tabitha last Christmas that I'd get tickets and take them when it came nearby. They were so excited, and I didn't want them to miss out. I booked them last year, but they've only just posted out the actual tickets. There's three tickets.'

'Are you seriously proposing taking my children to the theatre?' asked Claire, incredulously.

'No, of course not,' said Emily. 'But I thought you could? It's supposed to be a great production, and I thought they might enjoy it. I miss them. I just … it might be fun for them. For the three of you. Like I said, I promised them. It was supposed to be their belated

Christmas present. I know you hate me, Claire, but it would be a shame for them to miss out, especially Tabitha. You know how much she loves *The Lion King* – she knows all the words to the songs.'

Claire did indeed know. She'd had to listen to Tabitha's, in truth rather tuneless, renditions many times.

'I can't take these. Is this just to try to make yourself feel better?'

'Oh please, Claire. It just seems such a shame for the tickets to go to waste, when the children would enjoy it so much. God, nothing would make me feel better about any of this. Nothing. I've made such a mess of things, I've made such a mess for you, and I'll never, ever stop being sorry for that. You're not really going to lose the house, are you?'

'No. He's being quite decent about that, and says I can stay here. And your mum found me a good lawyer if he does change his mind and decide to be a dick about things.'

'Oh, that's good! I was so relieved when Mum said she'd put you in touch with someone, though.'

Suddenly Claire's anger exploded into life and the rage starting burning.

'Emily, you're literally the reason my marriage ended, how can you have the NERVE to be "relieved" I have a good lawyer? I wouldn't even NEED a lawyer if it wasn't for you. How could you DO this to me?'

'I don't know,' said Emily in a small voice. 'I honestly don't. I didn't think any of this would happen.'

'Jesus fucking CHRIST, Emily, are you stupid? What did you think would happen? You slept with my husband! And deceived me and betrayed me every single bloody time you texted him, and worse than that, every single time you looked me in the eye while you were sending him dirty photos of yourself and pretending to be my friend.'

'I wasn't pretending,' sobbed Emily. 'I wasn't. I was your friend, I am your friend, you just always had *everything* and I wanted that too.'

'How did I have everything? What did I have that you didn't? Look at you. And look at me. How can you say *I* had everything? Lydia and Martin bought you anything and everything you ever wanted. You were spoiled rotten.'

'I didn't want all that stuff. I wanted what you had, a normal family. Tessa and Jonathan. Mark. The dogs. The cats. I wanted people to look at me like they did you.'

'What are you on about?'

'People look at you differently to how they look at me. They always have – the girls at school, men, everyone.'

'Stop feeling so sorry for yourself. Every single time we've ever gone out, you've been surrounded by men, buying you drinks, asking you to dance. I felt like the ugly sister standing next to you, so don't give me that bullshit.'

'Men would come over because I've big tits and long blonde hair. And once they started talking to us, who did they ask out? Who did they want to keep talking to, when they just wanted to get me drunk and into bed? You. Because people like you. They just like you, and they don't like me like that, and I've always just wanted people to like me the way they liked you straightaway. No one ever liked me like that, except you. And making friends was easy for you. I was always scared you were about to go off and leave me and I'd be on my own, and now you have and it's all my faaaaullllt.'

Emily ended on a snotty howl reminiscent of a thwarted toddler, and Claire just about resisted the urge to slap her extremely hard.

'What are you talking about?' said Claire in confusion. 'People like you too.'

'Because I was your friend. And they don't like me like they like you. Men *like* me, but not enough to marry me. Not the way they always liked you. Mostly they just wanted to fuck me. That's why I'm "Poor Emily" now, that's what everyone whispers. "Poor Emily. She's pretty enough, I can't understand why she can't keep a man. Poor Emily."'

Claire realised guiltily that even she on occasion had said this about Emily. And there was a tiny bit of her that couldn't help but be pleased that Emily thought people liked her better than herself.

Emily was still crying, so Claire handed her a box of tissues, because she could hardly thrust her out into the street wailing like a randy tomcat. The neighbours would all be peering out to see what was going on, and Colonel Mousicles would probably attack, thinking his patch was being encroached upon, and then Claire would have to endure another lecture from his owner about how very Sensitive and Highly Strung he was.

Claire suddenly decided that since Emily was here, and because she was already having a fairly miserable day, she might as well push the issue of the affair, and maybe finally get some answers.

'I keep asking myself this, but what did you think would happen? How did you possibly think this could end any other way? Did you think I wouldn't find out? Did you think I'd find out and go, "Oh hey, no worries, Emily, you can borrow my husband just like you borrowed my Tiffany earrings," only you broke them and fucked it all up too, didn't you? WHAT DID YOU THINK WOULD HAPPEN?'

'I don't know. I don't know what I thought. I suppose I thought you wouldn't care. All you ever did was moan about him – how he didn't pull his weight in the house, how annoying his breathing was, why did he wear those fleeces. You didn't seem to want him. And when I met him that night, he was so nice. I'd always been jealous of him taking up your time, but I'd just had such a shit date, and he was so kind and he listened to me, and he wasn't at all like how you'd made him out to be, and I didn't think you'd even be bothered.'

'You didn't think I'd be bothered? Because sometimes I needed someone to vent to, because relationships are hard, and sometimes we need a moan about our partners, so you thought I wouldn't mind, just because I said he never took the fucking bins out until I asked him to? Emily, do you even remember when we were fifteen, and Jake Crosby broke up with you, and then at Tara Lewis's birthday party he snogged me, *he* snogged *me*, remember – I was not a willing participant in the embrace, but it was the nineties – and yet you were SO FUCKING ANGRY AT ME! Because a horrible spotty youth that had already dumped you had come up to me and stuck his tongue down my throat in the queue for the loo, but you still were furious and blamed me *even though I hadn't done anything*, and yet despite that, you thought "I wouldn't care" if you SHAGGED MY FUCKING HUSBAND!'

'Oh God, I know, I know. It was so stupid of me, but we got through that, Claire, we were still friends despite Jake Crosby, weren't we?'

'This isn't even slightly the same thing. How can you imply it is? Emily, how many times do I have to say this? You slept with MY HUSBAND! Worse than that, you came to my house, days before you screwed him. You sat here with me, laughing and joking and drinking my wine, like you weren't planning on destroying my life later in the week. How could you do that? How? That's what I don't understand, really. Not why but *how* you could do this to me?'

'I wasn't going to go through with it. With Andrew. I was getting cold feet. I knew he was your husband, I knew it was wrong. And I hadn't seen you in weeks, you'd been so busy, I was almost able to pretend it was all a bit abstract, you, me, Andrew. And then the closer it got, the more I realised this was happening, and I wanted to stop it and I didn't want to stop it. I knew it was wrong, but I wanted so much for one night to feel like you, not to be Poor Emily, to be the one someone wanted most. But it would be so wrong, to do that with him, but I didn't think I'd be strong enough not to do it, because at the same time I wanted to so much, I wanted to see how it felt to be *you*.

'And then I thought, I'll go and see Claire, and that'll be it. I *won't* be able to do it when I've seen Claire, it will make it all real, what I'm going to do. And I wasn't going to. We had such a nice night. But then Andrew came home and you were just so indifferent to him. You looked at him, talked to him like he was barely there, just another irritation in your life, and I thought, "Sod it, Claire really won't care."'

'So you just, what, decided it was OK to shag my husband because I wasn't thrilled enough when he came home? What would have changed your mind? If I'd flung myself into his arms shouting, "Darling, life has been meaningless without you"? If he'd bent me over the hall table for a quicky while you put the bottles in the recycling? Marriage is *hard*, Emily, and you don't know anything about it, and yet you decided to destroy mine without having the least understanding of how it feels to live with someone for fifteen years, day in, day out.'

'Well, thank you so much for reminding me of that,' said Emily tartly, 'lest I ever forget my place as Poor Emily. Admit it, you felt superior, didn't you? Because you'd managed the husband and children, and I hadn't!'

'No,' said Claire, blushing through the lie. 'Anyway, even if I did, what gave you the right to take my husband and wreck my children's lives?'

'You're right,' said Emily. 'You're right. And why shouldn't you have felt superior? You had your life all together, whereas mine was just a car crash largely due to my own bad decisions. And here we are again – it's still a car crash, due to the worst decision I ever made, and I've lost my best friend, which is the worst thing that's ever happened to me.'

'And me,' choked out Claire. 'And most of the time I was jealous of your so-called car-crash life, your freedom, your clothes, that never had mysterious sticky marks from children on them.'

'It isn't all that. And I guess neither was yours all those times when I was feeling so jealous of you.'

'No,' said Claire sadly. 'It wasn't. Maybe we weren't as honest with each other as we thought we were.'

'Maybe we just didn't listen properly. I've missed you so much.'

Claire was properly crying now, as was Emily.

'I've missed you too. But Emily, I can't go back. To how we were. This … it's all been too much.'

Emily sniffed and blew her nose. 'I know. I mean, I'd hoped, of course. But deep down I knew. I wish it was different.'

'Christ, so do I.'

'You know I'll never forgive myself for any of this. For being so selfish. So self-centred. I wouldn't even mind how much it hurt *me* for the rest of my life, if it meant you hadn't been hurt by this.'

'Oh, stop being so fucking melodramatic,' said Claire with a laugh, through the tears. 'You always were one for lurid speeches.'

'Sorry,' said Emily with a half-laugh cry too. 'Sorry about all of it. But it's not all bad, is it? Only you look great, Claire.'

'I saw Jen in B&Q today and she told me I looked tired!'

'Jen's a cunt,' said Emily indignantly. 'Always has been, always will be. Seriously, you look amazing. Better than you have in ages. Not that you looked bad. But you look less stressed. And you've got

Sadie. You always wanted a dog so much and Andrew would never agree to it, so maybe one day you can forgive me, even if we can't be friends again?'

Claire looked at Emily, and thought of all the hate and bitterness of the last months, and all the happy years between them before that, and all the misunderstandings and half-truths that had led them to this place.

Claire nodded slowly. 'Maybe,' she said. 'Not right now, but maybe one day.'

'Thank you,' said Emily with a tearful smile. 'I should probably go now. I just want to say one more time how sorry I am, and how much I love you. I hope you're happy, Claire, and I hope life gives you everything you deserve, because you didn't deserve Andrew or me. You ought to have a wonderful life, filled with people as amazing as you, and I really, really hope you do. Bye. And bye, gorgeous, look after your mum, she's a special one, like you.'

Emily paused to scratch Sadie's ears as she walked out the room, and out of Claire's life.

After Emily had left, Claire slumped on the sofa and cried very, very hard. She had not cried like this since the first days after she found out about Emily and Andrew. Sadie sat anxiously beside her, licking her face in an attempt to provide comfort, and helpfully removed the last few traces of Tabitha's pink paint that the tears had not washed off. Claire finally wiped her eyes, feeling that strange, drained, calm sensation you only get after a really epic bawl, and gave Sadie a big hug.

'She was right, you know.' She sniffed into Sadie's head. 'At least I've got you.'

As Claire cried on, she thought about some of the things Emily had said. How Emily hadn't thought she'd care. About how indifferent she was to Andrew sometimes. Claire hadn't been indifferent to him, of course she hadn't. She had loved him very much – he was the father of her children. But the last few years, *had* she tried as hard as she could for their marriage? All this time she had been blaming the whole thing on him, but could any of the fault have been hers? Had she really made enough time for him, for Andrew as a person, for them as a couple? Or had she been so busy trying to claw out a little bit of time for herself that she'd forgotten about him?

That had been one of Andrew's unkinder comments, during the many rows after Claire found out about Emily, that cut her to the quick – that Emily had at least had time for him. It was doubly painful because, after all, it was *Claire* that Emily was supposed to have time for. 'And whose fault was it that we had no time for each other anyway?' she'd shouted back, before pointing out that maybe if Andrew was that upset about Claire not having time for him, he should have done something slightly more constructive about it than fucking Emily to make himself feel better.

But at the same time, Claire now realised, she could have done something about it too. She could have said no to the constant presence of friends, to the dinners and barbecues and holidays. Andrew enjoyed them, of course, but if Claire had said no, they needed time to themselves, he wouldn't have objected. But Claire hadn't. Because deep down, perhaps, she too was afraid of what she and Andrew would find in their marriage when all the distractions and noise ceased. And increasingly, in recent years, when Claire had felt lonely or anxious or in need of someone to talk to, it had been Emily she'd automatically turn to, not Andrew. It was, however, Claire thought crossly, disliking this chain of thought, still *mostly* Andrew and Emily's faults – after all, he was every bit as guilty as she was for not prioritising their marriage, but he was the one who had decided to screw her best friend as a panacea, and Emily certainly could have said no. And if some of the blame lay on Claire for how this all arose, how could she fully continue hating them with her moral indignation and righteousness?

'I fucking hate being a grown-up,' Claire told Sadie. 'Really, it's pants. You don't know how lucky you are to have no concept of guilt or blame.'

Sadie licked Claire's hand in agreement, and suggested croissants might be a good cure for such a tangle of emotions.

22

The next day, Claire had to go to Lucy's life-drawing class. She'd been very tempted to cry off after Emily's visit, but once she was there, she was glad she hadn't. Alone in the house, it was easy to think you were the only one having a bad day, but it turned out everyone else was too.

While they were waiting for the model to appear, Kate had related her mother-in-law's tears and woe because Kate had failed to remember that today was the anniversary of the day that Susan had done a triathlon, and how could she be so thoughtless as to have forgotten that, such a great achievement, and not rung Susan's mother to talk about how proud her mother had been of her, or better still, gone to see her mother so they could have looked at photos of her doing the triathlon and her other sporting achievements, because Susan had been so good at sport.

'Susan hated sport, and I hadn't even met her when she did the triathlon, which she insisted was the stupidest thing she ever did. Her mother loathes me, though, that's the thing. She never ceases reminding me I stole Susan's childbearing years from her. I know she's grieving and feels guilty, but for Christ's sake, doesn't she realise I'm grieving too? And feeling guilty that Susan and I didn't have a baby, that I don't have some part of her left? God knows what she'd do if I ever did have a baby on my own.'

'She wouldn't help? See you as a surrogate daughter?' asked Claire.

'God, no. She'd just go on and on about Susan at best, or have a coronary on the spot at worst. I'm probably doomed to a barren life because I don't want my mother-in-law's death on my conscience. Maybe I should just get a cat instead of pretending to have one to leave book clubs early.'

'Yes! Get a cat!' said Lucy enthusiastically. 'Or better still, a Border terrier! They're dogs that are clearly part cat, so it's like having both! And Bingo has never fucked me over like men have. I mean, he did do a shit in my raspberry LK Bennett court shoe, but still, give me dogs any day!'

'Another bad internet dating experience?' asked Kate.

'When will I learn? If a man is holding a fish in his profile picture, steer well clear! But every time I tell myself, well, maybe *this* man is perfectly nice, and just happens to really like fishing, rather than casual misogyny.'

'What happened?'

'Dick pic from an incredibly creative angle that managed to incorporate his arsehole. I didn't even know it was anatomically possible to take such a photo of yourself. Of course, I'm *assuming* it was a selfie. I was out when he sent it, so it was a couple of hours before I saw it and blocked him, so I also got a barrage of abuse between his sending and my blocking because I hadn't immediately responded to this marvellous work of art by sending nudes in gratitude. Anyway, I only mention it due to the very unusual angle. I've become almost immune to dick pics and men telling me I'm an ugly slut because I won't show them my tits. I'm definitely over internet dating. I know I say that every time, but this time I really mean it. Dogs are the way forward. Anyway, Claire, you're very quiet. What's new with you?'

Claire took a deep breath and said, 'Emily came round.'

'Emily? Horrible husband-stealing ex-best friend Whore of Babylon Emily?' chuntered Lucy.

'Yes. She brought round tickets to *The Lion King* that she'd apparently promised the children.'

'The two-faced slapper thought she could take your kids on a nice day out?'

'No, they were for me to take them.'

'Lucky, they're bloody expensive. Are you going to go?'

'I don't know. She left the tickets on the mantelpiece.'

'If you're not going to use them, can I have them?'

'LUCY!'

'Sorry, Mary, but you don't ask, you don't get! I just thought it would be a shame for them to go to waste, that's all. Anyway, she came round to give you the tickets. Was that all?'

'No, she came in – it was raining so hard – and Sadie was trying to say hello and getting wet and Emily couldn't find the tickets, so she came in, to keep Sadie dry, and then she kept trying to say she was sorry, and all this time I've just wanted to know *why* she did it. If I knew why, maybe I could understand. So I asked her.'

'And what did she say? Did she say, "Because I'm the Worst Person in the World?" asked Lucy, agog.

'No. She said a lot about wanting to be more like me and thinking I didn't care about Andrew. I still don't really understand how or why she could do it. I'm not sure she really understands it herself. I felt sorry for her. She asked me to forgive her.'

'WHAT?'

Claire sighed. 'Do you know what? I think I'm going to.'

'But Claire, you can't!'

'She did such a terrible thing.'

'No, no, don't let her guilt you into this.'

'Why do you want to forgive her, Claire?' asked Kate.

'I don't know. Because she was my best friend? Because we've so much history?' said Claire. 'Don't get me wrong. I'm not going to go back to being friends with her. I probably won't even tell her I've forgiven her. But we were friends for too long, I hate hating her.'

'I think you're right,' said Kate. 'As long as you hate Emily and are angry with her, she's still controlling your life and emotions. If you forgive her and let it all go, you're in charge of that. You're in charge of your life again. Sorry, I did lots of reading about moving on and letting go and anger management after Susan died. There was a fair bit about taking charge of things you can control and letting go of things you can't. But I think this is a really healthy thing for Claire to be doing.'

'Do you? It's still hard, to let it go. Especially when she still couldn't really give me a solid reason why she did it.'

'Sometimes there are just no reasons. Shit simply goes down. I think that's why people turn to religion, isn't it?' said Lucy. 'It offers reasons for things, it's God's will or part of his plan, or of course there's a reason but only God knows. That's why I got thrown out of Sunday school. I just couldn't get on board with a god that let all this crap happen, for mysterious reasons of his own, and we were just to accept it was all God's plan. Pointing out that a plan that let millions of children die from starvation or that had let the Holocaust happen was maybe a bit of a bollocks plan went down quite badly, actually.'

'SHHHHH,' said the art teacher lady. 'Neville, we're ready for you, if you'd like to come out.'

'What did your Sunday school teachers do?' asked Mary, 'when you told them you didn't believe in God because he let too much shit happen to possibly exist?'

'Mostly they just shouted "INEFFABLE" at me. "Why are there famines, if God is so fabulous?" "INEFFABLE." "Why did that child that I saw on the news get murdered?" "INEFFABLE." "Why is there a gender pay gap, why weren't women allowed to vote for so long, why are women forced to shoulder the burden of emotional and domestic labour, why are there so few women at senior levels in STEM subjects?" "Ooh, those ones aren't ineffable, they're Eve's fault for eating the apple." "Why am I destined to grow up to a life-time of oppression by the patriarchy just because some imaginary bint quite fancied a Granny Smith?" "For fuck's sake, Lucy, because it's FUCKING INEFFABLE!"'

'Did your Sunday school teacher really tell you it was "fucking ineffable"?' said Claire in astonishment.

'SHHHHHH!' said the art teacher again. 'You'll distract the others with this chatter. Our model is ready now. Come along, Neville.'

'No, of course not. It's, like, against the Sunday School Teachers' Charter to swear at the little darlings. It would make the Baby Jesus sad. Mostly they just told me to stop asking questions or I wouldn't get a sweetie at the end.'

'And did you?'

'For a bit. They had Quality Street. That's how they lure you in, you see. Oh fuck!' said Lucy, as the life model sauntered to the front of the room, clad in a rather grubby towelling robe.

'Oh fuck,' echoed Claire and Kate, as Stinky Neville from the book group flung off his robe and revealed himself in his full glory, smirking as he did so.

'What does "ineffable" actually mean?' asked Mary.

'Do you know, I've no idea. I always thought it meant "Don't ask me any more questions."'

'It means "incapable of being expressed in words",' Kate said. 'Like my feelings at the prospect of having to draw Neville's penis!'

On cue, Neville leered at the class, and, spotting Claire, Kate and Lucy at the back, winked lasciviously at them.

'What's wrong?' hissed Mary.

'It's Stinky Neville from the book group where we met Kate,' Claire whispered.

'The one who called you "fair wenches"?'

'Yes.'

'BE QUIET!' snapped the art teacher, 'or I shall have to ask you to LEAVE,' as Lucy gave a moan of despair and Claire dissolved into giggles. Once she started, she couldn't stop. A combination of Neville's extremely unimpressive appendage and sitting at the back of the classroom in trouble again, just like she was fifteen once more, had quite overcome her.

'I can't,' she sobbed through tears of laughter. 'I can't draw it.'

'Right,' the art teacher thundered, looming over them. 'This is your last warning.'

Claire pulled herself together and attempted to deconstruct Neville into simply planes and angles to be drawn. It was quite difficult as he kept scratching himself, and Claire kept dissolving into silent hysterics again, as did the rest of the Sisterhood, judging by the suppressed snorts and shaking shoulders.

Afterwards, they compared their drawings. They'd all pretended to run out of time before any 'details' could be added.

'Oh, that was awful!' said Claire. 'Awful but fun! Can we not do it again, though? Or at least can we go to a different class, because I'm not sure we'll be allowed back into that one?'

'Knowing my luck, the next class will probably have Morag as a substitute teacher, urging us to sculpt our own vulvas,' said Lucy, still wiping tears of laughter from her eyes. 'But you're right. It was grim, although I did enjoy the laugh.'

'I wish I'd started trying new things years ago,' said Claire. 'Maybe that's what forgiving Emily should be counted as – trying a new thing.'

'If you forgive Emily, will you forgive Andrew?' asked Kate.

'I suppose so,' said Claire thoughtfully. 'I might make a wax effigy of him and stick pins in it first, though …'

'Maybe that's what was wrong with Neville,' said Mary with a shudder. 'All that scratching …'

'Ugh,' said Claire. 'That means some poor soul has sculpted … that … oh shit! He's coming out. Run! I feel itchy looking at him.'

'Cooooeeeee! Ladies! Remember me? What about that drink?' yodelled Neville after them hopefully, still scratching vigorously.

23

A week later, Claire came home from work to find a parcel sitting inside the porch. She opened it and found a large bundle of old plastic photo albums, and some newer-looking, smarter ones, and some large envelopes. There was a note on top.

Dear Claire,

I couldn't bear the thought that you had lost all your photos and memories because of me. I've been through mine, and taken out all the photos of me. And I've been through all my old photos that were still at Mum's and put in all the best ones. I took most of them, so I wasn't in them, so that was easy. Please, please accept this. I've taken enough from you; you deserve the photos. I know this doesn't make up for anything, but I thought you might like to have them. We wore some terrible clothes in the nineties.

    All my love, always.

    Emily

PS I don't know if you got the invitation to the school reunion, I assume so, but I just wanted to say, I'm not going. If you want to go.

True to her word, there was not a single photograph of Emily. Claire sobbed again as she looked through the photos, overwhelmed with happiness at having them back, and sadness that Emily wasn't there laughing over them with her. There were school dances and university balls, there were parties in parents' houses, and ones at dubious student flats where you could almost feel your feet sticking to the floor as you looked at the picture. There was Claire with the keys to her first flat, and her housewarming party. There were a lot of photos of Claire draped over various early-nineties youths, complete with curtains haircuts and dodgy sweatshirts, followed by a grungier vibe a few years later.

Tabitha and Lucas came in, as Claire was smiling over a photograph of her standing with her friends Elizabeth, Sarah and Lindsay and their partners at their first school dance, a sea of dangerously flammable-looking lurid taffeta skirts and velvet bodices, badly fitting tuxedos and spots poorly concealed with Rimmel's Hide the Blemish.

'What is THAT?' demanded Lucas in horror.

'It's Mummy and her friends going to a dance, when I was about fifteen,' Claire explained.

'Mum, what happened to your hair? Did you get electrocuted?' asked Tabitha anxiously, peering at the photo.

'No, darling, Mummy had a perm.'

'What's a perm? And what are you all wearing? You've got a big bow on your dress – it makes your bum look massive!'

The bow *was* rather unfortunately placed, reflected Claire, and oh for the innocence of a generation spared the knowledge of a spiral perm.

Lucas held up another photo. 'Is this you too, Mum?' he enquired in disgusted tones.

'Yes, yes, it is,' beamed Claire.

'But Mum, you're KISSING that boy.'

'I think that's Oliver Armstrong.'

'And he has his HAND on your BOOB!'

'Right, well, that's enough of these old photos,' said Claire hastily, sweeping the albums and loose photos back into the box. 'Must be bath time. Or bedtime, or something. Come on, darlings.'

'I can't believe you just went round kissing *boys*,' grumbled Lucas in appalled tones.

'I can't believe boys *wanted* to kiss her with hair like that!' said Tabitha with all the wisdom of an eight-year-old fashionista.

'Don't be so cheeky, thank you very much! And I'll have you know, Kylie had a perm like that when she was in *Neighbours*.'

'Who had a what when they were in what?'

'Oh, never mind. Go and get ready for your baths.'

After the children were in bed, Claire got out her phone and stared at it for a long time. Finally, she sighed, opened it up and unblocked Emily's number. She texted 'Thank you' and hoped Emily wouldn't see this as the thin end of the wedge and start trying to contact her all the time again. Two minutes later, her phone buzzed with a text that simply said 'XXX'. She left Emily's number unblocked, but there was nothing more from her. And on Saturday, to Tabitha and Lucas's joy, she took them to see *The Lion King*.

24

Claire dithered for a long time about whether or not to go to the school reunion. There had been reunions before, but she had never bothered to go, assuming it would be full of Getting-a-Pony-Mirandas and Head-Girl-Hatties all smugly congratulating each other about their perfect lives. But in the spirit of Kate's insistence that they all needed new experiences, and remembering, looking through Emily's albums, how many people she *had* liked at school and had lost touch with who might be there, she decided to go to the reunion and throw caution to the winds. What was the worst that could happen? She'd be stuck talking to Miranda Johnson all night.

Claire still quite regularly stalked Miranda online, along with anyone else she could find with poor privacy settings, and had discovered thanks to her Facebook profile that although they had *not*, in fact, got a pony (little Miles turned out to have allergies), these things were still the case for Miranda:

Works At: Full Time Mummy.

About: My children and my husband are my life.

Miranda's profile pictures consisted of perfect smiling photos of adorable moppets on the first day of term that Claire hoped had at least been taken in the one tidy corner of the house, or outside the front door to hide the shit tip inside, and had involved Miranda screaming, 'JUST SMILE, FOR FUCK'S SAKE, SMILE. I JUST NEED ONE DECENT PHOTO OF YOU. FUCKING HELL, WHY IS IT SO HARD TO SMILE FOR JUST ONE SECOND?' like Claire's own first-day-of-term photos. But further stalking of Miranda's Instagram account suggested not. Her tasteful home was a sea of Farrow & Ball and artisanal wooden furniture, miraculously unmarked by Sharpies, or dented by verboten indoor games of football or WWF wrestling re-enactments. Claire had been very worried about Lucas when he concussed himself after a particularly overenthusiastic demonstration of The Rock's apparently 'classic move', but at the same time, as she made a mercy dash to A&E to get him checked over, she couldn't suppress a tinge of irritation that her new coffee table would probably forever have one leg wonky now.

So it was that she had sent back the acceptance email to Head-Girl-Hattie, who was clearly still in charge of Organising Everyone Ever, despite Google revealing through a *Financial Times* interview that she now had six children, including two sets of twins, a terrifyingly high-powered job in the City of London and positions on the boards of various national charities. On reflection, Claire thought she'd much prefer to spend the night talking to Miranda than Hattie – Miranda might at least be able to provide some useful tips on how to get stains out of soft furnishings, for how else could her house look that immaculate, whereas Hattie probably had staff for such problems.

Claire agonised over what to wear even more than she had to the book club. Obviously, she needed to look FABULOUS and like she had barely aged at all, but at the same time she didn't want to appear like she was wearing something far too young for her in an effort to be hip and cool and Down with the Youth.

Unlike the book club, though, Claire now had the Sisterhood to consult as well as her mother. Kate had come to the rescue, lending Claire a little black dress (Tessa would have been delighted) of such utter exquisite simplicity that it was clearly very expensive, Kate still being able to wear nice things on account of not having sticky children. Kate also generously contributed a pair of extravagantly understated boots from her child-free wardrobe that Claire had to practise walking in. Once she had mastered that, the overall effect was of effortless elegance.

Claire had had to ask Andrew to take the children for the Friday night as she was going to stay at her parents' house after the reunion. He'd agreed, but couldn't pick them up until after work, which meant Claire had to get ready at home and then go pretty much straight to the event. Andrew's face when she opened the door and saw Claire in Kate's dress and Kate's boots was worth the bother, though.

'Wow!' he said, as the children charged down the path, shouting a casual 'Bye, Mum' behind them.

'What?' said Claire innocently.

'I just … you look … I mean, wow!'

'Oh, this old thing?'

'Where are you going anyway?'

'Out.'

'Where? Who with?'

'Friends.'

'What sort of friends? Where will you be? What if I need to contact you?'

Claire had no intention of relieving Andrew's very obvious jealousy over how good she was looking by admitting she was going to a school reunion and then would be going to bed under her Laura Ashley duvet in her parents' house. Let him think she was going off to be ravished by some hunk. With a huge penis.

Claire looked at him and smiled sweetly. 'You don't need to know where I am, Andrew, and frankly it's none of your business.'

'What if something happens to one of the children and I need to get hold of you?'

'You can call me.'

'What if one of the children wants to talk to you?'

'They can call me.'

'What if I want to talk to you?'

'What about?'

'I don't know.' Andrew looked at Claire sadly. 'You're going on a date, aren't you?' he said mournfully. 'Oh, Claire. You're moving on.'

'Andrew, please. Yes, I'm moving on, but that involves more than just going on dates, you know.'

'So you're *not* going on a date?'

'No.'

Andrew's face became immediately more cheerful.

'But I might go on a date.'

He looked deflated again.

'Anyway, I really have stuff to do now, and your children are waiting for you in the car. Thank you for taking them, I really appreciate it. Byeeeee!'

'Ha,' thought Claire, as she waved them off. 'Take THAT, sweet girl from Tim's team!'

Claire loaded Sadie and her bags into the car, dropped Sadie off to stay with Lucy and Bingo for the night, and set off for Tessa and Jonathan's.

Being dropped off outside the school by her dad made Claire feel like a schoolgirl herself. All she needed was a pot of Body Shop cherry lip balm and a squirt of ex·cla·ma'tion perfume, which, smelling as it did of peach schnapps, had once been considered the very height of sophistication.

'I feel a bit sick,' said Claire.

'Why?' said Jonathan in surprise. 'What is there to feel sick about?'

'What if they're all super-successful and judge me? What if they all have perfect lives and families, and sneer at me for my failed marriage? What if they think I'm rubbish?'

'You're being silly,' said Jonathan briskly. 'If they're that "super-successful" they won't care about judging you. You know by now that no one has perfect lives and families; I can guarantee you're not the only one in there getting a divorce. And they didn't think you were rubbish at school, did they? Why would they think that now? Look – go in, knock 'em dead, and if it's grim I'm only in the Lion and Unicorn round the corner. Come and find me, and I'll buy you a gin and tonic and a packet of pork scratchings, then I'll walk you home. I'm ditching the car tonight anyway. Now enough of this, darling. On you go, and have a lovely time.'

The reunion was being held in the converted church next to the school, which did service as the assembly hall and gym hall, with the lunch hall downstairs in the old church's basement. As Claire walked through the doors she was met with the familiar smell of St Catherine's – dust, a hint of damp due to the Edwardian-era central heating not working very well, the stench of generations of rubber plimsolls and sweaty gym kits left abandoned too long in forgotten bags in the corner of changing rooms, and, wafting up the stairs from the lunch hall, ancient cheese sandwiches and black cherry yoghurt with the persistent whiff of boiled cabbage and baked potatoes. Claire felt her shoulders slouching forward into a teenage slump and had to make a conscious effort to pull herself back upright again. God, why were they having it *here*? Why couldn't they have the reunion in a hotel or a restaurant or something, like normal schools did?

An efficient-looking woman was sitting at a desk in the foyer as Claire came in.

'Hello!' she cried brightly as Claire approached. 'What's your name and I'll find your badge? No, wait, let me guess. And you can guess mine, it's fun!'

She clapped her hand over her left boob to cover her own name badge as she studied Claire through narrowed eyes.

'Hmmmmm,' she pondered. 'Let me see … AHA! Got it! Claire Roberts!'

'Yes, well done.'

'Oh, it was easy, you haven't changed a bit! And of course, I teach here now, so I pass all the old photos every day on the stairs so I'm reminded of all the familiar faces. Go on, now it's your turn.'

'Ummmm …' Claire was stumped. She had been going to guess Head-Girl-Hattie, but of course Hattie was a super-duper high-powered city slicker, not a teacher, and also there was no way Hattie would have tolerated the duff job of sitting on her own in a draught, handing out name badges.

'Louise. Louise Wilson,' the cheery lady finally announced slightly less cheerily when Claire ran out of ums and ahs. Claire looked at her blankly. She had literally no recollection of a Louise Wilson.

'Games Captain?' Louise offered, slightly dejected.

'Oh, LOUISE! Louise WILSON!' said Claire desperately, as she brought to mind a young Louise, who had indeed been just as chirpy and enthusiastic as she was now, trying tirelessly to instil a proper regard for sport into the girls of St Catherine's. She'd enjoyed little success in this, apart from with Head-Girl-Hattie and her ilk, like Hattie's sidekick Alison Walker, Deputy Head Girl to Hattie's Head Girl, who all turned out dutifully for the hockey team every Saturday morning. Louise, meanwhile, would wring her hands at the rest of them while lamenting it would be so nice if there was just a little more enthusiasm and they *could* manage an A team AND a B team, despite the fact that even with Hattie and Alison on the A team, St Catherine's lost every week, so God knows what the calibre of players would have been in the B team. (Louise had been raised on jolly books about girls' boarding schools in which the Games Captain was elevated to almost God-like status, so it was of immense disappointment to her that most pupils at St Catherine's were of Flora Poste's persuasion and preferred to run *away* from the ball than towards it, Claire herself being no exception to this, to the point that the first time she read *Cold Comfort Farm*, Flora's experiences on the school games pitch immediately convinced her that Flora was a Kindred Spirit.)

'And how are you, Claire?' asked Louise.

'Yes, fine, good! So you teach here? What do you teach?'

'Well, games. PE. What else?'

'Goodness. That's … very devoted of you.'

'We've an A team and B team for hockey now,' Louise said proudly.

'Gosh. Wow. How did you manage that?'

'I had to get the head to make it compulsory. I tried and tried to get Miss Pearson to do that, but she always said you could lead a horse to water, but you couldn't make it bully off, ha ha ha ha. Sorry, just a little hockey joke there. But childhood obesity has been an absolute godsend. I was able to persuade Mrs Greenwood, she's the head now, of the advantage of mandatory Saturday-morning sport in tackling obesity and screen addiction. Of course, the parents weren't best pleased, and I *am* disappointed in how few of them turn out to support the matches, especially the away games, but the girls are playing hockey. And that's what really *matters*, isn't it?'

'Yes, yes, I suppose so,' said Claire, with a grudging admiration for Louise, who from an early age had made two hockey teams for St Catherine's her life goal, and hadn't rested until she had achieved it. 'Do you win much?'

Louise looked slightly less chipper. 'Well, it's the taking part that counts, isn't it? It's *character building.*'

'Yes. Character building. Very important,' said Claire, feeling wretched at pissing on poor Louise's chips by reminding her that despite her pride in her two teams, St Catherine's calibre of hockey was still quite pants. 'Anyway, I suppose I should go in.'

'Oh yes, yes, on you go! In fact, you're one of the last, so I'll be through in a tick too, and we can have a proper catch-up. I'm trying to get an old girls' team together; I don't suppose you'd be interested in joining?' Louise asked, perking up a bit.

'Um, maybe?'

Claire was unable to crush Louise's hockey dreams any further. Doubtless if it came to it, she could claim work pressures, or life pressures, or that she lived too far away, or just good old Women's Troubles like she had at school.

'Marvellous!' Louise was full of beans again. 'I'll catch you in a mo and sign you up.'

Inside the hall the lights were dim, reminiscent of all the school dances held there, with the flammable taffeta and the spotty youths, Miss Pearson circling beady-eyed to make sure Nothing Amorous was taking place and smacking away the hands of any Filthy Boys that appeared to be Wandering. Coke cans had been surreptitiously topped up with vodka in corners, the vodka smuggled through in half bottles in inside pockets, fortunately invisible in the baggy dinner jackets that were the style in the nineties. There were no boys tonight, and no sneaky half bottles of vodka either. Instead, there was a table with very small glasses of red wine, white wine and orange juice. Claire picked up a glass of red, as the white was decidedly tepid, and looked around her. She couldn't quite believe she was here without Emily. Did she even know who she was among these people without Emily to giggle with and make sarcastic comments to about them?

'Claire Roberts!' someone boomed at her. Oh good. Head-Girl-Hattie, still head girling. Had no one changed? Louise with her hockey teams, Hattie still briskly taking charge, Alison there in Hattie's wake, ready to do her bidding like a good deputy head. Apart from lacking Emily, had Claire actually changed at all? Could she in fact feel her carefully styled hair flopping into her eyes, the better to peer out from under it rebelliously? Claire was suddenly seized by an urge to rush off to the loo and add several more layers of eyeliner and mascara. She licked her lips and was surprised not to taste the chemical tang of Rimmel's Heather Shimmer.

'How lovely to see you!' cried Hattie, air-kissing Claire on both cheeks, which meant Claire almost snogged her by trying to pull away after one 'kiss'.

'I don't think I've seen you since school, Claire. You've never been to one of these before, have you?' Hattie demanded in the same slightly accusing manner she used to ask Claire if she'd signed up to help with the lunchtime club for the younger years yet.

'No,' said Claire weakly. 'Sorry.'

'Never mind, you're here now. So, Alison will show you the ropes – drinks here, food downstairs later – everyone's here, do say hello, there's some teachers too, and of course, Miss Pearson's here, she's sitting in the corner over there. Alison, take Claire to say hello to

Miss Pearson,' and Hattie sailed off to corner another unsuspecting slacker.

'Come on, Claire,' said Alison brightly. 'SO nice to see you. How are you? You look very well – I like your dress. Do you have children? I have three, Millie, Olivia and Rosie, so adorable, all at St Catherine's, of course. Oh, here we are! Miss Pearson, it's Claire Roberts.'

And Alison trotted off back to Hattie's side, ready for her next set of orders. Alison had never taken the time to properly speak to Claire, she reflected, apart from when she needed to copy Claire's maths homework.

'Claire,' barked Miss Pearson. *Was* this Miss Pearson? That large and formidable lady – scourge of horny teenage boys and sex-pest flashers outside the school, and illegally shortened hemlines – looming large over her lectern at prayers as she belted out 'Jerusalem' or 'O Jesus I Have Promised', and sighing as she read out the weekend hockey scores ('Woodhill 13, St Catherine's 0. Really? 13–0? Oh dear'), and always but *always* lecturing her girls on the need to Do Their Best, Try Their Hardest, and also that You Can Do Anything, and Don't Let Anyone Dim Your Star. She was now a small, shrunken creature in a wheelchair, glaring myopically through her glasses at Claire. Yet her tone was unchanged.

'Still not paying attention, Claire Roberts?' she sniffed. 'How many times have I told you to stop dreaming and listen?'

'Sorry, Miss Pearson,' muttered Claire. 'But do you actually remember me?'

'I remember all my girls,' said Miss Pearson tartly 'You were a dreamer. Head in the clouds, hockey socks round your ankles. And your shirt was always dirty – you eternally had ink all over yourself, girl, I don't know why.'

'My fountain pen leaked.'

'Nonsense, your fountain pen didn't leak. You were covered in ink because you were always taking your pen apart and using it to make ink pellets to flick at your poor, benighted physics teacher,' snapped Miss Pearson.

'How did you know?' gasped Claire.

'I knew everything that went on in this school.'

'Why didn't I get in trouble?'

'Because you were a terrible shot and you always missed her. Girls will be girls. As mischief goes, yours was harmless. What was the point in dragging you over the coals for it? There was no harm done, and it would only have made you angry and resentful. Let the girls be, unless there was actual damage – that was my motto. You were a funny girl, though, always making other people laugh.'

'Was I?' said Claire.

'Yes. Aren't you anymore?'

Her old headmistress's eyes bored into Claire. Miss Pearson's body may have declined sharply over the years, but she still had the old commanding presence.

Claire hung her head. 'I don't know,' she mumbled.

'Hmmmm. Sit!' Miss Pearson gestured to a chair at the table beside her. Claire sat.

'Not just now, Alison,' Miss Pearson said as Alison dragged another latecomer over to pay her dues. 'Cara Forsyth, how nice to see you. Pop back in a moment, will you? Claire and I are just having a Little Chat. Now,' she said, turning back to Claire, her face kinder than Claire had ever seen it, 'tell me what has happened since I last saw you?'

'I don't know. Life, I suppose.'

'Oh, you do know. "Life" indeed.'

One couldn't lie or make denials to Miss Pearson. Claire felt like she was a child again, after she and Elizabeth had flooded the toilets by plugging the sinks with loo roll and turning on the taps for reasons Claire now couldn't recall, and they'd been sent to 'Have a Little Chat' with Miss Pearson.

'What do you mean by "life". Did something dim your star?'

'Um. I suppose so, yes. But actually it was … oh, nothing.'

'Nothing?'

Claire gulped. The little girl she'd suddenly become couldn't possibly tell Miss Pearson about anything that had happened. She looked at the floor and scuffed her feet.

'I'm going to say to you what I say to all the girls when I see them at these reunions. Don't fall into the trap of trying to do it all. So many women find themselves in the same trap. Before they know it, their hopes and dreams are buried under laundry and school runs, and they're sucked into exactly the domestic drudgery their mothers and I burnt our bras to try to avoid – and all this, and you've got to hold down a job on top of it. Am I right?'

'Mmmm,' said Claire non-committally, wishing the ground would open and swallow her so that she didn't have to hear Miss Pearson talk about burning her bra. Claire did not wish to think about Miss Pearson's brassieres. Claire wished she was anywhere but where she was. She took a large slug of her wine, accidentally finishing her tiny glass in one. The burning sensation in her oesophagus was at least a distraction from her burning embarrassment.

'Anyway, the important thing is that you've got to keep hold of who *you* are. You. Yourself. Not a wife, not a mother, not an employee, but *you*. Have you done that?'

Claire mumbled something into her empty glass. Of *course* she hadn't done that. Claire didn't know anyone who had. It was a nice idea, but Miss Pearson had no notion of what real life was like, what

marriage and children and family and commitment entailed. Before
Miss Pearson could interrogate Claire any further, Hattie came
bustling over.

'It's time to get ready for your speech, Miss Pearson,' Hattie
announced.

'Hurrumph,' said Miss Pearson. 'Can't I have another glass of
wine first?'

'Better not,' said Hattie briskly, wheeling her away. 'Do have fun,
Claire. I'm sure there are lots of old friends here!'

Claire tottered off to grab another glass of wine, very grateful for
Hattie's reprieve. She was astonished Miss Pearson remembered her
at all, and was slightly ashamed that she hadn't had more exciting
tales to relate of her amazing life and the use she'd put her expensive
education to. Now Claire scoured the hall for someone she recognised. A vaguely familiar short woman, with the sort of casually
tousled hair that Claire longed for but had never mastered, only
ever achieving the 'dragged through a hedge backwards' look, came
over to the table to help herself to a can of Coke.

She smiled at Claire, then looked at her name badge and
shrieked 'CLAIRE! Oh my God, how amazing, you've finally come
to one of these! You haven't changed a bit.'

A quick tit squizz by Claire revealed this was in fact
'ELIZABETH! How lovely! You haven't changed at all either.' (Claire
was quickly realising that this was the de facto greeting, regardless
of the recipient's appearance, as clearly 'Jesus, what happened to
you?' or 'My dear, you look positively hag-ridden' would be both
rude and frowned upon).

'Well,' said Elizabeth, 'I have a bit – I'm blonde now! I can't
believe you're here. I always look for you, and you never come.
Everyone's here – Sarah and Lindsay and Fiona. Come over, we

were just talking about you and whether you'd ever turn up at one of these. You're not even very easy to stalk on social media, with all your privacy settings!'

'You do that too?'

'Everyone does it.'

'I thought it was just me.'

'The internet was literally *invented* for stalking, of course it's not just you. Look, everyone, look who I found, lurking by the Booze of Doom. It's Claire!'

'I thought that was you I saw being sat down for one of Miss Pearson's Little Chats,' said Lindsay.

'Well, obviously,' said Sarah. 'She's not been before, so she must be one of the few who hasn't had The Little Chat. Miss P was hardly going to miss the opportunity, was she?'

'It was quite mortifying,' said Claire shyly.

'Yeah, she's not lost the knack of making you feel like a naughty schoolgirl,' sighed Elizabeth. 'Do you remember when someone stole the lollipop man's lollipop and the godawful row there was that went on for weeks. I had *no idea* what had happened to that damn lollipop, but every time she stood up at Prayers and reminded us this was a criminal offence and demanded the culprit hand themselves in, I could feel the guilt rising and my cheeks burning, and I was so sure she'd see and think it was me. Who was it, in the end? Did they ever find out?'

'They never found out,' said Claire 'It was me. Well, me and Emily. Emily and me, I mean.'

'Seriously? Where did you put it?'

'Behind the boiler. It's probably still there.'

'And *why*?'

Claire shrugged. 'I think just because we thought it would be funny. We had no idea of the awful fuss there would be.'

'We should have known it was you and Emily. You were always doing mad things like that. The pair of you were hilarious.'

Claire opened her mouth to say something but found the pressure to be 'hilarious' too much.

Luckily, before anyone noticed, Sarah said, 'What's Emily up to these days? Do you still see her?'

'No,' Claire said, braced for another inquisition. 'We just … drifted apart.'

'Oh, that's a shame,' said Sarah. 'Oh look, Hattie's getting the microphone out, it must be nearly speech time.'

'Yes, Hattie was talking about a speech when she wheeled Miss Pearson off. Miss Pearson was demanding another glass of wine and Hattie was saying no.'

'Hattie keeps a strict count of how many glasses Miss Pearson has had after she got hammered two years ago and made a rambling speech about how her advice to girls leaving school would be to get a dog, because dogs never break your heart.'

'She what?' said Claire in astonishment.

'In fairness, Miss Elliott had just died and she was still very raw,' put in Sarah reprovingly.

'Miss Elliott, the geography teacher? Were they friends?'

'Rather more than friends,' said Elizabeth drily. 'Hadn't you heard? Though according to my mother, everyone is wrong and they were just Great Chums – she has rather Victorian views on such things.'

'Miss Elliott and Miss Pearson?' gasped Claire in astonishment.

'Yes, by all accounts they were absolutely devoted to each other.'

'Like *devoted* devoted?' Claire asked, wanting to make sure she had not the wrong idea.

'Devoted devoted like a couple devoted,' Sarah confirmed.

'Wow,' said Claire. 'I had no idea. I was just thinking "What do you know? You're an old spinster" when she was giving me bossy life advice, but I guess, what do *I* know? You can never really tell what's going on in other people's lives, can you?'

'Nope! Oh, here we go.'

'Good evening, girls,' boomed Miss Pearson through the microphone, her stentorian public-speaking voice in no way diminished by age. 'I shall keep this short. I'm quite sure you'd rather chat among yourselves than listen to me, or at least that was the impression you always gave me at Prayers.'

Claire giggled. Was Miss Pearson being *funny*? Truly this was a night of revelations.

'I want to talk about the future tonight, girls. Your future. I know for many of you – most of you, in fact – life has not turned out the way you envisaged. For some that is a good thing, for others not so good, for some it's just different. Be that as it may, the past is not something we can change. The past has shaped who you are today, but it doesn't have to shape who you are tomorrow. You are still, compared with me, young women. Some of you may have lost sight of who you were, who you are or who you want to be. Don't let that stop you. You can *still* be whoever you want to be. You don't have to let the past stop you from having the best future you can, from being the best person you can be. But only *you* can make that happen. No one else can do that for you. Remember our school motto, girls, written by our founder, Miss Janet Crosby-Dawson, and say it with me – "With hope in our hearts and courage in our souls, we will go on, for tomorrow dawns anew."'

Everyone obediently chanted the familiar words along with Miss Pearson.

'This motto has brought me a great deal of comfort in the last two years since Margaret passed away,' Miss Pearson said. 'And I hope that when you face difficult times as well, you remember it, and it brings you the hope and courage needed to go on as well. Because tomorrow does always dawn anew, and whatever mistakes we made today, whoever we were today, tomorrow we can be better. Thank you for listening, girls. *Now* can I have another glass of wine, Hattie?'

Everyone applauded, and Hattie dutifully wheeled Miss Pearson over to the drinks table.

'I haven't thought of the old motto in years,' said Claire. 'It's really quite cheerful, isn't it? It never seemed that way when we were droning it out every day!'

'I know,' said Elizabeth. 'And when she's not rambling on about dogs, the old girl's actually quite on the nail.'

'I know,' said Claire thoughtfully, pondering Miss Pearson's words. She wondered if they had been meant especially for her, after their Little Chat earlier? It was true, though. She had been so caught up in dwelling on the past for so long, despite the Sisterhood, despite the brave new world of Trying New Things, that she had sort of forgotten that her future was there to make of it what she would.

At that moment, Miranda Johnson sailed over to join them, vastly pregnant with Moppet#4, in a tasteful navy maternity frock ('It's the same brand as the Duchess of Cambridge wears when she's expecting, actually') to hold forth on the latest renovations to her tasteful Instagramable home ('We used the same interior designer as the Sussexes did, but of course we wouldn't have done if we had known how *they* were going to turn out').

'I mean, you've no idea!' Miranda was chuntering indignantly. 'It was dreadful, those builders were very rough and it was completely smashed in. My back door was out of action for a week and Tristan was *livid*! And it's *still* not right.'

Claire caught Elizabeth's eye and they shook with suppressed laughter. Sarah snorted beside her, Lindsay made peculiar noises, while Fiona gave up the unequal struggle and openly guffawed. Once Fiona started, no one else could hold it in either.

'Why are you laughing?' complained Miranda. 'It really wasn't funny at all. I couldn't even put anything in my back passage! I even had to move the hamsters out of there – it simply wasn't safe for them.'

'Oh stop, stop,' begged Elizabeth, as Claire attempted to hold her up.

'I shouldn't have expected any better from you girls,' sniffed Miranda, 'you always were all peculiar,' and off she stalked.

Everyone got a semblance of control of themselves again.

'Poor Miranda. Fancy the builders being so careless as to smash her back door in,' said Claire solemnly. 'No wonder Tristan was *livid* – Miranda's back door out of action for a week,' and they were off again.

'Oooooh,' wailed Sarah. 'Stop it, Claire, it hurts. Poor Tristan. Never allowed in Miranda's back passage again.'

'Not after the builders. It wasn't even safe for the hamsters,' gasped Elizabeth. 'Sounds like they had quite a time with Miranda's back passage.'

'And her back door still isn't right,' gulped Lindsay. Fiona had lost all power of speech. Every time she went to say something, she just started laughing helplessly again. Occasionally, she mumbled 'hamsters' and started herself off again.

'Look at me,' thought Claire proudly. 'I'm being hilarious. And I don't need Emily to be around to do it. A new day dawns tomorrow.'

25

One Saturday morning, a couple of weeks after the School Reunion, Claire was enjoying a lie-in with Sadie and contemplating a quiet weekend. The previous Saturday had involved a plethora of New Things, as Lucy had found a life-drawing class on the Saturday afternoon, at which unfortunately there *had* been a funny-shaped willy that had also caused much hilarity, and on the Sunday, aware that the good weather of the summer would not last forever, they had braved the wild swimming again. Wild swimming, they'd all decided, was very *bracing*. Or as Lucy had put it, 'By bracing, I actually mean fucking freezing!' They'd finally decided that maybe wild swimming was not for them. Kate had been convinced she had a leech on her nipple, but it turned out just to be pond weed.

Today, though, all Claire had done was potter downstairs to get some coffee and microwave two slightly stale croissants – one for her and one for Sadie, who was a great fan of croissants in bed and who got rather put out now on weekday mornings when she had to get up without her croissant. Claire had attempted to read a worthy and improving book that all the newspapers described as 'urgent' and 'important', and that she found rather turgid and dull, so was alternating between scrolling through Instagram and chatting on her various WhatsApp groups. Between the Sisterhood and the newly rekindled, though somewhat long-distance, friendships with her old school friends, the past two weeks had in fact been good weeks for Claire.

She was just judging Miranda's latest Instagram offering with Sarah when a notification from the Sisterhood popped up.

[Kate] HELP ME! At Sainsbury's and just come out and my tyre is flat and I DON'T KNOW HOW TO CHANGE IT and the AA said it would be at least three hours before anyone could get to me and I've bought a lot of ice cream and I can't leave the car here or it will get a ticket. WHAT DO I DO?

[Lucy] Tell them you're a woman on your own, and they'll make you a priority and get someone there faster. Also, if the AA man is hot, text me so I can come ogle.

[Kate] I tried that, and they said that doesn't count when you're in Sainsbury's car park and can just go and wait in the cafe! Apparently you have to be abandoned down a dark country lane with murderous hitchhikers lurking behind every tree armed with axes for that to count!

Claire felt bad for lolling around eating croissants with Sadie while everyone else was having a productive weekend and jumped out of bed while typing.

[Claire] I CAN CHANGE A TYRE! ON MY WAY! JUST PUTTING A BRA ON!

[Kate] I LOVE YOU! LIKE REALLY LOVE YOU! You might just save my ice cream. Did I mention that I love you!

[Lucy] So no hot AA man for me then! Thanks Claire. Some people are very selfish! 😒

[Kate] Sorry Lucy! Sorry! But I'm sure you're too much of a lady to shag the AA man in the back of his van on a first meeting. 😊

[Lucy] It would depend on how hot he was, tbh. I could not rule it out entirely. He'd have to take off the hi-vis vest though. Hi-vis is not sexy.

Claire flung on her clothes and popped Sadie in the car as well. Sadie loved an outing in the car, and they could go on for a walk afterwards. She found Kate pacing and wringing her hands next to her sporty little car that they all envied. It would not fit a child seat, or a booster seat, and indeed had no back seats at all. A bag of delicious things was perched on the passenger seat, blueberries, croissants and pains au chocolat poking out the top. Sadie, who'd insisted on getting out to say hello, sniffed at it hopefully.

Kate flung her arms around Claire in relief. 'Thank you for coming! No, Sadie, pains au chocolat aren't good for you. Oh fine.'

Kate opened the croissants instead and gave one to Sadie, who smirked.

'Sadie, you're SHAMELESS,' scolded Claire. 'And you're getting very fat!'

'Don't fat shame her, she's beautiful,' crooned Kate, scratching Sadie's ears, as Sadie nudged hopefully at her, suggesting another croissant wouldn't go amiss.

'DON'T give her another one, Kate. It'll be her third today! Right, do you know where the jack is kept?'

Kate looked at her blankly.

'OK, well, it's not a big car, let's try the boot. Yep, there it is, and the spare wheel, which unsurprisingly is a shitty space-saver one, so you'll need to get your tyre properly replaced soon, and don't go too fast on this one.'

Kate stared at Claire admiringly.

'How do you *know* all this?'

'My dad. He was quite adamant I should be able to change wheels and do basic car maintenance. Now, do you have your locking wheel nut?'

Kate looked even blanker.

'My what?'

'When you get your tyres changed, the nut they need to get the wheels off.'

'I just give the man the keys and go for coffee, and I come back and he says I've got new tyres and talks about something called "tracking", which isn't anything to do with finding parcels apparently, and charges me extra for it, and then I give him all my money and go home.'

'Oh, Kate! I must give you a crash course in cars. They're probably ripping you off about the tracking too. They always say it needs to be adjusted and there's almost never anything wrong with it. Do they show you the print-out?'

'Claire, I don't know what the fucking tracking IS, so what do you think I'd do with the print-out?'

'Right, fair point. The tracking is –'

'Claire, I don't mean to be rude, and I really appreciate you coming to help, but I've got Häagen-Dazs AND Ben & Jerry's.'

'Well, I can't change the wheel without the locking wheel nut.'

After a lengthy search – for such a small car, there were a lot of cubby holes and nooks and crannies – Claire located the nut and set to work. Kate hovered, trying to look helpful and Sadie sneezed hopefully for more croissants.

'No, darling, Mummy says no more,' sighed Kate, scratching Sadie's ears instead. 'How are you getting on there, Claire?'

'The fucking nut is seized,' grunted Claire, wrestling with the wrench.

'Are you ladies OK?' enquired a deep voice behind them.

'Yes,' snapped Claire, as Sadie whimpered and shot behind Kate.

'Can I help?'

'NO. I have this in hand!'

Claire wiped the sweat out of her eyes and stood up. Oh, for fuck's sake. Why did it have to be a handsome man who had stopped to proffer assistance?

'Are you sure?'

'Quite sure. Can I get past, please. I just need to get something out of my car.'

As Claire returned from her car with a torque wrench that Jonathan insisted she keep in the car for just such emergencies, she was most put out to see that the handsome stranger had helpfully nipped in and loosened the nuts for her.

'This lovely chap is helping,' cooed Kate, doing an excellent impression of a Bad Lesbian, as she batted her eyelashes at him. 'This is so kind of you, thank you, errr?'

'Dominic. Dom. Right, where's the jack?'

'I can do it,' insisted Claire. 'Really, we're fine.'

'Oh, I don't mind! Won't take a jiffy,' said the handsome stranger, already jacking up the car.

'See, Claire! Not a jiffy,' said Kate happily.

'And nice to meet you, Dominic,' cooed Kate. 'This is Claire,' she added, shoving Claire forward.

'Kate!' hissed Claire, hideously aware her unwashed hair was shoved in a bun, and not a sexy 'messy bun' either. And not only did she have no make-up on, she hadn't even brushed her teeth before her mercy dash to Kate and was wearing her very oldest, least-supportive, but most comfortable bra.

'Smile,' Kate hissed back.

'There we go!' said Dominic ten minutes later. 'All sorted. Right. I'll be off, then.'

Kate nudged Claire hard in the ribs. Claire suspected that was another hint to smile winningly at the handsome stranger. God, he was handsome. She wasn't going to smile, though, because it would be too hideously shameful when he returned to his gorgeous wife with a tale of a sweaty mad woman gurning at him in the supermarket car park. Oh, why hadn't she put on a better bra? And maybe some lip gloss. And a bit of concealer. He was such a very handsome man, and useful too. Oh God, he was still standing there. Were they supposed to pay him or something?

Dominic stood there awkwardly for a few seconds more, and then cleared his throat and started to say something, then stopped and raked his hand through his hair, which was nice hair, and his arms *were* rather sexy, thought Claire.

He cleared his throat again and then looked up at the sky and said, 'Oh fuck it. Claire, is it? Look, Claire. It's just … I … well … I've seen you here a few times. And I wanted to say hello, and never got up the courage. And now I'm here, I thought maybe I could ask for your number, and maybe see if you wanted to go for a drink sometime?'

'What?' said Claire in disbelief. Her number? The handsome man?

'Yeah, look, I'm sorry, this is all a bit awkward. I'm not in the habit of asking women out in supermarket car parks.'

Dominic stared at the ground this time.

'Um,' said Claire, trying very hard not to gape. The last man that had asked her out was Andrew (Sweaty Harry Hughes's attempts at seduction didn't count). What was she supposed to say? What was she supposed to *do*? Claire was dumbfounded, and also rather thrilled and terrified at the same time, and she still didn't seem to have the power of speech.

'She would,' said Kate. 'Here!'

Kate had been rummaging in her bag, and now scribbled on a piece of paper and handed it to Dominic with a flourish. 'Her number. Give her a call.'

'KATE!'

'Wow, thanks. I'll call you. I mean, if that's OK? You haven't exactly said yes, have you?'

'Yes,' said Claire in a strange voice. Oh God, why did her voice sound like that?

Dominic laughed. Damn – nice laugh, too.

'Amazing,' he beamed, 'I can't believe I just did that. God. Great. Uh, I'll call you! And yeah, I promise I'm not a mad stalker or anything.'

'OK, good,' Claire's strange voice said. 'Though you'd hardly say so if you were,' she added, attempting to recover herself somewhat and seem less like a stunned haddock.

'This is true. But I'm really not. Um. Well, bye then. I'll call you and we'll arrange something. Wow. OK. Bye!'

'What just happened?' said Claire.

'You just got yourself a date, thanks to your Auntie Kate,' Kate chortled. 'No need to thank me.'

'Oh shit!' said Claire 'How are we going to tell Lucy I got a date changing your tyre?'

'Well, he'll probably turn out to be an arsehole anyway,' said Kate comfortingly. 'I'd better go, I suppose, as otherwise I think I'll be drinking my Cherry Garcia. Come on, Sadie, you can stop hiding behind me and go back to your mummy. Is that your phone ringing, Claire?'

'Shit, yes! Lydia. Emily's mum. What does *she* want?'

'Hi, Lydia,' said Claire. 'How are you?' as Kate got in her car, waving and blowing kisses and mouthing 'BYEEEEEE!'.

Kate got out of her car again as she saw the colour drain out of Claire's face, and Claire said, 'OK, thank you. Let me know.'

'Claire?' said Kate anxiously. 'Are you OK?'

'Emily's in hospital. She's … she's critical and they don't think she'll make it, Lydia said. They've told Lydia to come as quickly as she can to say goodbye because they don't think Emily will survive, and Lydia wanted to ask me if I wanted to go too,' said Claire, and burst into tears.

Kate hugged Claire and held her tight as she sobbed. Sadie, extremely confused by the whole situation, and suspecting that her previous croissant benefactor was responsible for making her mummy cry, was torn between being unable to believe that someone who gave her croissants was so bad, and wanting to protect Claire, and so settled on making a noise somewhere between a growl and a whine at Kate.

'It's OK, Sadie, don't worry. It's just Kate,' sobbed Claire.

Kate reached into her car and extracted another croissant, which she handed to Sadie, who took it gently, and then, after a moment's longing consideration, with an air of great nobleness and self-sacrifice, for surely, as far as Sadie was concerned, there could be no ill so great that it could not be cured by an only very slightly slobbered-on croissant, she attempted to thrust it into Claire's hand.

'Oh, darling,' hiccoughed Claire. 'Thank you. But you have it.'

In what she considered to be the greatest gesture of her life, Sadie refused. It was Claire's croissant now. To make her happy, though Sadie indicated with a gentle head tilt that should Claire be unable to finish it, she, Sadie, could contemplate helping her with it. And so, Claire wept on in the Sainsbury's car park, Kate's arms around her, a scruffy little Staffordshire terrier pressed protectively against her legs, both of them trying to pour all their love and support into her, and a soggy croissant clutched in her hand.

After a couple of minutes Kate gave her a shake.

'Claire? Claire, I don't think we've a lot of time right now. Do you want to go to the hospital? You don't have to, of course you don't have to, but if you do, we should probably go now.'

Claire took a deep breath and tried to wipe her eyes. She had quite forgotten that she was still holding Sadie's croissant, and was not entirely successful. Kate took the croissant and gave it back to Sadie, who ate it with an air of satisfaction, as if to say, 'See, it worked,' and Kate handed Claire a tissue instead.

'I think I do want to go. It ... it can't end like this. Emily can't die. Not now. Not like this.'

'Come on, then, get in your car. No, not in the driver's seat. You're in no fit state to drive. I'll take you.'

'But your shopping! And you'll get a ticket if you leave your car here.'

'It doesn't matter. Nothing matters right now except getting you there to see Emily. Come on, Sadie, in you go.'

On the way, Kate asked if Lydia had said what had happened.

'She was hit by a car. That's all Lydia said. Emily was always dreadful for dashing out in traffic – she'd never wait for the green man. I'd always be left on the pavement shouting at her to come back, or diving after her yelling she was going to get us both killed. And now she has. Well, tried to. Hopefully not. I don't even know where or when it happened. Poor Lydia, she was in bits. She just said, "I need to say this and then go, or I'll break down, and I'm not doing that. Claire, Emily was hit by a car and they don't have much hope. I'm going now to say goodbye. They've taken her to Bramford Hospital, if you want to come too." That was it.'

'That's terrible. I'm so sorry, Claire.'

'I didn't think I'd feel like this. There's been plenty of times this year I wished her dead. I never meant it, though. What if I did this?'

'Believe me, you didn't. If ill-wishing worked, we'd all be hunchbacked, one-eyed, syphilitic troll creatures. It was an accident. A terrible accident. It was nothing to do with you.'

Kate dropped Claire at the entrance to the hospital and went to park, and as Claire was running to the reception desk to anxiously enquire where she might find Emily, she saw Lydia walking across the foyer, white-faced and blank-eyed.

'Lydia?' said Claire hopefully.

Lydia shook her head. 'No,' she whispered. 'My little girl … my Emily.'

'Claire … she's … she's … No,' and the invincible, unbreakable, unemotional Lydia dissolved in tears.

Claire tried to hug her, but Lydia pushed her away. Claire was so shocked by Lydia's grief that she didn't seem able to feel very much herself.

'I'm fine,' Lydia gasped, wiping her eyes. 'I'm fine. I just … they tried to put me in this ghastly room, a *family* room, they said. Such a stupid name, I don't *have* any family now, and the curtains were awful, and I just needed some air, to get outside. *Please* don't give me sympathy, Claire, it's the last thing I need.'

'Shall we go outside, then?'

'Yes. I need to ring Martin. Tell him what's happened. He's on his way as well.'

On a bench outside, Lydia stared at her phone and then said, 'How do you tell the father of your child that she's … something like *this*?'

'I don't know,' said Claire. 'I'm so sorry.'

'And I hope you never have to find out, darling. Right, I can't put this off. Poor Martin is haring over here trying to be in time. I need to tell him there's nothing to hare over for.'

Lydia pressed his number and Martin answered on the first ring, sounding wildly anxious.

'Lyds? Are you there? How is she? Is there any news?'

'I'm afraid there is, Martin,' said Lydia, suddenly sounding wonderfully calm and composed. 'Martin, I'm dreadfully sorry, but Emily –'

And Lydia stopped speaking and just made a dreadful hoarse, rasping noise.

'Lydia? Lydia? Lydia, what's happened? Is she OK?'

Claire could hear Martin shouting.

Claire took the phone out of Lydia's hand and took a deep breath.

'Mr Shaw? Martin? It's Claire, Claire Roberts. I'm here with Lydia. Martin, are you driving?'

'No, Grace is, she said I wasn't fit to. Will you just tell me what is going on with Emily?'

'I'm so sorry. Emily's …' Claire swallowed hard. 'Emily's gone. I'm so terribly sorry.'

Martin made a dreadful keening sound, and Claire could hear his wife in the background trying to soothe him.

For a little while, things were busy. Despite her protestations, Lydia needed to be looked after, and then Martin and his wife Grace arrived, and Claire was fetching tea, and propping up Lydia, and then they all went back into Lydia's family room. She'd been absolutely right – it was truly ghastly. Then two of Emily's half-brothers arrived, and a doctor came in to speak to everyone and to ask if Martin and Grace wanted to see Emily, and Claire suddenly felt like she was intruding. Martin and Lydia were locked together in their grief, and Grace and the boys were there to support them, and probably doing a far better job than she could. She said goodbye to Lydia and Martin, neither of whom really seemed to notice she was there, and then said goodbye to Grace as well.

'Give me your number,' said Grace. 'I'm sure Lydia will be in touch about what happens next, but in case she doesn't feel up to it, I'll let you know.'

'Thank you,' said Claire.

Claire texted Kate and met her outside.

'I'm sorry I was so long,' she said.

'That's OK. Sadie and I had a nice walk. I'm so sorry about Emily, Claire.'

'I ...' said Claire, and then the tears that had been kept at bay, while she held Lydia's hand and fetched tea, suddenly came.

Finally, Claire said, 'I'm sorry. Of all the people to be landed with this, this must be so hard for you.'

'Because of Susan? It's very different to what happened with Susan, though. Let's get you home.'

'What do I do now?'

'Now? Now, I'm going to take you home, and you're going to have a hot bath and a stiff drink. If you feel up to it, I'll stay and keep you company. If you don't feel up to it, I'll leave you with Sadie. Come on.'

26

Emily's funeral was on a muggily hot, oppressive day. Thunder threatened, but never materialised. Instead, everyone just sweated and tried to suppress the irritability the weather generated.

Claire had not been sure whether she should go or not. Lydia said it would mean a great deal to her if Claire came, but she completely understood if she didn't want to. Andrew said he didn't think it was appropriate for him to go, but he'd take the day off and look after Lucas and Tabitha, and even keep them overnight so Claire didn't have to rush back.

The Sisterhood had eventually talked her into it, pointing out that it would be Claire's only chance to say goodbye to Emily and actually get some real closure on the situation. They'd all offered to go with Claire too, for moral support, since Tessa and Jonathan were away visiting Claire's brother and his wife, but in reality the children were still off school for the summer, and Claire was well aware Lucy was juggling time off and childcare and work, just like she was, and Mary would either have to pay a babysitter or ask James to take a day off.

Claire appreciated the offers, though, and in the end went along with Kate's insistence that since she didn't have to hoard her precious annual leave to cover holiday childcare, she was quite happy to take the day off and come too. Claire was especially touched by this, as she suspected a funeral, any funeral, would be difficult for Kate so soon after Susan's, but Kate assured her that she'd be fine.

The church at least was mercifully dark and cold, and Claire could feel the sweat that was trickling down her back start to cool. It was remarkably hard to dress sombrely and respectfully in summer while not sweating your tits off. Kate had managed it with her usual customary elegance, in a black linen sleeveless dress and silk cardigan, but Claire was deeply regretting wearing tights, and wondered if she could nip to the loo and whip them off before she dissolved into a puddle of sweat on the floor.

Lydia also looked unruffled and as stylish as ever, not a hair out of place and her red lipstick immaculate. But there were new lines round her eyes, and her red mouth had a rather pinched look. Emily's father, Martin, looked shattered, and his wife Grace seemed to be actually holding him up rather than just holding his arm. Emily's half-brothers wore the embarrassed look of people trying to look appropriately sad, but really wondering how long it would take before they could surreptitiously check their emails.

Lydia had asked Claire if she'd like to say something, but Claire had declined. What could she possibly say? Lydia had said that was totally understandable, but there would be a short section at the end where anyone who wanted to contribute their memories of Emily could do so, if Claire changed her mind.

Claire couldn't quite believe that Emily was in the coffin. It seemed impossible that she was lying there, dead and cold and in a box. Claire kept looking at it, then looking away in disbelief. The vicar said his bits, and related Emily's life to them. Not for the first time at a funeral, Claire was left wondering if she was at the right ceremony, as the saintly, wonderful person being described did not appear to be the Emily she knew – though Claire got a mention, in the depiction of Emily's time at St Catherine's, 'where she met Claire, who became her lifelong best friend'. But I wasn't, thought Claire guiltily. I wasn't her friend to the end of her life. Not when she died. And now a vicar has lied in church and it's all my fault, and what if he's smote down with a thunderbolt for my sins?

Emily's brothers jointly read a poem that had clearly been picked from the first page of a Google search for 'poems to read at sister's funeral'. It was a nice poem, but it also bore no resemblance to Emily or their relationship with her, which had never been close, due to the considerable age gap.

Everyone sang 'All Things Bright and Beautiful', and then the vicar stood up and said, 'Lydia and Martin have asked that we take time in the service to share our favourite memories of Emily. If anyone would like to come up and speak about Emily, please feel free to do so.'

There was an awkward silence, then Suzanna, who was intense and intellectual and went to Pilates with Emily, stood up and read a long poem she had written about the sea. There was a confused silence afterwards. 'It's a metaphor for Emily, obviously,' she said before she sat down, looking rather annoyed that it hadn't received a standing ovation.

Emily's boss stood up and talked about what a team player she'd been (Claire recalled that Emily had referred to him as 'Gropey Granville' and his deputy as 'Sleazy Sean'), and a girl Emily worked with talked about her time being mentored by Emily. Finally, Claire couldn't stand it anymore.

'I'm going to say something,' she muttered to Kate.

Kate put her hand on her arm. 'Are you sure? You don't have to?'

'I know. But I want to. None of these people knew her. None of them knew what she was really like. They could be talking about *anybody*. Even the vicar. Even her brothers. I have to say some-thing.'

'Oh God, you're not going to make a scene, are you?'

'No! I'm going to be nice. People are looking because we're whis-pering, though, and if I'm not quick I think Suzanna might read another poem.'

Claire jumped to her feet.

'Hi. I'm Claire. Some of you know me. I was Emily's friend. For a long time. Since we were twelve. A lifetime. And I just wanted to talk about some of the good times we had over those years. Like when we'd find the only male teacher in school and lie to him that we needed to go to the chemists for Women's Things. He let us go every day – he must have thought us dreadfully afflicted. We were actually running a black-market operation, taking orders for the newsagents and selling on Opal Fruits and Mars bars at a consider-able mark-up. We spent the proceeds in Boots every weekend, on the No. 17 and Rimmel counters. I was clearing out the other day, and I found a box of sparkly eyeshadows that must date from then, in colours that didn't seem made to suit *anyone*, not even Emily. The nineties was a strange place.

'Then there was the school trip when we were thirteen, when our group jumped on a bus that was just pulling away before the teacher accompanying could catch us, and we spent the day roam-ing round town while she was tearing her hair out looking for us. Nowadays she'd probably just have called the police, but back then we met her at the final rendezvous point and no more was said. With hindsight I suppose losing six schoolgirls is what would now be called a "career-limiting event". When we were fifteen –'

And Claire was off. Silly stories, none of them involving any great originality or wit or cleverness on her or Emily's parts. Just the usual anecdotes that made up a life. But as Claire told the stories, the bitterness and anger left her. She forgot about what Emily had done to her, how Emily had hurt her. Claire was finally allowing herself to remember that there *was* a reason she'd been friends with Emily for all those years, that there had been so many good times, fun times, times when they had laughed till their stomachs hurt. And that was how Claire wanted to remember her.

Finally, Claire finished up. 'I still can't believe she's not out there somewhere, ordering a cosmopolitan like it's 1998 or shouting the wrong answers at PopMaster and insisting Ken Bruce must have got it wrong, not her. I just wish I could tell her how much she means to me, just one more time.'

After Claire sat down, the vicar stood up again. Intellectual Suzanna rustled her sheaf of poems at him quite menacingly, but he ignored her, for, after all, if he could ignore the temptations of the devil, Suzanna held no fear for him. He announced that the family would go to the graveside for a private burial, and the other mourners were invited to make their way to the church hall for 'refreshments'. The organ struck up and Emily began her final journey.

When everyone filed out of the church, and Lydia, Martin, Grace and the boys stood through the torture of shaking everyone's hands and thanking them for coming, Lydia hugged Claire fiercely.

'Thank you,' she said. 'You don't know how much that meant to me, and to Martin. To have someone who really knew Emily talk about her, instead of all those platitudes and soundbites. And I know how hard that must have been. Thank you. Would you … would you like to come to the grave?'

Claire swallowed hard. 'Do you mind if I don't? I'm not really sure …' She trailed off.

'Of course not. It's just a ceremony, isn't it? It's not really *Emily*. I just wanted you to know you're welcome, if you want to.'

'Thank you, Lydia. I appreciate it. But I think we're going to go now.'

'I understand. Thank you again. And do keep in touch, won't you?'

Martin shook Claire's hand and mumbled something, and Grace hugged Claire too. She shook the brothers' hands, and then Claire and Kate were back out into the grey, muggy heat.

'Well,' said Kate. 'Tea and sandwiches in the church hall, or shall we go and get royally shitfaced?'

'Royally shitfaced, please. But Kate, can we go somewhere that does cosmos?'

'Of course. Just this way.'

Many, many cosmos later (well, three cosmos, then they switched to white wine, as the cosmos were actually a bit sickly in large quantities), Claire poured Kate into a taxi and tottered back to the bar across from the church. After about ten minutes, she emerged again and made her way over to the churchyard. Emily's grave was easy to find, being the only new one, and Claire sat down heavily beside it and proceeded to remove the fruits of her final foray into the bar from her bag. It had taken some fairly hard negotiations with the barman to manage it, but Claire laid out two cocktail glasses and a large plastic bottle full of cosmopolitan beside the grave. As she poured the cosmos into the glasses, a figure loomed out of the dusk.

'Who's that?' a voice demanded sharply.

'Claire,' she replied defiantly, hoping she did not end the night getting arrested for drinking in a graveyard like a naughty teenager.

'Oh *Claire*,' said Lydia in relief. 'What are you doing here?'

'Came to say goodbye,' said Claire, gesturing to her booze picnic.

'Are you drunk? Did you go and get pissed afterwards?'

'Yes,' sighed Claire. There didn't seem much point in denying it.

'Good for you. God, I wish I'd done that.'

'You can have some of this,' said Claire generously, proffering the rest of the cosmo in the bottle to Lydia.

'Thank you,' Lydia took a gulp. 'What are you doing?'

'One last cosmo, for Emily and me,' Claire explained. 'Because I never got a chance to tell her I forgave her, and she thought I still hated her. So, this is as close as I can get to making amends.'

'Oh Claire, darling. You were well within your rights to hate her, and you've nothing to make amends for. And she knew you didn't hate her. She told me you'd sent a text, that she hoped meant someday you might forgive her. She knew things could never go back to how they were, but that text meant the world to her – she was so happy. So thank you. For being so generous. Knowing Emily didn't die with you hating her does make it easier.'

'I'm glad,' said Claire. 'I'm glad she knew. I'm sorry how things turned out.'

'We all are, sweetheart.'

Claire put one cocktail glass on Emily's grave, and raised the other one. Lydia raised her bottle.

'To Emily,' they said.

'Do you think I should pour it on?' asked Claire.

'I don't know,' said Lydia. 'Seems a bit of a waste.'

'Maybe we should pour a little bit on and drink the rest?'

'Good plan. Emily would hate to see a perfectly good cosmo going to waste, after all.'

After they'd finished the cocktails, Lydia said, 'Claire, is there anything you want? Of Emily's, I mean? Any books or jewellery, or that sort of thing?'

Claire thought for a moment. 'I'd like a photo.'

'Which one?'

'Just a photo of Emily.'

'Don't you have hundreds of photos of her?'

'I did. But, well, I was very angry and I burnt them.'

'All of them?'

'I think so. It was just a kneejerk thing at the time. I was so hurt and furious. Childish, I know. But now I don't have any photos of her left.'

'I'll get you some.'

'Thank you.'

27

Claire looked through her wardrobe, trying to find something suitable to wear to the Thai boxing class that Mary had picked as her Trying New Things thing, and wondering what it must be like to be one of those chic and elegant people who just instinctively know exactly what to wear.

She dreaded to think how much of her life had been spent agonising over clothes and worrying she wasn't wearing the right thing. She had only the very vaguest idea of what one wore to box, gleaned from a half-hearted viewing of *Rocky IV* with Andrew many years before. Claire didn't really have any idea what had been going on, except that boxing involved vests and unflattering shorts and possibly some kind of rags wrapped around your head. She owned nothing suitable at all like that, and when she attempted to wrap a silk scarf around her forehead she just looked like she was off to tell fortunes at the end of the pier. In the end she settled for leggings and a T-shirt, and set off to meet the others at the boxing gym Mary had found.

The others were waiting outside, looking a bit apprehensive.

'I've been googling this,' said Lucy. 'It looks quite violent, Mary.'

'Nonsense,' said Mary cheerfully. 'I don't think we actually hit each other or anything.'

'It looks like we do,' said Kate doubtfully, pointing to the photos in the foyer of bloodied men knocking the living shit out of each other.

'It'll be fine,' insisted Mary, as a very small and slightly scary-looking man came through and announced his name was Gary and that he was their instructor today.

'RIGHT!' he screamed when they'd got thought to the gym. 'AS YOU'RE BEGINNERS, YOU'LL JUST BE WORKING WITH BAGS TODAY, AND NOT ACTUALLY SPARRING.'

Everyone breathed a sigh of relief.

'UNLESS YOU WANT TO!' Gary bellowed. 'HERE ARE THE BAGS.'

'Um, sorry,' said Claire. 'But would you mind not shouting?'

'I'M NOT SHOUTING,' shouted Gary. 'DON'T INTERUPT ME WHEN I'M GIVING THE HEALTH AND SAFETY BRIEFING.'

An hour later, Claire had a definite headache. The boxing was hard work but quite good fun, and there was a certain satisfaction to be had in visualising punching the faces and kicking the torsos of everyone who'd annoyed her that week, from Tony in the office (who'd asked if Claire was 'on the blob' when she'd asked him for the second time to email her some information she needed urgently) to the utter, utter bastard who'd cut her up at a roundabout (leading to Claire making some very unladylike gestures at him out of her window). Unfortunately, Gary didn't seem to have any volume controls and continued to relay all his instructions to them by bellowing at the top of his voice.

'RIGHT,' he yelled. 'WHO WANTS TO GET IN THE RING?'

'ME!' cried Mary. 'I want to.'

'ANYONE ELSE?' Gary shouted. The other three women shuffled their feet and looked awkward.

'I would,' said Claire. 'But I've got this presentation next week, and I don't really want to do it with a black eye.'

'Yes,' said Lucy hastily. 'Me too, but I've got this thing, um, big work thing as well.'

'Passport photos,' said Kate sadly. 'Getting them done next week, so better not.'

'YOU WON'T GET BLACK EYES IF YOU DO IT PROPERLY,' Gary shouted at them sternly. Mary's face fell at the thought of no one to batter in the ring, and Claire was about to bite the bullet and volunteer, when to her immense relief Gary stepped up and announced that he'd go in with Mary.

'WOOO HOOO!' crowed Mary, leaping into the ring, and feinting and jabbing as Gary put on his gloves – 'Take that Mo-Fo! And that! HA!'

'RIGHT! LET'S GO!' screamed Gary.

Mary turned out to be a bit of a ringer when it came to Thai boxing. She sprang at their instructor like a cobra and proceeded to batter seven bells out him, while a slightly stunned Gary, who'd obviously not been expecting this, attempted to dodge around her. His embarrassment wasn't helped by Mary's great whoops of joy every time she landed a blow on him.

Finally, poor Gary croaked, 'OK. Time's up,' and tottered out of the ring, followed by a jubilant Mary, still shrieking, 'Hiiiii YAH!' and air kicking and punching as she went.

'Anyone else want a go?' quavered Gary bravely, in a more restrained register.

'Actually,' said Claire, inspired by Mary's example, 'I would.'

Claire squared up to Gary and tried to remember all the things he'd bellowed at them in training. To her astonishment, her first punch landed home, and suddenly a great swell of rage burst out of her – far more than the petty annoyances she'd been channelling onto the dummies she'd kicked and punched earlier. It was fury with Andrew and Emily, fury at Emily for dying before Claire could get the closure she needed from properly forgiving her and of robbing Claire of the chance to see if anything could be salvaged from the ashes of their friendship. And it was rage at herself for so blindly sleepwalking into a life of laundry and fishfingers and domesticity that was so very far from what she'd ever imagined as a girl.

'Tomorrow dawns anew,' she grunted as she tried to whack Gary again. This time she missed and failed to duck in time, and he managed to get a blow in. Oddly, instead of putting Claire off, Gary's punch enraged her even more, and she got back up and went in again twice as hard. By the time she finished, she was sobbing and sweating and shaking and gasping for breath. It was like there had been a big ball of hate and anger inside Claire that she hadn't known was there, and it had suddenly been lanced. All the time she had been 'getting on with things' and 'being brave' and 'putting her best foot forward' and trying not to wallow in self-pity, that nasty ball of misery had been getting bigger and bigger, and now it had popped. It hadn't quite fully disappeared, but was now suddenly considerably smaller. Claire stood there still sobbing, as the other women gathered round her in concern.

'Are you OK?' asked Lucy, putting an arm around her.

Claire nodded, still sobbing. 'Never fucking better,' she hiccoughed. 'Can I come back next week, Gary?'

Gary nodded, rather apprehensively, 'Um, yeah, great,' he said, trying not to look utterly terrified, as Claire finally got her breathing under control and, wiping the sweat and tears out of her eyes, tottered out of the ring.

'That was amazing,' babbled Mary afterwards, over sweaty glasses of Sauvignon Blanc and several pints of water. It had been an intensive physical workout, as well as a mental one – all that visualisation of visiting extreme violence on arseholes – and Kate had wisely pointed out that if they were having wine, they should probably rehydrate before they dehydrated themselves again.

'Oh my God! I can't remember the last time I felt so ALIVE. I'm going back too. I love it. I hadn't realised how much I had missed doing something just for *me*. I feel like me again. And you were amazing, Claire. God you just fucking went for it!'

Claire felt a bit shaky and drained after the emotional release of the boxing, and all she could do was nod.

'Are you sure you're OK, Claire?' Lucy asked again.

'I … yes … I just … I think I got a lot of stuff out in there. I dunno, I hadn't realised how *angry* I was. Am!'

'You've every right to be angry, especially with Andrew and Emily. They royally fucked you over,' pointed out Mary.

'I know. But I realised there, I'm angry at *me* too, for letting my life get to this point. For letting myself forget who I am, for buying into the fucking Boden-clad vision of being a wife and mother that was expected of me. And I can blame other people all I like, and rant about societal pressures and the fucking patriarchy till I'm blue in the face, and obviously that's part of it. But it was *me* who let it happen, *me* who let myself forget who Claire Roberts was, and I'm not going to do that anymore, I'm going to go back every week and punch the living fucking daylights out of poor Gary until I know who I am again.'

'Good for you,' everyone chorused.

Mary's face suddenly fell and her bottom lip trembled. 'I feel a bit like that too,' she muttered, all the bravado and excitement of the class suddenly leaving her. 'Not the anger bit, just the forgetting who I am bit. The kids take up so much of my time, apart from when I'm with you lot – I seem only to exist as a mother and bum-wiper and pasta-cooker. Oh fuck, do you think I'm having an existential crisis?'

'What?' said Claire. 'Oh Mary, why? How? I'm not a hundred per cent sure what an existential crisis even is.'

'I think it's just a sense of not being sure who you are anymore, or what you're doing with your life,' suggested Kate.

'Fuck,' said Lucy, 'I've been having one of those for years! I wish I'd known. It would sound so much better at parties than "I can't actually give you any accountancy advice right now due to a.) FSA regulations, and b.) because I'm at a bastarding party and I don't really want to talk about how you can minimise your tax liabilities because you're too much of a tight wad to pay an accountant of your own." I could have just said, "I'm so sorry, but I'm actually having an existential crisis, so I'm afraid I can't help you." Anyway, sorry, Mary. Why are you having an existential crisis?'

'Well, I'm not sure there's a "why" for an existential crisis. You just have one,' replied Mary. 'But I just … I don't know who I am anymore. And I feel so trapped. By the children. By hardly having any time to myself. But mostly, I think, by not having any money of my own.'

'Do you need money, Mary? Are you thinking of leaving James? Is everything OK?' asked Claire in surprise.

'No, James is fine, it's just … I just hate not earning any money myself. I feel like such a … parasite. And I know I'm bringing up the children, and I know motherhood is a valuable job that ought to be renumerated, and I know all the things people say about how fulfilling it is. And yes, it'll be easier now Lily's starting school too, and it'll only be Alfie at home with me. But sometimes I want to SCREAM if Alfie asks for the bastarding playdough one more fuck-ing time.'

'Playdough is the work of the devil,' said Lucy. 'The damn stuff should be banned. Even the smell of it is vile.'

'And I know James says it's "our" money,' Mary went on. 'But it doesn't feel like that. I don't feel like I can even buy him a birthday present, because I'm buying him it with *his* money. He might as well buy himself something he really wants, instead of me choosing something he might not like. It's only the last few years I've not made any money.'

Mary dropped her head despairingly into her hands. 'Oh God, listen to me! I was so happy ten minutes ago and Claire was remembering who she was, and now I'm whinging and bringing everyone's mood down, and I've made Lucy have an existential crisis she didn't even know about.'

'You can always whinge to us,' said Kate, hugging her. 'Let's think outside the box, though. There must be things you can do at home or with Alfie. Is it a career you want or just some money?'

'I know it sounds awful, but I just want some *money*. I feel if I had a bit of money of my own, it would give me back a bit of dignity and self-worth. I don't know what I can do, though.'

'OK, let's brainstorm,' said Lucy. 'What about ironing? People are always looking for people to do ironing on the local Facebook groups.'

Mary brightened. 'That's a good idea. I mean, I'm shit at ironing and I hate it, but maybe I could learn to be better at it. Like … learn what starch is for and stuff. I understand chemistry, so I'm sure I can figure out starch.'

'OK,' said Lucy. 'Ironing is on the list. What else?'

'What about dog walking?' suggested Kate. 'Again, people are always looking for a trustworthy dog walker.'

'Oh my God,' said Claire. 'Yes! Sadie has the loveliest dog walker, but she needs a hip replacement so she's retiring after Christmas and I'm having so much trouble finding a female dog walker who isn't fully booked! Sadie's her only dog now, though. She's only kept her on as a favour on account of Sadie's issues and would be more than happy to stop now if I found someone else. You'd be perfect.'

'Are you sure you wouldn't just be giving me Sadie out of pity?' asked Mary.

'No! Seriously. It would mean she didn't have to get used to someone new. And she loves you.'

'You could have Bingo too,' offered Lucy. 'He's been expelled by his dog walker for being a sex pest. Allegedly, there was an Incident when he tried to bum an indignant boxer. But he loves Sadie, and Sadie doesn't mind him humping her occasionally – she seems to quite enjoy it. So that's two clients already.'

'Do you really think I could do this?' Mary said doubtfully.

'Yes!' chorused everyone else.

'At least think about it,' urged Claire.

'You could get business cards made up,' said Lucy dreamily. 'I could help you, finally actually do something artistic but not have to draw willies! I could design them for you. Being creative again might ease my own existential crisis.'

'There you go, Mary,' said Kate. 'You've got to do it now, for the sake of the existential crisis you gave Lucy. And I can help with marketing advice.'

'Oh my God,' said Mary. 'I can't believe this is happening. To the Sisterhood! Thank you!'

'That's what we're here for,' said Claire. 'To help each other.'

'And to Gary,' said Lucy solemnly. 'I haven't had such a good laugh in ages as I did at the look on his face when you first walloped him, let alone when Claire then wiped the floor with him. He definitely wasn't expecting that. That'll teach him for being complacent about a bunch of women!'

28

A week later, Claire was mooching round Sainsbury's trying to think of meals for her children for the coming week that didn't involve pasta or pizza and incorporated some kind of green vegetables into their diet, when she rounded a corner and came face to face with Dominic the Carpark Man. Shit. Shit, shit, shit! She *knew* she should have gone to Tesco to avoid such a hideous confrontation, but Sainsbury's did the only yoghurt Tabitha would eat.

'Claire,' he said 'Hi. Uh, so this is … I tried calling you.'

'I know,' said Claire wretchedly, wishing nothing more than that the floor of the pasta and rice aisle would simply open up and swallow her, thus avoiding both this embarrassment, and all the complaints the following week when she mercilessly forced the children to endure the middle-class child abuse of eating penne because there was no fusilli left on the shelf.

'You never called back?'

'No,' agreed Claire.

'So, I guess that's what they now call "ghosting".'

'Is it?' Claire cringed. 'It really wasn't like that.'

'I mean, it pretty much was. You gave me your number –'

'Kate. *Kate* gave you my number.'

'OK, Kate gave me your number, but you didn't stop her. You

didn't say, "Actually, Mr Weird Over-helpful Carpark Man, don't call me." You said, "Fine" when I said I'd call you.'

'I know, it's just … it's complicated –'

'Complicated? What is this, your Facebook status? You could just have said no. I'd actually have much preferred a knockback there and then to my face, instead of spending weeks calling your voicemail and answering the phone to every withheld number hoping it was you calling back. Do you know how many call centres wanting to talk to me about my non-existent investments I've had to tell to bugger off?'

'No.'

'Twenty-seven. One of them just this morning, with my last glimmer of hope that maybe you'd lost your phone or something and had only just got a replacement, and were *finally* calling me. But no, it was Natasha from Investments 4 U calling to chat about my share portfolio.'

'You must be on a list somewhere. You'll have forgotten to untick a box saying you can be contacted by their trusted partners and someone will have sold your number on.'

'Do you think? Gosh! Never thought of that!' said Dominic sarcastically. 'Anyway. You're here now. You've made yourself clear and I've made an arse of myself, but it took a hell of a lot for me to come over and ask you out, so do me one favour please, and tell me *why* you ghosted me? Why you didn't just say no, or pick up the phone and say, "Look, this isn't for me. Sorry, my friend got a bit carried away," or even just block my number after the first call, so I got the message straightaway.'

Claire's ball of rage, admittedly much, much smaller after another battering session with Gary the day before, gave a sudden twinge, and instead of the polite 'Something came up' nice excuse she was going to give, she suddenly felt furious that she was expected to explain herself to a stranger when all she'd wanted was a bag of fucking pasta and some microwave rice. So why *shouldn't* she say what she was thinking?

'Men ghost women all the time! I bet you've done it loads. And they never get an explanation or a reason, so why the hell do I owe you one?' said Claire hotly.

'OK, fair enough. You're right. You've met me once, you don't know me from Adam, you don't owe me anything. But just for the record, I've never ghosted anyone. I wouldn't do that. It's rude. So don't explain, but don't blame me for the things all the other men do, because maybe not all men are bastards.'

'Most of them are.'

Dominic sighed. 'I apologise for the failings of my sex. There. Better?'

'Not really.'

'Excuse me!' said a couple in matching anoraks. 'Could you move, please? We can't get to the brown rice.'

'Sorry,' said Claire, and walked on. As her anger subsided, she wondered why she'd been so rude to him? He hadn't done anything wrong, except maybe be a bit entitled about wanting an explanation for why she hadn't taken his calls. In the grand scheme of things, that wasn't *that* awful. And it wasn't really him she was angry with. Claire wrestled with her conscience and her rage for a moment in front of the fishfingers, and took some deep breaths. He hadn't deserved that. There was being assertive and adult, and there was just being a bit of a twat. Andrew fucking her over wasn't really an excuse to shout at strangers in Sainsbury's, especially not rather attractive ones whom she'd been quite thrilled to be asked out by. She was moving on, Claire reminded herself. She cursed inwardly at the prospect of having to apologise for her twattishness and went back down towards the Brown Rice Twins. They were debating the merits of brown and wild rice mix versus plain brown, and was the organic worth the extra money, but Dominic was nowhere in sight.

She found him round the corner in the biscuit aisle, moodily lobbing packets of Mint Clubs into his trolley. That had to be a good sign, at least.

'Dominic?' Claire said. 'Do you like gravy?'

'What? Who doesn't like gravy?'

'What about dogs?'

'I don't like gravy on dogs?' he said uncertainly. 'I mean, I know in some cultures, but –'

'No, that's a separate question. Nothing to do with the gravy. Just "Do you like dogs?" Not to eat. With or without gravy. Just do you like them?'

'Yeah. I love dogs. Why?'

'It's just something that's important to me. That people like dogs.'

'Dogs are pretty important to me too. I don't have one right now, though. My old fellow died a few months ago, and I've not been able to bring myself to get another one. He was the best dog. He was just a Heinz 57 mongrel, but he was the cleverest boy and so loyal. Do you want to see a photo of him? Oh God, sorry, of course you don't. It's just I miss him every day. Sam. His name was Sam.'

Dominic's eyes were full of tears as he shoved his phone back in his pocket.

'I'd love to see a photo of Sam,' said Claire. 'Look. I think we've got off to a bad start. Something happened, right after I saw you in the car park, and I've not really been in a place to think about going for a drink with you, or anyone. Not that anyone else has asked me. But I had a lot of … stuff to process. And yes, I should probably have told you that, or at least texted and let you know, instead of letting you keep calling. But I kept thinking next time you called I'd have sorted myself out and I'd pick up. So, if you'd still like to go for a drink, I'd like to do that too.'

'Really?' said Dominic. 'Well, that's great. What about now? We could go now.'

'I can't,' said Claire. 'I've got ice cream and frozen pizzas; I need to take them home. I also should tell you now before you find out and get put off, I have two children.'

'I guessed you had kids ages ago from the stuff in your trolley,' said Dominic. 'And a dog, from the dog food and treats and poo bags. That was one of the reasons I liked you. The dog, not the children. Shit, I sound like such a stalker. But what I mean is, it's not a shock. Where are they?'

'With their father. We're separated. Well, obviously, or I wouldn't be picking up strange men in Sainsbury's. Look, I need to get this all back, and then maybe we could go for a drink this afternoon.'

'Yes!' said Dominic enthusiastically. 'Great! What about that pub by the park? It's dog-friendly, so you could bring your dog. About 3 p.m.?'

'Um, not really she has … issues,' said Claire. 'And I'm not sure I can make it for 3 p.m. I need to walk Sadie first.'

'I could come for a walk first. I miss dog walks. You feel such a twat walking on your own without a dog when you've been used to it, and I always feel if I walk past a playpark without a dog that everyone thinks I'm some dodgy paedo.'

'Oh God, this is awkward. You'll think I'm making this up, but she hates men.'

'Really? Why?' said Dominic, looking understandably suspicious.

'We don't know. She's a rescue and something has obviously happened to her.'

Dominic's face immediately softened at the news Sadie was a rescue.

'Poor baby,' he said. 'Sam was a rescue too. He was terrified of doors and it took a lot of work to get him used to them. But men are everywhere, like doors. Don't you think it would help if she started trying to get used to them?'

'Yes, probably,' said Claire. 'She should be OK if we're outside. But look, you can't get too close, and if she's scared you'll just have to go and do your dodgy paedophile impression. And I'll need to take her home before we go for a drink – she'll never cope with the pub.'

'I promise I'll do whatever Sadie needs,' said Dominic earnestly.

Dominic was as good as his word on their walk. He totally ignored Sadie at first and chatted with Claire from a safe distance. Sadie, initially shaking and bristling at his presence, had started to relax by the end of the walk, when Dominic had done nothing to threaten her or Claire, who tucked her into her crate with many treats and kisses and told her how very very proud of her she was, before going to meet Dominic at the pub.

The dog walk had been a good idea, Claire reflected. It had broken the ice and taken away the pressure of this being like a proper date, although they'd really only talked about dogs, present and previous, as both of them were focused on keeping Sadie as calm as possible, so couldn't really concentrate on anything deeper. Quite a lot, therefore, was riding on this drink, although Dominic's kindness and patience with Sadie were already huge plus points in his favour, though Claire wished yet again that she could text Emily and ask for her advice and opinion.

Over several gin and tonics (harder to accidently get hammered on than glasses of wine) for Claire and pints of beer for Dominic, they finally told each other a bit more about themselves. Dominic was a doctor, and originally from Yorkshire, but he didn't know James Herriot or a secret hack for perfect Yorkshire puddings. Claire had meant to play it cool and not tell him about Andrew and Emily, or Emily's death, but she somehow found herself blurting it all out in the first hour.

'Wow,' said Dominic, 'that *is* complicated. I see why you didn't call me back now. You really did have some other stuff on your mind.'

'Yeah. So, you know. We've done the date, and I understand if you want to run a mile. I've broken all the cardinal rules, haven't I? Talked about my ex, not been cool, blabbered on about a whole load of emotional stuff you certainly weren't expecting to have dumped on you. Sorry. This is the first time I've done this. It's all very new. To be honest, I wasn't really looking to start seeing anybody yet, I'm not sure I'm even ready. Thanks for trying to help with Sadie, though.'

'I'm a dummy run then?' said Dominic. 'Don't worry. I'm not sure what the rules are either. This is my first date in a long while too. In fact, asking you out that day was a sort of bet. With myself.'

'You asked me out for a *bet*?'

'With MYSELF. Not a *bet* bet. I just thought, you've been staring at the gorgeous girl in the supermarket for weeks, maybe she's not single, but she's not wearing a ring and you'll never know unless you say something. Now you've got a perfect excuse to go over and talk to her, but I bet you won't have the bollocks to do it and ask her out. And then I thought, what's the worst that can happen? She turns you down and you've got to go to Tesco's in the future. But at least you'll have *done* something, instead of feeling sorry for yourself.'

'Why didn't you go to Tesco's when I didn't call you back?'

'Really? Out of all the things you could ask, my shopping preferences are what you pick? Because I was still hoping I'd run into you, and there would turn out to be an answer to you not calling me that would soothe my bruised and battered male pride.'

'OK. Why were you feeling so sorry for yourself, and why are you still single?'

'Ah. I'm still single because it's hard to find a woman today who's willing to wait until after marriage for sex.'

'What?' Claire choked on her gin.

Dominic shook his head sadly. 'Yes. It's true. And they take umbrage when I explain that there can be no kissing until I've taken them home to meet Mother, and she has given her seal of approval.'

Claire choked some more. 'But I am a single mother. What will Mother make of that?'

'You have a pure look about you. I felt you'd understand that we must wait for the sanctity of marriage.'

'Um, look, I'm not sure this is –'

'I'm joking. My mother *is* religious – how else do you think I ended up being called Dominic? She named me after her favourite saint, and while I'm quite sure she'd be very happy if there was no sex before marriage and I did indeed bring home girlfriends for her approval before there was any snogging, I don't. Sorry. I shouldn't have made it a joking matter, not after you were so honest with me, but the truth is rather … I don't know. Embarrassing.'

'Embarrassing?'

'No, not embarrassing. That's not the right word. I don't know what is. OK, here goes. I split up with my long-term girlfriend last year, because she wanted children –'

'And you didn't,' finished Claire in disappointment, thinking that Dominic seemed so nice, but was just another selfish man-baby.

'No, I did. But it turned out I couldn't.'

'Couldn't … couldn't … rise to the occasion?'

'Oh no, *mechanically* everything is fine. But … I'm infertile. Firing blanks. A Jaffa, as schoolboys so tastefully put it. Mumps, when I was thirteen.'

'Oh shit. I'm sorry. But wasn't there anything they could do?'

'Oh yes. Lots. Donors. IVF. All that. But Carla didn't want to have to go through "all that". We'd both already endured various tests before we found out what the problem was, and she got an A* report for her reproductive system and wanted to have a baby naturally. And who can blame her? My bits are the issue, but she's the one who'd have had to go through all the invasive procedures and indignities. Well, I do blame her a bit. I think if she'd really loved me, we'd have found a way. But anyway, as she pointed out, she wasn't getting any younger, so off she went.'

'Did she find someone?'

'I don't know. We didn't keep in touch. I didn't think I could stand the idea of seeing her with someone else's baby in her arms, knowing that I couldn't give her that. Can't give anyone that. And then Sam died too, and well, it's not been the best year of my life either. But I'm trying, you know, to get back on the horse, so to speak.'

'Are you sure *you're* ready to start dating again?' asked Claire gently.

'I don't know. Probably not. But you were the first woman I'd seen who stopped me in my tracks. And more than that, you looked *nice*. Kind. As well as gorgeous. So, I thought I'd see what happened. And there you go, we've both just dumped a load of our shit on each other, so I guess that makes us even. Do you want to run a mile now?'

'No,' said Claire. 'I don't. I think you're really nice. And I think you're the first man I've met since Andrew left that has made me remember there are nice guys out there. Good ones. I don't think either of us are ready for this, though. But I *do* like you. Maybe we should just try being friends for a while, until we do feel ready.'

'Yeah,' said Dominic. 'I'd like that.'

Lucy was outraged when Claire told them about her date.

'You finally find a nice man, a really nice man, and it doesn't even matter about his shortcomings, literal short "comings", ha ha, because you don't want any more kids anyway, and you tell him *you want to be friends*. WHY? Send him to me if you don't want him!'

'It's not like that, Lucy. He's not ready either. He's had a bit of a time of it too.'

'Oh, I know. I'm joking, really. But seriously, if I end up single for the rest of my life, I'm TOTALLY blaming it on my parents for never teaching me how to change a tyre!'

'I promise, if Dominic is ready to start seeing people again and we're still just friends, I'll INSIST you're the first in the queue.'

'Thank you, Claire,' said Lucy. 'That's said like a true friend. And any other chaps you happen over in the supermarket … remember where I am if you don't want them! Unless they're standing at the fish counter holding a fish. That would definitely be a Bad Omen … all I want is a non-fishy man. Is that so much to ask?'

29

As the days shortened, Claire congratulated herself on how well she was coping with Emily's death. She no longer felt it like a physical pain when she thought about Emily, and she tried to limit how much she allowed herself to dwell on her. The weekly boxing sessions had calmed Claire's inner rage a great deal as well, and she really thought she was finally moving on, properly moving on.

One Thursday evening in the middle of October, however, Claire was sharply reminded of her loss and for once all her coping mechanisms went out the window and she thought there was actually an excellent chance she might just curl up into a ball and start screaming about the sheer UNFAIRNESS of it all, or punch out every window in the house in fury.

Tabitha had started it all by announcing at dinner, as she pushed her shepherd's pie around her plate, 'Mummy, I've been thinking, and I've decided, I think I'm a lesbian.'

Claire had been slightly nonplussed by this, as although since turning nine in September, Tabitha thought she was now immensely grown up and an expert on all things, it wasn't the sort of conversation Claire had been anticipating having *just* yet, especially because last week she'd had to have a chat with Tabitha when she'd fallen out with Ophelia Hughes, after Toby French (of the Bear Grylls wild living at Forest Fields fame), who'd apparently been Ophelia's 'boyfriend', had 'dumped' her for Tabitha.

Claire had sat Tabitha down and explained they were all far too young to be even thinking about having boyfriends or girlfriends. Right now they should just be friends, as there was plenty of time to think about all that later. Tabitha had seemed unconvinced, if for no other reason than to annoy Ophelia, which Claire had pointed out was not very in keeping with the spirit of feminist solidarity. But she had certainly not expected Tabitha to take their little chat quite so to heart.

'Errr,' Claire said. 'Why do you think that, darling? I mean, it's perfectly fine, and I'm glad you feel you can tell me, I'm just wondering what makes you so sure?'

Tabitha looked at Claire scornfully. 'Isn't it *obvious*?' she said, 'I told you I didn't like meat, so clearly I'm a lesbian!'

Lucas choked on his forkful of shepherd's pie. 'Oh my God, you're soooooo stupid,' he crowed. 'You're not a lesbian, you mean you're a vegetarian.'

'I *am* a lesbian,' insisted Tabitha. 'A lesbian is someone who doesn't eat meat.'

Claire suppressed the politically incorrect thought that this could be a very vulgar definition of a lesbian, and tried to let Tabitha down gently.

'No, darling. Lucas is right. Someone who doesn't eat meat is a vegetarian, not a lesbian.'

'Oh, well what's a lesbian then?'

Claire intervened hastily before Lucas could offer his own explanation cobbled together from Sex Ed lessons and his verboten forays onto the Urban Dictionary, and explained, 'It's a lady who has girlfriends not boyfriends, and if she wants to get married, she'll get married to another lady.'

Tabitha thought about it. 'Hmmm. OK, I'm *definitely* a vegetarian then. And I might be a lesbian as well, because boys are stupid and smelly, and I think it would be better to get married to Ella or Amy than a boy.'

'Right,' said Claire. 'That's fine, darling, and you've plenty of time to think about things like that. And about the being-a-vegetarian thing, you know that means you'll have to eat vegetables, yes?'

'What? NO, not vegetables! Why do I have to eat vegetables if I'm a vegetarian?'

'I think the clue is sort of in the name, darling.'

All of a sudden Claire found herself choking back tears, as unthinkingly she'd reached for her phone to relay this entire daft conversation to Emily, with some comment along the lines of maybe Tabitha was right and they should also have renounced stinky boys at a tender age and got married. And then she remembered that she couldn't tell Emily anything ever again. She swallowed hard and turned to the sink, so the children couldn't see her crying, but they were too engrossed in fighting, Lucas winding Tabitha up about her confusing lesbians and vegetarians, and Tabitha screaming at him to shut up, he was stupid, she hated him. The noise was too much, and Claire completely snapped.

'STOP IT,' she howled. 'Just STOP IT. I can't stand it, the constant fighting and bickering. That's ENOUGH!'

Both children looked at her in astonishment as she broke down and started sobbing. Lucas got up and guided her to a seat, Tabitha dashed to the fridge and pressed a brimming glass of white wine into her hand. Claire sniffed hard. All this time she had kept herself from breaking down in front of the children, and what was the point? Now she had. Lucas patted her shoulder in a manly way.

'It's OK, Mum,' he said kindly.

'Don't cry, Mummy. Here, have your wine,' said Tabitha equally kindly, lifting the glass to Claire's mouth and attempting to force it down her throat. By the time Claire had coughed the Sauvignon Blanc out of her lungs and could breathe again, she'd got a grip of herself.

'Sorry,' she said in a small voice.

'We're sorry,' said Tabitha. 'Sorry we upset you. But we weren't *really* fighting.'

'Weren't you?'

'Nah, Mum,' shrugged Lucas casually. 'It's just like, banter, yeah? Not *fighting*.'

'But you sounded like you were going to kill each other.'

'We were just having a laugh.'

'I don't want to kill Lucas. He told Toby French in front of everybody that he was a knobhead and would never get a real girlfriend because he doesn't treat women properly, because it turned out Toby told Gertrude she was his girlfriend as well as me, and now none of the girls will talk to Toby, and they all think I'm lucky to have a big brother like Lucas.'

'You did that?' said Claire in wonder. 'Also, Lucas, maybe don't call people "knobheads" at school.'

Lucas gave another casual shrug. 'It was nothing, Anyway, she's a lesbian now, so it doesn't matter, does it?'

'I'm a VEGETARIAN and YOU are an ARSEFACE!' shrieked Tabitha.

'Tabitha!' said Claire. 'Enough. Where did you even learn a word like that?'

'I taught her it,' said Lucas proudly.

'He also taught me that it's OK to say "bastard" because it's in Shakespeare and you can totally say the C-bomb because it's in Chaucer,' Tabitha announced smugly. 'Anyway, Mummy, about me being a vegetarian?'

'I really don't think it's OK to use those words,' Claire insisted. 'They were not as shocking then. And like I said, if you're a vegetarian you'll have to eat vegetables, and you always tell me you *hate* vegetables and threaten to call Childline if I give you them.'

'That was when I was *little* I said I was calling Childline,' said Tabitha with the great dignity of a wise nine-year-old looking back at the foolishness of her eight-year-old former self. 'What if maybe I just didn't have to eat shepherd's pie anymore, but I still eat chicken and sausages? And instead of shepherd's pie, I cook dinner once a week?'

'You want me to teach you to cook?'

'No. There's like loads of YouTube videos I've been watching, and I want to try.'

'Yeah, and Mum, after dinner, I'm going to take the lock apart on the bathroom door to fix it. There was a YouTube video about that too, so you won't be able to use it for about an hour, if that's OK. But it will mean no one will get locked in there again like Ella did last week.'

'Fine,' said Claire, in astonishment at these much kinder and wiser children her offspring had become, even if her nurturing and mentoring parental role in their lives did seem to have largely been replaced by YouTube.

'See, Mummy,' said Tabitha, waving her iPad in Claire's face, 'here's one recipe I want to try, and actually it's vegan and gluten-free, so totally healthy. In fact it's probably the sort of thing that you'd eat at Gertrude and Ophelia's house.'

'That's marshmallow fluff!' said Claire, looking at the recipe.

'So?' said Tabitha. 'It just shows you're *wrong*, Mummy, about having to eat vegetables when you're a vegetarian, because this is *vegan* and it has *no* vegetables in it AT ALL!'

'You're not making marshmallow fluff for dinner,' said Claire in horror. 'You might as well have jam. In fact, jam would be better – at least it has some fruit in it.'

'Jam is also vegan and gluten-free,' Tabitha informed her smugly. 'And like you said, it has fruit in, so can I have jam instead of this horrible shepherd's pie?'

'No. I'll make you a vegetarian alternative if you're really set on being a vegetarian, but it won't involve any jam or sugar or anything else like that, and it will most definitely contain vegetables. Oh, and you do know that if you're a vegetarian, you can't eat Haribos,' Claire added with casual cruelty.

Tabitha went pale. 'No Haribos? But why?'

'Gelatine,' said Claire, with the same smug air that Tabitha had employed when explaining the health benefits of living on jam to Claire.

'What's gelatine?' said Lucas innocently.

'It's the boiled-up bits of pigs' feet and skin and bones and tendons and all the other bits that don't go into even the nastiest sausages,' Claire explained with relish. 'It's what gives Haribos their jelly texture. That's what it is – sugar and E numbers and boiled-up pig bits. Maybe cow bits. Yummy, eh?'

Both children looked aghast.

'I'm never eating Haribos again,' swore Tabitha.

'Eurgh, nor me,' said Lucas. 'Why did you let us eat them? That's sooooo disgusting!'

'I didn't *let* you eat them. I've tried for years to discourage you from eating Haribos – I never buy you them. You get them in party bags from evil parents, or else your grandparents buy them, and even then I try to hide them before you eat the revolting things because they turn both of you into some kind of screaming Tasmanian devils, bouncing off the walls and wittering at me at high speed like chipmunks on amphetamines. So don't blame *me* for your Haribos addiction!'

'What's amphetamines?' asked Tabitha.

'Never mind,' said Claire hastily, hoping to end the evening on a parenting high of convincing them out of eating Haribos and into a path of clean-living vegetarianism, rather than an in-depth chat about the differing effects of various recreational drugs.

30

Claire picked Lucy up to take her to the climbing wall, as Lucy's car was in the garage. Lucy was uncharacteristically quiet on the way there.

'Are you OK?' asked Claire in concern.

'Yes, fine,' Lucy replied abruptly.

As no one really knew what they were doing with regards to climbing, they'd booked a group lesson and even Kate's jaw dropped when their instructor appeared, a tanned, blond Australian sex god who looked like he'd walked straight off Bondi Beach.

'Wow!' breathed Claire, nudging Lucy.

'Niiiice,' sighed Mary to Kate. 'Why am I married?'

'To be honest, that arse is making me question whether I'm actually a lesbian,' Kate whispered back. Only Lucy was silent.

'Are you *sure* you're OK?' Claire asked Lucy again, once they were all trussed up in their harnesses and checking out the climbing wall. Lucy didn't even appear to have *noticed* the instructor's arse, hadn't made a single *double entendre* or joke about bondage during their safety briefing nor even responded to the fact the instructor was blatantly attempting to flirt with her, something that had not gone unnoticed by the others, who were all slightly envious.

'I told you, I'm *fine*,' snapped Lucy. 'FINE.'

'Right,' announced Chris the instructor brightly. 'We'll start really easily on this beginners' wall, then we'll see how we go and maybe move on to something trickier. And if we've time at the end, we can even try some abseiling, if anyone's up for that.'

Lucy turned green as Chris pointed to her and said, 'So, Lucy. Would you like to go first? Don't be nervous, I'll be right beside you, showing you what to do.'

Lucy shook her head in a panic. 'Come on,' said Chris encouragingly. 'Don't worry, a lot of people feel nervous at first, but you're totally safe – you're all roped up, you can't fall even if you try, and like I said, I've got you. I'm right here.'

'No,' said Lucy. 'No, I can't, I can't, I CAN'T!'

Lucy started to breathe in a heaving, gasping, raggedy way.

'Christ, Lucy, are you having an asthma attack?' asked Claire anxiously. 'Have you got an inhaler?'

'She's having a panic attack,' said Chris calmly, putting his arm round Lucy and guiding her to a seat.

'Don't worry, happens all the time. That's it, Lucy. Close your eyes, and take some deep breaths, come on darlin'. You're going to be OK. You don't have to do anything you don't want to. Just breathe, yeah? Just focus on your breathing – in through the nose, aaaaand out through your mouth. That's it, good. Want some water?'

Lucy's breathing calmed and she nodded that yes, she'd like some water, and Mary dashed forward with the water bottle that Lucy had dropped.

'There we go,' said Chris comfortingly. 'Fear of heights, is it?'

Lucy rubbed her face despairingly. 'Something like that.'

'Don't worry. We get that a lot here. People either come to try to get over it, or sometimes they don't realise how much they *are* afraid of heights till they're halfway up a wall and look down. Now that's fun, trying to get Big Kev from the marketing department down twenty feet when he's sweating like a pig, swearing he's going to shit himself with fear and insisting he's never coming on another corporate team-building day again. It's much better when someone has a wobble *before* they start climbing, so we know to keep an eye on them. Also, when they don't weigh nineteen stone and have halitosis *and* BO,' he added.

'I de-odourised and brushed my teeth,' said Lucy indignantly.

'I know. And it's much appreciated, believe me.'

Chris twinkled at her, but Lucy still didn't respond to the very obvious admiration in Chris's eyes.

'So, feeling better? Want to try again? You only need to go up half a metre. And if you're OK, then you can go another half-metre. And maybe another one. You don't have to do anything you're uncomfortable with. Or do you want to let your friends go first?'

Lucy took a deep breath and stood up. 'No. I'll go. I can do this.'

She walked over to the wall, Chris attached a rope to her harness, she put her foot on the first hold and reached up to grip the nearest handhold.

'Well done, Lucy,' encouraged Chris, as she attempted to pull herself up. But Lucy flung herself away from the wall, scrabbling at her harness.

'No no no no,' she sobbed. 'Get it off me, get it off, please get it off.'

Chris rapidly undid Lucy's harness but before he could even attempt to calm her down again, she had fled back in the direction of the changing rooms, while Claire, Kate and Mary looked on aghast.

'I'll go,' said Claire quickly.

'We'll come too,' said Kate.

'No, you stay. I'll text you if I need you. Try to do some climbing,' and Claire belted off after Lucy.

The changing room was mercifully empty, and Claire found Lucy sobbing in a corner.

'Luce?' she said gently, putting her hand on Lucy's shoulder. Lucy wept harder. Claire sat down beside her and held Lucy while she cried, as if she was Tabitha, though Tabitha's last major crying jag had been over the gross injustice of a limited edition Build-A-Bear selling out before Tabitha was in receipt of sufficient funds to squander on it, having failed to heed Claire's warnings about putting some of her birthday money aside to save for things she really wanted instead of wasting it all on cheap glittery tat. Somehow Claire felt Lucy's breakdown was possibly over something a little more serious.

Lucy finally took a deep breath and tried to wipe her eyes. Claire considered giving her the tissue in her pocket, but remembered just in time that she had spat on it to wipe the remnants of Coco Pops off Tabitha's face just before Andrew picked the kids up, since Tabitha's idea of what constituted washing her face and Claire's idea were two very different things.

Instead she said, 'Hang on a sec,' and dived into the loo and came back with a handful of loo paper for Lucy to dry her eyes on and blow her nose.

'This isn't just about heights, is it?' said Claire gently.

Lucy sniffed hard and gulped.

'I'm fine,' she said. 'Really, go and have fun.'

'You're not fine,' Claire insisted. 'You've not even noticed how ludicrously hot Chris is, nor the fact he's quite blatantly trying to get off with you.'

'Yeah, right,' muttered Lucy. 'What would some sexy Aussie guy want with a middle-aged mother of two, especially one who's scared of heights when he's a fucking climbing instructor?'

'Because you're gorgeous,' said Claire. 'And funny and kind.

What wouldn't he want with you? It's more, what do you want with him other than a hot piece of ass? Though it is *very* hot. Even Kate noticed it. So if you didn't, something must really be wrong, because you've been telling us for months how much you want a shag, and there's a fit bloke out there who you don't even have to talk to online first, who's clearly up for it, and you've not even registered. So what's really wrong, Lucy? Please tell me, because I'm worried about you. We all are.'

'Nothing,' sighed Lucy. 'Nothing. Nothing's changed. Nothing's wrong. I'm just so tired, Claire. So tired of doing it all myself. So tired of picking up the pieces for my kids from the messes my fuck-ing ex leaves behind, so tired of "getting on with it", and I'm so bloody *tired* of being brave, Claire, of "facing my fears" and putting a brave face on it. And I hate heights, I really hate heights, but I didn't want to piss on Kate's chips by saying that. She came and drew Neville's penis for me, for fuck's sake, but I couldn't, I just couldn't. I wanted to, but I just had nothing left. I'm so scared all the time and I can't ever show it, and I just couldn't pretend to be brave about another thing. It simply wasn't there.'

'What are you scared of?' asked Claire, handing Lucy more loo roll as she started to cry again. 'And why do you think you can't show it?'

'Because,' snuffled Lucy, 'because if I let Matthew see how scared I am, he'll use that against me. And if I let my mum and dad see, they'll be too worried. And if I let anyone else see, well, no one will like me if I do. Because you only like me if I'm being funny and not being a bother or a drag to you all. If you knew the real me, you wouldn't want to be doing with me. And don't say it's not true,' Lucy went on, as Claire opened her mouth to staunchly deny any such thing. 'Matthew knew what I was really like, didn't he, and he left. And Lolly and Jacinta and Figgy, they couldn't get away from me fast enough. And all my old friends, from before children and from university have drifted away – we're still in touch, but I couldn't *tell* them anything, not anything important, not confide in them.

'And I'm so scared of being on my own. I know everyone much prefers fun, silly Lucy, joking about how sexually fucking frustrated I am, than they would to how I really feel, which is so lonely, so alone, knowing it all comes back to me, that I'll end up making all the decisions about the kids on my own, because Matthew's too much of an arsehole to be bothered. But I don't even get the autonomy of really being a single mother, because even though he can't be arsed with my kids, he'll still interfere and undermine and criticise the decisions I make just to make me feel like shit, and some days I don't even know if I can get out of bed, but that's not what anyone wants to hear, is it?'

Lucy started sobbing uncontrollably again, and Claire pulled her in for another hug as she wept. When Lucy had finished crying, Claire gave her the remnants of the toilet paper and also gave her a gentle shake.

'Lucy,' she said sternly. 'You've been really very foolish.'

'I know,' nodded Lucy soggily. 'I know. I'm so stupid.'

'No,' said Claire. 'You're not stupid. But you've been foolish, not to see what you mean to us. We worry about how much you laugh everything off and about how you never really open up, how you turn everything into a big joke, usually with yourself as the butt of it. And we love that side of you, but we all know there's more to you than that. And you can show us that part of you too. Lucy, you're one of the kindest people I know. This last year, I don't know how I'd have got through any of it without you. Kate and Mary too, but you – you were the one who made me see that I had choices, that I had to shape my own life for myself, instead of letting Emily and Andrew define it. Because of you, because of the things you said to me, that first night, when I was the one crying at you, my life has changed, and for the better. It's been hard, but I'm happy now, when I wasn't – and hadn't been – for a long time. And a lot of that is down to you, Lucy. For helping me realise that there's more to life than a miserable marriage.'

As she said this to Lucy, Claire realised in astonishment that she was happy. She truly was. There were still down days, and days when the grief for Emily threatened to crush her heart, but overall Claire was happy, in a way that she'd forgotten was even possible. And she realised as well that she was proud of herself too, that she'd got *herself* to this place. She'd had some help from the Sisterhood along the way, admittedly, but the main architect of Claire's happiness and the person she relied on to maintain that happiness was herself. And more than that, between the boxing, the wild swimming and all the other new things they'd tried, she was discovering not only a sense of herself again, but a sense of her own self-worth as a person in her own right, not as someone else's wife or mother or friend. And she didn't intend to ever let that slip away from her again.

'Lucy, please let us in. Please let us all help you, the way you help us. We'd so much rather see all of you than half of you.'

'Really?' said Lucy in a small voice.

'Really,' said Claire firmly. 'Including Chris. He definitely wants to see *all* of you.'

Lucy managed a small laugh at this.

'Come on,' said Claire. 'Let's go and get a cup of tea.'

'No,' said Lucy, standing up. 'Let's go and climb this fucking wall. After everything, I'm not going to be beaten by that.'

'Are you sure? You really don't have to.'

'I want to. But Claire, will you stay beside me while I do it? And help me if I get scared?'

'Of course I will. I'll be right beside you the whole way. I won't leave your side, I promise.'

'Well, you could maybe leave it for a bit if it really does look like I'm in there with Fit Chris,' said Lucy with a shaky laugh.

'OK. I'm by your side every step of the way until you give me the nod that you're up for a good rogering, and then I'll discreetly retire,' promised Claire.

'Thank you,' said Lucy. 'For everything. For being my friend.'

'Thank *you*,' said Claire in surprise. 'I mean it. I don't know what I'd have done without you.'

'Me neither,' said Lucy, giving Claire a quick hug. 'Come on, then. At least if I am to fall to my death, according to you I'll have a nice view as I plummet through the sky. Let's go and see if this arse is as good as you claim.'

'It is,' said Claire. 'It really is.'

31

In late November, Claire was attempting to marshal the children along the road from the school with Mary and Lucy, a process rather like herding cats. The children had all just been given their parts in the school show, and Ben and Lucas were swaggering ahead with the self-importance of worldly-wise eleven-year-olds who'd just been given the lofty job of being the narrators of the Christmas show, instead of such lowly roles as robins and snowmen.

Tabitha, Ella and Amy were trailing a hundred yards behind, which at least meant that the wittering budgieness of their indignant twittering was dulled somewhat as they chuntered about how Ophelia had borrowed Millie's Smiggle ruler and she hadn't given it back, and Ophelia said it wasn't her, it was Gertrude, but Millie said it *was* Ophelia, not Gertrude. Amy's sister Lily hovered on the edge, awestruck by the wonder of nine-year-old sophistication that the girls exuded through ratty friendship bracelets and Paperchase lunchboxes, and Claire, Mary and Lucy trudged somewhere in the middle, calling to the girls to hurry up and the boys to WAIT, and Lucas, LUCAS, do NOT GO IN THAT HEDGE, the man is LOOKING, and if you haven't found your Lego in there yet, you're never going to. Claire's phone rang, and to her surprise it was Andrew.

'I'd better take this,' she said. 'I don't know why he's calling at this time. Hello, Andrew. What's wrong?'

'Claire. Look, I know this is probably a bad time, I'm sorry. Can you talk for a minute?'

'Um, yeah. What do you want to talk to me about?'

'Christmas. I just realised we haven't talked about Christmas.'

'Shit.'

'Yeah. It's my weekend for them. And I was going to suggest, you know, we did the civilised thing, and we all spent it together. I was going to offer to cook Christmas dinner, well, go to Marks & Spencer and reheat their Christmas dinner, but the thing is my mother –'

'What's she done?'

'She's booked this amazing ski chalet in France, and she wants me and the children to come along too. I said, no, that wasn't fair on you, but she's nagging me and nagging me to at least *ask* you, so I said I would. It's totally your call. I'm happy for us to stay here and make Christmas dinner for all of us at my flat.'

Claire sighed. 'How amazing *is* this chalet?'

'Like, *fucking* amazing. Hot tub, mountains, walk straight out the door and ski. It's like something out of those books you love.'

'The *Chalet School* ones? I don't think they had hot tubs.'

'Yeah, but you know what I mean. It would be an awesome experience for the kids. Like once in a lifetime. If I took them it would literally just be for a few days, though. You could maybe do an early or late Christmas with them.'

Claire groaned to herself. 'I don't know, Andrew. Let me think about it, OK?'

'OK, great, thanks, Claire. You're a star for even thinking about it, I really appreciate that. And no pressure either way. I'm happy to do whatever you want. Or, what about if you came with us to France? How about that?'

'I think that would be weird. Also your mother hates me. And I'm not mad on her. But thanks for the invite. I'll let you know as soon as possible.'

'Well, she enjoys tormenting you, so she'd probably be quite happy if you were there for her to wind up. But you're right. Be a bit strange. Anyway, I'll let you go. Thanks again, Claire, for even considering it. I won't forget this.'

'Everything OK?' asked Mary, as Claire caught them up. 'Was it an emergency? Oh shit! Alfie! Alfie!'

Mary belted off to retrieve Alfie, who'd found a particularly foul puddle to investigate.

'Andrew wants the kids for Christmas,' Claire told Lucy. 'His mother has booked some amazing ski chalet in France for all the family.'

'Fuck. Hadn't you arranged Christmas access with him?'

'No. With the naivety of the newly separated, neither of us had thought to nail it down. Oh Jesus. What am I going to do? He's right, though. It would be a once-in-a-lifetime experience for them.'

'What will you do if the kids go away?'

'I dunno. Go to my parents? Except I can't. Dad's taking Mum on a cruise. He thought Mum should have a proper break for Christmas after years of running round like a blue-arsed fly after everyone every Christmas. It was very thoughtful of him.'

'I'm supposed to go to my smug brother's, though I can't say I'm looking forward to it, or I'd say come to me. What about handsome Dominic?' asked Lucy. 'Could you spend Christmas with him?'

'Bit soon? And Sadie? And anyway, he's working, I think. A&E still needs doctors, even on Christmas Day.'

'Why do we need a doctor on Christmas Day?' asked Mary, arriving back dragging a sodden and howling Alfie.

'Andrew's mum's booked some amazing place for Christmas and he wants to take the kids. Like once-in-a-lifetime amazing,' explained Claire again. 'So, we were just running through my options for Christmas if I let them go, because I suppose I have to think about what's best for them, not what I want.'

'Oh, that's a tough one. What are you going to do? ALFIE! Oh my God, what are you eating? Did you find that in the puddle?'

EPILOGUE

Claire woke up on Christmas morning to the familiar sight of Sadie grinning happily at her from the pillow. What was slightly less familiar was Dominic's face, beyond Sadie, also grinning at her.

'Morning,' he said. 'Can I just say, the gusts of morning breath are Sadie, not me?'

'Yes, she's not the most fragrant to wake up to. But she has such a nice smile.'

'She does. She has the second-nicest smile of any girl I know.'

'I'm going to be very up my own arse here, and say I presume I'm the one ranked higher than Sadie? I'd bloody better be, anyway!'

'Obviously you are,' Dominic assured her. 'Though you only *just* pip Sadie at the post. She has a *very* nice smile, don't you, darling?'

Sadie agreed by giving him an enthusiastic lick.

'My God, I never thought I'd see the day,' said Claire in wonder. 'She was *so* scared of men! Well, she still is. It's only you she can tolerate.'

'She knows I'm special,' said Dominic smugly.

'Right. Nothing to do with the months we spent desensitising her to you, then?'

'Nope. Special. God, I'm so glad you called me last night after the kids went to the airport.'

He attempted to lean over and kiss Claire, but was stopped by an indignant headbutt from Sadie. She butted him again, demanding ear scritches.

'I think Sadie's under the impression you're here for her benefit.'

'I have to say, it was nice waking up with a dog again.'

'Thanks!'

'You know what I mean.'

'Ah, I see. You're only here for my dog. My very *disloyal* dog, may I add? Sadie, stop it, you're shameless!'

'She is. She's the best girl. The best shameless girl. Yes. You're a good girl, Sadie, aren't you? Because all that time I thought you were just a cockblocker, but then once *you* decided I was all right, so did your mummy, didn't she, darling? Yes. You told your mummy, didn't you? "Uncle Dominic is a nice man, Mummy," you said, didn't you, Sadie? "Why not give him a little booty call?" Yes, you did. Yes, you did!'

'It was not a booty call!'

'No?'

Dominic looked up from scratching Sadie's tummy and raised his eyebrows. 'What would you call it, then?'

'I don't know, a ... I don't know!'

'Actually, all joking apart, I hope it wasn't. Because that suggests something more meaningless than what I want with you. I don't just want to be a casual fuck, Claire. I think this could be something serious. I *want* this to be something serious. Why do you think I waited all this time, till Sadie would let me in the front door? When she let me come in and have coffee last week, I wondered what would happen next. Was she simply an excuse and you really just wanted to stay "friends"? I'm happy to take this slow, Claire, but I want to be more than a friend with benefits.'

'Like Sadie's Uncle Dominic?'

'For a start. What do you want?'

'I need to take this slowly. I really do. There's the kids to think about, apart from anything.'

'I understand.'

'But I'd like us to be more than friends with benefits too.'

'Excellent. Well, in that case, Merry Christmas! And I've an hour before I need to leave for work, so we've time for some of those benefits as well.'

'Shit, is that the time? I need to leave for Mary's soon, too. If you want benefits, you can put Sadie out this time. I'm not having her thinking I'm the bad one putting her out and Uncle Dominic is the kind, saintly one who lets her back in. Go downstairs and get her a croissant. That will lure her down!'

'A croissant? For your dog? Really?'

'You want benefits, Sadie wants croissants!'

'Right. Come on, Sadie. Follow Uncle Dominic.'

Kate passed Claire's house on the way to Mary's, and they'd arranged that she'd call in for Claire and Sadie, and they'd walk to Mary's together. Unfortunately, Dominic's benefits had taken a little longer than anticipated and he was just leaving Claire's when Kate arrived.

Kate kept an impeccably straight face as she wished Dominic a very Merry Christmas, but as soon as his car pulled away she turned to Claire laughing, and starting singing.

'Claire and Dominic, Sitting in a tree, S.H.A.G.G.I.N.G.'

'Shhhhh,' hissed Claire. 'You'll corrupt Colonel Mousicles with such songs and I'll have his owner out complaining again. Come on!'

'Sure you can walk all right? You look a bit bow-legged to me.'

'Kate!'

'What?'

* * *

As soon as they arrived at Mary's house, Kate carolled chirpily, 'GUESS who I saw leaving Claire's house just now?'

'Who? Who?'

'DOMINIC!'

'KATE! You're very indiscreet. For all you know he came round to drop off a Christmas card.'

'A Christmas card?' said Kate. 'That's why he was attempting to suck out your tonsils on the doorstep and had his hand up your jumper.'

'What! What are you talking about?' said Lucy, coming through the back door. 'God, thank you so much for this, Mary. I know I shouldn't be glad my brother's kids have chickenpox, but this is going to be so much more fun. Who had his hand up Claire's jumper?'

'Dr Dominic,' smirked Kate.

'TELLY, CHILDREN! ON YOU GO! Sky +, if you go now, I'll take the parental controls off!' shouted Mary hurriedly, shepherding the innocent souls out the room. 'Don't start on the details without me,' she shouted over her shoulder.

'He was just wishing me a Merry Christmas,' insisted Claire.

'A very Merry Christmas!'

'Someone open that fizz,' instructed Mary, returning from TV duties. 'Right, Claire, tell ALL!'

'Oh, all right. He did stay last night,' Claire admitted. 'The house was very quiet and lonely when I got home from dropping the kids off at Andrew's to go to the airport, and he's been working so hard on getting Sadie to like him that she's OK with him in the house now, so I just rang him and asked him if he'd like to pop over for a friendly Christmas drink.'

'Very friendly!'

'And one thing led to another.'

'And there you were, Claire and Dominic, Sitting in a tree, S.E.X.I.N.G.,' carolled Kate.

'Sexing?'

'Well, I sang it earlier with " S.H.A.G.G.I.N.G.", but it didn't really fit. The two Gs were a bit of problem. This fits better.'

'It's also not a word.'

'You knew what I meant, though!'

'It's all HAPPENING for you, Claire!'

'God, this bottle's finished already. James, James, can you open another one? I think he's hiding in his shed, so I'll do it myself.'

'Aw, it's so lovely,' said Lucy emotionally. 'Claire's had a shag. I've had a shag. Several shags. Actually, I'm not really seeing Chris anymore. His arse was to die for, but he was quite dull. But you know what, he was amazing in bed, and gorgeous, and it's made me feel so much better about myself.'

'Couldn't you just have kept him on for the sex?' asked Claire.

Lucy blushed. 'We *may* have agreed an arrangement to our mutual benefit as long as we're both single,' she admitted. 'A sort of no-strings-shag kind of a thing. Does that make me an awful person? It's just, well, I'm fine on my own. I don't want to settle for anything second-best. But I *do* like sex. And he didn't want to settle down or anything either, so no one's getting hurt. But mainly I feel better because of all of you making me go to the doctor and finally getting anti-depressants, as well as using the health insurance from work to see a therapist, after being convinced for so long that they'd all be like that awful counsellor I saw after Matthew left. I'd spent so long joking about everything, I don't think I even realised how depressed I was until I started feeling better. So thank you. And thank you for not thinking I'm a twat.'

'We'd never think you were a twat,' said Kate firmly. 'And I'm so glad you're feeling better, Lucy. I feel better too, a bit like a weight's been lifted. I've made a decision about something, something important.'

'A baby!' gasped Mary.

'Yes. Well, no. That's my decision. I don't want to have a baby. All my reasons were wrong for having one. Having a baby because Susan wanted one wouldn't somehow give *her* a baby. And I don't want to do it on my own. And all the new things we tried. When I got to the top of the climbing wall, even though I was terrified of heights too, I thought THIS is what I want to be doing!'

'Climbing?' said Claire in confusion.

'No. New things. Exciting things. Things that challenge me. Maybe one day, if I met someone, yeah, we might have a baby. For now, I don't want one. I want to keep doing new things. And I thought I'd feel guilty if I made that decision, but I just want to look to the future. I'll never ever forget Susan, but I can't live the rest of my life making decisions based on what Susan might have wanted. And Susan would never have wanted me to do that either. So yeah. It's a bit of a shit announcement, actually, isn't it! "I'm not having a baby!"'

'Well, congratulations on *not* having a baby,' said Claire.

'Yes, congratulations,' everyone chimed in.

'I feel like my news isn't very exciting compared to Kate's not having a baby, and Claire's shagging and Lucy's getting better,' said Mary, 'but I bought James a Christmas present with my own money that I earned from dog walking, and it felt amazing. I mean, I'm very far from rich, and though I love dog walking, I'd still really like to do something to use my degree one day, but just earning my own money, it feels so liberating. And again, I couldn't have done that without you all. Giving me the idea, and then letting me have Sadie and Bingo as my first dogs, and knowing you believed in me. It made such a difference. Thank you!'

'Thank *you*,' said Claire. 'All of you. I don't know how I'd have got through this last year without all of you. Out of the shittiest year of my life has come the best thing that has ever happened to me (apart from the kids, but you have to say that, don't you? And Sadie, *obviously*). But meeting you. Our friendship. The way we're all there for each other. I've never known such love and support from anyone. You're the family I'd choose if I could. More than family. Nothing will come between us, especially not men. And we'll support each and every one of us when we need it. Because we're the Sisterhood, the Saturday Night Sauvignon Sisterhood. And together, there's nothing we can't do!'

'The Saturday Night Sauvignon Sisterhood!'

'Oh God, Bingo, stop doing that to Sadie! The Sisterhood!'

'Shit, we need *another* bottle. Dinner might be a bit late! The Sisterhood!'

'TO US! To friendship! To women!'

ACKNOWLEDGEMENTS

No finished book is solely down to the work of one person, and this one is no exception. There are too many people to thank individually, but here are some of the most important. As ever, I am enormously lucky to be able to work with an amazing team at HarperCollins, and I am eternally grateful to everyone there. In particular, to Lucy Brown, my amazing publicist, and to Hattie Evans and Julie MacBrayne, the marketing geniuses.

Thanks also to Claire Ward and Scott Garrett for the glorious cover design, which blew me away as usual.

Huge gratitude also to Mark Bolland, my brilliant copy editor, who may well be writing his own memoir 'Why the Copy Editor Drinks' after removing all my exclamation marks!

And a massive massive thank you to some of the most important people in this whole book process – the ones who get the books on the shelves for people to read – Tom Dunstan, Alice Gomer, Caroline Bovey and the rest of the sales team, and Marie Goldie and all the amazing people at the warehouse in Glasgow. And a special thank you to Sarah Hammond, for keeping everything on track despite my sometimes rather rambling excuses.

Three very special women were a huge part of making this book happen though – Kate Elton, thank you so much for your patience and kindness in the early stages. Jenny Hutton, thank you always for your excellent editorial advice and suggestions, including alerting me to the fact that horrors like class camping trips actually exist (though this one was purely fictional). But most all, Katya Shipster, my wonderful, incomparable editor. I always knew I couldn't do it without you, and you nearly proved me right. Thank you so much for everything.

Paul Baker, my fabulous agent at Headway Talent – thank you once again for putting up with me, you have the patience of a saint.

And finally, my friends and family – too many people to mention by name, but special thanks to Lynn Robertson, Mairi McGeachey and Tanya Hall for inspiring the title of this book with your friendship, and for all the red wine, gin and nights singing into spoons. And Georgia Hillman also deserves a special mention for providing the vegetarian story.

And of course, thanks to the dogs, Buddy and Billy, for keeping me warm and forcing me out the house for walkies, though I could have done without the repeated attempts to delete the entire book by sitting on my laptop, Billy!

And last but not least – enormous thanks to my lovely husband, who has rescued burnt dinners forgotten in the oven while I was working, fed ravening children and dogs, and held the fort more times than I can count. And to my darling children for so bravely surviving sub-optimal snack situations because I was busy, for making me laugh and for the cups of tea (and glasses of wine).